The Breast of Everything

Lori Berhon

"Truth is a pathless land,
and you cannot approach it by any path whatsoever, by any religion, by any
sect."

Jiddu Krishnamurti

"Forgive, O Lord, my little jokes on Thee
And I'll forgive Thy great big one on me."

Robert Frost

"Did you see? Did you cheer?
Or did you just refuse to hear?
Where did She go? Why don't you know?
The Revelation won't be televised!"

Tash Loving

CONTENTS

IN THE BEGINNING

A few years ago, in a country lead by a faith-based political party, in a city still nursing the scars of attack by zealots, a Being surfaced with a message of good will and reasoned enlightenment.

Why don't you know about this? The signs that Something was about to happen were there for anyone to see. Unfortunately, most of those who saw them didn't know how to read—or found the idea too inconvenient to contemplate.

The Reverend Dr. Hiram Crockertt, shepherd, author and advisor to presidents, saw the Signs and Rejoiced because he knew that in the next world, as in this one, he would sit at the right hand of the Throne; and meanwhile, his Halliburton stock was going up.

Rodney Oswald "Roddo" Hendron, the self-anointed Warrior President, was told a little about the Signs during a Cabinet-level briefing but he confused it with both the status report on the Occupation and the results of the latest polls. Anyway, he was a Hendron; as far as he knew, all signs pointed to him.

On Israel's West Bank, in the settlement town of Bet Halacheh, the fifteen-year-old daughter of Yitzhak Abramson placed her fingers on her eyelids as her mother had used to do, and greeted the Shabbos. Yitzhak watched the candlelight spill across the table and kiss the faces of his other four surviving children. He saw the Signs and knew he had been right to hold firm in this place, that Hashem was blessing their fortitude. On the other side of the half-built fence, sixteen-year-old Ismail ibn Ibrahim knew equally well that Allah was with him as he completed taping a farewell to his family, so that they could prove they qualified for the pension. He placed the video in an envelope, together with the photographs he'd autographed for the local girls who had always ignored him. Standing before the mirror, he wondered if the other virgins, too, would smell of lemons and spice, and he strapped on the heavy vest.

In other patches of desert, not all that many kilometers away, a Great Rebbe and a Great Mullah equally noticed the signs. They read them all too well, thereupon dismissing them as unclean and, ergo, deceptions sent out by the Darkness to corrupt the Righteous.

The Pope saw, but had alas reached the point in his own frailty where he no longer believed the witness of his own senses. None of his advisors officially noticed anything at all; there was precedent for ignoring signs until they had lapsed into the past.

The Buddhist monks noticed signs but had no application for them, as the next Dalai Lama had already been located and was even now being safely nurtured in an undisclosed location. The Hindu priests were distracted by the sheer volume of Divine temperaments they had to juggle on a regular basis to note any additional signs from an unnamed wellspring.

Not one of the uniquely spiritual individuals in Los Angeles noticed at all. Why would they? The Revelation will not be televised.

Only Una Goes-Beyond, until this day Tribal Council Leader of the Malawahnee, read with a true heart. She sat on her folded blanket, looking down with faded eyes into the great canyon she had chosen as her last sight of this earth. Her time came, as she had foreseen it would. Her heart slowed its beating of 88 years and her soul escaped on her last breath to join the Great Spirit. She rose from her carapace of flesh and bone as the rising sun glittered pink and gold across the streaky rocks. Hovering over the canyon, Una Goes-Beyond had a vision, and her last breath was a laugh.

1 - THE INVISIBLE WOMAN

"Three," Susan counted as the plaid plastic tote bag banged into her leg. The woman whose bag it was didn't even nod in acknowledgement. Eyes staring straight ahead, she continued her deliberate stomp down the platform as if on schedule to intersect with an incoming train.

There was no incoming train. There hadn't been for the ten minutes Susan had already been waiting on the nearly empty downtown platform at Columbus Circle. Monday nights after nine were notoriously slow for the New York subway system. People weren't supposed to be out after work on Mondays, they were supposed to be too exhausted from pushing themselves back into the rhythm of another frantic week after a too-short, too-full weekend. Susan herself had mixed feelings about Monday nights. Sometimes she imagined how much more relaxing it would be to have Workshop on Tuesdays or Wednesdays and have Monday as a short warm-up day for the rest of the work week, the way most people did. Other times, she thought these prolonged Mondays were a necessary kick in the pants, forcing her to jump-start her energies for the week and remember what her life was supposed to be about.

"A kick in the pants, or a bang in the leg," she thought now, rubbing that beleaguered limb. That third collision of the night had been a hearty thwack, and those square plaid bags, with their harsh surfaces of some mysterious fibrous texture, hurt like hell. There would be another bruise in the morning.

Having been hit by most of them, Susan considered herself a connoisseur of the standard portables lugged around by the restless population of the "Capital of the World" (or was it "The World's Hometown"? The Mayor seemed to change the slogan every week). To the bangs of Puerto Rican luggage, her legs could compare the brutish bite of various wheeled cases, the gentle rasp and occasional paper cut of shopping bags with cachet, and the thin-shrouded thump of generic plastic sacks. Traveling north along her compact body, her ribs and back were familiar with the thud of the overfilled messenger bag and strap-slung laptop case, usually worn by men. Women had better control over shoulder-held bags. The exception was the girls who crammed too much into fat little purses, which they let swing free and wide from thongs or chains, to sail with a cushiony smack, right into her upper arm. Gym and dance bags, slung over tall shoulders from short straps, were most likely to knock her on the back of the head. She'd lost a few hats and earrings that way. From the reverse angle, her face had been contused on more than one occasion by a book-filled backpack. Even when she lagged five or six steps behind one, she seemed unable to avoid the deep sure-to-produce-a-bruise poke of the golf-sized umbrella carelessly carried up a flight of stairs. Still, a bruise was better than losing an eye. And at least she no longer had to shield her eyes—or sleeves—from the flying embers of people who simultaneously smoked and talked with their hands.

Susan was a city girl, specifically a New York City girl, from birth and to the bone, and living in a city is a contact sport. A certain amount of collision damage is to be expected. She'd always accepted this with good humor, as she'd accepted other things that non-urban folk, with their acres of personal space and armored vehicles, find unpalatable or laughable. Then, somewhere around her 35th birthday, Susan began to notice a troubling pattern. Not only had the number of such collisions in her personal experience escalated, but far too many of them were totally unnecessary. She'd find herself in a situation where, in order to collide with her, the other person would have to go completely out of his or her way. For example, this wasn't the first time that she'd found herself standing on a nearly empty subway platform, with yards of empty cement on every side, only to have another person walk in her direction and veer close enough to slam into her. So many of the early incursions had been from young men in giant pants and hooded sweatshirts that she'd assumed she was the inadvertent participant in some kind of gang rite. Maybe something like the old Iroquois custom of "counting coup," where the premise was that if you touched a potential victim, you'd come close enough to attack and therefore earned your props. It didn't thrill her, but at least she could shrug philosophically and think, "If it means so much to you to smack into me, that's your pathetic problem." After a while, however, she noticed that it wasn't only these boys, but men and women of all ages and from all walks of life who were performing this routine. It was as if they were all meteors and she was the nearest planet, her gravitational pull sucking them in. Susan was heartily sick and tired of being slammed, but what troubled her more was that not a single person ever acknowledged her. When she was a child, along with giving up her seat for the older or infirm or visibly pregnant (who had tacitly ben categorized as infirm), she'd been taught that even when you bumped into someone accidentally you still had to apologize. In the rare packed train or sluggish escalator when she was the bumper instead of the bumpee, she continued to do just that, despite being met with increasingly hostile reactions from other people who seemed to take her inadvertent trip or foot-tread as an act of aggression, even as she was apologizing for it. Yet people who'd had to go out of their way to ram into her always passed her by without so much as a glance. Even families of immigrants from politer societies, and sweet looking older ladies in going-to-church hats, would knock into her and stride on by, her presence registering less than that of an I-beam or trash can.

She couldn't remember exactly when, but at some point Susan had begun to suspect that she was actually invisible. There could be no other reasonable explanation. That said, the question was, what had caused this?

She'd heard a few theories about what makes a person invisible to others. Primary among these was the concept that you become invisible by blending into a crowd. This makes easy sense if the crowd is homogenous. An average-build visitor of European stock doesn't register at all in Oslo. Put that same person on the streets of Beijing and you've got something as obvious (and entertaining) as a tricked-out circus clown. In New York, however, the crowded streets are everything but homogenous; everyone, even the most tabloid-prominent celebrities, can disappear. That didn't explain why Susan was so often buffeted in lonely places like the empty subway platforms and stairways where you might think that *any* breathing human being would be highly conspicuous.

Television crime shows dote on the theory that any type of uniform obscures the person wearing it. We don't focus on the face, the walk and scarcely even the race or gender of a uniformed cop, a mail carrier or, unless our lives are at stake, anyone in scrubs; in a boardroom full of dark suits, one is much like the other; and a person in a chador might not even be a woman - who would know? No, that couldn't explain it either. Her fashion sense wasn't noteworthy, but what Susan wore hardly qualified as a uniform.

Avoidance results in the most powerful invisibility. Susan thought this was the big one, because she knew she sometimes did it herself. If you won't look someone in the face, you make him or her invisible. Social prejudices turn entire groups of people into wallpaper, and if noticing a particular person causes discomfort, distaste or fear, the eye can decide not to see what the heart might grieve after. We pretend not to see schizophrenic street people, and look away from amputees or strangers with disfiguring scars. It's a more nuanced invisibility that the monied matriarch imposes on the trophy wife, and the trophy wife on her flight attendant and cocktail waitress sisters further down the ladder. The poor are notoriously invisible to everyone except each other.

None of this was explaining Susan's own degree of invisibility to her satisfaction. It was interesting to think about, on a Monday after Workshop when her brain wanted to exercise itself, but it was irrelevant.

Irrelevant. That was it. She was irrelevant. No one depended on her, not financially, not emotionally. She had no husband or other male complement and no children. Her widowed mother was, fortunately, healthy, independent and living in a senior community on the other side of the continent. Susan Roth didn't run a company, not even a department within an office of a company. She was neither a doctor, accountant nor hair stylist. In other words, if she quit work not so much as a single person would be discomfited by her absence. While she had her group of friends, some very

5

good friends, she'd never been the life of any party. To top it off, she was statistically irrelevant. Meeting none of these other qualifications and possessed of limited (when converted into New York dollars, downright minuscule) discretionary income, Susan wasn't so much demographically undesirable as nonexistent. To the powers that ruled her world, the politicians and the marketeers, she literally didn't count.

A middle-aged, middle-class single woman of unremarkably pleasant appearance, who worked at an innocuous job that barely covered her expenses, Susan Roth lived imperceptibly in the world, causing not a blip on anyone's radar. This wasn't all bad, she considered. There were times when it was convenient to be invisible. Crowd control and security personnel waved her through without a thought. In summer, she could sit for hours under a tree in Central Park and be as private as someone stranded on a desert island. Everywhere, people would say and do things in front of her that they would be shocked to learn had been witnessed, no less recorded.

It can be ideal for a writer to be more of an observer of life than a participant. Ideal for writing that is, but not, as Susan had been forcibly reminded earlier tonight, for a writing career. Unfortunately for her own career, Susan wasn't living in the age of Jane Austen but in the age of media freak shows and too much information. A writer didn't have to have something to say or the skill with which to say it. All that was important now was to be "sexy," to have an eye-catching "hook" that was easy to sell. Susan, bad luck, wasn't a brand or a rogue who could become a brand, but merely a good writer. On bad days, she'd reread her rejection letters and wonder what life could be like if she were only a nymphomaniac heiress, or the winner of *Geek Factor* (a TV game show where first round contestants had to bite the heads off live chickens), or that transsexual who'd carried to term an embryo germinated from a donor egg and his/her own sperm. Or simply Macintosh Wing.

Susan wondered if there was a word that meant the opposite of "mantra." She had to remember to ask Raju. If there was, hers would definitely be "Macintosh Wing," two words that caused her instant agitation. Macintosh Wing personified everything Susan wasn't. She thought of him as a boy, though Raju, who seemed to know everything, said he was probably around 25. A beautiful creature, all polished bones and dewy eyes, Wing sported a wispy soul patch on his chin and dimples to either side of his pouting and naturally rosy mouth. A titillating quantity of coffee-colored skin showed through his perpetually unbuttoned shirts and fray-ripped jeans. Men, women, even the horses under the mounted police, turned to stare when he walked down a street. They couldn't help it; anywhere he was, was bed. The world was his mirror and his writing pretty much reflected that. Yet as they'd learned tonight, Macintosh Wing was the only member in the five-year history of the elite Harrison Levy Professional Writer's Workshop to score an actual book deal. And he'd pulled this off without having written so much as a proposal, no less an entire manuscript.

According to the brief (inarticulate, rather than modest) announcement he'd made at the top of class, with their rent-a-mentor glowing behind him, Wing's book, purchased from a "pitch," was to be a memoir of his barely-lapsed childhood. What Raju had overheard later in the men's room and told Susan during their customary Starbucks postmortem, was that the boy had strolled into the offices of a venerable publishing house, allowed his insinuating gaze to glide over the receptionist and murmured, "I'm a straight man with gay and lesbian parents, and I need an editor for my book." He didn't need to tell her he was biracial and gorgeous, the receptionist had eyes. She was probably just out of Smith, as ambitious as she was dazzled and had realized at once that he wasn't so much a book, as a best-selling book jacket. Of course she'd lifted the receiver and buzzed upstairs to a senior editor. "Thanks to Jesus Christ," as Wing had concluded his own telling, before sprawling across his usual pair of seats. Except for Susan and Raju, the class gave him a standing ovation.

With an eye always on the potential for networking, Raju had instinctively risen with the rest of the class. His parents having left Bombay for Queens when he was less than five, he'd been raised in the city and, enterprising even in childhood, he'd assimilated as easily as curried mayonnaise. Recently however, as a marketing gambit of his own, Raju Nayar had begun a campaign of cultivating his vestigial ethnicity. Tonight, he'd ostentatiously resumed his seat at Wing's closing phrase. It wasn't, as he'd reminded Susan, that he had anything personal against Jesus. A Brahmin with a stone lingam proudly displayed on his kitchen altar, he was tolerant in the extreme and, unlike Allah, the Christ had cast no recent political shadows over his extended family. The gesture was his way of actively emphasizing his own cultural identity.

Susan had never left her seat at all. She couldn't. Her healthy stockpile of worldly cynicism, a graduation gift from the New York City public school system, told her that it was par for the course that Macintosh Wing, who couldn't successfully write "you suck" on a subway poster, was getting published. It was funny, in that grim way of things that really hurt. But Susan found herself picking at the thought like a sore.

Wing had a book deal. And the rest would soon be history. "Thanks to Jesus Christ," indeed. What an important use of God's energies, getting The Macintosh Wing Story out to the thirsting public.

This was another of life's great puzzles to Susan. She understood the need people had to believe in something bigger than themselves. What confounded her were the manifestations of that need. A couple of years ago, she'd found herself on an Amtrak train that had to pull over to a siding to allow a late-running freight train to pass on the single shared rail. They'd stalled there for about 15 minutes. When they started up again, a woman across the aisle threw her hands in the air and ecstatically sang out "Praise Jesus! I do praise His Name!!" To which the man seated in front of Susan called back "Amen, Sister!" Her initial impulse to laugh had been quickly squelched by a kind of horror, as she realized that there were people who truly did believe their God deliberately runs the trains. She'd never been able to wrap her head around the idea of a redemptive savior, but if there were such an entity, it would be distressing in the extreme to imagine He/She/It would maintain a laissez-faire attitude towards large-scale manifestations of Man's inhumanity to Man, but would find it essential to intercede in professional sports, awards shows or, well, publishing deals and Amtrak trains. More than distressing, she found the idea entirely unacceptable. Yet it was becoming apparent to her that she was bucking a trend.

At the dawn of the Third Millennium (CE), God seemed to be everywhere, and not in the omnipotent/omniscient sense. "God" was everywhere like "Coke" or "Mickey D's" and, like those and "Jacuzzi," was becoming a neutered brand name, used to invoke a quick consumer identification with other products. "God" stood for "Values," and both of those meant that someone was pushing an agenda that brooked no discussion. If you believe God has chosen you to live in a certain manner or to take a specific action, then that manner or action must be Right and, therefore, no one can possibly argue against it, and compromise is not an option.

Susan sighed, partly with fatigue, partly with nostalgia for the future of her childhood, when compromise was going to save the world and toleration rule it. Her eyes scanned the off-hours riders waiting with her on the subway platform. On the other side of the kiosk, the woman who had banged her with the plaid bag was now reading the flyers plastered over the metal accordion shutters. From previous experience, Susan knew them to be decorated with drawings of crosses and stars and hands forming horns, and that they variously extolled the virtues of "Mrs. Maria," "Sister Catherine" and "Madame Veronica," all of whose prayers could heal your broken heart, calm your troubled soul or help you find money. A few I-beams further down, a Pakistani man in a pale blue leisure suit kept a weather eye on the platform, checking out the others who were waiting. His eye and Susan's had met more than once tonight. The first time it happened, she'd smiled. He'd turned away. Slung across his shoulder was a dozing child kept up well past bedtime. Close to his side, an umbrella stroller with another sleeping tot sheltered between them, two women kept their eyes downcast as they spoke quietly across the handles. Both wore headscarves, but while one's was lilac to match her shalwar kameez, the other's was a plain black and tossed almost casually above her turtleneck and jeans. A pimply young man sitting on the wooden platform bench with a cracked leather briefcase was still growing into his black suit. His old-fashioned black hat rose and fell over the thick book in which he was entirely, nearsightedly, absorbed. The other end of the bench was occupied by a wizened black gentleman whose body was shrinking away from his pressed grey-striped suit. His sat ramrod straight, his eyes half-closed, and clutched a shabby canvas tote bag with the faded logo of the Church of Christ. And, nearest to Susan, a chubby little Filipino woman rested against the flat side of a thickly-painted steel beam, her lips moving as she read from the onionskin pages of a pocketbook bible. Susan wondered how many of them were praying for the downtown A train, and how many would give thanks to their higher power when it eventually, as scheduled, would arrive.

It was arriving now. To those who frequent the subway, the change in air current announces the arrival of the train even before the sound and lights. A train was now in the air and everyone on the platform shook themselves aware and moved briskly to their favorite positions.

"Fuck," Susan muttered, as the rolling stroller barked inevitably against her shins. That made four collisions tonight. And then she screamed. The coming train had roused another platform occupant as well, a pigeon gone astray. An underground bird, like a beached whale, is the kind of disquieting sight that usually brought Susan an instinctive shudder. This confused bird rose hysterically in a trajectory that took it just past Susan, its beady eyes glittering, its tiny heart pumping frantically in concert with its pale wings. As it narrowly cleared her head, claws brushed her hair. That's when she screamed. Not that anyone heard above the rumble of the train.

Susan boarded, shaken but determined not to touch her hair. She was sure she'd find bird shit and would rather wait until she was under a shower. At this time on a Monday night, the train was sparsely filled but she didn't waste any time trying to find a seat. The moderate number of riders had expanded to fill the perceived vacuum, filling additional orange and yellow shells with their bags, outstretched legs and ball-airing spread knees. At one end of the car, the corner group of five seats was walled off by a pair of youngsters too young and too broke to get a room. The junkie in the hoodie didn't stink, but it was wiser to give him a wide berth in case he suddenly woke up and forgot where he was—or remembered. Susan found an unoccupied door and leaned, illegally, against it. She pulled her emergency Trollope out of her bag and started to read.

For the past eight months, Susan had found herself coming home to an apartment that felt uninhabited. She'd never lived alone until now.

Way back at the dawn of adult life, she and her college roommate Diane had found the place listed in the *Voice* and subleased it from the tenants of record who were themselves gambling on homesteading in Tribeca. By the time Susan had gotten on the lease herself, Diane was long gone, her place in what had been designed as the living room having been taken by a string of fresh graduates Susan found by the simple expedient of ringing up their alma mater's Career Guidance office. Vassar hadn't been any help with her own career, but they'd been Johnny-on-the spot when it came to supplying her with a continual stream of optimistic, hard-working and intelligent roommates. Susan valued all three qualities equally. Optimism was not only ballast to her own increasingly darker temperament, but insured she would never come home to a body in the bathtub. Hard working meant the other half of the rent and utilities would be forthcoming. Intelligence, well, if you had to share your living space, it was nice to do it with someone with whom you could have a conversation. There were philosophic differences that would never be resolved, like Tara's faith in Jesus or Vicky's in Ayn Rand, but the discussions were usually fascinating.

The roommates came and went, moving on to husbands or lucrative promotions, while Susan beavered endlessly away as office-worker-by-day, anchoress-of-literature-by-nights-and-weekends. She got older, and they seemed to get younger and younger. At first, she'd found their bright enthusiasm contagious, then amusing; ultimately it was utterly demoralizing.

Tara had been the final roommate. When she'd announced she'd finally be moving in with Michael, subsequent, of course, to a proper Christian wedding (the dismayingly Hebraic heritage of Michael's mother notwithstanding), Susan had automatically gone for the Guidance Office number. The telephone already in her hand and the area code dialed, she'd stopped. She was a middle-aged woman and she was still calling a college to look for a roommate. Feeling more pathetic and defeated than even she'd thought possible, she'd burst into tears. Tara had found her in the kitchen and, with a quick prayer for guidance, put on a kettle to boil and set briskly to work. She was in mutual funds and knew money as well as she knew her Scriptures. After a couple of hours and a quart or so of Red Zinger, she'd handily reorganized her older friend's finances, showing how a better use of the 401K deduction would increase take-home pay, and that exchanging the ragged portfolio of bits and pieces stocks left by Susan's late father for shares in one of Tara's own funds would increase investment income. In the end, barring a long-overdue raise in salary, only a few minor economies would be necessary for Susan to be able to carry the expenses on her own. There would be no more roommates after Tara had gone. Unless, God willing, Susan were to find Mr. Right (as Tara, thank you Jesus, had), and for some strange reason he wanted to move into a tiny one-bedroom apartment in almost-Chelsea.

Tara was probably the most practical Christian Susan had ever met. She was also the kind of bouncy cheerleader that everyone wants to hate but can't help loving. Her sweetness was too genuine and she had the grace of a sense of humor. Susan was very fond of her. Despite wanting to live on her own, she missed the girl once she was gone.

The front room had been returned to its intended state by the removal of the false wall of too-dilapidated-to-sell prefabricated wardrobe and shelving units, and an amateurish coating of "uh-oh" paint. The raise in salary had yet to come through, so the economies held firm. It hardly felt like a living room. Apart from the television, which she'd rolled in from her bedroom (now "the" bedroom), the room held nothing but a stick lamp Tara had left behind, a rag rug Diane had made before her daughter Lindsay decided her favorite color was purple not green, and a mottled leather chair Lisa had thrown out when redecorating Alan's office. There was no overhead lighting, and with the lamp turned on Susan always felt she was in some Edward Hopper painting, marooned in a corner, picked out to be stared at from the other side of the dark void.

After eight months, it was still strange to push the door open and find that gaping space. Its near emptiness made her every movement echo from the moment she turned the key in the lock. She'd formed the habit of rushing quickly to her bedroom and staying there most of the time. Not that Tara had been around much, having almost from the beginning spent much of her time with Michael, but her presence had still been felt. Now, with only Susan's furniture and Susan's things and Susan's life to fill it, the place seemed hollow.

It seemed especially empty tonight. Workshop nights usually left her in a good mood, or at least with a renewal of purpose. Tonight she'd been too pissed off to be inspired, and even laughing with Raju hadn't helped. That wasn't true. It wasn't fair to blame Wing when her mood was as much about that other thing she had hanging over her.

Susan finished blowing her hair and faced herself squarely in the mirror. "You did good," she told herself, trying for a smile.

She deserved a smile, or some kind of pat on the back. Diane said that if you can't open up to your friends, you're an emotional paraplegic, but Susan didn't see it that way. She hated herself when she was being self-pitying; she didn't want her friends to pity her as well. In any case, she didn't like to bare her soul that way. It was a waste of resources. She'd always clung to what her college writing professor used to say, "Save something for the paper."

She was proud that she hadn't said a word to Raju about it. The question was, could she be that strong on Saturday with the girls?

The Macintosh Wing story was a big hit at the monthly "girlfriend's lunch." Everything was funny when the four of them got together, except when something was very much not and then they rallied to support the wounded.

11

The women had been friends since college, bonding over deadlines and break-ups, and using each other as mirrors as they tried on potential selves. As years went by, and days got busier and lives diverged, they still managed to stay close. Phone calls and (later) e-mails were never enough, so even before chick lit and cable had made it popular for girlfriends to arrange for regular, tipsy gatherings, they'd had their monthly lunches. Lisa's husband Alan liked to crack that she'd even included them in the pre-nup.

It had been hard for them all when Steffi "retired" and moved West. Everything was more buoyant when Steffi was around. There was something breezy about her, something that spoke of whooshing through various incarnations of water with sails and skis. It was a quality that embodied forward motion and triumph over obstacles, while shrugging off what couldn't be controlled. This quality had made her so successful selling commercial real estate in New York that she'd been able to chuck it all a year ago and move to Arizona, where she lived off her investments when she wasn't making sporting forays to wetter climes. This was the first time she'd returned to the City since then. It was only having her back for the week that made them acknowledge the gap they'd felt in their circle.

"Champagne!" Diane had crowed, but Lisa decreed champagne to be passé. Instead, they went trendy and ordered a round of one of the house special cocktails. Steffi, eyeballing the list, had claimed she was curious to find out what lemonade, pomegranate liqueur, pear vodka and sake might possibly taste like. A bit like Hawaiian Punch, Susan thought, and therefore stealthily potent. They were floating merrily even before the breadbasket guy arrived.

Now they were beaming at each other over their baroque salads. They were complete again. The comfortable rhythm of these lunches dictated they begin by catching up. Susan had so little to say that she always came with a prepared story to tell to start off the day. This time, with so much she didn't want to say, it was even more important to get a laugh and then she could sit back and enjoy listening to the others.

Everyone cooed over pictures of Diane's children, the only three among the four of them if you didn't count Lisa's stepdaughter who was old enough to be taking her SATs and had anyway, even before Lisa's marriage to Alan, always lived with her mother. Susan was the only one who regularly saw Diane's trio in the flesh. Diane philosophically attributed this to Susan being Sophie's godmother, and chose to appreciate her attention rather than reproaching the others for neglect. Susan's own hunch was that she was the only one with a void in her life that needed to be filled by someone else's kids. While the others moved on to Steffi's adventures in early retirement, she surreptitiously fondled the tiny stuffed animal Diane had slipped her at the door, a gift from Sophie. Apparently they scented toys these days; this one was trailing a whiff of sugar. She'd made a mental note to call her goddaughter and say thank you.

Around their second bottle of Viognier (Lisa having vetoed the Sauvignon Blanc), Lisa pulled out photos of the sofas she was considering for the new media room. Even Alan had to accept that with Megan heading for Berkley, it was a waste of real estate to maintain a bedroom for her use. He'd stood mesmerized before the enormous flat-screen television in the Bose showroom and given Lisa the green light to redecorate. Should his daughter improbably be inspired to visit, she'd be perfectly comfortable in the lovely, if generic, guest room.

"So, Sue," she said, fanning the photos on the table between them, "which do you think? I'm leaning towards the red leather, but Alan's going through this textile phase."

"Too Italian," Steffi said, tapping her tanned finger on a photo. "I like the nubby stuff."

Diane craned her neck across the table. "That'll be filthy in a week," she said with the conviction of a woman who was raising three children and a golden retriever.

"Doesn't matter what you two think," Lisa said bluntly. "Suze is the only who counts." It was common knowledge that Alan thought Susan knew everything. Whatever might have started that attitude, it had been set in stone when she'd discovered the first Harry Potter book on a trip to London and predicted the phenomenon more than a year before it hit the US. "I swear," Lisa often said, "if it were anyone else I'd be jealous." Susan never knew whether to be flattered or insulted.

"Steffi's right about the leather," Susan said. "It looks like the interior of a sports car." She shifted the other photos under her nose like a game of three-card monte.

"I was afraid you'd say that," Lisa said bluntly. "Can't you lie? You know he'll want to go with whatever you say."

She didn't know if it was the effects of too much wine on a breakfastless stomach or undependable peri-menopausal hormones, but she blurted it out. "At least somebody appreciates me." Even Susan herself was surprised. Once it was out, it couldn't be unsaid.

It was Diane, in automatic maternal mode, who jumped in. "You can't let that boy get to you," she said stoutly. Over the years, they'd heard plenty of stories about the various members of Susan's various workshops. As entertaining as she'd made the Macintosh Wing story, they'd understood how much it had demoralized her. "Big deal. He still has to write a book. You already have one."

"Two," Susan mumbled, embarrassed.

"Two," Diane nodded, as if this proved a point. "And you'll soon have your own book deal, thanks to Tara."

Which, coming as it did with the waiter topping off Susan's wine glass, was exactly the wrong thing to say. "There isn't going to be a book deal," she said, fighting the sudden lump in her throat.

"That's ridiculous!" Lisa objected. "You haven't even had a meeting."

Tara's new mother-in-law was a literary agent. And not just any literary agent, as Susan had informed the girls, practically drooling, when she'd first found out. Janet Ruben-Pritchard was one of the best in the business, a legend for ferreting out new talent and taking it all the way to the top. While the two were sorting out their triangular relationship with Michael, Tara had been unwilling to ask favors but once the bargain was sealed and it was a love fest on every side, she'd passed Susan's preferred novel to Janet and begged a meeting. Tara had called it a housewarming gift. Susan's friends had been waiting to hear about it for months.

"I wasn't going to talk about it, but she called me in last week." Susan had swallowed it down so far that she hadn't discussed it with anyone, not with Raju, not with her closest friends. Janet Ruben-Pritchard had seen her, yes, in her expensively shabby offices that reeked as much of critical acclaim as they did of financial success. Trembling as nervously as in a doctor's waiting room, Susan had perched at the edge of a tapestry armchair for a mercifully brief period of time, trying not to stare at the shelves and shelves of Janet's authors' greatest hits. She'd been ushered into the inner sanctum only five minutes after the time set for her actual appointment. Janet Ruben-Pritchard, a petite woman of probably-60, had risen from behind a hulking mahogany partner's desk to cordially greet her at the door. She'd cleared a pile or two of papers from the sagging tapestry couch so that they could sit there together.

"I should have known right then," Susan tried to say it lightly. "The minute she sat down next to me, I should have known she had no intention of doing business."

Steffi nodded her agreement. A negotiator like Janet Ruben-Pritchard wouldn't give up the traditional across-the-desk power play.

"Her assistant came in with a tray. What's that china your grandmother left you, Di? The set with those beautiful flowers?"

"The Spode?"

"Spode," Susan nodded. "That's what they were, the cups and the plate with the cookies. A plate that elegant, I guess I should call them biscuits. Let's just say I got a top of the line brushoff."

"What did she say?" Lisa would naturally be the one to ask outright.

"She said I was a good writer. I'm fluid, I have command of the language and my voice is clear. She said there was no question of my talent and ability." Not only that, there had been decades of confidence in that pronouncement.

"You call that a brushoff?"

Susan nodded. "It came with a but." She'd felt some small pride that she hadn't asked it herself. She'd simply smiled and nodded, leaving the silence until Janet had been compelled to continue. And so Janet had. "She said I wasn't interesting." The woman had not been unkind, simply matter-of-fact. She'd even claimed to be paying Susan a compliment by being frank.

"So she told you that you were good and then she turned you down?" Diane was bewildered. She was raising her children according to the belief that if you were good at something and worked hard, you could succeed.

"She said she needed something to sell." If Susan closed her eyes, she could see the tasteful manicure resting lightly atop her manuscript on Ruben-Pritchard's rosewood table. "I don't see anything here," is what she told me.

"What did you say?"

"I said 'other than good writing.'" She had, and she'd said it a bit more sharply than she'd intended. Janet had smiled in a way that Susan chose to interpret as rueful. "Good writing and what else? What can you give me, here?" The manicure had pointed squarely in the vicinity of Susan's heart.

"I had to tell her I was a pretty ordinary person," Susan continued. "She kept insisting 'there must be something unique about you, something special.' I'm telling you, she sounded so sincere that even if she hadn't held my potential career in her hands I would have wanted to give her an answer that would make her happy but, cold hard truth, I couldn't come up with anything." She took a big swallow of wine.

The bigger truth was something Susan couldn't bear to say to anyone who mattered to her, but which she'd impulsively spilled to Janet Ruben-Pritchard. "I may have breast cancer," she'd said, and then listened to the words take voice for the very first time since she'd thought them, after she'd gotten the call that her doctor had scheduled a do-over of her mammogram.

Janet's eyes had grown visibly kind, and she'd briefly patted Susan's hand. "That's a shame dear," she'd said, "it really is." She'd sighed. "But it's just not interesting. It may have been twenty years ago, but not now."

They'd chatted in a desultory manner for a while longer, just so that Susan wouldn't feel she'd been given the bum's rush. At the end, Janet had shaken her hand warmly. "Keep writing," she urged, "and if you ever have something for me, please, let me know. I'll take your call."

Twenty years ago, when breast cancer was still interesting and Macintosh Wing was arguably still in Pampers, Susan would have been overjoyed to hear this from Janet Ruben-Pritchard or her equivalent. Now, complimentary or not, it was simply another "No." She'd left with a smile, gone back to the office (this had been her lunch break) and blocked it out for the rest of the day. That night, she'd taken a twenty-minute shower, sobbing violently the whole time. The following week came the Wing bombshell, followed by her second mammogram on Thursday. She expected to hear from her doctor on Monday. Susan prided herself on coping, but too many things were piling up at once. It was getting to be more than she might be able to bear.

"I can write," Susan announced to the girls, gesturing for someone to top off her wine again. "Hell, I'm a fine writer. But I'm not interesting. I have nothing to say that anyone wants to hear, and my life is boring. Here's to me."

"Aw, Suze, she's just one person. Okay, she's important, but she's still just the one." Steffi always tried to put things into perspective, even if she sometimes had to skew the perspective to make things fit.

"She's Janet Ruben-Pritchard," Lisa said, clearly impressed. "She really said she'd take your call? Sue, that's a big deal. So you write another book."

"Just like that, sure," Susan said. "If I ever become interesting before I die, I'll be sure and sit down and do just that."

"We think you're interesting," Diane said, getting up to hug her.

It was that hug that made it all spill out of her: the feelings of invisibility and futility, the loneliness of the empty house. And ultimately, the worst thing of all, the fear that a single pronouncement from Dr. Snyder might make it all be over.

2 - KEEPING ABREAST

Sunday is usually the shortest day of the week for a working stiff, flying by way too fast towards the unavoidable Monday-through-Friday. But with "Monday, late morning, early afternoon" holding the threat or promise of Dr. Snyder's call, this Sunday looked like an Everest. Susan might have blown her brains out if it hadn't been for Steffi.

Susan being the only one of the girls to still maintain a nine-to-five job and therefore not as available to hang with visiting friends, she and Steffi had planned to spend this Sunday together. Steffi arrived at the apartment bright and early, her arms full of bagels and the Sunday *Times*, both of which she insisted they consume picnic-style on the living room floor. "You have to start owning the space," she explained to Susan as she spread the only clean bath towels under the patches of morning sun that checker-boarded the floor. "If you want to banish the negativity, you have to fill your space with life."

To Susan, inhaling her second cup of coffee, that sounded like borrowed philosophy. "So where did you pick up that line?" she asked. There was more acid in her voice than she'd intended but it didn't matter. Cynicism had always rolled off Steffi like raindrops off a slicker.

Steffi laughed heartily and wiggled her toes in a sunbeam. Dust motes swirled around them like snowflakes. "Touché, Suze. Even if I didn't say it that way, it's what I've always thought. It came up in my discussion group, at this personal enrichment center down the road from the house."

"Personal enrichment center? Don't tell me the Southwest New Age pod people have sucked you in already!" Susan was surprised how sad that made her. She liked to think of Steffi as the last great Independent.

Steffi laughed again and reached for the "Styles" section. "Everything is always so extreme with you, Suze," she said, opening the paper from the back. "Do or die; never any greys." She started flipping pages. "Me, I take what I find I can use and then I move on. A sculptor I met at the pool turned me on to a place that has a good schedule for yoga and a fantastic massage therapist. And when it turned out there were interesting people to talk with, I didn't think it was selling my soul to hang around and talk back." Steffi stopped and looked up at Susan, amazed. "Didn't Lisa date Norbert Burgess, back in the day?"

Susan snatched back "Styles." "Let me see!" There he was, Lisa's Junior year squeeze, looking middle-aged buff and a bit smug as he posed in matching profile with his partner, a thin-faced man whose eyes, even in the grainy pixels of a *Times* photo, twinkled irrepressibly behind his wire-rims. Susan recognized the partner without having to read the caption. He was the bible-runner—the keeper of the storyline—for a venerable network daytime drama. Once upon a time, Susan had taken his "Writing for Soaps" course and vied for the advertised internship. She'd been told, with twinkling eyes, that while her writing was surprisingly competent (could a compliment sound more like an insult?) they had "stylistic differences" that would make it impossible to work in such a close team harness. The plum had gone to Lance Esposito who was still learning colloquial English but had a tight bum and long eyelashes.

"So much for calling it the 'woman's sports pages,'" Susan cracked weakly, slipping deeper into her gloom.

Missing the real reason behind this reaction, Steffi tossed aside the pages with a snort. "It's all bullshit anyway. For most of these losers, it's the only way they'll ever feel important. I'm single by choice and damned happy about it. Who needs a man anyway?"

"Norbert Burgess?" Susan suggested. Steffi laughed harder than this deserved. "And I have bad news for him," Susan added, rallying. "He ain't getting one." Maybe two years after the soap internship, Lance Esposito had shown up at a Writer's Network Storytelling Bootcamp for Women and Minorities. His English had gotten much better and he'd had stories to tell.

This time they both laughed. "I know what," Steffi thought aloud. "Let's go see a crappy movie!" She reached for "Arts & Leisure" and started tearing through it.

They had to wait until the one-o'clocks, because Susan had promised to call Sophie after Sunday school, then found a sexy English gangster film that wasn't crappy at all. It was a long window-shopping walk back home. They ordered in pizza, which they ate, once again, on the living room floor. Steffi was meeting someone at seven, to see a play at Signature Theatre. When she stood to brush the crust crumbs from her sweater, she flashed Susan a thumbs up.

"Thanks," Susan said, inadequately. "I needed that." The day was mostly over.

"Hey," Steffi shrugged, slinging her bag across her shoulder. As they started together for the door, she patted the bag like a horse and grinned. "You don't know how much I get ragged about this in Sedona. 'Why do you carry such an ee-NOR-mous bag?!'"

"Looks normal to me. Do I see you again before you leave?"

Steffi shook her head. "You'll have to stop finding excuses and come visit me." They hugged and Susan opened the door. Steffi paused for a minute, looking back over Susan's shoulder.

"What?"

"I was wondering where you planned to put Lisa's old sofa when it comes."

"Too bad you're not taking Feng Shui at your enrichment center. Go, you'll miss your curtain."

Susan pushed her friend out the door and waved goodbye. Then she returned to the living room floor to finish off the wine so that she could fall asleep and make Monday come more quickly.

An unscheduled Monday morning staff meeting is the business world equivalent of a pop quiz. They staggered, bleary-eyed, into the large conference room like the cast of *Dawn of the Dead*, each clutching a mug in one outstretched hand and a yellow pad in the other.

Evelyn, officious as always, her arms assertively crossing her chest, stood at the door and watched them all dribble in. The meeting might not have shown up on the schedule, but Evelyn had clearly planned it. She wasn't that much older than Susan, but she continued to have her hair "done," in the manner of their mothers' generation; it had obviously been "done" that weekend, and she was wearing her pearls.

There were separate Management meetings for Vice Presidents, Directors and Chiefs, meetings that Evelyn was only occasionally invited to attend. Meetings run by Evelyn were for support staff only. To each staffer that entered now, she gave a tiny nod and an almost subliminal raise of one eyebrow. "Your presence has been noted," this said, "and it pains me to have to acknowledge you, you worthless drudge."

They were the standard-issue New York City support staff. At their core was a clutch of mothers under 35, who were there to bring home a requisite second income. Barely above them was a file of professional assistants, well-groomed women, usually between the ages of 45 and 60 and usually divorced or widowed, who had once been ambitious and were now merely frustrated, mired by the lean-mean-money-machine corporate structure that lacked middle-management positions that might once have allowed for internal promotion. Having been plucked from their ranks, Evelyn hated this group most of all.

Many of the remaining slots were crewed by the night-schoolers, the 20-somethings who were either working by day and going to CUNY by night, or had realized that today's BA/BS was yesterday's high school diploma and were investing their off hours in mobilizing credits towards an MBA or LLB.

They came and went, making many a temporary ruckus but rarely a lasting impression.

The current star in this cluster was Melissa, Steve's assistant. Steve, the self-satisfied VP of Marketing, had a regular flow of buxom young assistants grace the desk that guarded his glass-fronted office. Melissa was the latest and youngest, and flaunted two of the biggest assets the firm had ever seen. None of the men, and especially not Steve, had a clue how shrewd and ambitious Melissa was, and neither did Evelyn. Melissa always made a point of complimenting Evelyn on her print blouses and terribly tasteful jewelry, so much so that Evelyn had appointed her the official note-taker at these events. To be fair to the girl, Melissa found ways to compliment almost everyone, at least occasionally, and somehow managed to sound sincere. She could also be depended on to cover phones in an emergency, and was always bringing in plastic tubs of Godiva chocolates that she said her brother, who worked for Pepperidge Farm, picked up in the "seconds" shop for practically nothing. Despite wanting not to, Susan liked Melissa. Everyone did.

Even the cable and chip squad, that elite squad of tech commandos who wafted through the corridors at will (except where they were urgently needed), would find the time of day for Melissa. The trio were each 22 and arrogant with IT knowledge. Despite payroll evidence to the contrary, they considered themselves not so much employees but saviors of the company. Staff meetings were a cross they had to bear, but grace was not required.

At the bottom stratum of the company was the mailroom, where Jamal, their token Reformed Offender who had done time for a gang-related holdup of a bodega, was getting his fresh start under the desultory supervision of Wendell, a discouraged man who'd lost his dry cleaning establishment in a fire only to learn that his insurance policy was a phony.

All in all, it was a pretty typical New York City office.

Susan took her customary seat at the far end of the room, with the two coworkers she most nearly thought of as friends. She sat next to Ayesha, who would keep her covered head modestly bowed over the Sunday *Times* crossword during the entire meeting. Ayesha always saved the puzzles until Monday on the outside chance of just such a crisis. Usually, she sat at the end of the table because Susan and Hannah liked to whisper, but in what appeared to be her twelfth month of pregnancy with child number five, Hannah needed all the space she could get and had taken that place. Unable to slide her chair under the table, she pushed it back as far as she could and tried to ease her swollen feet by propping them up on a trashcan.

They always took these particular three seats so that neither Hannah nor Ayesha would be in danger of having a man sit next to her. Susan was the buffer screen, shielding their sanctity with her body. It didn't seem to occur to the others that her tongue might be in her cheek as she did so, or perhaps they didn't care. They'd all long since agreed to respect the boundaries of their religious differences, and Hannah and Ayesha were able to share their amused pity for the unnecessary floundering of their unbelieving colleague. It was a civilized way for coworkers to behave. And they all liked each other; there were few enough people in the company that they could tolerate.

Susan took a long drag of coffee. She needed the diversion of gossip and looked across Ayesha's headscarf to try and engage Hannah. Hannah, who'd come to her faith rather than being born into it, often made Susan laugh the coffee up and out her nose with observations as deadly as the sharpshooters she'd trained for the Israeli army in her unlikely past. Right now, however, she was too exhausted to do more than lean her head against the wall. She rested with her eyes half closed, her beret, stuffed with her hair, acting as a pillow.

The rules and regulations of mankind's many religions (and sects thereof) seemed so arbitrary to Susan that she couldn't imagine following any one of them; nonetheless, she found them fascinating to contemplate. For example, she thought, looking at her two friends, why were there so many rules and taboos about hair? And did that mean that gay hairdressers were doubly transgressing or were they, like the untouchable Harijan caste, fated to serve a purpose? It was an interesting question, one that she was tempted to pose to Hannah and Ayesha, who always enjoyed an opportunity to instruct her. A good seminar might even make Hannah forget her fatigue and Susan forget...

Before Susan could open her mouth, Evelyn rapped on the table with her cocktail ring and called the rabble to order. Above and behind her, making her look for the moment like Citizen Kane, loomed an economy-sized piece of corporate headquarters art. Evelyn, too, seemed to be dreaming of a larger and grander venue.

She began the usual litany, almost all related to belt-tightening. The faces stacked around the table registered varying degrees of indifference and hostility. The exception was the techs, who always pretended she had no power over them. They sat up front, directly under her nose, cracking each other up with feverish texting.

Melissa's pencil skimmed across the surface of her yellow pad. Too many sick days were being taken, as well as unauthorized overtime, which would NOT be tolerated. People kept forgetting that, since Anita's departure (Evelyn cleared her throat suggestively), the night-receptionist position had been trimmed from the budget and it was necessary to put all phones on night service before leaving. Mr. McKitrick had noticed an alarming increase in the purchase of unnecessary office supplies. Starting immediately, supplies would need to be requisitioned in writing from his office. An e-mail to that effect, with the new order form, was in everyone's inbox. Somehow (Evelyn narrowed her lips even more than nature had), despite the institution of key codes, there continued to be an abuse of the photocopiers.

Someone covered a snicker with a sneeze. One of the assistants had a daughter who taught third grade in the Bronx. For a class of 39 students, she was never sent more than 10 copies of any text or workbook. The staff considered it a civic duty and a reasonable use of office resources to make sure those third-graders had what they needed. Apparently it was not as reasonable as the easily-absorbed costs of copying Mr. Danziger's wife's screenplays, the Nelson twins' college application materials, or the color catalogues for Steve's wife's jewelry design business, or even as reasonable as sending out—because they needed professional copying—each of the oversized designer's renderings that Judith Beale needed duplicated to send to her husband in London (that the overseas overnight shipping was also covered without raising an eyebrow, went without saying). With the arrival of the key code system, staffers had opted to share the school copying between them or turn a blind eye to those who did. A copy of "The Tortoise and the Hare" was waiting under a stack of file folders on Susan's desk this very minute.

Finally, Evelyn came to some new business and the main point of the meeting. Everyone was already aware that they would be upgrading all client files from their old custom software to a new industry standard application. Their current program was so sadly out of date that it was impossible to effectively convert the files (Evelyn looked directly at the techs, who smirked) and therefore it would be necessary to enter everything into the new program by hand. It had been decided to divide the work among the assistants (sharp intake of breath from that quarter of the room) as they were the ones who made the most use of the files. Evelyn assured them that Management could not afford to budget overtime for this purpose. It was expected that any efficient PA, anyone worth the attractive base salaries the company was already paying, would surely be able to fit the work into her schedule, though it might mean temporarily sacrificing some of those long (ahem) bathroom breaks and leaving early for the hairdresser (gratuitous cackle).

Since the 2002 staff cuts (support staff only; management had retained size and salaries), each of the PAs was already doing the work of two. Finding time for a large-scale project was not amusing. The only possible way to do it was with overtime, and with overtime not being authorized, it meant no compensation for either the skipped lunches or extra early or late hours. Nor could they do a thing about it. In the current weak economy, no one could afford to quit a job, especially not the assistants who were all, as women "of a certain age," employment agency poison.

"Why?" Susan was surprised to hear the word leave her mouth. She didn't know if it was the unfairness of it, or Evelyn's relish, that made her speak.

"I would think that's obvious, even to our resident Artist," Evelyn permitted herself another bark. Needling Susan was another thing Evelyn always enjoyed.

"I mean, why overstress the resources of an already overextended staff," Susan could not resist rising to pomposity, "when we could hire some college kid to come in nights to do the work?" There were murmurs of agreement from around the room.

"The HR budget doesn't extend to that."

No, Susan thought, but it extends to management bonuses, and the CFO's new wife spreading her decorating wings in the reception area. "It's a lot less than the overtime you say we can't afford, and faster than the year it will take if people have to cram it in between all their other jobs. Wouldn't that be considered a virtual savings?" Predictably, Li-Huan tittered at what he saw as a tech joke. At least next time her monitor turned cyclamen, Susan would be able to get it fixed before going blind.

"I'm sure Management has thought of that," Evelyn said primly, "and has a good reason for not pursuing it."

The staff members shook their heads or made discreet gestures of futility, sad but not surprised. The idea was simply too logical—too logical and not Evelyn's. Melissa scribbled furiously, so much so that her pencil broke. She went to fish a backup pen from her stripe-enhanced cleavage; Hello Kitty came dangerously close to strangling on Melissa's gold name necklace on the way out. Jamal, who had the best view, was riveted until jerked away by Evelyn's command that he explain the latest version of the oft-amended mailroom procedures to "the girls." In their cluster, the assistants exchanged telepathic queries as to who among them would have the privilege of murdering Evelyn.

A mere two hours later, Susan heard a deliberate throat-clearing in the entryway of her cubicle. Hannah stood there, one hand as usual on her belly, the other pressing against the small of her back.

"Melissa told Steve they should maybe hire a student to come in nights and reenter the old files into the new software. He thought it was a great idea and brought it in to McKitrick."

"It was mine. Evelyn blew it off."

"Eh," Hannah said with a shrug.

"Hannah, you were there!"

"So why didn't you go over her head? Like Melissa did?"

"Yeah, well Melissa's got a way of getting Steve's attention," Susan hitched up her bra suggestively. Hannah gave the earthy laugh that always shocked Susan, so loud it nearly blocked out the ring of her cell phone. Susan stared at the answerback name. She'd actually almost forgotten.

"Um," she said, swallowing, "I have to take this."

It was a precaution, Susan kept telling herself. That was what she told Raju when she forced herself to go to Workshop that night. That was what she told her family and friends for the next three days. That was what she told herself when she couldn't eat and couldn't sleep. A routine precaution, Dr. Snyder had said. It could barely be felt, and the needle taken in the office showed nothing, but you don't ignore a shadow that shows up twice in a mammogram. It's only common sense to double check. A formality almost. She wouldn't even have to stay overnight, though it was always sensible to bring a small bag just in case.

"Just in case?!" Susan would have thought panic to be the typical reaction, except that it seemed to surprise Dr. Snyder.

Dr. Snyder spoke calmly and firmly, as if to the six-year-old twins whose photos graced her desk. "Susan, if I thought there was a reason to worry, I would tell you. It's a minor procedure and I expect to find nothing there. However, I prefer to be prepared for the unexpected. Should I find there's something to be concerned about—that's a 'should' Susan, a 'just in case'— I'd like to be able to get right in there and remove it."

"If there was really nothing to be concerned about, you wouldn't be thinking along those lines."

Dr. Snyder's sigh whooshed against Susan's ear. "Susan," she said patiently, "it's the same as packing some underwear in your carry-on bag, in case the airline might lose your luggage. That's all. We're being prepared. Like the Scouts." Dr. Snyder liked to try and defuse nerves with a small joke. No one ever laughed at this one, but she used it just the same. She cleared her throat and continued, "There is nothing, I repeat, nothing to worry about."

"Then why," Susan wondered as so many have, "am I so worried?"

She packed her little bag and quite a large book that someone in Workshop once mentioned as having saved his sanity during recent jury duty. She tried to have a good dinner the night before, because she'd been told not to eat at all after eight p.m. and the surgery wouldn't take place until noon. She couldn't eat a bite. She didn't sleep much, either, and she couldn't have a glass of wine or even a cup of herbal tea to help her.

Walking into reception, Susan wished Dr. Snyder had slightly lower standards of practice. Seeing "Memorial Sloane-Kettering" on the building hardly set her at ease. If she couldn't possibly have cancer, why was she at the cancer hospital? Everyone was kind and seemed highly efficient, but if there had been any food in her stomach, it wouldn't have stayed there long.

It helped to have the distraction of filling out all those forms, but soon they were done and it was still only seven-thirty. The annoyance of giving blood and urine, and all the other tests that seemed identical to the ones Dr.

Snyder had done the week before, filled some time. Maybe that was the real reason hospitals required it. She sat in the hospital gown and paper shoes, unable to focus on the salutary book. The TV morning shows were full of chirpy people who made her want to scream. She picked up a phone, but realized she wouldn't be able to control her voice and she didn't want anyone to hear her that way. She wouldn't have even allowed Lisa to pick her up later except that the hospital insisted someone come; they wouldn't send anesthesia patients home alone. Susan looked at the IV drip taped into her hand and tried to imagine glucose molecules bursting, one at a time, through the end of the needle and then luging through her veins.

It was a mercy when the nurse finally came with the pill. 'Pat Angelopoulos' explained that she'd be there when it was all over, and that Susan should call her Pat because no one with a post-operative flannel tongue should have say Angelopoulos. She had a sympathetic face, so Susan tried to smile before swallowing.

The empty stomach must have jump-started the sedative. She sensed no time at all between that swallow and hearing Pat's measured call: "Susan? Susan?"

Susan pried her eyelids open. Pat's face swam above her. She closed her eyes again. "Susan," the voice repeated. Susan groaned. "Do you remember who I am?" Pat asked encouragingly.

Susan knew, but her mouth wouldn't work. "Angel...iss"

"You like to do things the hard way, don't you?" Pat wiped her face with a damp cloth.

"Pat," Susan exhaled. "Water." The words "Helen Keller" bobbed across her rippling brain and she wanted to laugh. It came out a dry painful cough. Her throat felt as if someone had stuck a tube down it. Oh, yeah, they probably had.

"I can't give you water until you can sit up," Pat explained. "We have to make sure you can swallow, or you might choke. See if you can open your eyes first. Take it slow."

Susan felt as if she were crawling to the last watering hole in the Sahara, one inch at a time. She had to open her eyes in stages; the light hurt and the world was spinning. To sit meant ratcheting up her spine, vertebra by vertebra, with Pat rearranging pillows behind her until her torso was perpendicular to her legs, and then to continue, individually, those last vertebrae that supported her head. She'd once heard that the average weight of a human head was eight pounds. Impossible. Her shoulder bag weighed more than that and was much easier to lift than this head.

She hoped that Pat would volunteer the information she most wanted to hear but ultimately, once she could speak, she was forced to ask.

"The doctor will be in to see you in a little while," was all Pat would say in that imperturbable nurse manner. For some reason, that didn't make Susan feel particularly good. "I'll have someone send you some juice and crackers," Pat said by way of compensation, and left her, for a while, alone.

Susan closed her eyes and tried to see inside her body. It didn't work. She didn't have to be a yogi to tell that there were bandages over her breast, but what was beneath them? It felt to her as if there were still a breast there. Whatever it was that she wasn't being told, it didn't seem to have been an emergency mastectomy. Of course, she'd heard of amputees who felt phantom limbs, often for years afterwards. She stared at the walls and tried hard not to be terrified.

"How's the game going?" she asked the orderly who came in with the tray. She didn't follow sports, but there was always a game of something somewhere or another, and she was desperate to engage him in conversation and keep him in the room.

He looked at her strangely. "Didn't even start yet," he said. "I guess you lose track of the time when you've been out."

There was no clock on the bedside table and she hadn't brought a watch with her, so she asked him. It was only 1:15. Her surgery had been scheduled for noon. An hour and fifteen minutes to be scrubbed, incised, have whatever done, closed back up, brought upstairs, come to, and even have a snack order delivered? She sipped the juice—she had to or she knew she'd pass out—but she couldn't dream of swallowing a cracker. What could they have done in that operating room that would take less time than television surgery?

"It's inoperable, isn't it?" she demanded when Dr. Snyder came into the room, followed by Pat and a petite Chinese woman in a white coat. "You didn't take it out. Oh my God!"

"Calm down, Susan," Dr. Snyder tried the Mom voice. "It's not a cancer." Pat came over and tried to soothe her by rearranging the pillows.

"Not what we expected to find," said the other woman, who turned to Dr. Snyder. Susan remembered her now. It was Dr. Zhu, the surgeon; Dr. Snyder didn't cut. "Didn't you notice...?"

"Last time I looked at it, it was hardly even a mass."

"There's a mass?" Susan gulped.

"Susan, do you have a friend waiting for you?"

Susan stared at Dr. Snyder, horrified. "I have someone coming to pick me up when I call to say I can leave. That is, if I can leave. Please, Dr. Snyder, just tell me the worst. What's going on?"

Dr. Snyder turned to Dr. Zhu and shrugged helplessly.

"Well, Ms. Roth," she began, "there is a rare biological phenomenon—"

"Oh no," Susan shook her head and smiled meanly. "Bad news, doctor. You can't intimidate a writer with words."

"Susan, Dr. Zhu isn't trying to intimidate you, she's explaining—"

"Developing an explanation, to be more precise." Dr. Zhu actually looked sheepish for a moment. She was used to knowing exactly what was what and what to say. She fingered her stethoscope. "Ms. Roth, as simply as I can put it, in rare instances, a monozygotic twinning results in one complete fetus plus a cell cluster that fails to differentiate or develop beyond a certain point. Occasionally, this tissue forms as a cyst within the thriving embryo."

"It becomes part of the body of the child that's born," Dr. Snyder put in helpfully. "Inside." Susan was too focused on Dr. Zhu to take her own doctor to task for being patronizing.

"The cells that might have been another embryo present as a form of tumor. During an exploratory procedure, what is discovered is a mass of tissue that is, in effect, an unborn twin."

"I've heard of that," Susan was intrigued for a moment. "Hair, fingernails...oh, God! That's what you found in my breast?" She faced Dr. Snyder accusingly. "And you couldn't even find a lump?"

Dr. Zhu shook her head. "No. I said I was attempting to develop an explanation. Your situation might be similar, but there are significant, um, differences."

"Such as?" Susan found herself blinking back sudden tears. "This isn't helping me at all, you know." Dr. Zhu turned to Dr. Snyder, who opened her hands as if to set something free.

Dr. Zhu moved closer to the bed, unfastened the hospital gown and peeled it down. The air on her skin was a threat. Dr. Snyder peered over her shoulder as Dr. Zhu carefully removed the bandages; there weren't all that many. At a gesture from the doctor, Pat passed Susan a hand mirror. Susan took it tremulously. "I feel like I just had plastic surgery," she said with a nervous giggle.

Cautiously, afraid she'd drop it, Susan moved the mirror until she could see her breast. Beneath the iodine stains, she realized with boundless relief that it was whole and... "What the hell!?" she blurted out. The cut was so small it would have been invisible were it not for the tape holding it together. She'd done worse to her fingers by slicing carrots with a dull knife. "That's it?!" The doctors and Pat watched her, silent and apprehensive. She rotated the mirror, looking for whatever the doctors had been talking about. "It looks fine," she said, perplexed, "like always." She touched her nipple with a fingertip.

Dr. Zhu gave an undoctorly jump. "Careful!" Pat handed her a wipe and she gingerly swabbed some iodine from off the nipple. "Do you see it?" she whispered to the hovering Dr. Snyder.

As Susan watched in the mirror, she thought for a moment that some of the cold-crinkles had taken on the shape of a pair of lips. She blinked. Hard.

Dr. Snyder peered closer. "I'm not sure," she said, and prodded the area with a tongue depressor. The breast twitched out of the way. "Whoa!"

"What's happening?" Susan was definitely panicking now.

"That's what happened when I made the cut." Dr. Zhu spoke in an almost reverent hush. "And then..."

The lips, because now Susan could clearly see a pair of lips in the ridges of her breast, moved.

"Well what would you do if someone took a knife to you?" the Breast asked.

Susan screamed.

3 - WHAM BAM

They sent her home. They had to. She didn't, after all, have cancer—or any other diagnosable ailment. She had...The Breast hadn't spoken again and she refused to think about it.

"Why, sometimes I've believed as many as six impossible things before breakfast," the White Queen had told Alice. Well, Susan had yet to have breakfast, or even the dinner before that, and was still finding this impossible to believe.

She called Lisa. "Clean bill of health," she told her, which was the utter truth if not the whole of it. She put on her clothes, checked herself out and stood at the curb with her small bag and her large, unread book. It was sunnier out than it had a right to be.

"You look like shit," Lisa sympathized as Susan got in the car. "It's the anesthesia that really takes it out of you. Did I just hear your stomach talking?"

Susan's heart froze in mid-beat, but no, there had been no sound.

"You must be starving. Don't worry, all taken care of." She told the driver to stop by Shun Lee, where a takeout order was waiting for them.

"You thought of everything." Not only did Lisa think to arrange for food, trust her to know that Shun Lee does takeout.

"I remember when I had my boobs done," Lisa continued, oblivious. "Even with all the pain, I was starving. And all I wanted was Chinese."

Susan had no appetite. Lisa ate nearly half the food herself before Susan, with the excuse of needing to sleep off the anesthesia, threw her out.

It turned out she really did need sleep. She put her head down on the pillow and closed her eyes for just a moment, to stall her headache. When she was awakened by the telephone, it was dark.

It was her mother, frantic at not having heard from her and angry at having embarrassed herself by screaming at the hospital receptionist for being too stupid to find her daughter.

It was Susan's own fault for not remembering to call as soon as she'd gotten home. She could use the excuse of having something else on her mind, but she wasn't ready for the discussion that would have to follow. Instead she apologized briefly, knowing it would be accepted and not acknowledged, then kept her eyes closed as her mother raved on against her ear. It was only fair.

Suddenly she was starving, and what she specifically wanted was Chinese. She could almost laugh. Her know-it-all attitude often made you want to prove her wrong, but generally even Lisa's stranger pronouncements ended up on target. Her mother was running out of steam. Before she had to say something, Susan padded to the kitchen to forage for leftovers.

"Okay, Mom, okay. I said I apologize. Look, I'm home, I'm fine, there's nothing to worry about."

"But what did they find? You still didn't say. They must have found something, all those top doctors they have in that place. That place, ach! If you knew what was going through my head with you in that hospital. If anything happened to you, I couldn't live with myself."

"It's just...well...a mass of tissue." It was a fair way to explain it. She couldn't imagine her mother's reaction if she tried the truth. As she reached into her refrigerator for the orange chicken, her robe swung open. She couldn't help but peek down. It didn't look like anything at all. If the doctors hadn't heard it too... "Not even much of a mass."

"And it's not malignant?" Her mother had a firm belief that direct questions were the way to get the truth. Perhaps, but as any attorney could tell her, they had to be the right questions.

"No, it's not malignant," Susan was able to assure her. "At least," she added, darkly and under her breath, "not so far."

"Don't push it," said the Breast.

Susan coughed loudly. "What was that?" her mother said.

"Look, Mom, I'm still kind of punchy. Why don't I call you tomorrow?"

"It's those hospitals. You can catch things. Never put a well head in a sickbed, your grandmother always said, and she was right you know."

After a few more dire pronouncements, Susan was allowed to hang up. Of course, she'd lost her appetite. She sat at her little faux French café table, poking chopsticks into the plastic containers. It felt like something to do. She poured a glass of wine and took a sip. Immediately as she held it in her mouth, she wondered if it would hurt the Breast. She decided she didn't care and swallowed it down. A few more swallows made her much calmer.

"You'd better eat something," said the Breast. "We'd both be a lot better off if you did."

On some level, Susan clung to the thought that if she ignored it, it would all go away. She didn't reply. She took another sip of wine. Something that wasn't a talking Breast told her that food would probably be a good idea at that. The orange chicken was good cold. So were the prawns. The dumplings weren't half bad either.

After all that sleep, Susan wasn't ready for bed. Usually a wakeful night was a bonus for her, she could sit and write for hours. How could she concentrate on fiction when this strange thing was really happening? She couldn't read anyone else's stories either, not that so-recommended large book and not even her old favorites. It was a bitter night indeed when she couldn't find comfort in *Gaudy Night*.

She prowled restlessly through the rooms. It was a very small apartment, though it felt so cavernous on a silent night. What she needed were voices around her, to discourage the Breast from making its own. Television was full of *Law and Orders* she'd seen too often and news she didn't want to see at all. She settled for a home improvement show marathon. What a difference she might be able to make in this living room, if only she had $1000, a professional designer and a carpenter with his own power tools. After the third hour of befores and afters, with their accompanying sagas of near-disaster and ultimate gasps of surprise, she switched off the set with a yawn and toddled drowsily off to bed.

She really thought she'd made herself tired enough to fall asleep but as soon as she stretched out, her mind was flooded with a terrible alertness. She usually slept on her side, but that was the side... and for some reason, the other side just didn't fit as well. She put on a CD that often helped lull her, but tonight she found herself actually listening to the music. She turned it off with a sigh. Lying on her back felt peculiar. There was a crack in the ceiling she'd never noticed. It was probably time for a paint job, but then she'd have to take all her books and files off the shelves, which was such a miserable job. Of course, once they were down, if she were painting already, maybe it would make more sense to move that stuff into the living room. She could find some shelves and maybe customize them with crown molding, like they'd done on the show... This wasn't getting her any closer to sleep.

She tried deep breathing, but quickly found herself in that awkward position of being so conscious of it that she was terrified that if she stopped concentrating, her breath would stop.

"I can't take this." She spoke aloud, as she often did. Sleeping alone, it was safe.

"You could try talking to me," the Breast said.

"I have nothing to say," Susan said. It was the first time she'd spoken directly to It.

"I'm not going away, you know."

Susan pulled her pillow up around her ears to shut out the voice. "Why not?" she whimpered. The Breast, wisely, kept silent. Susan must have gotten some sleep that night; each time she looked, the numbers on her alarm clock had jumped ahead.

Sunrise found her awake and tired, and tired of feeling alone. She needed the sound of a human voice. If ever there were a time for a little help from your friends, this had to be it. She waited until it was Diane's usual hour to make breakfast for the kids and then picked up the phone. From her own closet kitchen, Susan could visualize another scene: Sun pouring through the picture window, glinting off the copper pans and kindling a glow in the honey-colored wood; Lindsay in her riding gear, sipping the one cup of coffee she was permitted each week; Sophie trying to tease Max into playing with her, and then getting her hair pulled in return; Taffy sniffing around in case a strip of bacon decided to fall. It was all so comfortingly normal, or at least what she'd always thought normal was supposed to be.

Somehow, Susan managed to relate her story fairly calmly. As she spoke, she could hear how ridiculous it sounded, but Diane took it as much in her stride as she would Sophie's contention that a leprechaun had stolen her toothbrush. This was Diane's way and why Susan had chosen to call her before anyone else. If someone said something absurd or did something outrageous, Diane would accept it quite calmly. Her assumption was that her refusal to react would take the fun out of it for the perpetrator.

Susan had wanted and expected this lack of reaction. She nonetheless thought Diane must be silently thinking that she'd lost her mind.

"If you tell me it happened, it happened," was what Diane said. When confronted outright (the Helen Roth technique), she replied, "No, I don't think you're crazy. Max, take that moldy dish off the table."

"It's pond scum, for my science fair."

"If it's not edible, it doesn't belong on the table."

"Who's crazy?" Sophie had a penetrating little voice.

"Auntie Susan...no, she's not crazy. She's telling me a story...Max, what did I say about that dish?"

"Pond scum is too edible!"

"I love you Auntie Susan!!!"

"She loves you too. Max, no scum. And don't tease Taffy with your bacon, it's cruel. Look, Susie, why don't I come down this afternoon, when Bob gets back from golf and we'll talk." Diane must have surely thought she was having some sort of post-operative, or maybe peri-menopausal, crackup. Dr. Bob was never considered capable of babysitting his kids.

"I want to talk to her!" Sophie screamed, and the phone went dead.

Diane came, with a pan of just barely warm cinnamon buns. Lisa and Alan, having also been called, came too. They came with hugs and kept their eyes focused above Susan's shoulder level at all times. It was a regular council of war, or an intervention, depending on how crazy any of them thought she was.

They sat on the living room floor, on Lindsay's ex-rug. With pastries and a pot of coffee in the middle, it was like being back in college, except that Steffi wasn't there and Alan was.

"I'm too old for this," Alan had remarked, trying to find a comfortable cheek to rest on.

"If you'd decide on a sofa for our living room, there'd be one here," was his wife's unsympathetic retort. It was also the last diversion she allowed. Lisa wanted to cut to the chase, which for her began with a wounded wondering as to why Susan hadn't confided in her the day before. This gave everyone an opportunity to vent some emotion on an irrelevant subject.

When they'd settled down, Susan began. She was nervous of course, seeing as how she wasn't an idiot. "This doesn't make any sense to me," she said in a rush, "so I don't expect it to make sense to you, but this is what happened," and she stepped them through the events, exactly as they'd unfolded. She had their complete attention and, when she finished, a moment of total silence.

Finally Diane said, "Wow."

"Well," was Lisa's contribution.

Alan nodded his head. "Yeah." Susan was underwhelmed by this eloquent outpouring. On the other hand, what had she expected them to say?

"It's not that we don't believe you, because we do," Lisa continued.

"Of course we do!" Diane got to her feet. "Should I put up more coffee?"

"Yes, of course," Alan hastened to agree. "But it is, well, a bit, well, unlikely, I think is the word I'm looking for."

There was some uncomfortable fidgeting and a series of "ahems." Then Lisa said briskly, "Well, Sue, bottom line, seeing's believing."

Susan instinctively crossed her arms over her shirt. "There is no way you're seeing my boobs!"

"It's not your boob," Alan said reasonably. "Something like this isn't personal, Sue. It's public property or whatever. After all, it's, uh...it's like..."

"An oracle."

"Exactly!" Alan agreed, "Like Delphi or..." He froze with his finger poised in midair. It wasn't Susan who'd spoken. They all looked for the source of the voice and their eyes stopped at Susan's chest.

"Holy crap!" Lisa breathed. "Was that It?"

They craned their necks discreetly, trying to reach closer.

"It really speaks," Diane marveled.

"It doesn't stop," Susan grimaced. "I knew you thought I was crazy."

Their denials were interrupted by the mesmerizing twitching of Susan's shirt. It was something like being at a picnic and seeing a napkin jumping around on the grass because a tiny frog was trapped beneath it.

"You have to let me out," the Breast said.

Susan was taken aback. "I'm supposed to expose myself?"

"Not yourself. Me."

The others were fascinated.

"It's like watching Shari Lewis," Alan marveled.

"Or a schizophrenic." Lisa was blunt as ever.

"I'm not..." Susan burst into angry tears.

"You see why I have to get out there?" the Breast was insistent.

"Lisa, she's not—" Diane rushed to comfort her.

"I know!" Lisa was affronted. "I was just pointing out what it sounded like. People are bound to say it, you know. Once it happens in public—"

"In public?" Susan groaned.

Diane ordered Alan from the room. He was reluctant to leave. Before the responsibilities of fatherhood and marriage had been sprung upon him, Alan Stark had made significant headway in post-graduate anthropological studies with a specialty in magical thinking. It had been a lifetime ago, but he kept his interest alive through watching endless hours of documentaries on the occult and scheduling vacations around an international calendar of obscure festivals. If any of them might be equipped to deal with the situation, it was he. He had a right to be there. Diane explained that "rights" had nothing do with anything. In full mother mode, she was implacable.

With Alan gone, Diane spoke as soothingly to Susan as she would to Sophie. "How bad can it be? Let's take a look." She started to unbutton the shirt, but Susan roughly pushed her hand away. "It's alright now, it's just us."

"Come on, Sue," Lisa had the nerve to sound exasperated. "How many times have we seen each other's boobs?"

Weary and resigned, Susan unbuttoned the shirt herself and pulled back one side. Diane and Lisa could immediately see that, despite the warmth of the room, the nipple was rigid and the aureole deeply puckered. The closer they looked, the more they thought they could make out a mouth. It yawned, and Lisa yelled "Holy Fucking Shit!"

"What happened?" Alan called into the room.

"It yawned!" Lisa said.

"That's much better," said the Breast. "So, you're the friends, eh?"

"Whoa!" Lisa breathed.

Diane, who had been extremely well brought up, automatically said "Uh, nice to meet you. How do you do?"

"Well," replied the Breast. "Though I think things could be much better."

"This is the worst bad dream," Susan muttered.

"To begin with, Friends," the Breast continued, "how would you feel about her attitude? If you were me?"

"So who are You?" Lisa asked, almost normally.

"Who are *you*?"

It was an ordinary question with an almost-programmed response "I'm Lisa. I'm..." It was as if she were at a cocktail party. "Well, I was in sales. Wholesale knitwear. For years. Which is how I met Alan, my husband. Now I do some fundraising for a group that helps homeless women prepare for the workforce."

"All very nice, especially that last part," the Breast remarked. "But those are the things you *do*. Who *are* you?"

Lisa was confounded. "That's not exactly easy for me to put into words."

"Then why should it be so for me?"

Out in the hallway, Alan laughed. It was rare that someone got the better of his wife. Lisa rose to the challenge. "So this is like a Zen thing, a what, a koan, is it? Okay then, so what are You? Like a spirit or...?"

"I prefer not to define myself. I think it sufficient to say that I exist."

"I am that I am!" Alan was delighted. "Yes!"

"That, Alan, would be plagiarizing." If a voice could wink, this one did.

And so it began. For nearly an hour, Lisa (curious) and Diane (polite) and Alan (beside himself with excitement) played "getting to know you" with whatever it was that was speaking through Susan's breast. Susan tried to keep her eyes closed. It was just too weird to watch her friends intently addressing her chest. It wasn't the most enlightening conversation one might imagine having with an inexplicable phenomenon. They probably gave away more than they discovered.

She (for they all agreed it was logical—if logic could be said to apply under these conditions—to consider the entity as female) suggested they address her as "Mam," which delighted Alan even more.

In addition to refusing to identify what She was, Mam couldn't explain how She'd gotten there or why, other than "I'm here to communicate."

"You must have so much to tell us," Diane said.

"I don't know yet," Mam replied. "First I need to listen." It was like a fortune cookie, Susan thought. She had a talking breast and it sounded like a fortune cookie.

Alan especially tried to coax more information from Her. Mam continued to evade, but they each couldn't help thinking that whatever supernatural consciousness was manifesting here before them, It must have some kind of axe to grind. It had to be, because this was happening. It was real. Not for a moment did any of them think that they might be imagining things, or that Susan might be pulling off the world's most extraordinary display of puppetry.

As to "why Susan?" When asked, Mam claimed to have no idea, but agreed there must be a reason.

"There is no reason," Susan said. Spoken aloud to the room with her eyes closed, her flat-voiced retort took on the gravity of a pronouncement. "It's random, like everything else."

"Surely you don't believe that?" Mam seemed genuinely curious.

"Not always," Susan admitted, "but at least for the past ten–fifteen years."

"Maybe that's the reason," Alan tried to sound enigmatic. He only succeeded in making everyone laugh, including Mam and even Susan.

Soon after that, Mam announced She was tired. She would get stronger in time (Susan groaned again) but for now, this was as much conversation as She could handle. Susan was relieved to button up her shirt and call it a day. She'd had a sinking feeling she'd be sitting half-naked on the floor until midnight, listening to her friends getting nowhere fast.

Lisa poked her head out to find Alan. He'd dragged one of the wire-backed café chairs from the kitchen and was having difficulties unfolding himself. He'd been so enthralled, he'd forgotten about his bad knee and was now limping like a pirate. He was also grinning from ear to ear.

"That was amazing," he said in Mam's direction, as they all walked to the door.

"I don't know what to say," Lisa said, kissing Susan's cheek. "Uh, Mam? It was, uh, nice meeting you."

"Likewise. And you, too, Alan. I look forward to continuing our discussion."

"I'd be honored. Of course, I'd prefer to meet you face to face, as it were."

"That is in Susan's hands. As it were."

Susan smiled ruefully at both of them and shrugged. Alan moved to hug her, as he usually did when saying goodbye, then pulled back appalled. "I am so sorry!" he stammered. "No disrespect..."

"Thank you," Susan said, and leaned closer to give him a peck on the cheek. "Thanks *all* of you."

"So, you going to be okay on your own?" Diane asked.

"She's not on her own," Mam said.

Diane bit her lip. "Give her some time, Mam. Please." She gave Susan a firm warm hug, then dug into her bag for her car keys. "I can't believe you're going to work tomorrow."

"I have to pay the rent." Susan exhaled sharply. There was a catch in her voice. "Damn it, Di, what's happening to me?"

Diane put her hands on Susan's shoulders and looked into her eyes, the same as she did when any of her three were in trouble. "You're at a crossroads. Whatever this is, you're moving to a new road. You have to believe that everything will be fine. Have some faith. Hey, if anyone should be able to have faith right now, it's you." She smiled and Susan had to smile back.

Susan locked the door behind her friends. "If you care at all,' she said, conversationally to the empty room, "I happen to hate crossroads."

She wondered if her bra would hurt It. She hadn't worn one since the hospital. Bare to the waist, she stood before the mirror and looked at the Breast. It looked normal. She could almost believe she'd dreamed the last three days under anesthesia. She cleared her throat. Nothing happened. Warily, she prodded her nipple with a finger, steeling herself not to scream if the thing jumped.

"Um, excuse me," she said. It was the first time she'd initiated a conversation and she felt more than a little certifiably mad. "Mam? Are you, uh, awake or whatever?"

"Yes."

"I have to get dressed. For work. That is....Damn! I don't know what to explain or how..."

"No need to. You only think I was born yesterday."

Susan let that lie there. Another epigram. She couldn't decide if It was being deliberately provocative, or how to—or even if she should—reply. "I'll get dressed then," she said.

Putting on the bra was like running an egg and spoon race with a raw egg and a plastic spoon. She put it on the "wrong" way, the way the corsetiere to whom her mother had taken her twelve-year-old self had said never to do, starting with the band wrapped back to front around her waist and fastening it, then hitching it around, then slowly fitting herself into the cups before, finally, slipping her arms through the straps and lifting it all in place. It seemed to take hours. She hated front-hook bras, but maybe she'd have to start wearing them.

The subway was another challenge. Shielding your breasts in a rush-hour train isn't easy. Collisions are unavoidable, and a large percentage of them are the genuinely accidental result of crowded cars and jolting brakes. Most women with any frontage get used to being bumped. Now, however, Susan had an extra issue to contend with. She had no idea what might happen if anyone made contact with Mam, and she didn't want to find out. It was astounding to her, but she found herself empathizing with suicide bombers: How did they ever get to the target site, having to go all that way with explosives strapped to their chests? For once, arriving at the office was a positive relief.

Susan would have been thrilled to hunker down in her cubicle with her mug and dissolve into the boredom of routine. It figured that there would be a network message flashing across her monitor: Evelyn had called a staff meeting. Another one.

Distracted by her own concerns, at first Susan didn't notice that Hannah was missing. She slipped into the third-seat-from-the-end, leaving the others empty for her friends. Two of the working moms plopped themselves down in the seats to her right.

"Can you imagine the relief?" the one with the airbrushed nails was saying. She turned to Susan. "Did you hear? After four girls, Hannah had a boy!"

The other woman laughed knowingly. "Poor thing can finally shut up shop."

Susan felt her breast give a lurch under her shirt. She hunched her shoulders to conceal it.

"Without girls we couldn't have more people," Mam said, thankfully sotto voce. Susan hushed Her in total panic.

"What?" the closer woman asked.

"Nothing," Susan said hastily, "just happy about Hannah's baby." Fortunately, Ayesha arrived and interrupted them with a few distracting details about breaking water and the Long Island Expressway.

Evelyn looked more grim than usual. When the lights were dimmed and the projector turned on, they all knew it was serious. There were pivot tables. Evelyn hated specifics and would never show tables if it weren't imperative to do so. The room hushed. Slide after slide flashed by with a single message—trouble.

Revenue was down for the fourth consecutive quarter. The cost of medical coverage had risen again. The repairs to the Stamford office building had not been fully covered by the insurance.

"And—I know you will all be shocked by what I have to say—" Evelyn's lips grew white around words that must have tasted unimaginable. "It has been learned that Mr. McKitrick has, uh, apparently disappeared, and a large sum of money is unaccounted for."

The stare of a Gorgon couldn't have frozen the buzz that went around the room. Even the members of the chip-and-cable crew were agog. Evelyn gestured for Melissa to turn up the lights. The whispers faded to apprehensive silence. It was bad; they all knew that. But what was going to happen, and to whom?

The other shoe dropped. "In an effort to obviate the necessity of layoffs," as Evelyn explained it, "The support staff are being requested to take a voluntary 20% reduction in their work hours. With an equivalent reduction in compensation."

There was a roar. Melissa spoke out in disbelief, "You're cutting us to a four-day week?"

"Not four days." Now that she'd left the treacherous neighborhood of an Executive disgrace, Evelyn was back on firm ground. She raised her eyebrows in scorn. "Five shorter days. It's obviously essential that we retain coverage throughout the standard business week."

One of the moms smacked her hand on the table. "So I need to have my kids in daycare every day? The same as working full time? How'm I supposed to pay for that?"

"You'll each be interviewed this week while HR fine-tunes the restructuring," Evelyn said coldly. "Remember, we're trying to prevent layoffs. We're doing our best. And thank you for your cooperation. Now back to work, everyone."

Susan had been so horrified by Evelyn's announcement that she hadn't noticed when the twitching had begun. At this dismissal, she felt her breast give a lurch and a voice rang out. "What if the managing directors stopped rewarding their failures with seven-figure bonuses?"

People stopped in mid-step, with their hands in the air, with their mouths open, to turn in the direction of the voice. One person started to applaud but immediately broke it off in fear. With one eye on Susan and one on Evelyn, no one moved a muscle.

Evelyn took a visible breath. "Surgery can be very traumatic, after all," she said with steely "understanding." "Perhaps, Ms. Roth, you came back a little too soon."

Susan swallowed hard. Her face was flushed and her hands like ice. "Perhaps," she whispered.

"I believe you have some unused days coming to you for this year?" Susan nodded. She had some unused sick days and a week of vacation. "I suggest you take them all—now."

Evelyn swept from the conference room, followed by the staff. Only a few of the bravest souls turned to look back at Susan, who found herself unable to move. When everyone had filed out, she sank back into her chair.

"What did you do that for?" she whispered intently.

"Like you weren't thinking the exact same thing?"

"That's not the point."

"Stubborn, aren't you? Well, at least you're finally talking to me."

"No I'm not."

"Yes you are. We're opening up a dialogue. Susan, how do you feel about injustice?"

"I hate it, Mam, but—look, I don't know where You come from but here, well, sometimes there's nothing you can do about it."

"There's always something that can be done. You have to stand up and fight. If you all resist..."

"Please Mam. Not now. Do you understand what the woman was saying? 'Resist' means losing my job."

"You don't like the job anyway. You should quit."

"I may not have to. Don't you...? Oh! I don't know about you, Mam, but I have to eat. You should have kept your mouth shut."

Mam was quiet after that. Susan hoped she'd made her point. Oracles are not all that practical in the real world.

Rinsing out her mug, Susan wondered if she should leave it in her cubicle or take it home. She had a few other things too: A picture Sophie had drawn for her, some Mardi Gras beads one of the girls had brought back last year, a framed photo of the Cobb at Lyme Regis... She started opening drawers to see what else there was. Would she need a box?

Melissa tapped on the metal frame to get her attention and slipped into the cubicle. She was as avid as ever, but her voice was sympathetic.

"I spoke to her," she told Susan. "You're not fired. You're lucky she can't believe you had that kind of guts, so it has to be you being sick. So, see you in two weeks."

Susan's knees buckled with relief. She hated her job, but she couldn't afford to lose it. Even with a 20% pay cut, it paid better than unemployment. And she needed the health coverage, especially now.

"It was pretty amazing." Melissa's eyes sparkled with admiration. "You'd a been the last person I'd imagine... That took real guts."

"It took stupidity."

"Yeah, that too," Melissa laughed. "Anyway, you're my hero. Probably everyone else's. E-mail me while you're out and I'll keep you filled in." She waved and ran off.

Susan put her mug upside down on a paper towel in its usual spot on her desk. It was, it seemed, still her desk. It was piled with things that needed to be done, but Evelyn had said "now," so all she did was clip a few notes to the things other people might come looking for, and arrange them in plain sight. She put her phone on night service, turned off her lamp and monitor, and picked up her bag. She left the building and squinted out at the partly cloudy day.

It was mid-morning on a weekday, and she was off from work. It was a peculiar feeling. Midtown Manhattan streets are always busy, throughout the working day, but in comparison to the a.m. and p.m. rush, they seemed half-deserted to Susan. Without the lemming pull of those crowds, her feet slowed to an almost-stroll. She noticed people around her with cameras, reading maps. They must be tourists. So many of them. She'd never really noticed. There seemed to be an unusual number of delivery trucks as well. It was almost as if, with the majority of the population walled up in their office cells, another shift took over the city.

Passing a bookstore, she realized she could go in and spend as much time as she wanted to. She went in. She tried to make it past the front table display of inspirational and motivational books in their telegenic jackets to where the real books were, but she didn't have the energy. She turned away and walked out. Susan was dazed. She'd had a near-unemployment experience, a miraculous reprieve and Melissa taking her side in office politics. And now she had two weeks to figure out what to do about the uncontrollable voice in her chest. It was too exhausting to deal with.

What she really wanted to do was curl up under a blanket and go to sleep forever. To sleep, perchance to dream. Hamlet had looked at things the wrong way, Susan thought. To her, the "rub" was waking up; she didn't fear the dreaming. Usually her sleeping dreams were pleasant, or else entirely forgotten. It was waking life that was often so hard to bear. It could be so numbingly non-existent, her life, and with no way she could find to change things excepting for the worse. Like now. Eternal dreaming sleep might be a very nice alternative.

For a split second, she thought about throwing herself under the incoming subway, but almost immediately felt too guilty about the driver and all the inconvenienced passengers to follow through. The moment passed. There was a seat on the train. There were many seats at this time of day. Susan didn't sit. She was so unaccustomed to it that two stops had passed before she realized there were seats available. And then she didn't sit because she was afraid that if she did, she would never stand back up. She could imagine being sucked down into the seat, her back and buttocks melding with the orange plastic, her legs taking root in the linoleum. The lassitude in her body would let her mind roam free and she would not realize that she was shuttling back and forth between terminals for weeks or months or maybe even years.

It was a kind of waking dream, this vision of having a waking dream. Standing and swaying with the rails, her hands gripping a center pole and her mind turned inside out, she didn't notice someone in the car noticing her. Pat Angelopoulos, a raincoat thrown over her turquoise scrubs, boarded at 42nd Street with another nurse and took a seat. When the car is half-empty, standees attract attention. Noticing Susan, Pat's face lit up with recognition, and then with something more. She nudged her companion, pointed discreetly and whispered something in her ear. The younger woman's eyes widened and she quickly made the sign of the cross. Then she pulled her cell phone from her bag. It was a camera phone. Susan never saw her snap the picture.

4 - MITRA

Susan realized almost immediately that she had to go somewhere. If she stayed home for two weeks, she'd never leave the apartment again. She decided to take Steffi up on her open invitation. She had no great urge to see Arizona, no matter how beautiful people said it was, and it was kind of a waste to go there in June but at least it would be different and miles from here, and being around Steffi would have to help. It seemed the perfect plan, until she was on her way to JFK the next morning.

From the moment she'd gotten Steffi on the phone, everything had moved so fast that she'd scarcely had the time to do what had to be done: to get a ticket; to arrange with Wayne on the third floor to take in her mail; to let Diane and Lisa and her mother know where she'd be. It had taken so long to convince her mother that she wasn't lying about checking into a hospice, that she'd been able to pack her entire suitcase while on the phone. She'd eaten a strange salad tossed together out of whatever was perishable in the refrigerator, arranged for a car service, taken a shower and fallen into bed in time to catch a few hours before having to wake up at 5 a.m. She'd slept better than she had in days.

It didn't hit her until she was giving the security nails in the windows a final once-over. She hadn't heard a peep out of Mam since being sent home by Evelyn the day before. She hadn't tried to initiate a conversation either. What was Mam thinking all this time (and, could She be said to "think?" It was really an interesting question if only it were happening to someone else). How could Susan be sure She wouldn't start talking in the middle of the inflight movie? You can tranquillize a dog or even, if you're that kind of person, a squalling child. Could she put Mam out of commission without knocking herself out in the process? Even if she knocked herself out, would it work? Susan had been out cold in the operating room, and that's when Mam had shown herself for the first time.

With five minutes to go before the car was expected downstairs, Susan found herself looking down at her breast and delivering a lecture on airline safety and public paranoia. "I'm begging you..." she said several times. "Not a word." There hadn't been a sound. Susan couldn't tell if Mam was asleep (or whatever might pass for sleep) or angry. All she could do was keep her fingers crossed.

It was just her luck—or did she look that nervous?—that she was pulled out in the second-tier "random" security check. The stocky female guard in her ill-fitting made-for-a-man's-body navy uniform gestured for Susan to spread her legs and stretch out her arms. She held her breath and complied. It wasn't that she expected the wanding to produce any beeps, Mam not being metal. It was the idea of being patted down that froze her blood. The pat-down was cursory and nothing was disturbed. She was sent on her way with a pleasant thanks for her cooperation. Maybe it had been random after all.

The flight was half-empty. Tucked into the curve of the window, Susan was grateful that there would be no one in the seat next to hers. She looked forward to the hours of peace. Unlike the subways, airplanes created a comforting capsule of limbo. There was no sense of time or responsibility. Control was surrendered to the invisible pilots and equally invisible currents of the air. When the cabin crew trundled by with their carts, she straightened up with temporary expectation and received her beverage or food with a pleased "Thank you." Flying, Susan thought, munching on a cracker, was a reversion to infancy.

The movie was something with Ben Stiller. It would be funny. She snuggled under the tissue fleece blanket to watch. After the movie, there were episodes of a bland sitcom she had never watched ten years before. There was also a "where are they now?" segment about a singing family that had been popular in the 70s. Susan dozed off during a nature film about koalas.

Twice in her life she'd traveled to places where she'd been talked into flying into the nearby local airport. After the second experience of a delay that made her miss the connecting flight and kill the better part of a day wandering around a terminal, she'd sworn never to do that again. So, she didn't land at "America's Most Scenic Airport," but at Sky Harbor, Phoenix. Sedona was two hours away by Land Rover, which was how Steffi had come to meet her.

It was Susan's first Land Rover and the height surprised her. Climbing up was like mounting a horse. She'd ridden a horse once or twice in summer camp and never forgot the feeling of towering over the land. With her outside hand, she gripped the side tightly, the same way she'd had to grip the pommel on that horse's saddle. Steffi drove like a cowboy, Susan thought, with great speed and a casual confidence; and she looked so... "Western" in her white shirt and worn jeans and boots. Feeling the stare, Steffi looked as Susan and grinned broadly.

"Well, if it finally got you to visit, it must be a miracle!" In the airport, she'd only given the briefest quizzical glance at Susan's chest.

With her inside hand, Susan frantically tried to keep back the hair that was blowing into her eyes and mouth. "Steffi, it's no joking matter!" She had to shout to be heard.

"Who's joking?" Steffi shouted back. "Don't you believe in miracles? You'd better," she waved her hand at the landscape. "You're in God's Country now!" They were halfway to Sedona and all around them in the distance, beyond the strip malls and the rooftops of condos and footprints of ranches, the sky glowed blue against rocks that were as ruddy as they were in photos. Everything seemed in sharp focus. Steffi'd turned on the radio and for a moment, Susan had the strange sensation that she was actually in a movie, soundtrack and all. She took a deep breath. The air held a faint trace of something astringent and bracing. It was almost too vivid to bear. Steffi caught the expression on her face and nodded sympathetically. "I know. Amazing, isn't it?" Susan could only nod.

The view from Steffi's wall of windows and from her redwood deck was spectacular, almost Martian, if you ignored the lower tier of roofs and desks and the corner of the pool. They had lunch out there, and after the nap Steffi insisted she take, she hoped they might dine there, too. She wasn't in the mood to get dressed and go to a restaurant. Steffi, however, had made plans and headed down to the carport.

"Take a warm sweater for later," Steffi called back. When Susan came downstairs, Steffi was stowing a cooler in the back seat. "We're having a picnic." She tossed Susan a scrunchy. "We've got a long drive ahead of us."

"Where are we going?" Susan asked, obediently hopping up into the Rover and binding back her hair.

"Somewhere that'll give you some perspective."

Oddly enough, it wasn't until they were nearly there that Susan realized where they were going. Steffi had timed it perfectly. The sunset had just barely begun as they reached the viewpoint on the rim.

Rim. A word to describe the edge of a teacup or cereal bowl. It was hardly sufficient for the edge of the fissure that yawned before them, just as "Grand Canyon" seemed ridiculously terse as a name for the chasm itself. Over hundreds of years, thousands of people had gazed into these depths. It had to be assumed that some of those who had gazed into these depths had been pretty fair wordsmiths, yet words had failed them in the naming. This was not a sight for words.

Steffi hit the CD player. Not Grofé's suite with its clomping burros, but a haunting flute wove around them, calling out to map the depth and breadth with its echoes. The piper led them to receive the vastness of the landscape in their ears, while their hungry eyes roved impossibly far and wide. The glory of the colors, an earthbound rainbow of stone, was both more subtle and more intense in the glow of the setting sun. The ridges and gulfs and scrub threw shadows that played tricks with perspective. The land breathed. The chilly wind was alive.

"Thanks, Steff," Susan said in a tiny voice.

"Sure." Steffi sighed with satisfaction. "Now that's what I call a symbol of the feminine principal."

"Kind of humbling," Mam said. It was the first time She'd spoken all day, and the first time Steffi had ever heard Her. Steffi tore her eyes from one wonder to look in the direction of another.

"Can you see, Mam?" Susan marveled. "I hadn't realized."

"Some. Better without the cloth."

Without hesitation, Susan took off her sweater and moved her T-shirt out of the way. It was hard to be small in this place.

Steffi watched in wonder. "How does It see without eyes?"

"How does She do anything?" Susan said wryly, trying to wrap her sweater around her shoulders. The temperature must have dropped 20 degrees.

"Quiet, girls," Mam whispered. "It's too beautiful."

Twilight poured in like an ocean.

Standing on the deck with her morning coffee, her hands resting on the weathered rails, Susan stared out over the landscape. She took a deep, deep breath and let the air course through her body like a medicine. Slowly, she unbuttoned her shirt so that Mam could share it all, the mountains and the air and the sky. It seemed natural, and only fair, to do so.

"I'm glad we came here," Mam said.

"So am I," Steffi said. "Both of you." After all that driving yesterday, Susan thought Steffi would sleep in, but she'd been up with the sun. "Too excited to sleep," she'd said. "So, ladies, what do you want to do today? We can hang around, hit the pool. Or I can take you around town, show you the sights?"

Susan laughed.

"What?" Steffi hadn't thought she'd said anything funny.

"The way you said that. Like we're two people here."

"I'm assuming you are."

"Thank you," Mam said.

"But you're so, I don't know, so nonchalant about it. I mean, Steff, you have to admit it's strange."

Steffi shrugged. "Not here it's not. Well, not so much. I know, how about a Vortex tour?" Susan looked at her blankly and Mam didn't say a word.

"We've got a lot of energy vortexes—is that right, 'vortexes?' or should it be 'vortices?' No? So these energy vortexes, different kinds of energy, are all over town and some people have them mapped out and do these tours. You go from site to site and, well, open yourself up to the power I suppose. I've never done one myself. It's supposed to help you connect with the Divine or the Great Spirit or whatever you believe is out there."

"I'm kind of trying to connect with what's in here," Susan said.

"Oops." Steffi was embarrassed. "Maybe you're right. Maybe I've been so busy being open that I haven't actually absorbed this."

"We can explore the vortexes another time," Mam said kindly. "It might be interesting to see what would happen."

Susan was aghast. "I'm just starting to handle you the way you are."

"What about after lunch we go to Mitra?" Steffi suggested. "That's the place down the road I was telling you about. Shall I make a call?" She quirked an eyebrow at Susan. "I'll bet you're feeling a little less judgmental these days."

No reply was necessary. Susan wasn't the same woman she'd been two weeks earlier. Who she was now was neither someone with whom anyone in the world would be expected to identify, nor something that could even be explained. She needed some kind of help and understanding, even if it could only be partial and pieced together. It seemed a shame to be in Sedona and not take advantage. Of all the available resources, Susan and Mam agreed that it would be more comfortable to test the waters in a place where they had a personal introduction.

The center was down the road from Steffi's condo, just as she'd said. It did help to know which road and exactly where to turn as there was no gate, only a rough archway of sculpted stone. Not until you were on top of it could you see the sign, a modest copper plaque, newish but already starting to oxidize in its post:

Mitra Center for Personal Enrichment

Susan was surprised at the wealth of trees and generous gardens. The lush green seemed hedonistic in an area where water should be precious, but Steffi assured her that it was all local flora and highly ethical. The center itself waited at the other end of the long drive. It was a low spare building of the same stone as the archway, mostly a veined clay white but with the occasional startling splotch of deep mustard yellow. The enormous door of blackened wood looked as though it had been looted from Japan. It took a gentle push to make it swing into a large open space full of light and calming colors. Music that must have been aboriginal to some place or other wafted softly through the sound system, in pleasing counterpoint to the trills and tinkles of the glass water wall. A trace of sage and cedar permeated the air.

The denizens of Mitra lounged on low divans, talking and reading. As well as the usual jeans and active-wear, there seemed to be a vogue for loosely woven hemp that had never touched dye. Many wore caftans or hapi coats of a distinctively-printed cotton. Occasionally, Susan noticed someone wearing white from head to bare toes.

"Leaders," Steffi informed her. "Teachers, instructors, guides, whatever you want to call them."

Looking around, Susan could see a glass-brick counter that seemed to be a juice bar and a small shop filled with books, candles and some of the cotton printed robes. Here and there, she noticed discreet arrows pointing the direction to Crucible and Pantheon as well as the only slightly less obscure Energy Healing, Sensory Suspension and Balancing Chamber.

If there were any other Personal Enrichment Centers, Susan thought, this was bound to be the archetype. "What is all this?" she asked nervously.

"Mind, body, spirit," Steffi said. "They do the whole package here."

"I thought you came here for yoga."

"Me, yeah. Yoga and deep tissue massage. Sometimes, when I'm up for it, tai chi on the lawns at sunrise. You, however, have other needs. Lucky for you, I've gotten into some interesting conversations hanging around the mineral pools. They're fake, by the way, but you'd never know it. They're great."

The front desk was a slab of fossil-pocked stone, propped on two pillars of glass brick. Behind it stood a woman haloed in hennaed frizz. Catching Steffi's eye, she made a temple of her hands and bowed her Namaste.

Steffi returned the greeting. "Hazel," Steffi said, "this is my friend Susan I called about." Susan waved. She didn't think she was Namaste material.

"You're expected in the Fulcrum," Hazel smiled solemnly.

Steffi nodded and led Susan past the desk and under a row of Tibetan prayer flags. From there, the corridor seemed to spiral inward.

"The Fulcrum?" Susan whispered, once Hazel was at a safe distance.

"It's a kind of meditation room. I set up a meeting with the guys that run the place. If there's one thing I learned in my past life..." She noticed the expression and Susan's face and laughed. "Oh, for Christ's sake, Suze, I mean my life in real estate! One thing I know is how to get a meeting."

"What are they like?"

"No idea. I hear they're into all sorts of things and that they're pretty bright. They say Bear was a Rhodes scholar."

"Bear?!"

Steffi shrugged. "Here we are." She opened a door and pushed aside a handful of yellow silk. The small tranquil room was a circle, the draperies continuing all the way around and gathering on the ceiling around a skylight. There was little else to see, except for the midnight-colored cushions heaped on the floor, and the three men who rose from them by scissoring their legs in a single fluid motion.

"Hi," Steffi said, with the breezy confidence that had made her enough money to retire at 45. "Steffi Cicollilo. I spoke on the phone with...?"

The tallest man was not merely bald. The muscular golden body above and below his hip-slung dhoti appeared to be entirely hairless. He held out both hands to Susan and looked into her eyes with his probing black ones. "I am Bear," he said.

"You're Bear?!" If any of the three were a "Bear," Susan would have thought it would be the chubby redhead.

He caught her hands between his own warm ones. "My spirit guide," he said with a trace of humor in the dimple by his mouth. Susan was not the first person who'd found his name a surprise. "I was Told to expect you, but I don't know who you are."

"Susan Roth," she said.

"Susan Roth," he repeated. She thought he sounded a little like Leonard Nimoy on Star Trek. "This is Patrick..."

The one who stepped forward had a wide-open face with red cheeks, framed by the flyaway hair that had escaped his ponytail. He looked as if he'd be more at home in overalls than the caftan and Jesus sandals he was wearing. "Hey," said Patrick with an easy grin.

"...and John Robert."

Last of all was the ruddy teddy bear with flecks of white in his curly beard and boisterous springs of red poking out of whatever skin his jeans and T-shirt left uncovered. "Namaste," saluted John Robert, his round eyes staring behind his rounder wire-rimmed glasses.

"So now, Susan Roth," Bear continued, as they all scissored back down to their cushions, gesturing for Susan and Steffi to follow suit, "why have the guides lead you to this place?"

Susan looked at Steffi, who was trying to find a cushion that had no embroidery. Steffi gestured as if to say, "I did my part, now it's all up to you." Susan sighed. "Might as well get it over with," she thought. In a single quick gesture, like ripping a bandage off a healing wound, she pulled off her shirt. Before any of the men could say a word, she pointed to her breast.

"Gentlemen," Susan said, "I'd like you to meet Mam."

Mam yawned. "Nice place you've got here," she said. "So what can you boys do for me?"

"Prodigious!" said Patrick, in awe. John Robert seemed to shrink with silence, and Bear began to weep.

As Steffi had heard, the three were into all sorts of things. Between them, they'd had any number of experiences as they'd sought wisdom and enlightenment around the world. They'd taken advanced degrees at universities and apprenticed themselves to shamans and sangomas. They'd climbed frozen mountains, crossed deserts, sweated in lodges and made pilgrimages to ancient cities. They'd swallowed mushrooms and suffered lengthy fasts. By the time they'd come together in Sedona, they didn't know what they believed in, but they knew It was powerful and that Mitra would call it to them. They had prepared their whole lives to receive a visitation. Now here it was, and it turned out that they were only three men in an Arizona wellness center and they were dumbfounded.

"Anyone want a cup of tea?" Patrick asked brightly, while Bear began to chant "Ishtar, Astarte, Inanna, Anat...," with tears running down his cheeks.

"Great idea," said Steffi, jumping up. "I'll go get some."

Susan shot her a dirty look as she fled the room.

"Uh, Mam, is that right?" As blessed out as he was, Patrick was coping better than his two friends. Bear continued chanting, "Isis, Shakti, Cybele..." and John Robert had yet to say a word. "Mam, if you don't mind me asking, what are you anyway? Are you like a spirit or a goddess or what?"

"Holy Mary Mother of God," Bear had come to.

"Now that is definitely wrong," Mam said sharply. "Stop that!"

As if he had been slapped, Bear came to and shook his head vigorously to clear it. "I have abased myself before you Madam," he said, lowering his eyes. "I am an infant, an insect. I am ashamed."

"Mam, not Madam," Mam corrected. "And don't be so hard on yourself. The first time Susan met me she screamed. Didn't you Susan?"

"I did," Susan agreed. "And after that, you can't imagine what a bitch I've been. It's a lot to handle."

"Is this really happening?" John Robert's voice trembled from behind his hands.

"Abso-fucking-lutely," Patrick breathed.

"Praise be to whatever sent you!" added Bear.

"So tell us," Patrick urged. "Tell us everything you can. Like where are you from? Who sent you? How did you get here?"

"If She knows She won't tell us," Susan said.

"I can't remember," Mam corrected her. "That is, if there is something to remember. It seems to me that first I wasn't. And then, I was. Fully conscious and with a great deal of knowledge, but with little understanding."

"You didn't say that before," Susan said. "'I'm here to communicate' is what you told Alan. You've been acting like you know everything."

"She said She didn't get what She knew." Patrick thought he could explain. "Like the connections weren't there. She's missing the human factor."

Mam concurred. "I know a great deal about your world, and your history. I know much from a great distance. I seem to need to feel my way."

"To what?" John Robert asked tentatively.

"I don't know," Mam said. "I'm sure I have a purpose here, but I don't know what it is. I think I have to learn by being with you, with people."

"It is we who must communicate with You." Having found a thread to guide him, Bear had come back to himself.

By the time Steffi returned with the chamomile and Saint-John's-wort, the men were basking in their favorite type of discussion, a bemused Susan trying to sort through the noise.

Was Mam earthly or divine? She was a sentient being, that much was clear, but what kind? Was She a goddess? What was a goddess? Did a god have to be a creator or simply be divine, and what was divinity? Not all powerful entities are gods. Mam might be any of a number of spirit beings. Perhaps She was an angel. "Or a demon," John Robert reluctantly suggested. "Some people might say She was a demon."

"She could even be an alien," Patrick joked, or Susan decided to think he was joking. The others seemed to take it seriously. Was it any less likely than the other possibilities? And what was an alien? Weren't there some that theorized the Old Gods had been aliens, or that maybe even Jesus was?

This wasn't getting them anywhere. Did it really matter what Mam was? Wasn't it more important to find out what Her purpose might be in being here? Did She bring a Message for Mankind? Did She come—or was She sent—to enlighten, or did She come to learn? Did one preclude the other? Was one necessary to fulfill the other?

The men were so caught up in their seminar that they hardly noticed that Mam spoke only when directly addressed, and then usually deflected the question. From the evidence of Her tone of voice and a few trenchant murmurs, Mam seemed to be enjoying listening. Even Steffi was absorbed.

To Susan, the meeting had turned as riveting as a lecture on prostate disease. "Gentlemen," she was polite but firm. "Time out." While they'd clearly been having a grand time, she thought it politic to sound grateful. "I appreciate all your time and trouble, but I think we've gone as far as we can go."

They couldn't believe that Susan wasn't as fascinated as they were. "We've only just begun the journey," Bear said. "You must have patience."

Steffi was surprised. "You didn't expect instant results?"

Susan shook her head. "I don't know what I expected," she admitted. "I think I was hoping that people who'd gone a bit further off the beaten track might come up with some ideas I hadn't already had. Some historic precedent or guidelines for living with alien possession or something. Or maybe I just wanted to see if you'd be as freaked out as people who aren't so used to weird things. And as for Mam, not to put words in your mouth, but I don't think this is getting you what You need, either."

"We can seek the answers together," Bear said, once again capturing her hands between his and fixing her with this obsidian stare.

"We could sit here for weeks and never get any answers, because there aren't any." She felt a little bad at being so blunt, but she was somewhat put off by the Mesmer routine.

"How do you know?" John Robert naturally had to reply.

"Have you ever found any? Any of you? In all these years?"

"It is the seeking that is the journey," Bear was unfazed.

"I've never understood that," Susan said honestly. "Okay..." She fumbled around in her brain for a way to say it. "There's some part of me that's beyond my flesh and bones. But I don't need to go analyzing it any more than I need to be able to read my DNA."

"But someone knows how to read your DNA," Steffi pointed out.

"Yeah, well, someone has to be an expert in everything. And anyway that was a bad analogy. DNA is concrete, it's tangible. Someone with the right knowledge and tools can study DNA and reach practical conclusions. If that's what they want to do."

"Then you agree there is a place for those who seek," Bear insisted.

Susan shrugged. "As long as they don't go killing other people in the name of it, they can have any hobby that makes them happy. I just don't get why this does, why all that searching makes them happy. I must be more of a commuter than a seeker. I think there ought to be a destination."

"For us, it is the seeking that is the conclusion. We seek, because through the act of seeking we have already achieved our goal."

"Which is?" Susan was exasperated.

"The Truth," Bear said, rather sharply for a spiritual leader, Susan thought.

"And what would you do with it if you got it?" Mam spoke up.

"Thank you!" Susan said. "Exactly."

It was as if someone had tossed a grenade into the silk cocoon. The circle burst apart, limbs sprawling, mouths and eyes agape. Susan was baffled by the reaction. With all the questioning these three had experienced, had no one ever asked this one before?

"John Robert," Mam said, "you haven't said much." For a burly middle-aged man, John Robert was looking a lot like a frightened sixth-grader. She kept her voice encouraging. "What would you do with the Truth?"

His face as red as his curls, he hemmed and uhmmed and scratched his head. "I don't know," he finally said, "I never thought about it. I was so busy searching." There was a catch in his voice. "The searching, all that trying, it seems to give it meaning, all of it."

Susan felt bad for him and patted him on the shoulder. "Okay," she said.

"Tell me more," said Mam.

Drawing on their own extensive questing experiences, the three men tried to explain to Mam what they assumed everyone already knew. They spoke of fear, especially fear of the unknown, which culminates in fear of death. They evoked the emptiness of futility, of living to no purpose. They described the consolation of ritual and pattern. They expressed the yearning to be part of something greater than their individual selves and the intoxication of those hard won moments of connection. Susan and Mam listened with equal intensity; they both wanted to know.

"I actually agree," Susan said in the end, "that we're all connected. There's some kind of energy out there that we all belong to. All of us, probably everything alive is woven together in some way." She saw the optimistic gleams and shook her head firmly. "But I think that's it, that's the end of it. Nothing more. That's your Truth."

"Susan," Mam inquired, "what do you do if that is the Truth?"

"Live with it. The Truth is just there; it doesn't do anything. It doesn't change the way things are. So, like with anything else you can't do anything about, you just try to be a good person and live the best way you can."

"Anything else like me?"

Susan had to laugh. They laughed together. Steffi grinned with relief. She wasn't sure why, but the meeting had turned out to be just what the doctor'd ordered.

Patrick, Bear and John Robert were confused. It wasn't funny to them, to have the core of their existence abrogated in an afternoon. Yet, there was no denying they'd had a unique experience. Mystical. Inspirational. It would provide food for thought and discussion for a long time to come.

"In every end there is a beginning," Bear whispered.

"When God closes a door, He opens a window," John Robert agreed.

It was Patrick who asked if they'd consider talking with some of the other leaders at the center. Susan and Mam both thought it was a good idea. Mam wanted to meet as many people as possible. Each time she listened, she learned so much. Susan saw the idea as a test of the philosophy she'd just so openly, if accidentally, embraced. Mam was here, why ever and whatever it might mean. Susan had decided to accept it. Diane had been right about the crossroads; time to get going and see where her road might lead.

Susan relaxed and enjoyed the rest of her unplanned holiday. One morning, they woke up at four to experience the Red Rocks from a hot air balloon. Another day, Steffi took them to the workshop of a Hopi weaver from whom she'd ordered a rug. Susan's eyes filled with colors more nourishing than food.

The day that made the biggest impact on Susan was the day they went to Canyon de Chelly. This more modest canyon, unlike its Grand cousin, had been home to several waves of human culture. Susan's coastal eye was used to the idea of villages built on green shores. To look at a cliff of ivory rock and find houses of tumbled stone tucked within a crevice was strange and wonderful. More wondrous still were the dwellings cut in the living rock. These seemed unimaginably ancient to Susan. She climbed the kiva ladder to peer into the dark cramped hole that had been someone's home—several someones if the archaeologists were correct—and found herself dizzy with the remote past. "What do you think, Mam?" she whispered. "Can you see?" She began to fumble with her shirt, having to juggle her bag and her disposable camera to do so, and nearly lost her footing on the slippery wood. Steffi gave a shout from below.

"I can see," Mam said. "Probably more than you can right now." The cave had been hollowed out of the living rock and the opening that was the only window or door was small, admitting little light. The ceiling was black with antediluvian soot. It didn't require a spectrometer to sense distance in the dating of that carbon, nor to imagine how many years of dusty feet had shed the layer of beaten earth that crusted the stone floor.

"What do you think?" Susan's voice was hushed, and not from fear of being overheard alone at the top of the ladder.

"I admire them," Mam said. "They reached."

Susan thought about that, over and over again. Later, their guide led up a set of Moqui "steps" cut into the canyon walls. As they climbed, they spotted a row of petroglyphs. The iron oxide, the color of dried blood, showed clearly against the pale stone: spirals, a dotted cross and other-worldly men, some on horseback; and handprints, too, all too far above the ridge for a human hand to touch. They reached.

Other days, Susan and Steffi lazed around on the deck and luxuriated in doing absolutely nothing at all. Or else they visited Mitra.

The occasion of their second visit, a few days after their first, was the assembly Patrick had quickly organized. They gathered on what Steffi called the tai chi lawn, a larger crowd than Susan had anticipated. All the guides, instructors and such were there, even those who worked from home and rarely set foot in the center. They sat in a ring, but where Susan and Patrick sat was clearly its head. Obscured by Susan's shirt, Mam twitched excitedly.

Tired of stripping in public, Susan had bought a cheap bikini in Target and cut a peep-hole for Mam. They made an agreement that when they got to a place where She couldn't be seen—a restaurant, for example, or, later on, the streets of New York—that discretion would be the rule; no speaking unless spoken too. At Mitra, Susan wore the bathing suit with her jeans and an open shirt. At that first symposium, Susan found herself enjoying the drama of the moment, the stillness as she removed the shirt, the sudden intake of breath when Mam began to speak.

At first, it was similar to what had happened with her friends in New York, or with the original trio at Mitra. There were gasps and some tears and spontaneous chanting. The initial questions were the same ones of "What" and "Why." This time, however, Susan and Mam could draw upon experience. They knew what to expect, and Susan felt she'd learned something of how Mam wanted to proceed. Together they converted the questions into a general discussion. Tongues loosened and once again Mam learned more than She gave.

Not being a teacher, Hazel hadn't been invited, but she'd known something unusually exciting was happening and had gotten Ruta from the juice bar to cover the front desk. With her Pre-Raphaelite hair and mirror-embroidered tunic she was very visible, as well as being the only slightly familiar face that Susan saw. Susan gave a friendly wave that Hazel would never forget. She didn't even need to write it down, though she did, along with every word that she heard and engraved on her memory. It was hours before she could get home and type it all up in her blog.

The next afternoon, Steffi brought Susan back to try the therapeutic pools. The main pool had been designed to look as much like a natural pond as possible, and the water to mimic a natural hot spring in temperature as well as mineral content. Susan enjoyed her buoyancy and the way the water seemed to leech the tension out of her body, but Steffi had warned her not to stay in for more than fifteen minutes. No one should the first time, and there was no way of knowing how the extreme heat might affect Mam. So while Steffi stayed gossiping with some acquaintances, Susan had gotten out. Swaddled in towels, she was lounging on a chaise and wondering how long she could keep her neck feeling so loose, when Hazel approached with an offering from the juice bar.

Susan appreciated the gesture. She hadn't thought of it until she'd spotted the glass, but suddenly fruit was the only thing she wanted. After she'd expressed her thanks and finished the juice, Hazel continued to linger. The penny finally dropped.

"Would you like to talk to Mam?" Susan asked. Hazel nodded like a child asked if it wants to stay up past bedtime. "Come on, then. Say hello." Susan unwound the upper towels.

Hazel moved cautiously. She sat on the edge of Steffi's adjacent chaise and leaned closer to Mam. For a minute, Susan thought she was going to stretch out her hand, the way you do when meeting a strange dog. It was hard not to laugh.

"Hello, Hazel," Mam said.

Hazel swallowed and wet her lips. "H-h-h-hello. Mam."

"Namaste," Mam said.

"Omigod!" cried Hazel. Before she might faint, she jumped up and fled.

Steffi arrived in time to see a streak of red and purple disappearing between the trees. "What did I miss?"

Susan shook her head. "I must be really stupid, but it hadn't crossed my mind. Steff, Hazel just had an Elvis encounter...and we're Elvis."

Steffi fell back on her chaise and laughed. "Of course you are," she said fondly. "You really are a moron." Susan was so disturbed by the concept that it fell to Steffi to try and explain it to Mam. Mam was fascinated.

Twice more during Susan's time in Sedona, they came to use the pool. One of those times, they stayed to another meeting in the Fulcrum. Each time, Susan became more aware of the whispering and watching from the Mitrans in the lobby or on the grounds. Emboldened by her moment by the pool, Hazel made a point of greeting Mam each time they passed her. Mam always returned her greeting, by name. When others stopped to stare at her in turn, Hazel basked in the reflected glory.

The night before Susan returned to New York, there was a party at Mitra in Mam's honor. Patrick and Bear and John Robert had tried to describe to Mam what ceremony meant to human beings. In asking permission for the party, they explained that those at the Center who had met Mam, or even heard Her from a distance, had been shaken. Whatever they *didn't* know, they knew they would never be the same. This party was a ceremony that they needed.

Susan agreed. This was something she did understand. Having never been married or had children, having never purchased a house or had career moments to celebrate, she hadn't had a milestone ceremony in her own life since her college graduation. She felt it as a surprisingly powerful lack. There were moments in life that needed to be marked, to be framed in some way. Susan needed a party as much as the Mitrans did. Besides, it would be fun.

To Mam, the party would be another opportunity to mingle and learn.

Everything was set up around the pool, with heaters arranged to compensate for where the water's warmth wouldn't reach. More chairs were pulled out on the tiles, and cushions were arranged on the desks of the hot tubs. At the edge of the lawn, long plank tables were heaped with food. Strings of lanterns—rice paper, pierced tin, and colored glass—wound through the trees, and tiki torches studded the grass. Patrick had plugged in the outdoor speakers and the music brushed up against a multitude of wind chimes. In the elusive light, the celebrants glimmered in pale colors. Everyone seemed to float, the earth for once seeming as buoyant as the waters.

Susan was lead to a place of honor, a heap of cushions at the far end of the pool. While Steffi and the three leaders rarely left her side, others came and went. There was a pattern to this at first. People approached with respect, sometimes swimming up through the pool. They stayed for what appeared to be a carefully determined amount of time, then made their respectful goodbyes. As the night wore on, the atmosphere got looser and happier. By the time only the most dedicated were left, any formality had disappeared and everyone sprawled on cushions to laugh and say aloud whatever came to mind.

Early on, as inconspicuously as possible, Hazel appointed herself handmaiden. Bringing food and wine was a good way to stay near Mam and insure she could hear much of what was being said. Not only was she longing to hear, but now she had a responsibility to her readership. Since her first entry about Mam, "witch_hazel.com" was getting so many hits. It had been exciting to have more to write about than herbs and the local vortex scene. Hazel was resigned to the fact that tonight's report would be her last hurrah and she wanted it to be awesome.

It was the night of the full moon, which I have to think was a Sign. . . .

All the major Healers and Readers in Sedona were there, even people who aren't part of Mitra . . . .

P. had started a joint, but when he passed it to S., she passed it along saying "My reality is distorted enough as it is." I thought that was a good line to remember when you want to say "No!' S. does drink wine, but that's about it. So wine is okay with Mam.... . . .

Someone asked about prayer. This always comes up, as you could guess. In studying at Mitra and other places, I've learned so much about the power of prayer, but what Mam says is that we, meaning people, have forgotten what it means to pray. She says that we pray for things thinking it means we have to get it, which is the wrong attitude. It reminded me of when my father used to say "are you asking me or telling me?" "You refuse to yield" is exactly what Mam said. When P. said that wasn't true at Mitra where we know about prayer, S.

asked then how come the other day she heard someone in the garden chanting for a Hummer. . . .

I personally heard Her speak to people in three more languages, including Hopi. Even S. was surprised. . . .

Finally, I want to close with a part that I hope I get right. I kept wishing I had a tape recorder, but anyway, here is how I remember it going. Someone asked Mam what would make the terrorists stop, which is the kind of question she doesn't answer. Instead, S. said something like "how can there be peace when you have two different sides and each one swears that God is telling them what to do." (I know this isn't exactly right, but you get the idea). So Magda, the Regression Therapist who you probably remember from other mentions in this blog, tells S. that you can't think of it logically like that, because God expects blind faith, not logic. Well, this is where Mam DOES speak up and she says, and this is an exact quote, "How do you know what God wants?" Then S. says, "Right, who's spoken to God lately? Raise your hands." Which of course no one does. Then S. looks down at Mam, which is always so amazing because it really reminds you how Mam is there, inside her body. S. says to Mam "doesn't it drive you crazy when people say they know what God wants them to do?" or something like that. And Mam basically says "People use God as an excuse to do what they want to do anyway." Then S. said something about it being the same idea as when criminals say that Society made them do something. And Mam said, sounding really surprised, "Does that really happen? Don't human beings ever take responsibility for their own actions"

Which totally blew me away. So that's what I'm leaving you to think about as I sign off for tonight (this morning really!) Namaste.

Susan was a little hung over when she descended from the Land Rover in Sky Harbor a few hours later. Sedona had open arms, and Steffi had urged them to stay, but they'd agreed they had to go back. If Mam had been meant to stay in Sedona, they reasoned, She would have manifested there and not in New York City.

"What happens now?" Steffi asked, handing Susan her bag.

"We'll figure it out," Mam said.

"You still have to keep your mouth shut on the plane."

None of them knew that Hazel had been up all night, feverishly typing.

5 – AN UPLIFTING TURN OF EVENTS

Usually, early summer bathed the City like a blessing, but after Arizona everything seemed dull and dirty and the apartment dark and cramped. Susan felt compelled to buy flowers and stock up on fruit. She found herself longing for light so much that, a few hours after she landed, she ran to the Home Depot. That she might be out of a job in two days didn't signify. She was a body in motion and it was forward all the way.

When Lisa and Alan showed up on Sunday, they had to step carefully so as not to trip on the rolled up rug and a pair of oversized cushions. A breeze from the open windows stirred a set of wind chimes newly suspended above the entry to the living room. The room itself was a soft clean yellow, and they were just in time to help raise the self-assemble bookcases from the floor. Leaning against the old chair, in a cheap Plexiglas frame (but framed nonetheless), a poster of the Grand Canyon waited to be hung.

"You call this a vacation?" Lisa said. "Have you slept at all?"

"I had plenty of rest in Sedona," Susan said, sweeping her damp hair off her face with a smile.

"You look great." Lisa poked Alan in the ribs. "Doesn't she look great?"

Susan had automatically dressed for home improvement in her cut out bikini and an old pair of drawstring pants. Alan hadn't said a word since they'd entered the house. He was too busy staring at Mam.

"So, Alan, what do you think?"

It took Lisa a moment to realize that it wasn't Susan asking the question. In the ordinariness of the moment, Lisa had forgotten about Mam. Alan hadn't. When Lisa yelped, his face lit up with joy. Susan laughed and started dragging cushions around so that everyone could sit comfortably. She and Mam had a lot to tell them.

Lisa only wanted to know what their plans were. As soon as she'd heard about the Mitrans turning out to meet Mam, she envisioned a rally in Central Park. There could be T-shirts. Her native sales mind started to race. Alan cradled the small stone goddess that had been a gift from Bear. He was as excited as Lisa, but his imagination turned to other tracks. He saw a group of carefully selected scholars bent in years of quiet dedication. Susan, and Mam, dismissed them both in turn. They had no plans, they told their friends as they had told Steffi. Mam would listen and learn while Susan went about her day-to-day routine. They would see where that led them.

"That's ridiculous!" Both Lisa and Alan said the same words if not exactly simultaneously. There was no way that Susan really believed she could go back to her frankly pretty humdrum life. You can't take a talking breast to the office every day on the subway, or any other way for that matter.

"I have to eat," Susan said reasonably. "Pay the rent, little things like that. For Mam as much as for myself; after all, She's living in my body."

True, they agreed, but it wasn't fair to Mam, or to humanity who had so very much to learn from Mam. Her voice needed to be heard. Susan assured them that there would be plenty of opportunities for Mam to meet people. Nights, weekends.... They objected strongly. How do you shunt aside the mission of an oracle (for that was what Alan continued to call Her) and jam it into a few off hours? Susan was more than a bit affronted. Mam might be a new thing in her life, but she was fiercely used to the idea of squeezing a voice into stolen hours. She'd been writing that way for twenty years. Interesting how no one ever seemed to wonder—or care—how she'd managed that.

Mam, as Lisa and Alan were surprised to hear, agreed with Susan. Their plan, She told them, was to have no plan. Susan was going back to work tomorrow, and what would be would be.

Things went surprisingly smoothly.

Susan still had a job. The shakeup at the office had resulted in a major administrative reshuffling, as a result of which, Evelyn had received what amounted to a promotion and was feeling rather charitable. No one had been let go, and the new COO had promised to reassess the 20 percent reduction at the end of the quarter. Mam kept to Herself at work, though Her evening conversations with Susan proved that She was absorbing large amounts of "human connection."

Susan went back to Harrison Levy's workshop, though it crossed her mind that it might now be difficult for her to write. Still, she knew Mam would find it fascinating to listen to what went on. She was almost disappointed when MacIntosh Wing didn't turn up. Raju said that while she'd been away, Levy had announced, with parental pride, that the boy was spending the summer polishing up his manuscript at the McDowell Colony. Raju also reported that according to the grapevine, the infamous editor was realizing that she'd bought the emperor's new clothes. With gleeful malice, he repeated the speculations that had Wing, and a ghostwriter, virtually chained to a desk in a rooming house in Fishkill until something would come of it. It wasn't that Raju presumed to be a literary writer himself. On the contrary, he was honestly out to cash in with a potboiler, but he was canny enough to know the value of a prestigious artists' colony and it galled him that Wing was once again rising triumphant.

Ordinarily, Susan, whose aspirations were rather loftier and who had been repeatedly unsuccessful in qualifying for The Colony and its fellows, would have been equally provoked, but just now she was distracted by a colonization of her own. In lieu of their usual storefront tête-à-tête, she invited Raju over to her place for coffee that first Monday back. They sat on Lisa and Alan's newly arrived old sofa, and she introduced him to Mam. It was the first time she'd ever seen Raju speechless.

It was the same old life, but wondering what Mam might say made it seem a little more interesting.

One morning, as usual, Susan stood in the rush hour subway, trying to read. At 34th Street, when the population of the car redistributed, she found herself sharing a pole with a petite Latina in three-inch heels. The other woman kept reaching too high above shoulder level, with the result that her hand would slide down the pole and hit Susan's. Each time it happened, Susan would startle and the woman would apologetically remove her hand to a higher spot on the pole, again moving far too high. Hardly unusual, but after it had happened several times, Susan felt the woman staring at her. Once she'd gotten over the surprise of having someone acknowledge her existence on a subway, she was annoyed; after all, it was the woman who kept hitting *her*. She looked up, preparing to argue. The woman blinked and looked away. When they were stopped at 42nd Street, Susan felt a tap on her wrist, a deliberate tap. The young woman was still staring. She held a deeply creased piece of paper in her hand, which she showed to Susan.

"It's you," she whispered shyly. "You're her, right?"

Susan's instinct was to ignore her and look for another pole, but something about the paper caught her eye and she looked more closely. It was her own face. A bad picture, it looked like a digi-cam with insufficient resolution, but it was clearly her. Underneath there was something written in Spanish.

Susan didn't speak Spanish. "Where did you get this?" she stammered. "What does it say?"

"This girl in my bible study class, her sister's a nurse up at the hospital. It says... Does it really... " her eyes shining with hope, she leaned close enough for her lips to touch Susan's ear so that her whisper would be heard above the moving train, "talk?"

Susan was taken aback. When she and Mam had said they'd see what happened next, somehow she hadn't expected anything to happen. Or if she had, nothing like this bizarre New York moment. "Uh," she said elegantly. "What's your name?"

"Rosa. Rose."

"Rosa. Umm, this isn't really the time or the place."

Rosa's eyes glowed. "So then it's true!" She rapidly crossed herself. "Madre de Dios!"

Susan panicked. The last thing she or Mam needed was a riot in a subway car. She tried to hush Rosa, who was giddy with excitement.

"You got to come and talk to my girls. We meet every Wednesday." She was fishing in her shoulder bag, "I'll write it down. You got a pen?" She pulled out a lip liner and wrote an address on a bit of the flyer, which she tore off and gave to Susan. "Seven o'clock, okay?" Susan was too stunned to say a word. "Please," Rosa begged. "It's like you have a responsibility. Ai! I'm gonna miss my stop!" Her heels wobbling dangerously, she flew off the train. It was lunchtime before Susan could concentrate on anything and even then she made sure to avoid fish.

The next Wednesday after work, she found herself on the D train to Brooklyn. Susan's familiarity with Brooklyn consisted almost entirely of bus rides to events at the Brooklyn Academy of Music. It was an undiscovered country to her, rattling past the monotony of battered elevated station stops with strangely Kafkaesque names, the Avenue Js and Avenue Qs and so on. All she could see from the windows were stained cement platforms and dilapidated roofs. She couldn't read the book she'd brought; she had to stay glued to the signs or she knew she'd lose track of where she was, or, since she literally as well as metaphorically had no idea of where she was, at least of whether or not she'd reached the station Rosa'd told her to use. The tension of getting lost on the train, or the danger in crossing under the rusted girders that seemed to be supporting the rusted tracks, or the disorientation she found in the low houses and prewar red brick apartment buildings that alternated like rows of corn and beans was so strong that she had little room to fear what might happen when Mam would meet a bible study class.

When Father Hubert had started a women's study class at St. Agatha's in the 1970s, he was trying to integrate a growing stream of raw immigrants into the community. Many of the newcomers were from small country villages, the women being particularly unsophisticated about city life and prone to folk medicines and other old ways. His women were as much encouraged to exchange stories about child-rearing and local shop keeping practices, as they were lead to learn scripture. Deep bonds were formed—a kind of sisterhood—and new generations considered it a rite of passage to be allowed to attend the meetings. Even after the good Father had passed on, the women continued to perpetuate the society. They met, not in the church or parish house, but in the homes of members, in living rooms like Rosa Santiago's where the small shrine of statues and prayer cards and photos of the dead had its corner next to the television or alongside the knickknacks from Disney World, Atlantic City and the home country. It was questionable whether Father Martin, the current overworked parish priest, even knew that such a group existed.

Despite the popularity of the group, the women had busy lives and it was unusual for more than a dozen or so to make it to any one weekly meeting. This week, it seemed that every single member had managed to attend and Rosa's tiny living room was crammed to bursting with women. Those who lived in the building had brought extra chairs from their own apartments and these, together with the ones from Rosa's kitchen, were pushed so close together that three women could share two chairs between them. Even after her son's playpen had been moved to the bedroom (her son himself having been sent with his father to his uncle's house), they couldn't fit enough chairs to seat everyone, so there were women standing along the walls.

Susan was a bit daunted by the size of the crowd and the charge of anticipation that filled the room. She smiled hard at the women as Rosa led her to the place of honor on the sofa, beside Vanessa, the hospital nurse with the camera phone. Rosa settled on her other side, bumping Vanessa's sister Julia to perch on the sofa's arm where she had to lean her head to avoid hitting it on a shelf of souvenir shot glasses. Vanessa, who she'd never met, introduced Susan to the ladies.

She acknowledged their applause and unbuttoned her shirt. From the window in the bikini bra, Mam winked out and said "Hola, senoras." Only those in the front row could see Her. They turned pale and hurriedly crossed themselves. The others nudged each other in confusion.

"Hello everyone," Susan addressed the room. "It's kind of you to invite us." She had no idea as to what might be expected of her by a room full of presumably God-fearing Catholic women, but then she'd been unable to predict much of anything since Mam had arrived on the scene. "Um, we usually kind of do a question and answer kind of thing..."

"Susan, let me get things started," Mam said, cutting in on Susan's speech. The two overlapping voices penetrated the room. This time, all the other women crossed themselves, and several began to mutter prayers. Rosa, dumbstruck beside her, could not keep her eyes from Mam. "Ladies, senoras," Mam's voice rose above the murmurs. "I am honored to be with you tonight and to hear what you have to say." And then, She repeated the same in Spanish.

There was total silence. Then a number of women spoke up at once.

"Are you the blessed Mother?"

"My son has the asthma bad. Please, will you help him?"

"My brother in San Turce, he lost his house in the hurricane. He wants to rebuild it. Is it safe?"

"Ladies!" Mam's voice was loud and firm, but not unkind. "I am not your Mother Mary. I do not heal. I don't tell fortunes." She continued to repeat herself in Spanish, ensuring that everyone would understand.

"But you're a miracle," Rosa said, puzzled. She seemed to be speaking for them all. "You have to do something." She looked to Susan for a human explanation. "Doesn't She do something?"

Susan shrugged helplessly. "She talks. But mostly She listens."

"There has to be some reason for Her."

"We don't know what it is. She says it's to communicate, but I can't honestly say I understand."

"Let's not talk as if I'm not here," Mam said tartly. Rosa blushed and Susan sighed. "Ladies," again she addressed the room, "don't think of me as a miracle. Think of me as a visitor from far away. Let me know what worries you in the world. Tell me your questions that have no answers. I don't know if I can help, but I want to know."

The women thought about this. They were clearly a little disappointed; they'd expected more from a miracle than just talk. Still, they were witnessing a miracle, and that in and of itself was too special to allow it to end.

Julia poked out her hand, as if she were in a classroom trying to get the teacher's attention. When Susan pointed to her with a nod, urging her to go ahead, she tossed her hair diffidently, nearly upsetting the shot glasses in the process. She spoke in a low, shaky voice. "My baby's papi, Mam, he was married and I knew it before. I didn't care. I wanted him. Will God punish me?"

Everybody knew about Julia's baby's daddy, including Father Martin because she confessed it on a regular basis. She'd done a stupid thing, the way girls do. She's done penance for the adultery and hadn't compounded the sin by having an abortion. The baby, two years old and healthy as a little pig, had been duly baptized and Julia was a good mother. Nothing unusual, except that the girl wouldn't let it go. They waited to see what Mam would say.

"I don't know about God," Mam said. "If you're worried enough to ask, then you're punishing yourself. You don't need God or anyone else to do it for you."

"She did her penance from Father Martin," said Vanessa with sisterly defensiveness. "The idea of penance is to get forgiven. She don't need to be worrying about it no more."

"That's interesting," Mam said. "I would have thought the idea of penance would be to make you reflect on what you'd done so that you wouldn't make the same mistake again."

"So okay, maybe," Vanessa conceded. "But mostly to get forgiven. She wouldn't be so stupid do it again with him, would you chica?"

"Julia, it's not about the man or even your baby, is it?" Mam asked gently. "It's that you think about the other woman. You put yourself in her place."

Again, Vanessa butted in. "It's his fault if his wife feels bad, not Julia's, dogging around on her like he does. He got babies on other girls too."

"Three, maybe four." Julia sniffed. "Besides also with his wife."

"It's not all his fault," Susan finally had to speak up. She didn't know if Mam had enough "human connection" to get the big picture. "I mean, clearly he's a shit, but how can it be all his fault when he tells girls that he's married and they still go around with him?"

"He shouldn't be doing that," Vanessa said.

"No he shouldn't," Susan agreed. "But if none of the girls would go out with him, he'd have to stop, wouldn't he? It takes two. That's why you can't let it go, Julia. You feel guilty for messing around with such a jerk, for enabling him to hurt you and his wife and even the other women."

"Respect," Mam said. "Respect has reflective qualities. You have to respect yourself, so that you can respect others. And because each of you is equally precious, if you don't respect one another, you don't respect yourselves."

The women, listening closely, eyes shining and hands aflutter, fervently voiced their assent. It was such a simple concept, Susan thought, basically the old golden do-unto-others rule. Surely someone in the Catholic Church must have preached this same thing to these same women, and yet they were receiving it as news, simply because it was coming from a talking breast. Susan wondered if their new conviction would last beyond the evening.

"Por favor Mam," a woman pleaded from the back row, her voice breaking into Susan's contemplation, "can we see you?"

The cut out bikini bra still obscured Mam from the view of those sitting to the extreme left or right of the room. The woman had spoken in Spanish. Mam translated for Susan who smiled ruefully. It was only fair, she agreed, but this was the part she would never get used to. She tried to act nonchalant as she unhooked the top.

"Tanto modestia!" said Mam. The women giggled. It was an icebreaker of sorts. From there on, the evening loosened up. There was even cake, though it was hard to pass it around. When it was time to call it a night, the women filed up to say goodnight and pay their respects to Mam face to face.

"Madonna?" To Susan's surprise, the tiny stout woman with a frizzle of grey curls was addressing her, not Mam. "Please, I think maybe I can help." She pulled a tape measure from her purse. "It's my work, at Corpo Céleste." Corpo Céleste was a manufacturer of high-end intimate apparel, so famous that even Susan had heard of the brand. Their $80 silk thongs were de rigueur in supermodel-rock star circles and recently, their hand-embroidered flimsies had been featured on a long-running sex comedy on HBO. Marta had sewn for CC for most of her life. She was now the senior sample maker, helping turn the designers' sketches into actual garments. There was nothing about the construction of a brassiere that Marta didn't know. She was certain that she could come up with something comfortable and supportive that would allow Mam to be seen while preserving Susan's dignity. "And pretty, too," she winked. "No nursing bras."

Despite the astounding commercial success of the show, the conference room assigned to *Duh News* was only rudimentary. Though filled with A-list awards, the metal-framed glass-fronted display case had the look of something salvaged from an elementary school circa 1962. Instead of being dry-mounted and matted, the handful of national magazine covers were tossed into chain store frames and hooked over existing nails. Instead of a conference table, there was a pair of mica-topped folding utility tables with matchbooks folded under two legs. Around it, in an assortment of thrift shop chairs, sat the writers and performers. The combined cost of the sneakers worn by the mostly male, mostly Ivy League crew amounted to far more than the cost of all the furnishings in the room, even when factoring in the price of the cappuccino machine.

As was usual for the weekly brainstorming meeting, the creative team sat around, and on, the tables, throwing around ideas and donuts. Lily, the production secretary and one of only two women in the room, stood at the rolling whiteboard, attempting to jot down some coherent notes that only she would ever copy.

Roger, a former member of *The Harvard Lampoon* and current on-camera member of the *Duh News* team, had been going on at length about a man who'd built a scale replica of the Taj Mahal entirely out of dog teeth.

Wendy could feel the guys to either side of her flinching in disgust. She wished they had the balls to speak out. She would speak out, but after six months, she'd already learned that as she didn't literally have balls, her outbursts tended to have the opposite effect to what she'd intended. She was on the brink of asserting her enthusiasm for Roger's idea in the perkiest possible way (a surefire idea killer) when Jack finally cut him off by throwing a pencil across the room and hitting him on the shoulder. It was only the eraser end.

"Enough already with the weird hobbies and freaky collections. There's got to be some real news out there." *Duh News* was a comedy show in the guise of a television news magazine, and Jack Rabb was its "anchor" and head writer. In his native Ontario, Jack had been classically trained to handle Shakespeare and Shaw. His present job was the end result of his appearance in a hemorrhoid cream commercial so wildly popular that it achieved a kind of cult status. He'd gone on to be interviewed on every morning chat show and most of the late-night ones as well, and had even hosted *Saturday Night Live*. Lots of face time but no pay. He'd been down to his last Canadian dollar before landing this gig, replacing the original host who'd gone on to make films for Scientology. After four years on the air, he continued to take his work very seriously; seriously enough that they'd named him co-producer. Most people didn't realize it, but he had a wife and two kids.

"Doesn't anyone have anything with some substance?"

"There's the Bake Sale for Automatic Weapons group in Idaho that—"

"Anything safe with some substance," Jack amended.

The network programming director's nephew, who habitually kept a low profile, cleared his throat and took his feet off the table. "There's something my assistant found on the web," he said. He was the only staff writer who had an assistant. "But it may be too weird even for us." He pulled a page out of a folder and slid it across the table to Jack. "Some nutso blogger in Sedona who works at a quote/unquote Personal Enrichment Center—"

"Wouldn't you say New Age cultists come under the heading of 'weird hobbies'?" Roger took everything personally and was in a perpetual snit, even when his stories were better received.

"Hey now, Roge, give me a break. I'm only saying she claims to have seen a talking breast." The room erupted: snickers, guffaws, the whole available gamut of nasty laughs. "Hey now, I wasn't trying to be funny. That's really what she says."

"She does," Jack looked up from skimming the printout. "Claims to have met a woman whose breast actually talks. With a mouth."

"And says what?" someone asked.

Jack shrugged. "Does it matter? It's different, I'll give you that. How long since we did a miracle story?"

Alec, the associate producer, consulted his laptop. "We had the Jesus on the underpass a few months ago."

"Before that, we had that haunted diaper genie in Cleveland," Lily reminded them.

"Yeah, well, that was more of a whatchamacallit, possession—"

"Let's do it," Jack said. "Who's up?"

"Ooo, a Girl Story!" Roger grabbed the paper and pushed it in Wendy's face. "Here Wendy, you're always complaining. It's all yours."

Wendy wanted to grab what was left of his hair in her fist and slam his face down on the table. Instead, she raised her eyebrows and flashed a smile. "Sounds good to me," she said brightly.

After the meeting, Wendy forced herself to stop fuming and got to work. Roger could stuff his arrogance up his ass, if only it would fit there. *Duh News* was just a day job for her, a stepping-stone on the way to her real goal. Wendy wanted to do television documentaries, like David Attenborough or Ken Burns or Terry Jones, multi-part in-depth investigations of items of substance. She even had some ideas. The first step was making herself famous enough to sell them. What she needed now was exposure. She was determined to take Roger's little joke and turn it into a spot good enough that they'd have to give her some major face time. Maybe they'd even bump one of Roger's pieces to do it.

To Wendy, "witch_hazel" seemed a common enough type, a GenXer who spent her life feeling she'd missed out on the 60s. The photo on the homepage showed a hippie-wannabee, channeling Janis Joplin. Hazel seemed to consider herself something of a healer. Her site boasted an extensive guide to the gathering and various uses of herbs and other plants, as well as links to mail order sources for the same, all rounded out by an annotated vortex map of Sedona and a number of ineffectual poems. Slogging through the blog itself, starting from a point about a year back, Wendy read perpetually awestruck accounts of Hazel's Mitran odyssey. She found it mostly boring, sometimes a bit sad, but never ridiculous. Only a shallow shit like Roger would want to make mockery of such an earnest attempt at self-discovery.

Finally, she reached an entry from a couple of months ago. A woman arrived at Mitra and met with the Center's three leaders. From the moment she walked through the door, Hazel had Known Something was about to Happen. Later that day, she accidentally overheard the three men talking about the astounding manifestation they'd witnessed—a mouth had opened in the woman's breast, and it had spoken to them. The next entry, a few days later, was an eyewitness account of the same phenomenon.

It struck Wendy that there was an immediacy to the writing of these entries, and a lack of the affectation that characterized the rest of the blog. She shifted in her chair and read on, with renewed interest. Her excitement continued to grow as she read Hazel's account of her first direct exchange with the creature or whatever it was. The disjointed but passionate attempt to capture the "goodbye" party had the ring of utter honesty.

"She says that we pray for things thinking it means we have to get it, which is the wrong attitude."

Whoever had said that, it wasn't Hazel herself. The alleged utterances of this "Mam"ifestation, whatever it was, lacked the warm-and-fuzzies that characterized the rest of the blog. And whoever's words they were, they had Wendy curious. What was the goal here? What did She (presumably) want? A certain amount of provocation was offered, but no reassurances and no precepts. As a conscious approach to start a prayer-for-money scam, it was supremely wrong-headed.

Wendy didn't know if it was *Duh News* or not, but she smelled a good story. It was definite: she was going to Arizona to meet this Hazel face to face. She wondered if the budget would let her take a camera. Continuing to read, she reached for her phone.

Marta was as good as her word. Having negotiated permission from the shop steward, she began staying late at the factory, trying to engineer a solution. Jimmy Touray, the head designer, watched discreetly until his curiosity became unbearable and he finally had to ask. She swore him to secrecy. It was an easy oath to for him to take, especially as it was more from kindness than from a conviction of necessity. It wasn't a believable story. It was even less so coming from a woman who kept a glass of water upside down on a piece of cardboard on the floor beneath her sewing machine, to catch evil spirits.

Susan was told to come by after work. In the city that never sleeps, the vestigial light-industry neighborhoods alone run by the union clock. Though at just past six p.m. the rest of New York was still at rush hour, Long Island City was as deserted as a Sunday morning. The cars were all gone from the lots and the check cashing storefronts were shuttered and locked. Walking south from the Queensboro Plaza station, Susan kept looking back over her shoulder.

A bored security guard in a mismatched uniform took her up in the elevator and closed the gate behind her. She'd never been in a factory before, no less one that was closed for the night. It was eerie to walk across the shadowy space, past the wire fencing that made a corridor between the offices and the stockroom on one side and the factory floor on the other, her heels ringing out in the silence. Where there was light from the dirty, chickenwire-sandwiched windows, dust motes and lint floated in the stale air. It smelled like cloth and machine oil and old linoleum. Sewing machines, shrouded in canvas, made strange and menacing shapes. The cutting tables stretched flat and wide, the rivets in the metal rulers throwing sudden glints from reflected light.

In all this gloom, the well-lit sample room glowed like an inn on a stormy night. Susan picked her way towards the light and Marta's voice.

She stuck her head in the door. Marta was sitting at her machine, one of four in the work island at the center of the room. One wall was covered with felt, on which samples of panties and camisoles and bras were pinned, along with scraps of fabrics and trimmings, and the occasional photo. There was an old poster of Madonna in a Corpo Céleste bustier.

Jimmy stepped away from the garment he'd been adjusting on one of the fitting forms. It seemed to be a demi-cup brassiere, except that one side had an open shelf-like underpinning in lieu of a cup.

Slipping it on, Susan had to admit it did wonders for her other breast as well. Marta and Jimmy fussed with it here and there, looking for a mysterious perfection in the fit. Admiring herself in the mirror, Susan decided that Corpo Céleste was selling more than just a label after all.

"I like it," Mam volunteered. "Would you make up a few of these?"

Jimmy had endured several decades of fitting women into intimate apparel by cultivating a clinical attitude towards breasts. He'd never before been addressed by one. Still, it would clash with his idiom to appear flustered. He blanched, but didn't twitch a hair of his fox colored toupee. Instead, he assumed his patented faux-casual air.

"Once we have the pattern fixed," he said coolly, "we can make up as many as you need." He pointed to a pile of fabrics on the worktable. "And we were thinking we'd work up a few variations for special occasions."

"What occasions?" Susan asked.

"We won't know 'til they happen," Mam said mildly. "But it's good to be prepared. You can tell which one of us is the fashionista, can't you Jimmy?"

With visions of *W* layouts dancing in his head, Jimmy laughed delightedly. Marta had been wrong—this wasn't a mere miracle, it was a Star. He wondered if it would be pushy to ask for exclusivity.

Once Jimmy and Marta were satisfied with the fit, the prototype was carefully removed from Susan and they all sat down to review the samples. A few of the fabrics seemed excessive to Susan, a Chinese silk brocade for example. Jimmy scolded her for "thinking small" and, to her chagrin, Mam agreed. Jimmy'd also sketched a few designs for robes. They were cut deep in front to display the bra, then floated from the tightly fastened empire waist. The sleeves were invariably long and graceful.

"Even in one of my brassieres, there are times when you might feel a little underdressed," Jimmy said. "Besides, the look is killer. Very Pre-Raphaelite, which if you ask me is due for a comeback." Susan didn't accept the designer's contention that she'd be starting a major trend, but she was grateful to him for what she realized was an enormous effort. She also appreciated his results.

When he hinted at wanting to spend more time with Mam, Susan invited him to come to the apartment one night. Her spontaneous invitation was the germ of an idea. Everyone who'd met Mam wanted to spend more time with Her. Why not have people over once a week, to talk? It would be like the meeting at Rosa's house, except without the bible study and with men.

Recently, Susan had been learning a lot about men and breasts. More than she really wanted to know.

Most women don't think any more about their breasts, on a daily basis, than about their ears or knees. Unless of course they've just begun a new relationship, or maybe have just been dumped. Then, of course, their breasts would be weighed and, inevitably, found wanting. Susan, having been blessed with a sufficiency of her own from the age of twelve, thought little about them unless she was buying a swimsuit or something to wear in hot weather.

Men, however, can't get enough breast. It was hardly a secret; you couldn't miss it if you tried. Bosoms were everywhere, spilling over every cover at the newsstand, rolling across billboards and posters, flashing from mail order catalogues. They popped up in films regardless of their relevance to the story. For a while, until it had become so predictable as to be boring, Susan used to play a game with a friend where they'd bet on how many minutes into a movie, any movie, it would be before the leading lady would take off her top. They also noticed that it was only in what Susan thought of as "dick flicks," the kind of action films that had ten minute vehicle chases and lots of explosions, that the leading men could be counted on to tear off their shirts and display their gleaming shoulders and washboard abs; that wasn't for the girls. On television, where actual nudity was rigorously blue-penciled out of the prevailing sex and violence, cleavage was abundant; only the nipple had to be concealed.

Men, who didn't have any of their own to lug around, couldn't seem to stop thinking about breasts. Not being able to possess them created the yearning, the grass always being greener when you don't have a yard. In assessing value, they considered purpose and were unable to decide whether breasts were about food or about sex. This made men think about sleeping with their mothers, which made them feel guilty, guilt feeding the thrill, the heightened thrill raising the value and so on.

Alan and Raju, to whom Susan explained this theory, shook their heads sadly.

"There's more than titillation, if you'll pardon the expression," Raju didn't so much as smirk. "It's a very beautiful form, in the aesthetic sense. I never understand why women don't appreciate that." This was after they'd spent a Sunday morning dragging her through the Metropolitan Museum of Art to view hundreds of years of breasts on parade "You should at least make yourself appreciate the iconography." He pointed to the stack of Museum postcards they'd purchased as reminders.

"There's a bigger picture and you're not taking it in," Alan said. He picked up the stone goddess that Bear had given her. It was little more than a bulbous rock, all breasts and buttocks. "Not my Mom," he said, "Mother

Earth. Where it all begins, all life, all worship, all art. You find these in every primitive culture, all over the world."

"Like nursing," Susan insisted, "like I said. Food. Tied to sex."

"Food and sex are both sources of life," Alan said.

"So you expect me to believe that men are fixated on breasts because they worship the source of life."

"Absolutely." Alan picked up the postcards and dealt them like a hand of blackjack. "Madonna with the Holy Child; obvious. Renaissance Venuses, look how they present themselves like ripe fruit. Gauguin's noble savages..."

"Then explain why every world religion treats women like garbage."

"In my religion, we have goddesses," Raju reminded her, somewhat smugly. "And there have been great women gurus."

"I have one word for you," Susan fixed him with a steely stare. "Suttee."

"Men fear what they don't know," Mam spoke up. "In Raju's religion, the Destroyer is also a woman."

"Yes!" Alan always got very excited whenever Mam joined in one of these discussions. "Woman, like the earth itself, is both giver of life and destroyer. And what is more womanly than a breast?"

"If you're really asking me and not being rhetorical," Susan said, "I'd say a womb."

"You can't see a womb," Raju was primarily logical. It was part of what made him so devastatingly successful with contracts law.

"Sue, if the breast wasn't that important, then why would Mam have chosen to appear in a breast?" As Mam consistently refused to admit She had any knowledge, no less choice or control, of Her origins, this was unanswerable and Alan knew it. He needed to stymie Susan just long enough that she'd consider his point. Whether or not Susan respected it, he wanted her to accept that the imagery of the breast was significant beyond stroke magazines and "Girls Gone Wild." She had a duty now to learn these things.

Susan sighed. She knew her guys meant well, with their excited deluge of books and websites revolving around mother goddesses and other female symbols of power. If only she could be as fascinated by their fascination. She hoped it would die down after a while, the way people stop fussing over a new baby once it's four or five months old.

Which reminded her, she really ought to visit Hannah while she was still on maternity leave and pay her respects to little Reuven.

Wendy tossed a coin, bet the lottery numbers in her lunchtime fortune cookie and signed a work order to take a cameraman with her to Arizona.

She'd have to do everything else herself, but she was used to that. Even so, she was putting herself on the line for a huge expense. She had an appointment to meet Hazel at her apartment in one of the older, adobe complexes in town. She also had the names and numbers of a man who had a power vortex in his bathroom, and a woman who collected cacti that were shaped like celebrity faces. If Hazel turned out to be toxic video, Wendy would need to come up with some other footage to justify the trip.

The sunshine in Sedona was impressive. It was perplexing how Hazel had managed to turn her little apartment into a Northern European cave. Having brought only a few lighting instruments, Wendy and Uri found they needed to open all the curtains and rearrange most of the living room in order to place two chairs in sufficient light. Finding two suitable chairs had been another challenge.

Hazel was disconcerted. Wendy's call had been such a thrill; she'd felt so proud to have done something so important as bringing Mam to the attention of a genuine cable television show. Yes, there'd been a moment of panic, when she'd wondered if she were really worthy to represent Mam in this way. So she'd turned to Patrick, who she'd always found the least intimidating of the Leaders. She could tell she'd surprised him, but he'd been so reassuring, even inviting her to bring the reporter over to Mitra, that she'd found her center.

She'd opened her blue door with a happy edge of anticipation. Wendy, friendly and pleasant on the phone, had turned up wearing a black jacket and no-nonsense New York air, both of which rather intimated Hazel, as did the camera and its large taciturn operator. With hardly a "may I," they'd taken over her home. It had taken weeks to map out the proper balances for her space, and they'd upset it all in less than an hour. They'd let her special tisane grow cold while setting up their lights. They'd even insisted that she change her earrings because they said that every time she nodded her head, the coins on the hoops caused a "ping" on the soundtrack. Dressed in her most extravagant layers, Hazel trembled in what now felt like a strange room. She crossed her legs nervously. Her body felt oddly extended this way; she'd become too used to sitting tucked up.

"And it never occurred to you that this woman might be throwing her voice?" Wendy asked, her voice implying Hazel surely was a fool.

"It's not possible," Hazel shook her head vehemently, setting the moonstones in her ears to swing wildly. If she'd stayed with the coins, she'd have been chiming like a carillon. "I mean, they'd argue. Susan would be in middle of a sentence and then Mam—She said we should call Her Mam— would open Her mouth and interrupt."

"It has a mouth?" Wendy didn't know whether to be fascinated or horrified.

"Lips really. No tongue or teeth, not that you can see. But definitely lips. They move when She speaks."

"So this Susan is a puppeteer as well a great ventriloquist." Everyone hired by *Duh News* acquired Roger's patented skeptical tone along with the first paycheck. Designed to turn almost any conversation into a joke, it could make "hello" sound like a sneer. What it did to an expression of skepticism was painful. Most of the reporters, like Wendy, were hardly aware of using it.

Hazel's distress was clear. "Oh, no! You have to believe me." She leaned forward towards to the camera that pointed, over Wendy's shoulder, directly into her face. Her eyes were wide and moist; her body trembled with conviction. "It's just like Mam said, you have to learn how to yield."

Uri, holding the camera on his shoulder, thought she was speaking to him. So would everyone else who saw the footage. He nodded curtly to Wendy. This was the place to stop. Wendy concurred. It wasn't going to be useful, but it was a good interview and it was finished.

After the lights were stowed and her living space restored, Hazel, much happier since being freed from her chair and her nerves, brought Wendy and Uri to Mitra.

They had to stop the car under the stone arch so that Uri could get a shot of the sign. He kept the camera rolling as Hazel walked them to the Fulcrum. They were welcomed by Bear and Patrick (John Robert, who had made some dubious life choices in the 70s, was camera shy). Bear was nearly naked, as usual, and Patrick wore his white caftan. Uri and Wendy both perked up. This was starting to look like it might make a segment after all.

Trailed by Uri and the camera, Wendy was lead on a tour of the Center, with special attention given to places where Mam had spoken. In common with the Fulcrum, both the pool area and a segment of lawn were newly marked with small stone figures and bronze plaques. Uri made sure to get the pool and a few attractive bathers into frame.

They set up in the Zen Garden for a formal interview. Both Bear and Patrick were eager to share their experiences of Mam. Mitra now offered a weekly hour where they passed along what they'd learned. Wendy asked if they'd like to sum that up for the camera. Bear and Patrick exchanged sage nods.

"All life is connected," Bear intoned. "Man seeks the truth because he is afraid there might be none to find."

"Actually, *you* said that last bit," Patrick said. "All actions have repercussions, that's more like what She said."

Wendy frowned. "Didn't Einstein say that?"

"Newton," Uri said, off camera. "Third law."

"Newton's Third Law," Wendy continued. "For every action, there is an equal and opposite reaction." She'd remembered the concept, she just couldn't remember who said it.

Bear nodded gravely. "It was Einstein who remarked that God does not play dice with the universe. Should we be surprised that the laws of physics are the laws of God?"

"Then you're saying Mam is God?" Wendy said, conscious this time of using the Roger voice while she tried to contain her outright glee. Now she'd get airtime. A man who looks like a bronze statue thinks he's heard God talk from a woman's breast. Who's laughing now, Roge?

Instead of agreeing, Bear looked troubled. He sighed deeply and glanced at Patrick.

"We don't," Patrick said. "Not if She won't. And She won't say."

"We accept the miracle of Her presence," Bear said, "without presuming upon it."

Wendy indicated that Uri should stop rolling tape. She already knew how to cut this to make it play.

On one of her half-days, Susan headed out to Kew Gardens Hills. She had a baby present to deliver. She also had a more selfish purpose. Mam had been exposed (in all meanings of the word) to people of a variety of religions and levels of belief, from the Mitrans and Raju to the ladies of Saint Agatha's and their Pentecostal neighbors. Now Susan wanted to give Mam the opportunity of meeting a devoutly observant Jew. The gamble was in how Hannah might react to Mam. It was a gamble Susan wanted to take; lately risk had become a lot less scary.

Susan had lived in New York for her entire life, but it never ceased to amaze her how many worlds the city contained. From the subway station, she boarded a bus that took her past blocks of apartment buildings, through a narrow swathe of single-family houses with lawns the size of doormats. As the bus crossed over the Grand Central Parkway, waving by the old fairground and the stadiums, it seemed to cross a border. The hilly streets were lined with row houses presumably designed for the returning vets of WWII. They were arranged in blocks with anglophilic names like "Regents Park" and "Kensington Gardens." At nearly 3 p.m., the light traffic consisted mostly of bearded old men in black coats and flocks of girls whose pleated school skirts, despite the lingering heat, covered their ankles. Women walked in pairs or behind twin-seat strollers, usually with a child or two skipping or stumbling beside. Often, two women would meet in the middle of a street, their two wide-load strollers and clutch of under-eights effectively blocking the entire sidewalk. Susan learned this the hard way almost immediately as she got off the bus. Detouring around the klatch, Susan started to walk along Main Street, looking for the corner Hannah had described.

While some neighborhoods in the outer boroughs supported their own branches of national chains, it was fairly usual to find, as here, only local shopping. What set communities apart was what the people who lived there meant by "local." Just as the district where Rosa lived was a slice of San Juan, this commercial street might have been airlifted out of some suburb of Jerusalem.

The shops Susan walked past had signs in both English and Hebrew. Drugstore windows advertised phone cards for Israel, and every pizza shop sold falafel. Other restaurants displayed placards indicating "meat" or "dairy," and bakeries posted assurances that everything they sold was "parve." The hardware store advertised the availability of a mikvah. Main Street it might be, but this sure wasn't Mayberry.

What made her sense of dislocation greatest, Susan realized, was the surprising lack of stores designed to entice shoppers into impulse buys. Everything here seemed so grey and functional. It was a world where all energy went into necessities. There were no stores selling video games or luxury soaps or cheap glitter. The only clothing stores for women were small and seemed uniformly stocked with long dark skirts and long-sleeved, high-necked tops. There was not a single shoe store. Susan was conspicuous walking through the neighborhood with her bare head and jeans, yet the people she passed aggressively ignored her. Here was a situation where she was invisible because she was too different to be seen.

It was with no small relief that she found Hannah's corner and made her way past the trashcans and the tricycles to Hannah's door.

The Hannah who greeted her, while smiling and pleased, wasn't the same Hannah with whom she exchanged Evelyn stories in the corner of the conference room. Susan had paid enough baby calls to not expect makeup or smart clothes. What she'd probably anticipated was the same bed-head and rumpled sweats as every other new mother she'd visited at home. Instead, in a long shapeless skirt and top, a cotton scarf wrapped around her head, this Hannah seemed like the great-grandmother of the one she knew. The standard hug-&-kiss seemed too unseemly. Susan wasn't sure what to do, other than smile back.

Hannah made tea and brought out some cookies, and they sat on the plastic-covered brocade sofa, catching up on small talk. She was curious to hear Susan's take on the McKittrick scandal, and how long the 20% reduction was likely to last. Aviva and Sorah Leah, the two youngest girls, ran back and forth between the cookies and their own plastic kitchen in the corner of the room. Susan was purposely vague about her recent adventures, but enthused about the beauty of the Arizona scenery, pulling out some photos from her bag. Hannah had photos of her own, of the recent family visit to her husband's parents in Ramat Gan, and they compared deserts. The older girls came home from school and were sent to the dining table to begin their homework.

There was no good time for Susan to take the risk she'd planned. She had just decided to forget about it and say her goodbyes before Hannah, needing to start dinner, had to throw her out. As she was about to make her move, Hannah mentioned that it was time to feed little Reuven. She took him from his carrier and matter-of-factly began to nurse. To Susan, this was a sign. She took a deep breath, pulled her shoulders straight and began to open her own shirt. Hannah was completely taken aback. She opened her mouth, but no words came out.

"Hannah," Susan said, "bear with me a minute. There's really no way to explain this or prepare you. There's someone I want you to meet."

"Shalom, Hannah" Mam said. "Susan's told me a great deal about you."

Hannah averted her head and spat three times through forked fingers.

"I won't cause you any harm," Mam said. "I simply want to talk with you." Hannah refused to turn back. She bent her body protectively over Reuven's. "I have so many questions, so much to learn. Isn't it a mitzvah, to help someone learn?"

"Please," it was a low sound, halfway between a moan and a hiss. "Please leave."

Susan nearly broke her leg on a toy vacuum cleaner as she ran to the door, buttoning Mam in as she went. Her hands shook and she realized she was crying. "I'm so sorry!" she sobbed, to Mam, to Hannah, to anyone to whom it might apply. She'd known it was a gamble, but deep down, gamblers, like those who pray, never expect to lose. "I thought...I hoped... I mean, everyone else has been so...so great. So excited."

"Susan," Mam said quietly, "think back to the first time that you saw me. Why should Hannah react any differently?"

"Because she has that kind of blind faith that I never had. And she didn't always, not until she was grown up and out of the army. She had an experience in the desert, she told me once, and after that... I really wanted her to talk with you. I was so looking forward to listening and finding out..."

"We still learned something," Mam said. "We'll have to figure out what it was."

The next day, after a sleepless and prayerful night, Hannah called Ayesha at work. She couldn't imagine talking to her husband or her Rabbi about this, not to a man, and she was afraid the women in her community would think she was crazy. Despite the enormity of their one essential difference, Ayesha was the person most like her, most able to believe what she had to say.

Melissa was talking to Ayesha when the call came through. She heard it was only Hannah, but when she saw the expressions on Ayesha's face, Melissa hung around. She could smell good gossip. When she pushed Ayesha to tell her, it was nothing she might have remotely anticipated.

"Hannah could never lie," Ayesha kept saying, shaking her head back and forth until Melissa was irresistibly reminded of a bobblehead doll. "But what does it mean?"

Melissa practically flew across the floor to Susan's cubicle, then stood staring wordlessly in the doorway. For once, Melissa was somewhat daunted. Eventually, feeling the stares on her neck, Susan looked up.

"What?" Susan asked, impatiently. "If you're looking for Steve's PowerPoint presentation..." She was behind schedule on several projects thanks to the reduced hours, but she would have thought Melissa would understand that.

"Is it true?" Melissa said, pointing to Susan's chest.

Susan sighed and rubbed her temples. She could imagine the chain of communication without being told, and she regretted it reaching Melissa, but there was no wishing it away. "Look," she said, "I'm having some people over tonight. Why don't you come by then?" Though she knew Melissa would be more than able to ferret it out from HR, she jotted the address on a Post-it. Let it be an official invitation and not a spy job.

On the whole, both Mam and Susan were pleased with what they called their "study groups." Like the Saint Agatha's meetings, the groups were gradually swelling as people who'd met Mam brought their friends to meet her. There was a pattern to first times, Susan had discovered. The more obvious marvel of Mam being Mam at all would initially be diminished by people's expectations of seeing the lame walk or straw turned into gold. Then Susan would notice them literally snapping to. She'd see it in their posture. They'd catch themselves feeling disappointment, and they'd be ashamed, and then amused, and only after that could they sit quietly and find their way into the conversation.

Tonight, it was Dr. Bob's turn. He hadn't wasted much energy on disappointment. He probably hadn't expected much. He probably hadn't expected anything at all. What Diane had described to him was biologically impossible and therefore there shouldn't be anything to see. He'd only come because Diane, having bribed Lindsay to babysit her siblings, had dragged him by the neck. Now he was sitting in the old chair, wrapped in his physician's cool, listening and giving nothing away.

Mam was pleased with each new encounter. So were Raju and Alan and Lisa, who were almost always around. Susan thought they'd taper off once they'd heard everything Mam was willing to volunteer. Raju was only half joking when he said "So? You and I have been talking about the same things for four years." It was a good point. There was always something new, maybe not from Mam, but something that would come up in the general conversation. For example, Marta would discuss different things in Tara's company than she would with the ladies of St. Agatha's.

"It's nice to use my brain for a change," was Jimmy's comment, "and talk about something besides who's wearing what or screwing who, or what you can't get tickets for."

The door was left unlatched and Tara was enthusiastically holding forth on the rapture of knowing a personal savior, so no one noticed when Melissa entered.

Wendy still wasn't sure how to handle this story. She kept running the footage through Final Cut, cutting and re-cutting. Thanks to Uri's quick and lethal eye, she had an embarrassment of riches. She could see a dozen ways to Sunday to turn what she had into classic *Duh News* material. But she was uncomfortable turning it into an easy laugh. These people, Hazel and Patrick and Bear, had been so serious, and it had meant so much to them. She thought they were nuts, but she had to respect their depth of feeling.

She powered down and decided to call it a night. Settling in a seat on the uptown IRT, Wendy set down her laptop and her gym bag. She was starving and her neck was all kinked up. Trying not to think about cheesecake, she forced a wide yawn and stretched her head until it massaged the top of her back. Her eyes noticed a sticker on one of the backlit advertising slots above the handrail. It was decorated with a lucky hamsa, a heart with a rose and, in the other two corners, an oddly distorted spiral.

"MEET MRS. SUSAN. SHE HOLDS THE ANSWERS NEXT TO HER HEART. MAM WILL CHANGE YOUR LIFE FOREVER."

Wendy stood to get closer to the sticker and read it again. Then she wrote down the phone number on her hand.

The woman with the faintly Spanish inflections gave Wendy an address and said they were having a bible study class on Wednesday. Everyone was welcome, she said, but sometimes lately they ran out of room.

Wendy couldn't even get near the door. A woman with a shoebox was giving out numbers. They would be meeting in three shifts, she told them, an hour apart. She asked, slightly embarrassed, if everyone would please find another place to wait for their turn. Someone had complained to the Housing about the crowds and Rosa had been issued a warning. Small as it was,

Rosa's was still the largest apartment. Until they could find another place to meet, they didn't want to lose it.

Wendy killed about forty-five minutes over a salad at the fast food place around the corner. She noticed a few of the others having a more deep-fried approach to the same idea. There was some jostling for position by the elevators, but they were all back in the hall, waiting patiently, when a pack of excited women filed out of the apartment and group two was called. Wendy was one of the last to enter and took a seat at the rear where she could stand if she needed a better view. She pulled out her Blackberry and felt the weight of it in her hand. She liked taking notes this way; it made her feel more like a journalist and less like a clown.

The room was warm with bodies. Perfume and cooking smells mingled and clotted the air. A smallish woman stood by the sofa and called them all to order with a china bell, a souvenir of the Magic Kingdom. Wendy recognized her voice from the phone. She recognized her face from the framed wedding picture on the wall. This then was Rosa. The seated woman, who would have been pleasantly nondescript if she hadn't been wearing an embroidered chiffon tunic with her jeans, must be Susan. Wendy surreptitiously rose halfway from her seat. The tunic neck was scooped out all the way down to the waist, giving a clear view of Susan's bra. One breast was bared to the room. With a thrill, Wendy realized this must be Mam. Suddenly she had no doubt that there really was a Mam, that everything she'd heard in Sedona would turn out to be true.

"Hola amigas, welcome friends!" A warm mezzo soprano voice rang out from the sofa and penetrated the room.

The women called back. Some of them crossed themselves.

"So, ladies, what do we want to discuss today?" Mam said, and as she repeated it in Spanish, Susan laughed, "I've got to start on those language tapes."

Wendy, wholly standing now, blinked. That comment had definitely occurred while Mam was still speaking. Even as she began to wish she had a camera, she realized that it wouldn't matter. It was too easy to fake something like this on video. No one would believe it without seeing it live, in person.

The hour flew by. At first Wendy tried to take notes, but she gave up. She found herself wanting simply to be there as part of it, not on the outside recording it. It was a bad attitude for a journalist to have and what was worse, Wendy didn't care. She was witnessing a miracle. Something impossible was happening right before her eyes. And that meant the world was a different place than it had been when she'd gotten out of bed that morning.

When their time was up, she couldn't move. She noticed that everyone stopped on the way out to pay their respects to Mam. She wasn't quite ready to do that. She put herself together slowly, allowing other women to push past. She had so much buzzing around in her head, not just the past hour but her day in Sedona, which she'd rerun so many times. She didn't know whether to curse Roger or kiss him. This was definitely not *Duh News*. It was real news.

There was a bit of a commotion up ahead. Susan cried out "Pat! Mam, you remember Pat!" and everyone in the room stopped to listen.

"How could I forget," Mam said with what sounded like a rueful laugh.

"It's so good to see you. Where have you been?" Susan asked. The woman addressed as Pat stood speechless. "Don't leave yet. Marta, take her to the kitchen. Vanessa's there. We can talk later." Pat nodded. Followed by envious eyes, she allowed the older woman to lead her to another room.

By the time Wendy had achieved the sofa, Marta had returned to her position, guarding a large glass bowl. Wendy noticed that, having made their nods, most women dropped in a few coins or a folded bill before moving on. The elderly woman directly in front of Wendy stopped to whisper a few words in Marta's ear. Marta beckoned to Rosa.

"Lupe wants to know if she can bring her neighbor who's Ilalocha."

"Who's what?" Susan's ear had picked up the unfamiliar word.

"Santeria," Rosa said with a small frown. "Priestess."

"And someone aksed before if we spoke to Father about this yet."

"Is this your first time," Susan addressed the distracted Wendy, who was blushing now in front of her, and nodded. "I know, it's a lot to take in."

"Come back again," Mam said.

"I will," Wendy stammered. She pulled her emergency five from her pocket and stuffed it in the bowl. Later she wished she'd opened her wallet and gone for a twenty. A movie was costing eleven bucks these days, and with all the special effects Hollywood could muster, no film could come close to what she'd seen. She didn't sleep at all that night.

The next day, she sat in front of her computer, unable to write a word. She went online and started running "breast," "goddess" and "oracle" through the search engines. She waited for a reasonable hour, then called Mitra and asked for Hazel. "I saw Her," she told Hazel. That's all she could say.

"Now you know," Hazel replied. They stayed on the phone for a while, saying nothing but sensing they were sharing thoughts.

When they hung up, Wendy found Rosa's number in her Blackberry. This time she introduced herself properly. She explained that she'd been there the night before and asked if Rosa could put her in touch with Susan.

"We knew something would happen," Mam said. "We didn't know what it would be, but here it is." Susan had to agree. She told Wendy yes. Then she went to the bathroom to throw up.

A few days later, Susan sat in her own living room with Jimmy fussing over her robe as a makeup artist friend of his dabbed crème foundation on Mam. "I told you there'd be an occasion," he said.

Two technicians were setting up lights and microphones. Wendy was discussing the camera angle with Uri. Raju, there for moral and legal support, was standing in the corner reading the release.

An occasion, Susan thought. That was one way of looking at it.

6 - A MASS IS CELEBRATED

Wendy had run her interview with Susan and Mam through Final Cut and burned a DVD in time for the weekly brainstorm. She sat quietly through nearly an hour of crass jokes and self-aggrandizing bull until, having run out of targets, Roger Haff finally fixed her with his beady eyes.

"Awfully quiet today. Something caught in your throat?"

"Nothing of yours," she said pleasantly. She walked to the DVD player and fed in the disk. "I have an interview I'd like to run past you. See what you all think." She mentally crossed her fingers and pressed Play.

The four-minute rough cut ran on the monitor to a room full of increasingly slack-jawed men. The lull that followed was long enough for Wendy to pop the disk out, slip it into its case and take her seat.

Finally, Roger snorted. "So who'd you blow to make him fake this for you? That must be some happy geek."

Wendy dismissed him with a perfunctory middle-finger salute. As far back as her first internship at a local cable station in Minnetonka, she'd found her biggest asset in television was having grown up with three brothers and five male cousins. She knew how to ignore. For some of the guys at *Duh News*, even that had been insufficient and she often found herself actively regressing to middle school. Compared to comedy, hard news was gay. "What a surprise, Roge. Any more constructive comments?"

Jack cleared his throat. "It's certainly a clever idea." When Jack saw himself as the token adult in the room, he tried to be diplomatic.

"Seriously, Wendy," Lily said, "the effects are awesome.

"Yeah," said Alec's assistant. "Whoever did it, you should give me the 411. We can maybe use him sometime..."

Wendy smiled serenely. "So you all think this is a hoax?" She was answered by an assortment of snickers and good-natured assent. "It's not like I wasn't prepared. I thought it would be nice to give you a chance." She walked to the conference room door and opened it. "Just what we expected," she called.

Susan entered from the hall, where Wendy'd set her to wait her cue. She found she was quite calm, with no need to swallow hard or wipe her palms on her skirt. Jack, automatically swinging into host mode, jumped up with an outstretched hand. She gave it a firm, dry shake. "Hello. Susan Roth."

"Jack Rabb, nice to meet you. Nice work."

"Thank you." She acknowledged the others around the table with a little wave. "Glad you enjoyed it."

Roger jerked his head in Susan's direction. "No offence," he said, implying the opposite, "but she looks perfectly ordinary to me. Bad luck Wendy."

Under Susan's white shirt, Mam started to twitch determinedly. "She is. I'm not. Would you let me out of here, please?"

Jack pulled back, horrified. Several of the boys jumped up so fast that their heels hit the table. Wendy smiled broadly. "Maybe we should all have a seat," she suggested.

Susan remained standing and unbuttoned her shirt. She was impressed by the way she'd started to take it in stride, presenting herself and Mam to a room full of strangers. She even thought she was getting rather good at it. She hoped she'd come across that way on screen. Wendy hadn't shown her anything yet and she had to wonder. Not that she'd been looking to be on television. On the contrary, it creeped her out to think of it. But it was another of Mam's "things that might happen" and she was learning to go with the flow. Right now, it was only important that these people stop thinking Wendy was crazy.

"So," Mam said, "does anyone here think I'm not real?"

"That isn't the point," Alec spoke up bravely.

"No?" Wendy said. "Two minutes ago, you were complimenting me, not on my excellent journalism in uncovering what might be the story of the century, but on my 'access' to effects. Oh, and Roge, by the way, thanks for the tip."

Roger was already the color of a pickled beet. "Enjoy your moment," he fumed. "Have fun, cause this is all you're getting. It's not like we can air that."

"Why not?" Mam asked. "Wendy told us that the people in this room make the decisions."

"For the most part," Alec fumbled. "But we have to answer to... There are many things we have to consider. Sponsors, ratings..."

"This would get ratings," someone said.

"Through the roof," someone else agreed.

"Are you people nuts?!" the programming director's nephew yelled louder than anyone imagined he could. "You want a Janet Jackson coming down on our heads?! We're on basic cable; we can't show a nipple!"

"It's not a nipple, it's an interview subject." Wendy had already thought this through. "As long as we present it that way. It's all in how the piece is cut..." She backtracked the DVD to a spot she'd bookmarked. "Look, see there, see how Mam is moving?" She aimed a laser pointer. "Now pay attention."

"Both sides insist there is only one God," Mam was saying, "and both claim to have God on their side. But they disagree."

"Tell me how that's possible?" the frame widened to include Susan. "I mean, logically?"

"Why do you expect logic?"

Wendy paused the footage. "Did you see...did you hear the overlap, how Mam's voice cut in over Susan's? We need to show it; let that fill the screen." Before anyone could interrupt her, she hit play again and turned up the sound.

"I'll bet Wendy is the same way. Both of you educated out of your natural human instincts." Mam's voice recorded well. She sounded clear and tranquil. Wendy kept using the zoom until Mam's lips filled the screen. "Logic is an unnatural luxury. 'My God's bigger than your God' isn't about logic—it's about faith; blind illogical unshakeable faith. Humans seem to be compelled to believe, not to think. That's why no one can ever win."

Wendy paused the image right there and let the words hang in the room.

"Wow," Susan said appreciatively into the silence. "It's different, watching it like this." It was something of a revelation for her. After her initial shock at their meeting and despite her often-bared chest, she reacted to Mam almost as if a voice were speaking in her own head. Looking at the monitor, she finally understood what it might be like for other people to hear Her. Susan felt something she'd never felt before: religious. "You're good, Mam."

"Thank you."

"How can we not air this?" Wendy pleaded. "This could change the world and we could be the ones who started it."

"I don't know what to say," Jack stammered. "This is... Even if it could be shown..."

"Why can't it?" Lily spoke up bravely. "We're supposed to be 'edgy,' aren't we? Our audience pushes the envelope. So we give them like the ultimate push." There were some rumbles of agreement.

Jack sighed. "But we're only a comedy show. This is serious stuff." It was demoralizing to have to say it. "It means something."

"Look, man, we mean something," Alec was affronted. "Okay, we're only borderline serious, but we educate our public. It's part of what we do, it's why we get awards." Except for Roger, who was too aggrieved to consider it, the general tenor around the table was positive. He made a fist and smashed it gently on the table to sell his point. "Wendy's got something here way too important to turn away from. I say we take it higher up. And if it doesn't go over," he shrugged pragmatically, "we pretend it was a gag for Halloween."

Jack was getting tired of being a joke, even a well-respected one. He didn't know where it would lead, but being part of this would certainly shake things up. He looked from face to face, weighing what he saw there, and tried not to be influenced by his own longing to say yes. Co-producer he might be, but it was little more than a courtesy title; this was far too big a call to make without solid support. If everyone else was behind him, he could maybe talk to the big guns. Not that he expected much success. "We'll have a hard time convincing the network," he said. "Apart from being off message, they'd be risking an FCC fine."

"We tell them that if they won't run it, I'll take it somewhere else," Wendy countered triumphantly. "HBO would leap at the chance."

"*Playboy* meets *The 700 Club*," mulled the programming director's nephew. "Hey, there you go. Yup, they'd snap that one up for sure. Let me get my uncle on the phone."

Nothing was leaked to the press. Even the onscreen cable channel guide showed a blank. One night, two weeks later, fans of *Duh News* clicked in as usual, completely unaware that they were on the brink of one of those "Where were you when...?" moments.

Jack, groomed as beautifully as a session at The Art of Shaving could guarantee and dressed in a very good suit, was seated behind the anchor desk, pretending to scribble on a yellow pad, just as he did at the top of every show. When the theme music finished playing, he looked up and addressed the camera with charming sincerity. Regular viewers wondered why he seemed a little nervous.

"Good evening," Jack began, "and welcome to a very special edition of *Duh News*. No, we're not having a sensitive discussion about bedwetting. And none of our reporters is suffering from a rare disease—at least not that I know of." He looked offstage in comic alarm. "Anybody? Whew. Good. Okay then. Tonight we're setting aside comedy to address a serious news story."

The live studio audience moved restlessly in their seats. They'd been hoping to see Jack interview one of the Clintons or Andy Dick. It had been a four month wait for tickets. Some of them were on vacation (or leave). They had no intention of wasting precious time. They hadn't come all the way to New York for more news.

"I know, I know," Jack continued, "a lot of you are thinking 'what comedy?' But you know, we here at *Duh News* have always prided ourselves on using comedy as a tool, to tell the truth in ways that more standard reporting can't."

In the control booth, the director pressed a button. When the show aired later that night, television viewers would be puzzled to see a banner scroll across the bottom edge of their screens:

"The following show contains adult content. Some images may not be appropriate for all viewers. Viewer discretion is advised."

"This time we've got a story that's beyond even our impressive talents, and we've decided to play it straight." The screen used for "in the field" reporting bits descended and Jack pointed to it. "Tonight, Wendy Smedstad reports on what I can only describe as a unique phenomenon. Pay close attention. And take my word for it, no special effects were involved in tonight's report. No e-mails or phone calls tomorrow, please. This is real. Wendy?"

The piece, as it was finally cut, began with footage of Wendy in her black suit standing in the Zen Garden. "Thank you, Jack," Wendy said on the screen, as if it were any *Duh News* report. "Our story begins here, at the Mitra Wellness Center in Sedona Arizona..."

Once the team had been given the go-ahead, they'd committed an entire half-hour episode to the story. Wendy had been given eleven minutes for her report, instead of the usual three. As well as extracts from the Sedona interviews, she'd included pieces of conversations she'd managed to hastily arrange with Dr. Snyder, Vanessa and Pat, and Rosa. There was also a full minute of a group meeting in Susan's living room, a particular thrill for Raju who was overjoyed to think he, too, would now be on TV before Macintosh Wing.

Everything led up to the one-on-two interview with Susan and Mam, and a final, unmistakable close-up of a woman's bare breast, the nipple slashed by a pair of moving lips.

The final image faded to black and the director in the booth switched to a close-up of Jack. He was pale and deeply serious, the way he'd been when he'd played Hamlet in Toronto. There hadn't been a peep out of the studio audience; they were sitting, frozen, at the edge of their seats.

"Thank you, Wendy. Now we're not fools here at *Duh News* and we know our viewers aren't either." He tried flashing an engaging smile at the camera and the studio audience. "Right?"

Someone in the studio audience called back, "Right!" more from nerves than anything else.

Jack was relieved. He'd had Lily stationed in the back, ready to jump in if no one spoke up. "And being no fools, despite what I said at the opening of this show, you're going to think that the report you've just seen must be the result of some pretty slick special effects."

This time a few more people called "Right!!"

"Well, this is live TV we're doing, right?" Jack ratcheted up the energy.

Now more than half the audience chimed in, including Alan and Lisa who'd been too scared to open their mouths before. They nudged each other, the only people in the audience who knew where this was leading.

"So hold on to your shorts and help me welcome our special guests for tonight, Susan Roth and Mam!" Jack stood up to meet Susan, who walked out in the Chinese brocade robe she'd thought she'd never wear. Wendy followed—Jack had agreed to have her sitting at the far end of the couch.

The studio audience went wild, stomping and whooping and whistling. Watching the monitor in the green room, Marta and Jimmy hugged each other with excitement. Raju was too busy typing into his laptop to be part of a hug, but he wore a wide smile. Now that there was no question about the success of the appearance, he had a broadcast e-mail to send.

Like most other live late-night shows, *Duh News* was performed and taped closer to dinnertime. If the taping had gone badly, the network would have pulled the episode at airtime and replaced it with a rerun. They'd had last year's Flag Day show standing by just in case. There was no need.

At 11:35 p.m., Susan curled up on her big chair and turned on the television. She shivered to think how many other people were doing the same thing. Fortunately, most of them were probably college students or unemployed artists. *Duh News* was popular, but it wasn't like being on *60 Minutes* or *The Today Show*. She didn't have to worry about being mobbed in the streets, and it was poor Wendy who'd have to sift through the e-mails. Still, so many people, and so very few were her friends. Susan poured herself a glass of brandy and pulled the afghan over her knees.

In Brooklyn, Julia Martinez pressed the record button and hoped the new DVD burner would work. It was so lucky the floor model had been on sale this week, since the old VCR had died just when she'd volunteered to tape the show for anyone of the Saint Agatha's ladies who didn't have cable, and for those like Rosa who weren't ready to let their husbands see what they were really doing in bible study.

In Darien, Connecticut, Lindsay Wilson curled up on the sofa in the family room, overjoyed at being allowed to stay up for *Duh News* for any reason, even something as weird sounding as this story about Aunt Susan. There was no way it was true. Clearly her parents hadn't been as straight during the seventies as they insisted and it was finally catching up with them. As Jack Rabb made his opening announcement, Diane put a protective arm around her.

In lower Manhattan, Yang Li-Huan was cruising the Pole Vault when *Duh News* came on. Waiting to see if Jack would be interviewing anyone attractive, he was flirting with the curly-haired guy down the bar, the one whose rolled up T-shirt revealed a bleeding heart tattoo on his left arm.

They'd just exchanged names when Li-Huan heard a familiar voice—a woman's voice, which made it more conspicuous in the male hubbub surrounding him. He tore his eyes from the gun show to look at the plasma screen. "Holy crap," he breathed. "I know her!"

"Jack Rabb is gay?!" Colm was astounded. "I really never saw that!"

"No," Li-Huan said testily, heedless of the effect on his potential conquest. "That woman. From work. I defragged her hard drive just the other week. Her!"

At the other end of town, Janet Ruben-Pritchard watched *Duh News* as she did every night: propped up in bed, glasses perched gently atop her greased nose, a stack of books and a large yellow pad beside her. It was one of the dozens of ways she kept her edge. She was already engaged enough to have started taking notes when she realized she knew that woman. Her eyes never leaving the screen, she reached for the phone and pressed speed dial.

"Let me speak to Tara," she said when her son answered. "Why didn't anyone think to call me? I want Susan Roth's home number, please, now." At midnight, with Jack Rabb still talking on her screen, she dialed it. Just as she'd calculated, hers was the first call to get through. Janet turned in immediately after; Susan, predictably, did not.

The buzz flew across the country.

When the tagline had been spoken and the show officially ended, Finity Barnstock of Saugus Massachusetts called her twin brother Will on the West Coast. She wanted to make sure he caught *Duh News* later. Will worked in CGI and she needed his professional opinion. Either this was an animation effect, or it was time for him to stop making fun of her religion.

In upstate New York, Macintosh Wing sat in the dark in the usually deserted TV room of Colony House, where he really was in residence and had written 27 pages all on his own. The person who'd given him his welcome tour had joked that the last time the set was known to have been turned on was for the 1969 Moon Landing. He knew this was a joke because it was a color set and had basic cable. He'd tried it the first week, until someone who'd seen him made a nasty crack at breakfast the next day. Colonists didn't watch TV, it seemed, though if paid well enough they would deign to write for it. He never would have dared to be there tonight, if he hadn't picked up his e-mail after dinner and found the message from Raju. He was glad no one had noticed him sneaking in. He hoped no one would see him sneaking out. He was thrilled that Susan Roth and her bizarre cry for attention would never be talked about by the Colonists, or by any other seriously important people. Damn it, though, who'd have thought Miss Mouse would have the balls to pull a stunt like that. And who did she get to do it? Maybe he could use them on his publicity tour, get his cock to talk. On the other hand, he remembered going with his dads to a movie like that when he was a kid, a comedy that pretty much blew. Still, there had to be a hook here he could use, somehow.

An hour later, in Chicago, a bunch of Alec Klocek's childhood friends switched off their sets in glazed disbelief. So did the Smedstads of St. Paul.

Yet an hour after that, in a trailer park outside Salt Lake, a lapsed Mormon spilled his illegal beer, ripped the illegal cable from his television and fell to his knees to pray until dawn.

Meanwhile, there was cheering in Sedona, where advance word had spread like karma and Patrick had set up a large screen in the Mitra Pantheon. After the show, someone turned up the music and people started to dance around the refreshment table. Steffi guessed correctly that there'd be no sleep at Susan's and called so that she and Mam could hear the cheers.

The impromptu address over the speakerphone at Mitra gave Susan the energy to face the call that came, as she'd known it would, at midnight Pacific Time. Helen Roth finally saw Mam with her own eyes and, after knocking back a traditional Valium, she called her daughter. Thank goodness no one in the condo ever stayed up so late that they could have seen that show, but at least Susan could have used a phony name. That said, it was comforting to know now that it wasn't early menopause, because Susan should know that her father's sister Gladys had had a very bad menopause and tried to run over Uncle Fred with a lawn mower. On the other hand, Helen was very worried and though she'd heard the doctors at Sloan Kettering were supposed to be good, maybe Susan should get a second opinion from someone at Johns Hopkins. On that jolly note, she was heard to yawn as widely as the Grand Canyon. The Valium had finally kicked in, to everyone's relief.

Unbeknownst to Susan, Will Barnstock, formerly of Saugus, Massachusetts, e-mailed an apology to his sister. It was a rare enough event that she would feel compelled to keep the e-mail in her inbox, to be noticed again in a few months time.

The leader of a group anticipating the arrival of a mothership at Mount Saint Helen's in February started to rearrange his calendar and a plastic surgeon in Beverley Hills called a car service to pick him up immediately and drive him to rehab.

So many people.

The next morning, the first thing Susan remembered was the phone call she'd gotten at midnight. Janet Ruben-Pritchard wanted her as a client. She had an agent, and such an agent that there was no doubt that she was going to be a published author. Of all the astounding things that had happened over the last five months, this was the only one that she'd ever imagined, and yet it had taken such unimaginable things to make it happen. Compared to being part of what could fairly be called a miracle, something that occurred on a regular basis all over the world should have been an anti-climax, but it had never before happened to her, and having a dream come true has a particular power over the dreamer.

Tired as she was, Susan began her day in a very happy mood. Mam was pleasantly surprised to hear her humming as she dressed. The last thing that Mam recalled from the night before was the call from Helen Roth, hardly a hum-worthy experience.

As usual, Susan went for coffee as soon as she reached the office. Unusually, she was mobbed. A bunch of the younger employees were laying in wait by the refrigerator. Li-Huan had soon learned that he hadn't been the only *Duh News* regular to have had a shock the night before. Only Melissa had been prepared, and she'd managed to keep her mouth shut. Of course, now that the word was officially out, she was having a ball bringing everyone up to speed. For once, people were genuinely interested in what she had to say.

When Susan came by with her mug, Melissa grabbed her, jumping up and down and kissing her on the cheek. "I bet you're going to be in *People*!" she exclaimed.

"Oh, no, I don't think so!" Susan was completely taken aback. Even after Janet's call, she hadn't given much thought to what else might happen as a result of *Duh News*.

"Can we see it...Her...?" Li-Huan had a date with Colm on Saturday and he'd sworn he'd have a scoop.

"Are you crazy?" Susan hissed. "Not here!"

"Steve's got a lunch meeting at Beale," Melissa volunteered. "We can use his office between..."

Evelyn, patrolled by, halted in front of them. "Is there a meeting I'm unaware of? Or has the Queen of England come to visit?" She couldn't miss the excitement, but she was totally oblivious to its cause. "Ladies, gentlemen...I'm sure you all have work to do." She stalked off with a sniff. Knowing she'd double back in a minute, everyone took their mugs, or at least a cover-story bottle of water, and prepared to disburse.

"She's probably never been up past ten in her life," Li-Huan whispered.

"Lucky for me," Susan added. The others had to agree.

That day, about a third of the staff found their way to Steve's office for at least a few minutes of their lunch breaks. So many people turned up in her apartment that night that Susan had to ask some of them to leave. The same thing happened at Rosa's the following week.

For the second time in less than a year, Susan realized she'd lost any semblance of control over her life. It wasn't that life was chaotic. On the contrary, in order to make it through the week, her schedule was so tight that she didn't have wiggle room enough to notice the leaves change. After work, she'd grab a salad or a wrap on the way to wherever she was bound.

No more Monday nights at Harrison Levy's. She'd had to give up workshop, which was a shame because the smarmy old goat could have been a help to her now that Janet had her working on a memoir of her life with Mam. He'd written an excellent, elegant autobiography a couple of years back. Susan wasn't much of a diarist, but Janet assured her that this would be a book people would want to read, and once she had readers, they could take a new look at her fiction. Each night, after a long hard day, Susan had to fight to keep herself awake long enough to write her mandatory pages. Sometimes Mam helped by putting her two cents in, but often she seemed to be exhausted as well and not a peep would be heard from that quarter.

In addition to the continuing three shifts at Rosa's on Wednesdays, Susan and Mam now spent two hours each Thursday at the Open Center (thanks to someone connected with the receptionist at *Duh News*) and kept open house at home two weeknights as well as Sunday afternoon. Most of the rest of the time, there seemed to be someone or other in the living room, helping with paperwork or just hanging out.

The mailman was getting annoyed. Just at the time that catalogues and other holiday mailings were weighing down his load, every day brought another wad of envelopes from people who had somehow found out Susan's address. Every evening, *Duh News* sent a messenger with all the letters and packages that had been received there.

Melissa had taken it upon herself to come over to Susan's and sort the mail into file folders that she kept in plastic crates. There were the prayers, the begging letters and the letters describing the inspiration the writer had found in Mam. The offers to speak went straight to Raju who, working tightly with Janet and Tara, had turned himself into a business manager. People wrote poems, and enclosed photos of themselves. Naturally there were also some rants and threats, but not too many; *Duh News* was excellent about screening mail before sending it on. The boxes and jiffy bags held all kinds of Goddess-related items—statuettes, drawings, medallions and more than one piece of art needlework. A tattoo artist, volunteering to work on Mam, sent sketches, and a woman in Manitoba sent a bra made of what she swore were eagle feathers.

Something had to be done, all of Mam's friends agreed. That's what had Susan feeling so out of control—she never got to make any decisions on her own anymore. It seemed that every time she sneezed, a dozen people had to give her advice on how to blow her nose.

"I think you need an office," Diane said, tripping over a stack of plastic crates one Saturday afternoon.

"We couldn't afford that," Susan said dubiously, peering into the basket. Many of the good letters included checks, money orders, even folded dollar bills. She still didn't understand how all of this had come from a single appearance on basic cable.

Tara looked up. "We have more than you think." Back when the collections from the meetings at Rosa's had begun mounting up to more than the cost of cake, Tara had insisted on opening a bank account. There were contributions from the meetings at the Open Center, and fees from a couple of lectures Raju had arranged through the New School. Susan had also deposited the check for the appearance on *Duh News*; she thought of that as Mam's money. The dollars had been mounting up, and Tara knew what to do with them.

"And we could earn even more," Lisa said. Raju and Tara nodded in agreement. Susan had always been an infant when it came to money. Thank goodness she had friends who knew better. "Especially if you'd quit your job and focus on this full time."

"That's impossible. I'm not extravagant, but there's no way I could make a living talking with Mam."

"You have no idea what a big business religion is." Tara's uncle had worked at the Crystal Cathedral.

"Religion?!" Susan was aghast.

"Oh, for goodness sakes, Sue," Lisa said, impatiently, "wake up and smell the coffee."

Whatever it was called, it was clear that being with Mam could no longer be a part-time job.

Raju and Janet wanted Susan to do more speaking engagements in the New Year. The deal Janet had negotiated with a major publisher for a "Mam and I" book, in print and audio, came with a significant advance, and she wanted to ratchet up the buzz. Wendy had suggested that the best way for Mam to reach people might be via webcast, which she'd said was relatively inexpensive and simple, as well as very effective.

"Those porn sites make a fortune," Melissa said enthusiastically. "They did a big story about it on the news."

"She's right," Alan agreed. Lisa gave him an interested look. "What? It's a sociological phenomenon. The more conservative the community, the more money there is in porn."

"Great," Susan said. "But Mam isn't porn. Anyway, the idea isn't to make a fortune. It's to communicate. And Mam likes to talk to people face-to-face...okay, face-to-face so to speak."

"No reason we can't have a studio audience for a webcast," Alan said. "People there for Mam to talk to in person, and meanwhile you reach a broader audience. Like when you did *Duh News*."

"Don't people write in?" Melissa asked. "Over e-mail?"

"Like IMs," Diane said proudly. "I learned that from my kids."

"Then someone reads the questions aloud to Mam," Lisa shrugged. "Works for me."

Raju shook his head and laughed. "No need. People call in over IP." Only Melissa seemed to understand him. "They use the internet to make a phone call."

"Now it's a radio phone-in show?" Susan said. "I don't think that's what Mam is looking for."

"So let's ask her," Alan suggested. What do you think, Mam?"

"Yeah, Mam. You've been awfully quiet," Susan realized. "Are you there today? Hello??"

"I've been thinking," Mam said mildly. "Do I understand correctly? This webcast means that people see and hear me? And the approach Raju suggests means I'd be able to hear their voices?"

"Yes," Raju said, "though I admit we can't arrange for you to see their faces."

"Or feel their presence, Mam," Susan added. "I'm still not sure which it is that matters."

"But you'd reach such a lot of people," Melissa said. "Maybe millions."

"We can try this," Mam said, decisively. "If I don't like it, we stop."

They needed an office large enough to do a webcast with at least a dozen people in a studio audience. That was what Mam wanted. Tara said it was silly to rent when they could invest by buying, and Steffi put them in contact with a former colleague who called one day with a lead on a five-story building in Long Island City. It was a bank repo, with a view of Manhattan. There were long-term tenants in the bottom two floors who couldn't afford to buy but very much wanted to stay, which meant there was assured income.

There was also some projected increase in cash flow. *Duh News* was putting out a DVD of the show, with additional footage from Wendy's interviews. The fee for a small documentary filmed specifically for the DVD was good news all by itself, but in addition, thanks to Raju who always thought of "just in case," Susan had never signed off on the subsidiary rights to the original material and now could name a substantial price. From another source, the owners of Corpo Céleste had told Jimmy to ask if there might be interest in an endorsement deal. Lisa took that as the beginning of a marketing plan that she could tie into the website. They could sell an exclusive style of Corpo Céleste bra, as well as bumper stickers and baseball caps. There'd obviously have to be a line of T-shirts, and maybe sweats. Lisa wondered if Jimmy would allow her to have copies made of the T-shirt he'd designed for Susan's everyday wear. It had a kind of sheer window for Mam to peek out. It would probably sell like hotcakes, especially on the Hooter's circuit. She also started to envision a silicone-filled talking Mam figure, but Susan nearly smacked her.

Once it began, everything happened so quickly. There was hardly time to absorb each move before the next one was made. What had been a group of friends sitting on someone's floor had become an official and serious company, with everyone finding their niche. The building was bought by a new corporation that Tara, against Susan's strenuous objections, had registered as a not-for-profit religious organization. She and Raju, finance and law, were the business team and were working 70 hour weeks to fit it in with their other jobs.

Lisa, awaiting her moment to spring into marketing gear, had put herself in charge of setting up the office itself. She organized a weekend painting party, a couple of dozen volunteers living on fumes and pizza. She polled other volunteers to find out what they could do and how many hours they would be willing to donate each week, and then she made trees and flowcharts and schedules until she'd run through two sets of printer cartridges. She found a second-hand office furniture warehouse right in the neighborhood, shopped for office supplies and nagged at the phone and cable companies until they moved the hookup appointments ahead to the date she wanted.

Mam Enterprises was a hive of activity from morning until night. Anyone who wasn't working in the building was squeezing every available hour out of their days to get things done.

While working on the new short for the *Duh News* DVD and otherwise trying to keep herself alive on the show, Wendy was working with Li-Huan to put together the equipment and personnel needed to do the projected webcasts.

In an effort worthy of a cable home decorating show, Marta, Rosa and Diane had partnered to design the room that would be used as the Gathering room. Lisa had been about to order folding chairs when Rosa stopped her. "Mam talks to people, not at them," Rosa said. "You can't make a room that looks like school or something." It was her the idea to fill it with soft furniture and floor cushions, to make a comfortable space where people would want to open up. She and Marta spent every spare minute measuring the thrift store sofas and armchairs they'd found, cutting the mill-ends Jimmy's contacts had provided for slipcovers, and distributing the work amongst the St. Agatha's ladies to be sewn. Diane had rallied her quilters' circle to run up hangings enough to cover the tall plaster-over-cinderblock walls. It made Rosa sad to think that Mam would no longer be leading meetings in her own living room, but it was a relief as well. Her husband was starting to complain about being thrown out of his home until midnight every Wednesday, and the Housing had been grumbling nearly as loudly. This new space, she reflected, was maybe three times the size. With the help of the others, it could be warm and welcoming as well.

There was little Susan could do—and nothing Mam could, of course—that others couldn't do just as well if not better. Everyone had decided there were more valuable ways for them to use the waking hours they had left while Susan saw out her notice at work. She and Mam kept up their usual schedule, paying only an occasional visit to the work-in-progress. Instead, in a distribution of efforts that was disconcerting to the casual observer, Alan talked with Mam in Susan's living room while Susan worked towards Janet's deadlines. He would sit with a notebook and fountain pen in the big chair, and they would discuss religion, social structure, human history, anything that seemed to come into play. He would take notes of things She wanted researched and served as a sounding board for Her own observations. At the exact same moments, Susan would be on the sofa with her new laptop, her ears covered by noise-reduction earphones playing Mozart, writing her own version of the story and transcribing her notes of what Mam wanted to have quoted in the book.

With February came the big day. At the end of that day, Susan stood in her cubicle. It was, like every other office cubicle that ever was, ugly and anonymous. A blue-grey tweed fabric stretched over the partitions, rubbed in spots, and studded with pushpins in others. A strip light, that had never worked properly, ran across the partition above the long end of the desk. The desktop was in an L configuration, laminated in some kind of polymer that had been treated to look like blonde wood. It bore the marks of Sharpies and a warehouse label that had never come off, and a permanent dull spot where Susan habitually kept her coffee, even though she'd always tried to put a napkin under her mug. Now she put a napkin around her nameplate and tucked it into the mug, which she wrapped in turn in some paper towels from the bathroom. She set it carefully into a corner of the cardboard shipping box that Jamal had brought her. Already in the box were her extra pair of shoes and an emergency umbrella, together with the Mardi Gras beads, Sophie's drawing and the photo of the Cobb. There was a bottle of clear nail polish, a tin of aspirin and a zip lock bag with a few tampons.

Suddenly she felt an overwhelming fondness for her stapler, though she'd always found it inadequate and hard to squeeze. She put it back and wondered who would be using it next—her stapler and her tape dispenser, and her blue in/out trays and the matching perforated plastic cylinder that held her pens and scissors. She dumped the contents of the cylinder onto the desk. Some of what was in that jar was hers, like the pen that Hannah had brought her from Israel, back in the days when Hannah was still speaking to her, and her souvenir letter opener from the software people. Susan had a bad habit of chewing on her pens. She figured the company wouldn't really want to keep any biros with bite marks, so she winnowed them out and slipped them into her carton, too. The windup Godzilla was hers. The mouse pad was hers, too: Munch's *The Scream*, a gift from the Christmas grab bag a few years back.

She'd already gone through her drawers and removed any personal papers, including a certificate from the year when they'd had Employees of the Month and she'd been August. She'd even pulled the top few pages off any partially used pads, so that they would be as pristine as possible for someone else. Her personal hanger had been removed from the coat closet, along with her air conditioning cardigan.

She closed the box with a sigh and sat, for one last time, in her chair. Her fingers rubbed the duct tape covering the tear on the right arm. She leaned backward, knowing the exact degree at which to stop so that she wouldn't fall backwards. She had hated this cubicle for fourteen years. Now she would never see it again. She blinked back a stupid tear. Change was scary. She hated the place and she didn't want to leave.

"You ready?" Li-Huan asked. He'd volunteered to help her with her box. He'd already helped her scrub her hard drive clear of personal writing, e-mails and scanned vacation photos.

"Yup," she said. She jumped up and smiled hard at him. On Sunday, he and the tech squad would be coming by the new offices to put the finishing touches on the network. People who were nodding acquaintances just a few months back were now supporters and friends.

"Let's go, Li," Mam whispered, "before she breaks down on us." Li-Huan grinned and hoisted the box. Susan followed him down the hall. Faces poked out of every cubicle to wave goodbye and wish her well. Anyone who didn't was kind enough to stay out of the way.

Melissa came running to the elevator to give her a hug. "I have a going away present," she said. "I couldn't wait 'til later to tell you—I just gave Evelyn my two weeks notice. Tara says you need a full-time assistant. I'm coming to work for you and Mam!"

Susan was nonplussed. "But Melissa," she blurted it out before she could stop herself. "There'll be hardly any men around!"

Melissa giggled. "Uh-huh. And even when there are, I'll be up against the only ta-tas that get more attention than mine."

"I didn't mean..."

"I know," Melissa grinned. "Hey, a girl uses whatever she's got, right? It's going to be wild to have people looking at me for my brains. Too exciting to miss!"

Li-Huan put her in a yellow cab to Long Island City. Unless it was to the airport, trips to Queens were considered a loss by the drivers of medallion taxis because they were unlikely to pick up a paying passenger on the ride back; it was like doing the run for half price. Still, the smarter ones were good natured about it. Generally, if they were kind to some poor slob who wanted to cross the river, they came out of it with a much better tip than the round-off that was the custom of the never-off-the-phone Don't-You-Know-Who-I-Am's who ran them up and down Madison and Broad. Susan's driver was not one of the smarter ones. He cursed her in a language she didn't know. The old Susan would have disappeared in silence or else started an argument that would have ended with her being dumped on the Manhattan side of the 59th Street Bridge.

"If everyone only did what was easy for them, no one would ever get help when they needed it," is what Susan said after eight months with Mam. "Because usually the things you need as help aren't easy for someone else to give." The cab driver scowled but kept his mouth shut. "I'm sorry you feel cheated," she continued. "I hope that someday when you need it, there'll be someone there to help you." She wasn't naïve enough to think her reasoning would have any positive effect on his outlook but she felt better for saying it. And she did give him a generous tip.

The elevator was slow and windowless, and nearly unnervingly rickety. Susan propped her box on the beaten-up handrail and distracted herself by trying to read the sgraffito scratched into the grey Formica; it mostly involved initials connected by hearts, and a few dates. As she stepped out, she was greeted with a booming "Surprise!" Li-Huan had phoned to say she was on her way, and everyone who'd been working had gathered on three to meet her.

The previous tenants had left behind a reception desk and a false wall that, since Susan last saw it, had been repainted a peachy color with an enormous gold M A M and decorated with an aspidistra courtesy of *Duh News*. Standing there, Susan found herself surrounded by happy, laughing faces. "Come and see!" someone shouted; she thought it might be Julia. Someone else grabbed the box out of her hands and made it disappear. She took off her shirt so that Mam could be part of things, and it too seemed to vanish on its own. Everyone cheered and she was propelled forward to have her tour. They lead her through the halls, proudly pointing out the features they'd worked so hard on. Everyone of her "Ooos" and "Aahs" was real.

Throughout the offices, what had once been dingy grey cinderblocks and worse was fresh with paint and bleach. The windows were sparkling clean and the fixtures had new bulbs. A big central work area had been cleared of partitions and fitted out with long tables, rows of phones and computers. The brand new office supplies and pristine while-you-were-out pads looked more alluring than they ever would again. Choice spots along the walls had clearly been claimed by the more devoted volunteers. Walking through, Susan spotted a few personal touches, including a copy of the flyer Rosa had shown her on the subway what felt like ages ago. The space was made festive with some helium balloons that Lisa had bought out of the budget. One room held nothing but file cabinets, all repainted the same creamy white. Another open-faced room had nothing but shelves. Two of Lisa's volunteer squad had been unpacking the first shipment of T-shirts when Susan arrived and they held them some up to show her.

On the same floor was a closed-off room with a polka-dotted Plexiglas door. "For the day care," Rosa explained with shy pride. It had been her idea. So many volunteers were women like herself who had children. If there were a room where they could bring their kids, they could take turns babysitting and everyone would be able to give that much more time to Mam. Right now the room had little more than carpet tiles and a ball pit that Diane's children had outgrown, but Susan had to applaud the brilliance of the concept.

Several of what had been private offices, with walls and doors, had been left intact. The one between what was being referred to as "the Pool" and the stock room was for Lisa. The walls, covered with corkboard, were already papered with charts, and the desk overflowed into the trash can. To Susan, it looked as if Lisa had been working there for months. Other offices were reserved for Tara and Raju; eventually, they'd be able to afford to pay people to work in them. Tara had insisted on there being a small conference room, though Susan couldn't imagine what use they would ever have for such a thing. Right now it was empty, but like the offices, it had a neat plaque affixed to its door.

Susan's own office was on the fourth floor, next to the Gathering Room. Her box was placed with some ceremony on her new desk, which also bore a bowl of forced paperwhites from Janet. With a few toys from Mitra and a small quilt from Diane, the office had the beginnings of a feeling of home. Outside it was an area she realized must be for Melissa. Looking closely at the desk, she smiled to notice that Hello Kitty was already in the house. The Gathering Room itself, thanks to heroic efforts on all parts, was very nearly finished. It was like a giant coffee bar, Susan thought, the nicer sort, but without all the little tables; exactly the cozy place the women had envisioned for long conversations and the opening of hearts. It beat the hell out of the Fulcrum, was the other thing that came to mind. "Wow!" was what she said. "This is gorgeous!" Rosa and Diane, and Marta, who'd just arrived with Jimmy from down the street, blushed and high-fived each other.

"And someday this will be a library," Alan said, pointing to a large unused space. "Think combination research and meditation. Nice shelving and a library table with some of those green-shaded lamps. Maybe some display cases for the artifacts people have been sending. Oh and I'd want something we could use for videos and the web. Li'll know what. But that can wait 'til we take off."

"I'm glad something can," Susan said feelingly. She couldn't imagine how they'd afforded to do so much already, not even with all the secondhand goods and leftovers and discounts and volunteer hands in the world. Her sense of this deepened when they took her upstairs. The top floor would house the webcast studio. She looked at the layers of soundproofing stretched to cover the walls and ceiling, at the professional-looking lighting instruments, and at the room that she guessed must be meant as a control booth, even though it was currently empty. She tried to imagine a camera and microphones and whatever equipment it was going to take to get it all on the web.

"This is costing a fortune!" she blurted out, unable to stop herself.

"Actually, the most expensive part is the glass we have to put in here," Lisa said, pointing to the front of the booth. "Triple glazing on an area that wide. Sheesh! But lucky us, it turns out Li's friend Colm has a cousin who's married to a girl whose father owns a glass place, so we're getting a discount. And of course, thanks to Tara, we're saving a fortune on sales tax. This not-for-profit deal really rocks!"

"I still don't see..." Susan rubbed her eyes.

"Anyway, this is money we have to spend. Because it's the website that's going to be bringing in the bread."

"Don't worry about it," Mam said gently. "Faith, Susan. Faith."

"Faith," Rosa whispered in agreement. "God provides."

Lisa looked at her watch. Six-thirty. "And right now, if we adjourn to the Gathering Room, Dragon Luck will be providing. Dinner, of course. Hopefully everyone else'll be here by now."

Almost everyone was. Most of their friends had left work a little early. Even Dr. Bob had driven down from Darien, bringing the kids. *Duh News* didn't air on Fridays, so Wendy brought Jack who'd been longing to come. They, like Alan and the Ruben-Pritchard party, had thought champagne appropriate, so everyone who was old enough had a paper cup full of something festively bubbling to toast the day.

"Shouldn't someone say Grace?" Tara asked, "Or something?"

The room went silent. Those few who had already bitten into an eggroll or rib stopped in mid-bite and tried to cover their mouths. They all turned to

Susan, who herself was holding a water chestnut in midair between her splintery chopsticks. Susan tried to go invisible, but it was no longer working.

"Susan," Lisa said, "it's a good question. Do we say Grace? Or whatever? What's the score?"

"What do I know?"

"A lot." Melissa was round-eyed in wonder. "You're like a prophet."

"Oh no. I'm like a custodian. Or, wait, I'm like someone who's in charge of a historic site or something. That's me. That's all."

"What does Mam say?" Alan asked, as usual.

"I don't want to impose any structure." Mam replied.

"That's a bit ingenuous from someone who's trying to start a new religion," Wendy observed.

"A new religion?" Marta was startled. Without realizing it, she crossed herself. Rosa and some of the others likewise murmured prayers.

"Susan, is that what we're doing?" Mam asked. "When Tara and Linda used the term, I thought they were discussing a legal status."

"Me, too," Susan said carefully, "at first. But once someone actually used the word, well...I couldn't stop thinking... Really, Mam. What else does a breast start talking for?" She was conscious that everyone in the room was hanging onto every word. She took a deep breath to steady her voice. "And frankly, Mam, it scares the shit out of me, seeing as I believe in absolutely nothing..."

"People start religions. I'm not people."

"But what are you?" Alan had to ask. "You told me once you were an oracle. A voice? That's all you are? Whose voice?"

"A voice. What you do with that is up to you."

For a full minute that seemed to stretch forever, no one said a word. It was Rosa, surprisingly, who finally spoke up. "It's a meal," she said stoutly. "Of course we say Grace."

7 – WHERE SHALL WE MEET?

The first significant change the new offices made in Susan's life was the last one she'd anticipated: she had time enough to write. It was a strange sensation to awaken after a full seven hours of sleep, shower, have an actual breakfast and then realize she didn't have to be anywhere until five or six o'clock. As most people worked days, the weeknight Gatherings were scheduled to start at seven. Not only could Susan choose to write all day, but it was actually in her job description to do so. The publishers had set a tight deadline for the manuscript of *Off My Chest*, as the book was being called (*Keeping A Breast* having been deemed too potentially controversial for Walmart, containing, as it did, the word "breast"). Janet had negotiated high. As there was every chance Mam would turn out to be a flash in the pan, they needed to get a product out there while the buzz was still fresh.

Susan was used to working at home. For years, any hour she could steal had been spent sitting at a slab of mica stretched across two tinny file cabinets next to her bed. What was relatively new was the simple experience of leaving her bedroom for another room that had a corner dedicated to her work, and to have no one else living in the house who might be playing their own music a bit too loudly or popping in for a friendly chat. The living room was still home, however, and being alone didn't mean being without distractions. Wearing her old sweats and feeling she had all the hours of the day stretching ahead of her, Susan would wander to the kitchen to rearrange her utensil drawer or have a sudden need to dig out her college yearbook to see if the Judith Miller she'd gone to school with resembled the reporter for *The New York Times*, or else she'd turn on the TV for white noise and find herself sucked into *The View* or the twelve millionth airing of *Peggy Sue Got Married*. Just as in the days before Mam, when she would often sit down on a weekend or Monday holiday with all intention of writing for six straight hours, chunks of time would dissolve without any words having been committed to the page. Now she was earning her living and the distractions could neither be afforded nor allowed. After four days of trying to write at home, she was tearing her hair out.

Mam (who said She'd been finding the movie breaks highly enlightening) asked why she didn't just use her new office. Susan was embarrassed that the idea hadn't even crossed her mind. Writing had always been a private indulgence, a hobby glorified by hope. It was something that she wanted to do, that had to be rigidly separated from the work she had to do. She'd never done any writing in a genuine office.

The next morning, Susan went to put on real clothes. She looked through her closet at the rack of safe shirts and dark, knee-length skirts that had been her corporate attire and wondered if she'd ever wear any of them again. Maybe she could give them to that clothing bank Lisa used to work with. It was too soon to tell. She might yet find herself having to temp for food. This was no time for negative thoughts. She had work to do. She pulled on a pair of jeans and one of Mam's T-shirts; she might be going to an office, but it was *their* office.

She didn't know if there'd be coffee in their office, so when she got off the F train she stopped at the bodega on the corner. It had been a long time since she'd been somewhere where the trajectory from subway to destination didn't pass a Starbucks or the like. She found herself smiling nostalgically at the traditional blue cardboard container with its legacy Greek diner motifs. The entire neighborhood gave her that feeling of having stepped back in time. Small buildings, mom-and-pop shops, sedans parked on the streets. When she was growing up, a lot more of New York City had looked this way. She crunched happily, if cautiously, through the lingering snow-plough backwash that didn't seem to melt at the same rate in the outer boroughs as it did in Manhattan.

In the elevator, she gave a friendly smile to the curious smoker who'd followed her in, and smiled again when he'd gotten off on the second floor. She imagined the old tenants had a great deal of curiosity about the new owners. She wondered if anyone in either the knitwear factory or Stewie's Stickers watched *Duh News*. It had become an habitual question for her. Soon she'd have to wonder if they'd seen her on the web.

Susan headed upstairs and set up her laptop on her new used desk. She played with the angles of her desk lamp. The heat in the building wasn't great, but she remembered her old emergency cardigan, which meant she had to unpack her box. An hour after arriving, she'd run out of distractions and had no choice but to work. During the day, all the activity was on the third floor. Apart from her fingers clicking on the keyboard, the only sounds were her own voice and Mam's. It was the same as having no sound at all. It had gotten so that talking with Mam was like thinking aloud—it didn't register on her ears. Once used to the ambient silence, she concentrated on her writing so much that a ringing phone made her jump out of her chair.

"Were you planning to eat before the Gathering?" Lisa wanted to know. It was well past 5 o'clock.

Susan scrolled through the day's work, amazed at how much she'd accomplished, most of it decent work. If she could keep up this pace, she'd make the deadline with days to spare. Writing in an office was definitely the way to go. She wondered, a bit sadly, if she'd ever get to write another book this way. Even if *Off My Chest* were as successful as Janet was betting, would it open the door to the kind of writing career she'd always dreamed of? Or would it turn out that there's only one story the public would accept from her pen?

"Have I sold my soul to the devil?" she asked aloud.

"I thought you didn't believe in souls," Mam remarked.

"Soul is the only thing I do believe in," Susan answered reflexively before realizing it was the truth.

The director Wendy hired, Ziggy Curtiz, was eager, enthusiastic and, like the industry, quite young. Ziggy had his generation's predilection for quick cuts and music. He had lots of ideas. As he was coming to Mam Enterprises directly from a technology convention where he was in charge of installations at seven different booths, he had only two meetings with Susan and Mam prior to the first webcast.

He'd barreled into the first meeting, bearing a video crammed with beautiful mountains and skies and assorted indigenous peoples. His idea, he explained, his fingers and face moving rapidly as he spoke, was to stream inspirational images while Mam was speaking.

"Don't you think that will distract from Mam?" Susan asked carefully.

"Hey, it's a visual medium. If you didn't want images, you'd be running a chat room, right? It's a multi-sensory reaction, you know." On his feet now, he contorted his body into what Susan had to assume was a pantomime of the effect of a five sense download. "You get your resonance from layering what you hear with what you see."

Susan would have thought Mam "visual" enough to satisfy anybody. She pulled her T-shirt over her head and pointed. "Tell me you need something more resonant than this," she said. "Mam, talk to the boy."

"I'm ready for my close up, Mr. DeMille," Mam said. She really had enjoyed watching those old movies, Susan realized with a grin.

Ziggy's jaw dropped. For nearly half a minute, he was entirely still.

"Exactly," Susan said.

"So okay, I get it," Ziggy said when he'd pulled himself together. He started to pace Susan's office. It seemed he was only able to think when he was in motion. "We need to keep the visual focus on... uh... on Her, doing the preaching thing."

"I don't preach," Mam informed him.

"Whatever," Ziggy said, barreling along. "But when She... you... look, there have to be breaks, right? To break it up. We can throw up some stuff then. And wait 'til you hear the band I found."

"Band?" Susan wasn't sure she'd heard him correctly.

"Yeah, this brilliant group I met last summer in Edinburgh," he clutched his ears and released them in delight. "All indigenous instruments from third world countries. Really brilliant."

"What do we need a band for?" Susan asked, afraid to find out.

"Oh!" he said, knowingly. "Studio's too small. That's cool. We pipe 'em in. And they'll be brilliant for the meditation DVDs."

"We don't do meditation."

He brushed it off. "Well, prayers or whatever you wanna call 'em."

"We don't do that either."

"I thought you were supposed to be the next Deepak Chopra or something." Ziggy was too thwarted. Wendy'd sold him on a hot gig and now it was sounding more like a public access vanity spot. He spun around, then slapped his hands on the desk. "Okay, look. You don't like video, She doesn't preach, there's no meditation, no prayers... What the hell do you do?"

"We talk," Mam said.

Ziggy was confounded. "Yeah, I can see that."

"Seriously," Susan said. "We talk. People talk to Mam, they ask questions. She talks back, answers questions. That's it. And," she stopped him from butting in, "people find it fascinating, just as it is. That's what they'll be logging on to watch."

"So you're a talk show." At least now he knew where he was.

"I guess." Susan hadn't really thought of it that way before. She hadn't really thought much at all except about how much easier it was going to be to not have to run to Brooklyn and everyplace else every week. "And people call in... Or 'e' in or whatever it is you call it."

"Yeah, Wendy said it was interactive. Eight p.m. we're streaming live is what she figures. Cuts across the time zones best for live interaction." He was practically dancing to his thoughts. "You keep that at the end, the questions; gives people time to log on. So what I'm thinking is, She, uh, Mam does like a monologue thing, and then talks to the audience. Wendy said you're having an audience in the studio, right? And then, like, time to interview guests and answer questions, maybe do a few bits."

"No bits. We kind of are a bit," Susan smiled ruefully and he had to smile back. "And no monologue, either. Just talking to people and answering questions."

Ziggy shook his head determinedly. "Gotta have structure. Otherwise, YAH!" He grimaced horribly while tearing his fingers through his very black hair, then sprawled backwards into a chair. "Which is boring as hell. Maybe not for the people who can hook into the live energy, but it sucks for the replay."

"What kind of replay? I thought the idea was a live webcast."

"Sure, yeah. But we record while you run. So later we post to an archive for people who missed out. They're putting together a monthly subscription thing, too, which I think is definitely the way to go."

"What kind of subscription?" Susan asked. "They who?"

"Wendy and what's his name Raju, and, uh, Tara. They said not to bother you with finance things."

"That was kind of them," Susan said dryly.

"You told them to leave you out of it," Mam reminded her. "You said you were 'not a money person,' your exact words."

"That doesn't mean...never mind. Fine, so we have structure," Susan threw up her hands. "And we make ourselves 'entertaining' enough for reruns. But we do it with conversation. No band, no monologue, no bits." She could tell he was unconvinced. "Look, Ziggy, I don't want to get off on the wrong foot but the customer's always right."

"Oh, that can't be," Mam was surprised. "No wonder you find business so confusing."

Susan explained the adage as she walked Ziggy to the studio. He listened to them talk, trying hard to understand why it affected him so powerfully. The "why" didn't matter, he realized. All he had to do was duplicate the experience. The studio pleased him. His color came back and he started to make notes. There would be two cameras, he decided, one always fixed tight on Mam, while the other would be hand-held so that it could pick up Susan and any guests that might be in the studio for the webcast. The area where Susan would sit needed to be large enough that Mam could have two or three guests. They probably wouldn't show the audience. The only reason they were having one was because Mam wanted it. He had a friend who could turn it around some kind of set by next week.

They had their second meeting in the studio, the Sunday before the first webcast. Ziggy's friend's people had been bustling around all day Thursday and most of Friday to install the set. It seemed a lot of time for what turned out to be a couple of projection screens and a pile of yellow cushions. Susan was pleased by the simplicity of the approach. Her relief didn't last long.

On Sunday, she anxiously watched Ziggy pace the room until he threw himself down on some of the cushions and smiled. "Cool!" he said, spinning his fingers in the direction of the screens. "I'm seeing lights. We can have some fun with this. Marvel, throw me a headset so we can get some sound checks!"

Popping on the wireless headset, Ziggy was back on his feet, raising Susan's anxiety level with every beat of his perpetual motion. Someone's hands affixed a tiny microphone by her hairline, and another one for Mam was set on her bra. Melissa had a special stool and microphone all her own, at a console with web access. It had been decided that she'd be introducing the callers and reading questions that came in via e-mail. Alan and Lisa and Raju, who had shown up to watch (Tara never worked on Sundays), were asked to play at being guests, and microphones were clipped to them as well. Ziggy liked a mix of voices for sound checks.

It was part of the process, Ziggy assured them, as his team aimed lights and adjusted sound levels. The goal was to get it right now, so that everything would be set up and comfortable for the webcast tomorrow. They were instructed to act normally, as if it were normal to be wired for sound and have lights glaring off your eyes at harsh angles, and react as Ziggy regaled them with his ideas for guests for future shows. He wanted to have people from a variety of religious backgrounds come and talk to Mam. The people at *Duh News* had passed him their overflow list, and he was in negotiation with several of them including, to his evident great delight, both a man who had the Passions of the Christ tattooed across his body and a highly visual snake handler in Tennessee.

"Do you think," Alan asked in a strained voice, holding Lisa down with one hand, "that these are the kinds of guests that will create the tone we're looking for?"

Susan was glad Alan had spoken up. Ziggy's idea of great guests made her uncomfortable, but she didn't think she was in a position to object. It had become difficult for her to consider anyone or anything as freakish.

Ziggy was dismissive. "I'm staying on message. I though you wanted discussion. I didn't know there were limits to what kind."

"I'm interested in knowing all kinds of people, Alan" Mam admonished gently. "And I depend on you to prepare me to meet them."

It was somewhat reassuring that Ziggy was also in touch with an Aboriginal Australian artist who was eager to discuss the Dreamtime and a former Roman Catholic priest and nun, now married to one another, who had five children and taught high school in upstate NY. And there was a firm commitment from a croupier at the Mohegan Sun and his grandfather, a shaman.

Susan had to admit Ziggy had been working hard. Alan anted up a former classmate who now worked at the Museum of Natural History, and Raju said he was feeling his way with someone at his temple. Lisa had a Persian friend at the gym that was a belly dancer.

"Not bad," Ziggy said. "We have to start small, but I'm thinking we'll get enough heat to bring in some big names. Shmueli Boteach, Al Sharpton..."

"Richard Gere?" Melissa asked breathlessly.

"Not that big. Maybe Uma Thurman's father." He informed them that it was highly unlikely they'd ever get a Scientologist. His fantasy, it turned out, was to book a Voudon or Santeria priestess.

"A llalocha?" Mam asked. "We know one. Lupe's friend," she reminded Susan. Susan nodded and Ziggy's face lit up like it was Christmas.

For the first week, Wendy and Ziggy had strategized that they keep things low key. Everyone needed to get used to working together, and to the overall feel of webcasting Mam. There would be no guests that first week. The first guest, sometime the following week, would be, appropriately, a Mitran. Patrick was being flown in from Arizona. Wendy had decided he was less likely to freeze on a live mike than Bear. Ziggy, who'd seen *Duh News* footage and thought Bear was too visual for words, had been disappointed.

The first webcast was terrifying for Susan. *Duh News*, with Jack's polished hosting, had been exciting, but reassuringly tried and true. It was a genuine long-running television show that she'd accidentally wandered into, and everything was so professional that she'd known even she would be fine. This was different. Somehow, she couldn't believe anything that had been created around herself could be anything more than a game. It seemed the worst kind of mean joke, to imagine Ziggy and his group of recent School of Visual Arts students would be aiming cameras and microphones at her and that people would be sitting at their computers, watching. She was certain they'd be making fools of themselves, and she'd be the only fool on camera.

Even Mam seemed a bit off her stride during the abbreviated Gathering immediately before. After the Gathering, there was no time to think. Susan ran up the fire stairs to the fifth floor. She was sure the old elevator would stall if she tried to use it, just because there was no time to lose. In the small dressing room, an assistant brushed some powder on her face against shine. He started to dab some kind if cream on Mam, then recoiled when She twitched.

"Give me that," Susan said irritably, pulling the sponge out of his hand. "Mam, keep still. This is the same as when we did *Duh News*, you need makeup or the lights will wash you out."

"It makes me feel stiff."

"Yeah, well, no pain no gain, okay?"

"What an odd concept."

They rushed into the studio, where the same hands as yesterday fixed the microphones on Susan in the spots they'd learned they worked best for her and for Mam. A few Gathering regulars had been invited upstairs to make up the first audience. They perched with pride and excitement at the edges of their seats, trying to beam reassurance.

Susan could hear Melissa clearing her throat at her console and saw her reach for a bottle of water. Someone, she realized, was more nervous than she was. At least she'd gotten used to speaking in public.

"Um," Melissa called into her mike, "Ziggy, what if no one...?"

"Won't happen," Wendy said from her perch in the booth. She'd prepared a worst-case scenario weeks ago and had Hazel on alert in Colorado, if need be, ready at a signal to type in a set of prepared backup questions.

"Quiet!" Ziggy called, splaying his hands like a climbing gecko. At least Susan knew enough by now to not let his gyrations add to her worry. He moved to the front of the booth where she could see him, his shock of inky hair like a negative halo above his glittering eyes. "Ready Susan in five, four, three, two," he pointed a finger at her and a red light flashed above the booth.

"Hello," Susan said, trying not to sound nervous. "Welcome to our first webcast. I'm Susan and this is Mam."

"If they're on line with us, Susan, I imagine they know who we are."

Melissa giggled, causing Susan to add, unrehearsed, "We're here tonight with a few of our friends and our assistant, Melissa Yazbek."

"Since our appearance on television in October," Mam continued, "so many of you have reached out to contact us. I've been looking forward to establishing a dialogue with you, to freely exchange thoughts and ideas."

"Only legitimate questions, please," Susan added. Her first thought, when the venture had been proposed, was that they'd be inundated with crank calls. "I'm going to ignore anyone who writes in asking if Mam is a prosthetic."

"Believe in me or don't, as you choose," Mam agreed.

"Or wants their fortune told, or..." Susan noticed Melissa waving to her frantically. "Wait, we've got our first question coming through. Wow! Go ahead, Melissa."

"Thanks Susan, Mam. This first caller is Elliot R., from Chicago, Illinois."

Susan found it hard to contain herself. Melissa had been listening to radio and noticed that female announcers never had high voices. In addition to self-consciously pushing down her usual shrill soprano, she seemed to be talking in slow motion. Susan was so tickled she was afraid she'd start to hiccup.

"Hello, Elliot," Mam took the lead.

"Mam? Is that really you? This is so surreal. I can't believe I'm the first caller. I saw you on *Duh News* and I thought you were amazing."

"Thank you, Elliot. Did you have a question for me? Or something you wanted to discuss."

"Both, I guess. I, uh, work for a small company. Privately owned kind of thing. Small. There's only eight of us work there. The owner, my boss, he's very religious. Well, he hasn't given out a paycheck in three weeks. Not to anyone."

"What?!" Susan was appalled.

"Yeah, so the first week we asked him what's happening. Was the company in trouble or whatever? Were we being laid off? 'Cause if that was it, we could file for unemployment. But he said no, the business was fine but there was a temporary cash flow problem. We should be patient and everything would be okay. Then last week I was talking with the bookkeep...," Elliot coughed, "I kind of found out he overdrew the payroll account to pay for his kids' parochial school tuition. That's why there was no money to pay us."

"That's illegal!" Susan said. "Even if it's privately owned. Isn't it?" She looked over at Melissa. She was so interested, she'd forgotten they were on the air. "Can we get Raju to check this out?"

"Susan, I'm sure Elliot has someone else to turn to if he wants to discuss legal issues. Let's hear why he called me."

"Thanks, Mam. It's not the first shady thing he's done and we've kinda been prepared. Still, I found it kinda hard to believe. I mean, you have to pay your employees, right? Or you don't have a business. I mean, the company's a service provider. So I asked him straight out. And he tells me, just as straight, that it's his religious obligation to pay for school. Didn't even look embarrassed. Which got me a little crazy. Most of us at the place, we pretty much live paycheck to paycheck. We don't get paid enough to save much. So three weeks of no pay is seriously messing us up in taking care of our own responsibilities. And here we have our boss telling us, like there's no room to argue, that giving his kids a private school education is more important than what we have to pay for, because it's religious. That's nuts! Isn't it? I mean, no matter what, how can it be religion to steal from people? Which is what he's doing. No matter what reason he thinks he has."

"Mam, isn't this what you're always saying, about people using God as an excuse to do what they want to do?" Susan was outraged, but striving to remain calm. If this was going to work, she needed to learn to act like a journalist.

"It sounds that way, yes. This man, Elliot's boss, implies that as long as he follows the letter of his laws, which I'm hearing seem to include the religious education of children, that he's morally free to use any means necessary to do so. I can't pretend to know all that I should about the various religions on earth..."

"And Elliot hasn't told us what religion his boss follows," Susan noted. "Or should I say purports to follow."

"I don't think 'which' matters for our purposes, Susan. Because whatever religion he claims, he definitely doesn't follow it."

There were murmurs from Her fans in the studio, most of whom were committed to their faiths. "You don't know what's in his head," Julia objected.

Mam continued, as much to her as to Elliot R. "One thing I've found in common with every religion I've explored so far is that they're all designed to provide two basic things for their followers: A system of ceremonies formulated to honor, and thereby bring them closer to, their God; and moral guidance to protect and nurture the community."

"What about faith, Mam? You're always talking to me about faith."

"Faith isn't religion, Susan. Faith is an emotion; religion is a structure of behavior. You can have one without the other. And this has nothing to do with Elliot's question."

"It doesn't?" Elliot sounded a little lost. "So Mam, tell me, what do you think? About my boss?"

"I think he's bullshitting you, Elliot," Mam said, kindly but firmly. "If he truly believes he can honor his God, whatever God he thinks he serves, by treating his fellow human beings like garbage, he's what I consider to be evil. There is evil, you know. It's a very real thing. On the other hand, if your boss doesn't honestly believe his own posturing but is hiding behind his religion to do what he wants, he's merely a nasty piece of work who needs to learn he's not the only person on the planet."

"So like what do I do? Am I supposed to turn the other cheek or something? Or, I don't know, smite him?"

"Someone's been reading a bible," Mam said. "Oh, Elliot, that's something I can't tell you. I'm not here to set down rules for anybody. I'm just here to help you think. You need to think about what you want to do. You have to think about the rules that feel right to you and use them, not his actions, as your guide. Whatever you do, be able to look yourself in the mirror and accept responsibility for having done it."

"You mean like on the day of judgment?"

"Every day is a day of judgment, Elliot. Whether people realize it or not. Because every single action has its repercussions."

"Yeah," Elliot sighed deeply. "You don't make things easy, Mam."

"No pain no gain, Elliot. Thank you for calling."

Susan tried hard not to laugh. "Thanks Elliot. Melissa, who do we have next?"

"Um, we have an e-mail here from Donna C. in Atlanta, Georgia."

Downstairs, all their closest friends were crowded around the computers in the Pool, watching the webcast. As Melissa began to read the e-mail, Lisa's cell phone began to play "Tapestry." She picked it up. "Hi, Steff," she said.

"How'd you know it was me?"

"Diane's sitting next to me and Sue goes without say." She hit the speaker button and set the phone down on the desk.

"I'm watching out on the deck. Who'd a thunk it?" Steffi couldn't resist asking the traditional college question.

"Not me," Lisa had to say. Whoever, anywhere, would have thought of this one? "Hey, it just occurred to me—who's sending this one in to *The Vassar Quarterly*?" She started to laugh, helplessly, in a very un-Lisa-like fashion. Diane and Steffi caught the laugh. It was the kind of uncontrollable laughter they used to share at two in the morning, the laughter of angst.

"Susan Roth and her talking breast, Mam, launched their new website," Diane chirped, before entirely breaking up.

"We always knew she had it in her!" Steffi sputtered.

The others in the room started to break up in the same hysterical laughter. It didn't take much to set them off, they needed the release that badly. What was happening was far too serious not to laugh.

Susan and Mam settled into a comfortable working groove. They spent hours each day writing. During the lunch break, which Lisa insisted they take, Susan would go down to three, and Mam would greet the volunteers. Their budget stretched to a very few salaried positions, so Mam Enterprises continued to depend on volunteer workers. After the first webcast, the mail exploded. People were ordering T-shirts and other merchandise faster than Lisa could push them through the door. Fortunately, new people kept showing up to help. For these new volunteers, meeting Mam became a rite of passage, and having Her remember their names, a badge of belonging.

Mam especially enjoyed meeting the children. Rosa's daycare room had been prophetic. Many of those who offered their time were young mothers. While one or two supervised the children, the others were free to spend an hour or two sorting mail, answering letters, processing orders, opening boxes, or anything else Lisa had that needed doing. After lunch, Susan would pop into the daycare room so that Mam could say hello.

Susan had been hesitant when Mam had first proposed it. She didn't want to scare the children, but Mam had been so curious. If She was going to know what it was to be human, She needed to reach across age as well as gender and culture. Susan broached the subject with Diane, whose Sophie had been the first child Mam had ever met.

Diane laughed. "You've got to be kidding! See, Sue, this is how anyone can tell you don't have kids. Mam wouldn't scare a child. She's no more frightening than a talking sponge or a fuzzy purple dinosaur."

They had to explain to Mam what Diane was talking about. Mam was intrigued. "Children don't fear the impossible?"

"Children don't even know what impossible is," Diane said wryly, "and teenagers think it's negotiable. Only adults fear the impossible."

"Adults fear so many things," Mam had observed, "particularly the unknown. Do children fear the unknown?"

"Yes. No... Not so much when a parent is with them, or someone else they love and trust." Diane thought for bit. "I think children fear being alone and unprotected. They can handle quite a lot if they're with someone who makes them feel safe."

"Remember when all it took to feel safe was a parent or a stuffed animal?" Susan recalled wistfully.

"What makes adults feel safe?" Mam wanted to know.

"Nothing," Susan said firmly.

"God," Diane said, just as firmly.

Mam sighed. "That was helpful."

The children, as Diane had anticipated, accepted Mam without so much as a blink. She would ask them about the games they were playing, and they would ask Her the same questions they asked any other adult in their world: What was Her favorite color? Where does the sun go at night? Which are better, boys or girls? Sometimes, Mam would tell them stories.

Susan found this part fascinating. Was this a recently acquired skill? Or had Mam always been able to tell stories? If it was new, then she had to assume Mam was succeeding in Her mission to learn more about how people ticked. And the one thing Susan felt was certain was that Mam always told the truth. If Mam had always been able to tell stories, should that cast a different light on anything She did—or didn't—say?

After the break, more refreshed than she would admit to Lisa, Susan would go back to her office and continue her writing until about five thirty. Each Monday through Thursday evening, she'd have a light bite (the bodega had turned out to make excellent soup) before putting on their makeup, getting into one of Jimmy's ensembles and walking across the hall to the Gathering room to meet with 150 of Mam's closest friends.

The Gathering room had seemed too large to Susan when she'd first seen it. She'd expected that many of the St. Agatha's ladies wouldn't want to make the trip to Queens. She'd underestimated how many of those who had thronged to Rosa's living room had no affiliation at all to the parish, or even to Brooklyn. She'd also underestimated how many people had been closed out of Rosa's small apartment and the Open Center. Even before the webcasts had begun, the Gatherings had been pretty full. After several weeks, people were being turned away. There was talk of adding a second nightly Gathering after each webcast, a weekend Gathering, and possibly, once Susan finished her first draft, a weekly morning coffee Gathering, but that was only talk.

The doors to the Gathering room opened at 6:30 so that those who'd arrived early could find a seat. As at Rosa's, there were no tickets and no entry fee. A pair of hollow Lucite pedestals stood on either side of the door, and people would stuff in coins and folded bills as they felt moved to do, usually on their way out. On the way in, the prime consideration was to find a good seat, different people being equally convinced of the superiority of different seats. Most people arrived early and jostled their way to the spots they liked best. Sinking into Rosa and Marta's cozy nest, they whispered, to friends and to strangers equally, of Mam and themselves and the issues on the news that day. Those who wanted to be quiet would focus on Diane's quilts or close their eyes.

At seven promptly, Susan entered through a private door and mounted the platform that had been devised to make it easier for Mam to be seen. A hush fell over the room, and all the faces turned like flowers. Susan smiled and said, "Welcome." Then Mam greeted the crowd and the Gathering officially began.

At seven fifty-five, Mam would say goodnight. Susan would slip out her door and go up the fire stairs. If there were no other audience members invited, a dozen of those who'd been at the Gathering would be asked, by the volunteer at the door, to attend. The webcast lasted an hour, after which Susan would walk to what was possibly the nicest subway station in New York, if one of the most deserted at night, and catch the train back home. She'd shower off the makeup and inhale her long-awaited and usually unhealthy supper in front of the television, where she and Mam would unwind to the most entertaining and distracting program she could find on a scan of 250 channels. Then it was time for a good night's sleep before starting it all over again the next morning.

Susan had always thought that she needed hours of downtime every day; she'd spent half her life recovering from the other half. It turned out she didn't need much spare time at all when she didn't feel her time was being wasted. Working with Mam, she had a longer work day than she'd ever had before, but it was also the first time that the work she was doing was work she wanted to do. It wasn't only the writing that she was enjoying. Something interesting was always being said, by Mam or to Her. She felt alert and stimulated nearly all the time. That might not have been as blatantly extraordinary as Mam herself, but Susan would have considered it equally impossible. After years of moving numbly through the days, she felt alive. She was enjoying being with Mam. Maybe that was the most unexpected thing of all.

There might not have been a "Mam Fever" sweeping the nation, but there definitely was some rising heat.

The webcasts grew more polished as the team knit together. Susan was learning camera savvy, as Melissa learned to screen questions so that the most provocative conversations would reach airtime. Subscriptions were enormously popular. There was evidence that people were re-watching broadcasts they'd already seen and Ziggy was designing a website poll to vote for favorites for the first projected "Best of Mam" DVD. Across the web, www.mamcam.com was showing up on hit lists and as a homepage hot link.

More Gatherings were indeed added to the schedule. After several nights of having to turn people away, they decided to make "after-cam" Gatherings ticketed events. There was no charge for tickets, which were offered on a first come-first served basis on the website. As early as the end of March, Susan was surprised to meet people who had traveled to New York specifically to be at "Mam-after-cam." She shouldn't have been. Tickets were being distributed into the summer. People didn't seem to mind that they might have to wait for their turn to come.

Susan's perpetual astonishment at the reach of the web put her, for the second time in her life, strongly on the wrong side of a generation gap. She might use all the technology she could afford to have available to her, but she didn't take it as given. When Mam received her first e-mails from Tokyo, Reykjavik and Doha, Qatar, Susan had to pause to digest the information. To Ziggy and Li-Huan, for example, mail from halfway across the world was par for the course. They expected it, nudged it aside and focused on bigger issues, such as whether their current ISP could handle the rising volume of traffic.

The volume of merchandise sales was likewise on the rise. After each webcast, the shopping area of the website experienced a major spike. The most popular item at first was, hands down, Jimmy's "MAM I AM" T-shirt with a kind of triangular spiral shape sitting modestly over the Mam breast. Jimmy'd doodled the logo on the back of a Playbill during a play that should have had an intermission. When pressed to explain the symbolism, he said that the spiral was an ancient symbol of the goddess while the triangular shaping was a nod to the equally ancient female trinity, the maiden, the mother and the crone. More practically, he was secretly pleased to have found an ideal substitute for the peek-a-boo window for which Lisa, not so secretly, still cherished intent. In black, white, carnation and beet, the shirts flew off the shelves. The logo was also featured on caps, mugs and shot glasses, and would appear, embroidered discreetly, on the upcoming Corpo Céleste bra (and matching thong).

At the same time, Lisa started a new line of what she was calling "Mamorisms" in response to what she felt was popular demand. Take Responsibility, There Are Always Repercussions and the enormously popular You're Not The Only Person on the Planet were printed on T and sweat shirts, sport cups, mouse pads and cleverly bound Japanese notebooks. Tara had been dubious about authorizing the expense, but merchandising was Lisa's baby and Tara ultimately gave way. The day after the mockups were first added to the shop, Tara downloaded the first pre-sale figures and had to read them twice. That day, she called Raju. They'd occasionally blue-skied the idea of quitting their current jobs and starting a management company together. It might not be such a fantasy after all. Their first private client was becoming an increasingly substantial one.

The last week of March, Susan finished her send-off draft of *Off My Chest*. Janet invited her to celebrate with dinner on Friday at the newest Jean-Georges Vongerichten restaurant. Steffi, who she called for advice on what to wear for such a trendy outing, was extremely impressed by Janet's idea of celebration and even more by her clout. "Marooned" in Arizona (as Lisa put it), Steffi somehow continued to know more about the city than most people who lived there. Many people, she informed Susan, were still finding it impossible to get into the hot restaurant Jean-Georges had opened the year before.

"Black pants," Steffi decreed. "And put your feet in something that doesn't make you look like a librarian." This was Steffi's traditional admonition. In fact, Susan owned a pair of rather extreme Italian shoes that Steffi had bullied her into at the Barney's Warehouse sale nearly eight years before. She'd worn them weeks later, on the last blind date she'd ever let anyone set her up on, then never again; they'd been more uncomfortable than the date. "Big earrings, and a funky shirt. Expensive, but funky. Go down to Century 21 and look through the racks. Get a pen, I'll tell you what labels to look for." But before Susan could gather up the energy to take on the bargain hunter's equivalent of a big game safari, Janet preempted it by asking that she wear one of Jimmy's bras.

"To a restaurant?!" Susan was appalled.

By now she was all too well accustomed to walking around with Mam on display, but a restaurant was hardly the same as a room full of friends or invited guests. Susan was old enough to remember when people wouldn't wear tank tops and shorts on the streets of New York, and if she was that old, Janet was at least the same. Even in today's overly forgiving climate, baring a breast in public would be pushing the envelope. What was Janet thinking, asking her to walk into a restaurant with Mam exposed?

"Mam is a celebrity, not a gland," Janet said, coolly. "We need to establish that, and the sooner the better. You wear one of those bras, with something pretty and transparent on top. Not those long schmates you wear for your talks. They're lovely, they really are, but they're a bit more, let's say "costume" than we want for a social engagement. I'm thinking haute, with an edge. Something that reveals, but only just. Maybe a silk gauze." Susan groaned. "Oh, call your people, they seem to know what to do. And full hair and makeup. Makeup for Mam, too. Be there at five after eight. I'll get there at five before. I want you to make an entrance."

Susan called Jimmy. No surprise, he was in complete agreement with Janet, castigating himself for not having thought of it sooner himself. "I should have started on a red carpet wardrobe months ago!"

"Are you nuts?! What, you think Mam's going to be invited to the Golden Globes or something?!" Jimmy snickered at her. "Okay, bad example," Susan admitted, "but not really. I mean, that would be a stunt and we don't do stunts. When Mam is, um, out there, it's to work. And yes, you were right on the money about what we need for that. But the last thing She needs is party clothes."

"Susan, even Eleanor Roosevelt needed party clothes."

"One outfit for one lousy dinner," Susan said, wishing there was a way she could back out. "No 'red carpet.'"

"It's a metaphor. For those situations when your average star sends her stylist showroom hopping. Leave it to me. And don't fool yourself that this is the last time you'll be taking Mam out for a night on the town. Janet is testing the waters. Mam's a public figure now. She'll have to have a presence."

"So was Mother Teresa," Susan said glumly. "She wore a full habit."

"You could still see her face," Mam said. "Are you finished whining now?"

Jimmy whipped up a discreetly embroidered black satin bra to be worn beneath a sheer black top that wrapped and tied and gaped where Mam would be peeping through. It looked, Susan had to admit, like something in a fashion magazine, and it went well with the rest of her Steffi-dictated uniform. With her hair and makeup done, she felt rather glamorous. She felt, at the very least, like someone who wouldn't look like a gatecrasher at the restaurant. She took a cab downtown, to complete the package—and because she couldn't walk more than a block over pavement in these shoes.

It was one of those restaurants where the staff had to look chic enough to be patrons. It was smaller than she'd expected, and had a simple elegance. No doubt the effect was meant to be cozy, but Susan was far too intimidated to relax. She was so intimidated that, for a precious minute, her only concern was being insignificant for the room. Then she surrendered her undistinguished wool coat and felt a slight draft on her chest. Immediately, she felt conspicuous. Mam whispered, "I think we look fabulous." Somehow, that didn't help.

The hostess, who was wearing a severe black dress even Susan could tell was worth more than any clothing in her own wardrobe, immediately spotted a bared breast as she approached and just as immediately looked away. Susan gave Janet's name, which seemed to score a point. Tossing back her curtain of glossy hair, the girl looked at Susan's face for the first time. She did a double take, then looked down at Mam and flashed a genuine, super-whitened smile.

"Mam!" she whispered, "This is such an honor. I watch you all the time."

"Thank you," Mam whispered back.

The girl was trembling as she turned to lead them to the table, where Janet was already seated as planned. In her wake, Susan carefully picked her way between the tables, terrified of tripping on the unfamiliar spike heels. She imagined Mary Queen of Scots might have had the same concern. Anyone who color-keyed the robes she wore for her own execution was bound to have worried about accidents that might spoil the final effect. While most diners aggressively took no notice of anyone not at their table, a few caught a flash of bared skin in black gauze and blinked. Susan pretended not to wonder or care what they might be thinking. As they reached her, Janet looked up and smiled warmly. "Susan, Mam," she said in a ringing voice, raising herself halfway to kiss Susan's cheek, "how lovely to see you." A dozen heads turned their way, several taking the invitation to frankly stare. Slipping into her chair, Susan wished she could keep sliding under the table.

Instead, she pecked Janet back and said "Janet, so good to see you too."

"I took the liberty of ordering you the house cocktail," Janet said, gesturing to the chunk of crystal at Susan's place. "I thought you might find it...refreshing." She winked. "I hope that's alright, Mam." It wasn't that her voice was loud, but it was clear and seemed to carry.

"It has no effect on me," Mam said quietly.

"Here's to the book, then," Janet said. "I'm very pleased with it."

Susan lifted her glass and took a bracing sip of something citrusy. She hoped there was a hidden kick. "Thank you."

"I am, very. I had every confidence in your abilities, you know that. But not everyone can meet a deadline. And this was such a demanding one."

"Thank you." A waiter who had obviously spoken with the hostess placed their menus before them. As he asked if they wanted him to recite the specials, his eyes slewed down for the tiniest second.

Janet waved him away, the corners of her mouth twitching upward. She leaned in towards Susan and softened her voice. "Relax," she said, ignoring the dirty look that was sent her way. "This is what's going to happen."

"Only if Mam's out in the open like this," Susan hissed through a beauty pageant smile. "I usually keep Her covered when I go out."

"You have to get used to it. People are starting to know who you are. We want them to. That's a very good thing for us, for the book."

"Can't they know who I am without...?"

"Susan, dear, the celebrity isn't you—it's Mam." She touched her manicure lightly on the table to emphasize her point. "People will want to see Mam. And we need to take control of that situation now, and frame the debate before anyone else does."

"I look forward to debating," Mam said.

"Not a debate with you, a debate about you. You control your website and your, ah, your Gatherings, yes? Yes. And almost by a fluke, you've managed face time on late night cable. The likelihood of that being allowed to happen..." Janet shook her head and smiled in tender reminiscence. "Ladies, we have a book to sell. At some point, there's going to be some attention from the mainstream. There had better be. And before that happens, we need to make it very clear that there is a difference between this" she flicked a discreet finger at Mam, "and Janet Jackson flashing a tit at the Super Bowl. Now, right from the start, we need to establish that Mam is a "who," not a "what," an individual, not a body part. Because Oprah and Barbara, no matter how powerful they might be, are subject to network censorship..."

"Oprah and Barbara?" Susan swallowed.

"Katie, Diane, Ellen, Pearl. Someone's going to jump on the story, dear, mark my words. It's only a question of time. And the fight will be to be allowed to air the story of the century intact. To interview Mam and prove it, by showing Her on network television. When that time comes, we will be ready." She leaned back with a satisfied smile. Challenges were harder and harder for Janet to find. This one was a whopper and she was planning to relish every minute.

"Janet seems to have thought this out very thoroughly, don't you think?"

"Yes, she has." Susan felt almost as shell-shocked as she had when the bandages were first removed. "I hadn't thought ahead much. I've been taking each day as it comes. This sounds so...too big."

"And I remember telling you that you weren't interesting!" Janet laughed like someone at a cocktail party. "Have you heard that story, Mam?"

"No, I haven't."

"We'll have to tell you some time, now that we can laugh about it. Oh, this is an exciting day, Susan! Imagine that you're Cinderella and this is your first step on the way to the ball."

"I...I'm sorry, Janet. I don't seem to be able to get into the spirit of things."

"I didn't expect the first time would be easy. But it had to happen sometime, and better in a place like this where half the people in the room are in the same boat." A man two tables away caught Janet's eye and nodded in a friendly manner. She flashed him a wave and a smile. "Graydon Carter," she whispered through her smile, "*Vanity Fair*. And did you notice who's sitting at the far table to my left?"

Susan couldn't help herself. She craned her neck to see past Janet's shoulder and spotted a celebrity couple so well known they didn't need to use their last names. He was facing Susan and as their eyes met, he gave her a startled and somewhat awed smile. She felt herself blush and turned away.

"Aha, you see," Janet was delighted. "You and Mam have more than one fan in this room. And you've only just begun."

Susan didn't exactly enjoy the evening. Even the superb crab dumplings didn't delight her the way they ordinarily would have. Maybe it was having to chew on so many other things at the same time. Each time she thought she'd settled into her new life with Mam, something would happen to push the boundaries and she'd have to start her adjustment all over again.

The first Tuesday in April, the witches came.

It was late afternoon of an ordinary day at Mam Enterprises. When the elevator dinged, Jonelle, the receptionist and the fourth full-time paid employee, reached for the shipping log. It was time for the daily pickup, and there were ten pages of packages to be scanned and counted. She looked up with a rueful sigh. "It's mostly T-shirts," she began.

Instead of Nestor, she saw three women standing by her desk. That all three were dressed in long drifty clothes, richly colored and textured, and hung with beads and silver and crystals, seemed pretty standard to Jonelle. She was seeing a lot of this sort of fashion statement since she started this job.

"Can I help you?" she asked brightly.

The oldest, a tiny hatchet-faced woman with a froth of white curls, twinkled up at her. "Oh, yes. We're here to see Mam."

"Great! Do you have an appointment?"

The youngest of the women rummaged nervously through her mirror-embroidered sack. "We have tickets."

Jonelle looked at the slips of paper, then checked the numbers against the log. When they began distributing tickets, Raju had insisted on the log as a guard against forgery. These were genuine, listed as having been issued to a Finity Barnstock of Saugus, Massachusetts. "Finity Barnstock?" she asked. The young woman nodded. "Great, you're clear. Only these are for Mam-after-cam, you know, which isn't until 9 o'clock. We can't let you into the Gathering room until after 8."

"We're aware of that," said the tall woman, whose indigo draperies managed a kind of elegance. "We'd like to see Mam before then. We have business to discuss."

"Um, can you wait a sec? I'll be right with you." Jonelle did what she'd been trained to do and buzzed what had become the conference room. "Lisa, hi, sorry to interrupt, but could you pop out here for a minute?"

"I knew we should have made an appointment." The flustered young woman had only been invited because it was her tickets they were using.

"She'll see us," said the oldest, serenely.

Jonelle didn't have to smile aimlessly for too long before Lisa strode towards reception, her right hand already extended. "Lisa Denton. Nice to meet you. How can I help you?"

"How important are you?" asked the oldest woman. The youngest winced.

"Hello, Ms. Denton. Stella Ravenswing." The tall woman took Lisa's hand firmly. "These are my Sisters, Hester Carl and Finity Barnstock. We represent the Assembly of New England Wicca."

"Ah," Lisa nodded thoughtfully.

"This year our region is hosting the annual Beltane Confluence for the Wiccans of Greater North America. It's a significant assembly from all across the US and Canada."

"Yes, the Beltane Conference."

"Confluence," Stella corrected. "On April 30, in the Berkshires. We know it's short notice, but we've only recently become aware of Mam. And it seemed so…Ordinarily we would have gone through proper channels but as one of our members," she nodded slightly towards Finity, who turned pink and poked her fingers through her hair, "had already procured tickets for one of Mam's Gatherings, we thought it expedient to put the question to her in person."

"We didn't want to interrupt the Gathering," said Finity, quickly.

"We didn't," Stella agreed. "Which is why we're here now. It's rather short notice, we know. But if her schedule allows…Ms. Denton, it would be such an inspiration to everyone if Mam would consent to open the ceremonies."

"Love the Berkshires. My husband and I do Tanglewood at least once a summer. And there's this great jeweler in Lenox. Is that where you got that fabulous ring?" Lisa pointed to the large black enamel bird on Stella's left hand.

"Are you trying to think of how to get rid of us?" the oldest woman asked with an engaging grin. Jonelle, who'd been eavesdropping, smothered a giggle. "We're not crazy, you know. Any more than your people must be."

"You did catch me a little off guard," Lisa decided to meet honesty with honesty. "We haven't had any requests for personal appearances. Not yet, though we did think we might eventually... Look, do you have a few minutes?" They all nodded. "Wait here," she said. "I'll be back in a minute."

Lisa ran into the conference room, where she'd left Tara and Raju going over some figures on a whiteboard while Susan and Melissa pretended to follow. "You have to hear this one!" she said. "We've got three witches out by the elevator." It was an attention getter. Everyone stopped what they were doing and turned their full attention to Lisa, who tried to explain. "They want to know if Mam would be willing to speak at some kind of conference in the Berkshires at the end of the month. Anyway, I didn't think the decision was mine to make."

Mam was immediately interested, but the others felt they needed to hear more details. Since *Duh News*, Mam and Susan never made an appearance that they didn't themselves control. What exactly was the nature of the organization, and of the conference in question?

"We should get Janet on speaker," Raju said. "As Susan's agent. And maybe Wendy? Would we call this a media thing?" Tara shrugged.

"Alan, too or I'll be sleeping in the library tonight. Three witches. Do they always travel in threes?" Lisa went to bring the Wiccans to the conference room while Susan ran up the fire stairs to the dressing room and swapped her T-shirt for a bra and robe.

Susan returned quickly, but not so quickly that it didn't turn into something of an entrance. "Oh, good, we're all here." The seat being kept for her, between Melissa and Raju, was at the far end of the room from the door.

The three women rose hastily as she passed, trying to find a place to set down their teacups. They bowed their heads in respect, the queenly Stella bending particularly low in an attempt to greet Mam "eye to eye." "This is an honor beyond imagining," she said.

"Namaste," Mam responded. Hazel once explained to her that it meant something along the lines of "the divine in me salutes the divine in you." Mam had found this to be a useful greeting. "I'm told you have an interesting proposal."

For more than a decade, the national organization of Wiccans with which the New Englanders were affiliated had held an annual convention of sorts, planned around their observation of the all-night Feast of Beltane. Stella explained it as the Wiccan May Day, a "welcome back" to the sun and a celebration of the return of life and fertility to the earth. It had proven to be tremendously popular, a way for Wiccans who ordinarily practiced in small, local circles, to make contact with others who shared their beliefs. Each year, a different regional group was selected to host the Confluence in a location of their choosing. When Hester implied that rotating the event was well advised, Beltane being a fertility feast by nature, Stella shot her Elder a dirty look. There were various elements to the festival, Stella smoothly assured Mam and her associates, from amongst which Wiccans individually chose. Honored guests were only invited to participate in a special few. She had been sent to discuss the opening ceremony specifically.

Each year, the hosting committee was faced with a political hot potato—choosing someone to officially open the Confluence. There being so many small, independent groups involved, it was pretty much a given that selecting a member of one group would be certain to cause offense to another, who would have been likely to lead his or her own ceremony back at home. After a few years of ugly scenes, the California group had been inspired to invite a famous singer-songwriter, a decision that had made for a resounding success. Subsequent host committees, less well-situated to provide an outsider of sufficient celebrity who would be both acceptable and accepting, had found it a greater headache to find the right person than to clean up the woods the morning after the feast. ANEW, having drawn a complete blank, were desperately about to call a somewhat senile member of an old Salem family, until someone had suggested Mam would be the dream candidate.

"We need some time to think it through," Raju told the Wiccans, taking command of the situation. "I'm sure you understand."

"Of course," Stella said, rising to her feet. The others put down their cups to follow. "You've been more than gracious in hearing us out. We'll be back later, for the Gathering."

They'd all almost forgotten the Gathering. Melissa checked her watch. It was almost time to run down to the bodega.

"If you'd leave a number with Jonelle," Raju continued, "we'd prefer to discuss it further before getting back to you with an answer."

"Ordinarily, that would be fine. You do understand how soon the Confluence is?" Stella asked. "April 30. We have to make arrangements..."

Raju held out his hand. "I'll personally commit to calling you tomorrow at 5. Would that be agreeable?"

Stella shook his hand. "Very." As Raju walked them out to the elevator, Finity Barnstock gave a last lingering glance over at Mam and sighed deeply.

There were many strong positives to the idea, as Mam's advisors saw it. For a first appearance outside Her own environment, it was unlikely they'd find a group more predisposed to be receptive to Mam than a group of Wiccans celebrating a fertility festival under the moon.

And it was time for Mam to try and venture off home turf, that was the sense that was growing off the website. If Mam's popularity continued to rise, there would eventually be a demand for her and Susan to appear in places away from New York. The cost of travel could never be offset by audiences the size of their own Gatherings, but up until now those were the largest live crowds that Mam had addressed. A critical question was whether Mam could reach a large audience, where many of those present wouldn't actually be able to see Her. This Confluence would be a good size for that test. And the Wiccan community was discreet enough that, if the appearance tanked, there would be little to no publicity. It would be worth a few hours drive into the mountains to find out.

The major negative, as Tara pointed out, was the risk of Mam being associated, in the public mind, with Wicca. "We wouldn't want Her appearance to be taken as an endorsement."

Rosa, who'd come in with the tea tray and stayed to stare at her first real witches, nodded vigorously.

"I agree." Over the speaker, Janet's voice slipped briskly over her daughter-in-law's. "Avoid labels. It's not in Mam's best interest to become affiliated with any one particular established religion."

"Oh, no!" Alan cut in, "After all, Mam is ecumenical."

"Ecumenical apart from Jews, Christians and Muslims, you mean," Wendy couldn't resist a wisecrack.

Lisa disagreed. "I think there's a place for Mam pretty much everywhere. I mean, as a lifelong agnostic..."

Alan couldn't help himself. "Agnostic my ass, babe! I'm an agnostic. You're a total atheist. Always have been. She always has been."

"Not total," Lisa was defensive. "I mean, not any more, you know. It's hard now, not to believe something."

"What do you believe?" Raju asked, in good earnest. "I've been wanting to ask, but it never seemed appropriate. I was raised to believe in many gods. For me, this isn't much of a stretch. But for the rest of you...Melissa?" Melissa looked at him in confusion and made a wavy motion with her hand. "Rosa, you're a good Catholic..."

"Yes, I am!" Rosa was agitated. "And Mam is a miracle! Like the stigmata."

"That's what your priest says?" Alan was genuinely curious.

"I...I haven't told my priest." Rosa said, and she burst into tears.

Tara went to Rosa and hugged her. "I guess I don't think it matters," she said. "Think about that woman who was here last week. As good a Christian as myself, I talked to her. And all her people handle snakes for God." Rosa continued to shake with sobs. Tara put a sheltering arm around her shoulders and gently led her out of the room. "There's all sorts of things like that, among people of faith," she crooned consolingly. "Things of power that you can't explain. You just offer it up to Jesus."

They left an uncomfortable silence behind them. Rosa could almost be said to have discovered Mam. From the first, she'd been so full of enthusiasm and support. If any of them had spent a moment thinking of the possible conflicts she might feel, they'd ignored the thought. She'd hid it so well. Or maybe she hadn't allowed herself to acknowledge it.

"Rosa?" Alan's voice came in tentatively over the phone.

"Tara's taking care of it," Lisa said.

"Good," Janet said, briskly. "She'll sort her out. Now where are we on the Confluence?"

"Susan, what do you think?" Mam asked.

Susan had been thinking hard, from the moment Stella had started to explain her invitation. She didn't know much about Wicca, but she imagined the parishioners would be something like the people she'd met at Mitra. She understood now that some kind of large crowd event was inevitable. It made a kind of pattern sense to make this Confluence the first. As to people thinking she and Mam were Wiccan, well, that was silly. That was like saying that those weeks with the St. Aggie's bible study class made them Catholic, or that going on *Duh News* made her a comedian. Mam was unique. She'd made it clear that Her agenda, of having no agenda, was equally unique. No one who followed Her story would ever make the mistake of thinking She was anything but Mam. Everyone else didn't matter, because they wouldn't be paying attention. "Who'll know we're there, outside the Wiccans?" she asked.

"Anyone we tell," Melissa said. "Like if you mention it on the show."

"So it's only people who already know who we are, right?"

Everyone had to agree.

"So then the positives outweigh the negatives," Susan pointed to the whiteboard, where Tara had been keeping track before she left. It was a first, for Susan to make this kind of decision.

Mam laughed.

Despite having made the decision herself, Susan regretted it almost immediately. There was so much fuss, about wardrobe and travel, and learning what exactly she and Mam were expected to do. Jimmy and Marta were working on a special costume. Hester Carl, who turned out to be the Eldress of her Woonsocket coven and unofficial ritual director of ANEW, came down from Rhode Island the Sunday before to teach them their part in the ceremony. Wendy was filming it all, for the feature-length documentary she planned to someday make about Mam. Susan could hardly refuse her after all she'd done for them, but it was an added level of stress to have a camera popping up in the corner of every situation. Meanwhile, the galleys had arrived for Susan to correct. And all along, she and Mam had to fulfill their usual schedule of Gatherings and webcasts.

They rented a Winnebago for the two days, to serve as Susan's dressing room and Wendy's production office. At midday on April 30th, too many people piled in. Susan and Mam had an entourage. Melissa, in her role as assistant, and Marta as official dresser, were necessary and comforting to have along. Alan came because he couldn't dream of missing a genuine Beltane observance, and because he'd appointed himself consulting anthropologist for Wendy's documentary. Lisa came to be with Alan. Raju came because he hated being left out. Wendy's crew included another camera operator in addition to Uri, two sound guys, and an electrician who followed in a truck with the generator.

The weather was clear, still mostly crisp but with a tantalizing glimpse of balmy days to come. As it was none of the several peak seasons for travel to the Berkshires, traffic was light. Before they turned off the turnpike, they stopped at Friendly's for lunch and ice cream. As Melissa pointed out, they didn't know when they'd be eating again—or what. That was no problem for Susan, who gnawed a breadstick and doubted she'd eat again until May 2nd.

When it came to taking the back roads, the men were all for following the map they'd gotten online. Fortunately, Lisa made them follow the hand-drawn map that ANEW had provided. After they hit Becket, there were back roads that didn't have signs, no less a presence on MapQuest.

Finity Barnstock, who was of little moment in ANEW and thus had no ceremonial part to play, had volunteered to be their liaison. She met them at the beginning of the dirt drive, marked only by a large white banner with a painting of a maypole, and led them to where they would set up. The Confluence was being held in a wooded area that fringed a large bowl-like meadow. They were to set up just where the woods began to nibble the grass, behind a thicket of old growth trees large enough to conceal their vehicles.

A team of workmen was already busy setting up loudspeakers in the trees, to carry the words of Mam and the other speakers all the way to the edges of the crowd. An enormous maypole was being raised in the center of the lawn, and a series of platforms locked in a ring around it. Wendy's crew was impressed by how professional it all was. For some reason, they'd assumed that Wiccans would do everything with sticks and stones.

While Wendy and her people busied themselves with cables, Susan was supposed to take a nap. She stretched out in the trailer on a sofa while at the other end, Marta got her costume neatly set out. Melissa sat on the step outside, reading galleys, Raju worked on his laptop on Chapter 3 of his very-slowly-increasing sure-to-be-a-best-seller legal thriller *The Case of the Missing Brief*, and Alan and Lisa left to poke their noses into whatever they could find. Alone in the trailer with Marta and the hiss of the steamer, Susan couldn't sleep a wink. She kept hearing a bird. She was a city girl, she told Mam, she couldn't sleep through birdsong. Marta suggested she was trying too hard. "The more you think, the less you can sleep. Forget it. Just close your eyes and try and get some rest. Don't worry about sleeping." Two hours later, she awoke and stretched. It was just beginning to grow dark. Everyone had returned and was sitting in the trailer, eating and talking quietly together. There was something peaceful about it, a kind of repose.

"We've got veggie wraps," Melissa said, noticing she was awake. Susan waved her away. "And look what Finity sent. 'Wild water.' That's what she called it. It's supposed to be like energizing. You want some?" She unscrewed the jar and took a puzzled sniff. "I thought it was some kind of moonshine. It smells just like water."

"Yeah, babe" Alan said, taking it from her. "Because it is. *Wild* water. As in not tame, you know? Free-flowing. Natural power and all that. Probably from a stream. Unless there's a spring nearby." He took a swig and passed the jar to Susan who did likewise. "Pretty great, huh?"

"Great," Lisa said. "Unprocessed stream water. You can both get Montezuma's Revenge or whatever they have in Massachusetts."

"You can drink water that's been running through rocks," Alan said scornfully. "It's naturally filtered."

Susan clutched her middle. All Lisa had to do was say the words. The last thing she needed now was a queasy stomach. Marta saw her.

"I don't get why you're so nervous," Marta said. "You do this all the time."

Susan shook her head. "This feels different."

An hour before show time, as Wendy insisted on calling it, Marta threw everyone out of the trailer. It wouldn't take an hour to put on the robes, but she thought Susan needed the time. Marta had helped to dress a lot of brides in her time, and she knew how calming the ritual could be. She brushed Susan's hair and fixed it on top of her head, the way they'd worked out would go with the headdress that Raju had insisted she wear. It was a simple band of silver and moonstones that rose up from her hairline and seemed to throw light across her forehead and cheekbones. He'd also found some earrings, and a pair of wide silver cuffs that Susan said made her think of Wonder Woman.

"You wear them," Marta said. "That Raju, he knows about jewelry." It was the expertise of growing up Indian with five sisters. Raju had also insisted she get a pedicure the other day, with silver polish. They'd been told that everyone would be barefoot at the Confluence.

They took their time on makeup, both Susan's and Mam's. Mam had agreed to allow a little blush as well as the usual cream foundation. It was a large field and the color would make her that much more visible.

Finally, Susan stood and allowed Marta to slip her into the white silk robes. They were long, to the ground, and trimmed with silver embroidery. It was a shame to think of what would happen to them, trailing behind her as she walked barefoot across the patchy early grass. They were very lovely. Susan stared into the mirror, willing herself to be large enough for the occasion. As long as she didn't focus on her own face, she could believe in this person she saw there. There was a knock at the door. Melissa poked her head in. "Wow!"

"Thanks," Susan said.

"Maybe she was talking to me," Mam suggested.

Melissa giggled. "It's time to get ready. We just got the first signal."

They left the trailer, carefully followed by Uri's powerful zoom lens, stationed up in a tree. Alan, Lisa and Raju came to squeeze Susan's hand and wish them luck; they didn't want to muss her with hugs. Raju gave her costume an approving nod and winked.

Susan passed by Wendy, who was perched on a folding stool between two trees, her PowerBook open in her lap and trailing cables. She gave them a quick thumbs up before returning her eyes to her monitor to watch the event through the eyes of the two cameramen. The meadow seemed full to overflowing, the atmosphere both joyful and solemn. The moon was clouded over, but there was a soft shimmer of light from the candles held by many of the celebrants. The platforms around the maypole, which had been lit for the convocation, seemed almost blindingly bright.

Wendy's stool was the best seat in the house, if you weren't a high enough ranking Wiccan to be in the first circle around the maypole. Melissa and the others stood watching over her shoulder. From where she stood, Melissa could keep an eye on Susan, who waited where Stella Ravenswing had told her, to make her entrance.

Susan held her head straight, almost grateful that the pressure of the headdress gave her something concrete to focus on. Marta kept circling her, tweaking unnecessarily at her skirts and sleeves.

There was a sound of flutes and cymbals. That was the second signal.

From five points around the periphery of the field, a line of white-robed dancers wove through the crowd, to meet in a dancing ring around the platforms. The chants of the dancers were picked up by those closest and rippled outward, the crowd starting to sway to the chant.

"You'll see," Marta muttered, giving Susan's skirts a final tug. "That Raju, he was right about those bracelets." She stepped back towards the others.

"Camera one, tight on Susan." Wendy's low voice crept magically from her headset up to Uri in the tree. "Camera two on the crowd."

"Still nervous?" Mam said.

"Yup," Susan replied. "You?"

Mam laughed. Someone shook a string of bells. The third signal. Susan took her first step forward.

As she broke past the trees, the clouds parted to reveal a full milk pail moon. Susan's white and silver robes glowed. As she continued to walk, the crowd began to sense her presence and parted to make way. With each step, Susan felt a growing confidence. The hush and the green smell of unseen trees seemed to buoy her up and she slipped like a canoe through silken midnight waters. The path opened before her. She felt the ruffle of soft air and the kiss of moonlight. She felt like someone in a dream.

Nearing the edge of the platform area, she raised her arms to greet the moon. Her wide kimono sleeves slid away and the bands of silver gleamed on her bared arms.

There was total silence.

Stella Ravenswing, in elaborate leaf-green robes, met her there and escorted her up the stairs to the ring of platforms.

The remaining honored Elders, four more from the local region and one from each of the other eight, were stationed on the inner ring. They all bowed their heads in greeting. Then, with her arms still raised, Susan slowly circled the outer edge of the platforms as she had so carefully been instructed, showing Mam equally to all sides of the gathered crowd. When she reached the point from which she'd begun, someone rang a bell. It chimed, enormously loudly, across the hushed assembly.

Mam spoke. "Greetings to all who honor Nature!" Her voice rang out as piercing and silvery as the bell. The buds on the trees seemed to quiver with it.

As one person, the crowd roared, "Mam!!"

Together, alternating phrases, Mam and Susan recited the invocation that Hester had taught them. Then Mam began to speak on her own, about the pulse of life that flows through every living thing. It was the first time She'd ever made what might be called a speech. Susan found herself as spellbound as any of those hearing Mam for the first time.

Listening, Susan looked out at the audience. She could see the faces of those closest to the platform. There were tears and smiles, and the glaze of awe. One man fell to his knees. People farther away, who could not see Mam as more than a speck of pink, would later claim that the hairs on the backs of their necks rose up. Even those so far back that Susan appeared only as an ectoplasmic blob would tell of an ozone shock that tickled the air. Seen or unseen, Mam sent a force through the assembly that lifted them, for a few precious moments, into a cloud where all their energies seemed to knit together as one and reflect back to be perceived by a sense they hadn't quite ever realized they'd owned.

After Mam finished speaking, Susan was supposed to descend and return the way she had come, while the Thirteen would sing a traditional song to open the crack between the worlds. Instead, as she approached the first step, she felt herself being lifted by a dozen hands. It seemed to happen in slow motion. As the flutes and drums resumed their call, she was passed in an outward spiral, over the heads of the celebrants until she reached the trees. Raju and Alan were there to catch her. They lead her, dazed, safely back to the trailer, where Marta met her with tears in her eyes.

When she saw the footage later, Susan was struck by how inevitable it all seemed, and as perfect as if it had been performed a thousand times before, an ancient and sublime form of prayer.

No one at the Confluence of Beltane that year would ever forget the feeling of that night, and most would spend the greater parts of their lives trying to recapture it.

8 - PERSUASIONS

The few who had accompanied Mam to the Berkshires couldn't stop talking about it. They'd driven home before daybreak in a kind of fugue, awakening midday in their own beds almost accidentally and half accepting that they'd dreamt it all.

Some of Wendy's raw footage was screened on Saturday in Lisa and Alan's media room, so that the rest of those in what inevitably was being known as the "inner circle" could share the experience. They reacted almost as intensely as those who'd stood under the moon. The Mam who spoke at that assembly was more than the benevolent oracle to whom they'd grown accustomed. She seemed to emit an energy through the crowd, an energy that transferred even across a video screen, that went beyond wise counsel or any other attribute to which Mam would admit. It was emotion stronger than any of them had felt the first time they'd met Her, or than anything Susan herself had experienced at any Gathering.

Was this something that should have been anticipated, that Mam would grow in some way, evolve, thanks to all Her human contact? Was it something to do with having an undiluted assembly of people unusually open and sensitive to the unseen world? The first people Mam had met, the ones in Sedona, had been similar to the Wiccans in that way, but there were so many more people at the Confluence than at Mitra. Had Mam, like many natural public speakers, simply risen to the occasion of a crowd many times larger than any She'd previously addressed and expanded as a result of this amassed focus of human emotion? The other possibility, the one that the inner circle seemed to be considering (whether consciously or not), was that Mam had always been holding out on them. The questions that had arisen over and over again, and been so glibly glided past, now seemed to take on more urgency. What was Mam? Why was She here? And what did She want from them? The questions loomed, but no one dared now to ask them again.

Over the past months, familiarity had been breeding nonchalance in the ranks of the inner circle, and in many of those less deeply immersed in Mam's world. Once they'd accepted that a voice, expressing cogent thought, was issuing from a human nipple, those who worked with Mam had lost the habit of amazement. Jimmy, for example, related to Susan and Mam in much the same way as he had to other celebrities he'd had occasion to dress: After a few fittings, the magic was gone, but the excitement of being part of something larger than everyday life had remained. There was plenty of enthusiasm and respect, but the awe, like the alcohol content of a flambéed dessert, was mostly burned off.

After the Beltane Confluence, things were never the same. It was as if everyone was meeting Mam for the first time, all over again. Susan noticed a change in the people around her, the ones who'd long ago grown accustomed to Mam. There was diffidence in their manner; not fear per se, but some reservation in speech and a kind of physical shrinking back. Sometimes she caught a head moving into what she could only describe as the beginnings of a bow. She started to feel like a Chinese emperor.

What made this new deference so particularly uncomfortable to Susan was that it had nothing whatsoever to do with her. Over the course of a year, Susan had moved from invisible and disregarded to conspicuous and respected. It had been a difficult adjustment, but not impossible to make because she had owned it at both ends of the journey. Up until now, she'd felt that she was in partnership with Mam, even if her part was little more than to handle it with grace and intelligence. She was part of the dialogue. Her opinions had weight. Once she'd raised her bracelets to the moonlight, her active role seemed to have ended. This new Mam, who had lifted that lawn into another realm, seemed so strong that Susan's cooperation was hardly necessary.

The most tangible result of the Beltane Confluence was the almost immediate decision to move ahead with scheduling a kind of lecture tour for Mam. For some time, fans across the country had been pressing Mam to come and meet them in person. With the web buzzing with Beltane-related blogs, the clamor had been rising. The decision to go on the road was made by Mam and her media and financial advisors. Mam, it seems, had been as excited by Beltane as any of the other participants. That it was Susan's body that would be shuttling from city to city didn't seem to factor into any of the discussions; her participation was taken for granted.

The big strategy meeting was a case in point. Raju, as manager, had been making his calls and doing his research, and he'd consulted as needed with some of the others. He was ready to finalize the itinerary and wanted to have everyone in one room, to talk them through it. In order to accommodate the more time-challenged among them, he planned it as a seven o'clock dinner meeting. This was the same time of day as the early Gathering, when Susan couldn't possibly participate, even if she had been told, but as Mam had already given her go ahead for the tour, the assumption was that details could be worked out without further consultation.

With the exception of Janet, who had to phone in from Chicago where she had a client on *The Oprah Winfrey Show*, those most concerned with the planning met in the conference room with a sack of sandwiches and chips. Raju and Melissa would be going along on the trip themselves, as well as Ziggy, who'd bring whatever assistants and equipment he might need to do the webcasts from the road. Some of the others might join up for a city or two, and there were Mam's costumes to consider, and the other detritus of such a show. Having spoken with several people who'd arranged tours, including some publishing contacts of Janet's and a friend of Alan's who turned out to have been in a boy band thirty years ago, Raju was convinced that their best bet would be to arrange the engagements so that at least part of the travel could be done by bus. The idea of hiring a bus put everyone in a festive mood. There was something so rock'n'roll about a bus tour. Lisa said she was ready to get going on the Mam in Concert T-shirts with a list of cities on the back. It was a perfect segue for Raju to turn their attention to the large foam core map of the US that he had already studded with flag-headed pins.

"I've assumed we'd all want to kick off in Sedona," Raju began, catching a drip of mayo with his tongue. He snagged a loop of bakery twine with a large green flag sticking out of the map.

"Like opening *Gone With the Wind* in Atlanta," Janet agreed over two layers of static. "You get the home field advantage."

"I spoke with Patrick and Bear myself," Wendy told the others. "They're good to go. To put it mildly. They're over the moon they're so excited."

"And flexible," Raju added. He saw some puzzled faces. "People, this is new territory. I have no idea how many tickets we're going to sell. Everywhere else, I had to make a guess and commit to x number of shows. We're planning two nights at Mitra, but if we sell more than we expect..."

"Patrick thinks we will," Wendy mumbled through her buffalo chicken wrap.

Raju shrugged. "If we do, we can push back a day and tack on an extra show. As long as we're in Santa Fe on September 9th."

"Santa Fe?" Alan asked. "Not Vegas?" Raju shook his head in a firm negative. "Why? Too much of a circus?"

"Too conservative," Tara said, waving a cherry tomato at the end of her fork. She laughed at the disbelief in the faces around her. "We're talking about the people who actually live there. You'd be surprised."

"She's right," Raju confirmed. "So no Vegas. We head straight to Santa Fe. An easy ride."

"And Stella said we'd get a good house," Lisa added. Everyone looked at her, questioning. "Ravenswing. I spoke with her last week." She continued somewhat defensively, "We have a lot to talk about. Market research. I figured that the solid Wiccan regions would probably give a strong turnout for Mam."

Wendy looked at the map. Raju, having linked Sedona to Santa Fe with his red thread was now moving north. "Colorado," she said, approvingly. "I hear there's a lot happening in Boulder."

"Telluride," Raju corrected her.

"Yes!" Lisa slapped her hands together. "Stella said that was a definite. Really hospitable. Also gorgeous, by the way."

"Telluride is hot!" Ziggy exclaimed, looking up from the Zen garden he was making out of artificial sweetener. "I am so up for Telluride!"

"You need two years ahead to book the opening of a door in Telluride," Janet warned. "It's not that big. And they seem to have a different festival in there every week."

Melissa was eating with her left hand so that she could keep taking notes. "So I'll put Telluride with a question mark, and list Boulder as a backup."

"I've already confirmed Telluride," Raju was the tiniest bit annoyed. Why did everyone seem to think this was open to debate?

"You have?" Janet was clearly shocked. "How did you...?"

"Research and negotiation," Raju said. What did she think he'd been doing for the past three weeks? "The weather starts to get iffy in the mountains by mid-month. I said we were willing to chance an outdoor space." He didn't add that the guy at the Chamber of Commerce had tried to talk him out of it. Raju was listening more and more to his instincts of late, and he felt it was going to be okay. He hoped he wasn't making a major mistake.

"This is fabulous," Lisa said enthusiastically, before anyone else could question the weather. "There's a town with a natural hot springs that I can't wait to check out, about an hour down the mountain."

"I didn't know you were planning on going," Diane said.

"Now that I'm going to have a second-in-command who can hold down the fort..." She smiled at Rosa, who'd recently been added to the payroll. "I know we said part-time, but it would only be for a week or so. Just to get the merchandise booth running. After that, Raju can hire someone local at each stop."

"Merchandise booth?" Rosa asked.

"Mmm. We've gotta sell stuff. People'll be asking for it. You know how it is at these things. There have to be T-shirts, of course, not just the tour ones but the regular ones and some of the usual stuff, whatever's doing well. I'm wondering if maybe we should have a tour jacket? Would that sell, do you think? If we can bring it in cheap enough? Or maybe just a tote and some new things from Jimmy. Ziggy's promised me he'll have 'Best of' volume 1." Ziggy gave a thumbs-up to the table.

"I'll talk to *Duh News* about a deal on copies of the Mam episode," Wendy volunteered. "I have a couple of things to talk about with them anyway."

"What about a program kind of thing?" Alan suggested. "Remember when we went to Elton John at Caesar's Palace, Leese, and they had that booklet with all the color photos? And shouldn't there be a poster?"

Diane laughed. "You want black light and lasers, Alan? I'm starting to think this really is a concert tour."

"It is," Janet said. "Sounds sexier than 'lecture tour.' It'll sell more tickets."

"What does Mam think about all this," Rosa looked troubled. "I mean, posters and things? It seems, I don't know, like it's not dignified, it's too..."

"It's paying a lot of the rent," Tara said, succinctly.

"Mam does her thing, we do ours," Lisa added.

"What does Susan say?" Rosa still wasn't happy.

No one had an answer. A few people shrugged.

"That's why it's called show business, hon," Janet remarked, "and not show art."

"But this isn't show business...it's a lot more serious."

"Nothing is more serious than show business," Janet chuckled ominously. "I'm sitting in a building owned by a woman who's worth more than the annual GNP of Andorra. Anyway, my client should have nothing to complain about. She wanted to be a writer. Well, she should see what J.K. Rowling puts up with."

Rosa didn't seem convinced. Selling things on the website was one thing. People had to go out of their way to find the store page, and they wouldn't be shopping while listening to Mam. But things were never sold at a Gathering. It wouldn't feel right, it would cheapen the experience of meeting Mam to walk out the door with some tote bag. Jesus wouldn't have sold T-shirts after the Sermon on the Mount. She caught herself, horrified. Was she thinking Mam was like Jesus? Mam was miraculous, yes, but not God. Rosa crossed herself, then darted a frightened glance around the room. No one had noticed; they were all too focused on the map.

By the end of the meeting, Raju's red thread had drawn two distinct designs to either side of the map, with a wide gap in between. Starting from Sedona, a kind of crook hooked up the Four Corners with the West Coast, where a neat row of pins connected Seattle, San Francisco and LA. LA, it was agreed, would either be a major disaster or the event of the year. All of this would be accomplished before the end of October. "So we don't have to deal with Halloween," as Melissa correctly surmised. A lonely flag waved over Chicago, which would be a three-day early November drop-in, all on its own. There had been similar caution in the South, where only New Orleans had made the cut. When Melissa brought up Key West or South Beach, Raju pointed out that hangovers often brought on prayer, but rarely guaranteed a spiritual mindset. After a break (apart from some book signing jaunts Janet and the publisher had planned), the straight line of the Northeast Corridor would begin in mid-January. Boston would technically be Cambridge, which ANEW had suggested as being a major university town as well as a convenient locus for their own member covens. While DC had been considered out of the question, both Philadelphia and Baltimore were good to go. Weather was a real concern, but Janet had encouraged Raju to strike while the iron was hot and not wait for April, as he would have preferred. If the roads were too bad for the bus, Diane pointed out, they actually could take the Metroliner.

Ironically, the only unconfirmed city on the tour was home. The dates for New York would entirely depend on what building they were finally able to book and as yet, Raju had been unable to find an available space that seemed right.

"I think the Garden would be fun," Lisa said dreamily.

"Talk about a rich fantasy life," Alan kissed her on the back of her neck. "Do you get how huge the Garden is? My wife thinks we're the Stones."

"Got to run, M'liss," Ziggy said, pointing to the orange plastic cuff that no one would suspect was a wristwatch. "Last thing I'm saying—the Beacon."

"Not unless someone else cancels," Raju said. "It would be perfect, I agree. But they're booked solid into next May. It's the same with Town Hall and City Center."

"We can't wait that long," Janet said decisively.

"I know that, Janet. I'm looking."

"We'll find a place," Tara said confidently, beaming up at Raju. "Look how great you did with the other cities. This tour is meant to be."

By the time Ziggy and Melissa reached the studio, Susan was already in place, miked up and worried. There was no precedent for handling things if either one of them missed a webcast. Maybe it was time to have a backup plan. She raised her eyebrows at the breathless Melissa who, settling in front of her console, gave a big thumbs up. "Everything's under control," she whispered, clamping down her headphones. "The tour is looking so great." With Ziggy giving the count, Susan barely had time to wipe the confusion off her face.

She couldn't stop thinking about it, and in the five minutes between the broadcast and Mam-after-Cam, she asked Melissa what had been going on immediately before air time. Melissa was delighted to bring her up to date with a quick, enthusiastic summary of the plans being made and promised that formal notes would be available in the morning. "Everyone was so caught up," she said apologetically, that she hadn't realized how late they were running until Ziggy had thank goodness checked his watch. It would never happen again. Susan thanked her, waving the apology away on the pretext that the meeting had simply slipped her mind. It hadn't. She'd never been told.

All throughout the Gathering, while Mam charmed and enlightened, Susan quietly stewed. When she wasn't thinking angrily about her closest associates, not to mention two of her oldest and dearest friends in the world, feeling it was appropriate to arrange her life without her, she listened to Mam handling the evening almost entirely on Her own and got angrier still.

At home that night, she couldn't seem to settle down. Instead of a slice of pizza or anything else that could pretend to be food, Susan ate her way through a container of strawberry ice cream as she flipped from cooking shows to true crime documentaries to faded episodes of M*A*S*H.

"Keep eating that and you'll get fat. I'll look terrible," Mam said lightly. Susan ignored Her. "Will you turn that thing off already and talk to me?"

"Why?" Susan erupted. "You don't care what I have to say. No one cares what I have to say. You, Raju, Janet, Lisa. Everyone's decision counts except mine. I'm totally irrelevant, apart from the fact that you're stuck on my chest." She was shaking when she'd finished.

Mam was silent while She considered Susan's outburst. "Whatever are you talking about?" She ultimately asked.

"Omniscient beings can't play dumb, alright?"

"Who said I'm omniscient?" Mam asked. Susan was silent. "Fine," Mam admitted, "I know what you're talking about. So let's talk."

"It's just too much." She needed to move and started pacing the room. "I didn't ask for this. I was happy in my own dull little life"

"No you weren't."

"So I wasn't. But I knew where I was and I wasn't scared half the time. I feel like I'm hang-gliding over a field of barbed wire." It was as if she were channeling Ziggy, it was that hard to keep still. "A national tour..."

"You're afraid of the tour?" Mam sounded surprised.

"Well I'm not Madonna, am I?! I'm a writer. At least I thought I was. All I wanted to do was make a living writing stories. I never planned to be a preacher."

"We don't preach, remember."

"Could have fooled me. You're the one who said 'people start religions.' People, as if they do it all by themselves, spontaneously combust into religious fervor. But I was out in that meadow. You were leading them into it. It was like a weird revival meeting. I half expected people to shout 'Hallelujah' and throw away their crutches. If that wasn't preaching, then what would you call what you were doing there? I'd love to hear. What?"

"That was an unusual occasion, Susan," Mam said, Her cadence soothing. "It's not how we work."

"Isn't it?" It was insulting that Mam thought she was thick enough to believe that. "It will be, when we go out on the road. That's what they'll want."

"What exactly do you think they want? And who are 'they?'"

Mam was being eminently reasonable. It was like arguing with Socrates. Or Freud. Maybe it would be simpler if Susan could figure out whether she needed a philosophy or a shrink. "Ecstasy, that's what they want. Everybody. Everybody out there who comes to Gatherings or watches us on the web. The people who are going to buy tickets if we go out on tour. They're expecting...I don't know, some kind of mystic leader or something. I'm in over my head."

"No one is asking you to lead."

"No, they're not, are they? They're asking you." Now Susan was confusing herself. Was she resentful because she, the ultimate non-joiner, was being pulled into a movement, or because she wasn't being asked to lead it? "And you're using me. I'm just, oh God, just a vessel!" She laughed sardonically. "I can't even say 'Oh, God' anymore without wondering what that means."

"Did you ever know? I thought you didn't believe in anything."

"Don't think you can change the subject. I'm talking about my place in the scheme of things. Am I an active part of this, whatever it is? If I am, why doesn't it matter what I think? Or does it turn out I really am just the world's largest piece of baggage?"

"You're part of the dialogue. We dialogue, remember."

"We used to dialogue. Dialogue means different voices. This is dialogue, what we're doing now. Not what you've been doing lately. That's monologue. I sat in that Gathering tonight and never opened my mouth except to say hello and goodnight. And no one even noticed. It didn't make a damned bit of difference."

"Everyone makes a difference."

"I could have bet money you'd say that, you know. You're getting a little predictable."

"Is there more value in unpredictability than in the truth? Everyone does make a difference, because nobody lives in a vacuum."

"You're not the only person on the planet? To coin a phrase."

"Just because Lisa put it on a T-shirt doesn't mean it's not true," Mam said tartly. "You have to know that you make a difference to me. You help me in what I need to do."

"So you're basically admitting I'm a tool. But maybe..." she faltered. What she needed, Susan finally allowed herself to realize, was to be valued. She'd always needed that, she supposed all people did. She'd never felt it until Mam had become part of her life, but she'd been so used to feeling invisible that it had been bearable. She'd even been able to make it something of a grim joke. Now that she'd had this year with Mam and had been able to feel, for the first time, that she had some genuine worth in the world, it was too painful to think of being without it. It always hurt more to lose something you had, than to long for something you never knew. Since Beltane, that had been the true fear, that she would be invisible again. "But maybe that would be okay with me, to be used, if I understood why, what it was all for. I need to know..." Before, Susan had always been afraid that if she pushed too hard, Mam might disappear. Now that she'd begun to face the idea of losing Her anyway, she was reckless. She took a deep breath and blurted it out. "Is there...? Are you God?"

"From what I hear, God creates things, God destroys. God judges and punishes and forgives." Mam's voice had a smile. "I don't do anything that sounds like God to me. I'm a voice, that's all."

"Enough with the 'I am a voice' thing!" After having been so honest herself, at least in her own thoughts, Susan was exasperated. "I am so, so tired of evasion. Whether you admit you wanted it or not, there's a religion happening here. Not just talk and advice or whatever—people are starting to worship you. And I'm having to along with it. Me, who never believed that anyone could know what God was or what God might want of us. I'm stuck now, I have to follow along with whatever you're doing and before this goes a step further, I think it's only fair of you to let me know what that is. Whose voice?"

"Does a voice have to belong to an individual? Can't a voice be wider than that and speak for something shared?"

"We call that democracy," Susan said. "If you're representing some great outcry, who elected you spokesman? The angels? The aliens maybe, like Patrick once said? Maybe some fairies from another dimension, because you look like something out of Hieronymus Bosch."

"I'm not dodging your question, Susan," Mam sounded more troubled than testy. "What I said in the beginning was the truth. I know that something happened, somewhere unseen. There was an explosion of some hidden force, a quake too vast to remain silent and what erupted was a voice. There I was."

"What kind of force? Could you be any more vague?"

Mam sighed. "I'm not making much sense, am I? You're the one who put it best into words."

"Me? But I have no idea what you're talking about. When? How?"

"That first time at Mitra. Don't be so surprised. You are the writer. Don't you think that might be one of the reasons you became my...what did you call it?...vessel? You said that everything alive is woven together by some kind of shared energy. That was your great truth. And when I asked you what you could do with that truth, you said..."

"Live with it," Susan murmured. "I remember that. Because they were so pissed off with me for saying it."

"Live with it. And try to live the best way you can. I think that's what I'm here to do," Mam affirmed. "Whatever brought me into being, there's a need for me, to help people learn that they can be better. And if that takes religion, to make your world a better place, if that's the only way that people will learn, then so be it."

"My world," Susan said curiously. "Not yours?"

"I don't sense that it belongs to me." Susan thought Mam sounded a little sad. "I know you think I'm using you, Susan. Perhaps I'm as much a tool as you are. And don't ask me whose. I told you. I don't know."

Susan let it go for the time being. It had been a dialogue. She'd said something, possibly even what she'd meant to say, and Mam had listened. Mam had said all that She could on the subject. Susan didn't know what difference it would make, but she knew she had to do some thinking. There was far too much religion in the world as it was, to her mind, and it did more harm than good.

A miasma of thought seemed to hang over Mam Enterprises. From her vantage point at the front desk, Jonelle noticed a lot of people walking around as if they were only half in the room. Whatever was going on, she hoped it was nothing bad. She was liking this job so much better than filling in all those forms at the eye clinic. Everyone was so friendly here, and usually they seemed to really like their work, which was different from any other job she ever had. Since that Gathering, as they called it, in Massachusetts, something felt different in the air. She decided to think positive, like her grandmother had always taught her. There couldn't be anything for her to worry about. People didn't seem unhappy, only distracted. Super distracted. She wondered what it was.

It was a direct result of not having been asked, Susan decided.

Susan Roth knew herself. Having come to some kind of terms with the whole Mam situation, she would have let things ride indefinitely, ignoring her own questions, swallowing down on unease whenever it tried to surface. Susan had always been like that. It was easier for her to let that conveyor belt move her along than to fight against the motion. Until, that is, something happened to set her off. It was always something that felt like a direct challenge. Funny how little that something always seemed to be. Not being told about that tour meeting had had been this something, just enough to make her want to challenge her own lack of control. She'd stopped coasting along and started bumping up against a lot of thinking.

There was comfort in her certainty that Mam wasn't actually God. Even Her inability to name the force She embodied brought a strange reassurance. Odd as it was, Susan had found Patrick's alien theory more acceptable than the possibility that Mam might be a messenger from some active, engaged deity. She'd never been a big fan of the idea of a personified God. Thinking of herself as a rational creature, she found it impossible to accept that another conscious being, particularly a superior one, might not be. Shouldn't morality be a trickle-down value, with the person at the top setting a good example for those lower down? A God who mows down innocent thousands in a tsunami while cosseting fat cat powerbrokers to a ripe old age is surely not making an admirable value judgment. The "reasons we can't imagine" theory carried no weight with Susan. There was no such thing as reason that couldn't be imagined, only reason that could be rejected as being misguided or faulty or downright perverse.

What was it that so desperately needed a voice that it had burst out through Mam? Clearly it needed the cooperation of human beings to achieve its goals, whatever those goals might be. Mam Herself was the only miraculous manifestation. Everything else was talk, all those conversations she and Mam had with all those people. Even that astounding speech in the meadow had been talk, albeit extraordinarily inspiring. They might have their personal quibbles, but Susan had no argument with the principles Mam broached. Mam suggested nothing more than that human beings should respect themselves and one another. Everything else, as Rabbi Hillel had noted long ago, was commentary.

That the words came from Mam made them resound in ears that might otherwise be deaf to them. Susan understood this. But while Mam might be the locus of energy, Susan's was the face people saw. Not unreasonably, some people believed that she and Mam were one and the same. If indeed a religion were organizing around them—and she knew intuitively that this would be a result of the tour, for what were groupies if not acolytes?—Susan's own responsibility would be enormous. It was almost shocking to realize, but her book, which she'd written as a kind of memoir, might end up turning into a gospel of sorts. She'd seen the things people did in the name of their religion. How could she shoulder such a weight? Was there any way to get out of it?

It was the Beltane Confluence itself that left an odd, private smile on the face of the most practical and earthbound person associated with Mam.

At various points throughout the day, Lisa Denton's usual businesslike air would suddenly fall away to be replaced by a moment of gazing into space with burning eyes. No one knew that late at night, she stood on the terrace by her lemon tree, looking up at the stars, or at least at the city lights that looked like stars. It made her feel as if she were back in the Berkshires, on that amazing night when she'd found herself believing something. It was a lot like love, what had happened to Lisa that night. Not like the love she felt for Alan, a comfortable, companionable kind of love, though she did love Alan very much. What she felt in the dark air, with the smell of damp earth and growing green in her nostrils, was an almost unbearable aliveness. She could feel her skin breathe. She could see across the river to Jersey as if she were wearing some kind of magic crystal glasses; everything was that clear and sharp and had at least one more dimension than she was used to. The world was so incredibly beautiful. Alan's sleeping head on the pillow beside her made her feel so tender she thought she might cry.

She was disappointed that Alan didn't feel the same. She'd tried to explain it to him, the power of what she'd felt, and he'd looked at her with that same sweetly puzzled expression he wore when absorbing Megan's allegiance to some band or noticing the sapphire in her nose. It was all fascinating to Alan, the puzzle that was his fellow humans, in an academic kind of way. Despite nearly 20 years in the rag trade, he'd never stopped thinking like an anthropologist. Post-industrial human society, he observed, was a seething mishmash of individuals who yearned to align themselves with a chosen tribe. Significant jewelry, for example, whether Megan's nostril stud or a charm on a chain around the neck, was an easily read signpost of belonging. There was no difference between the frenzy of true believers at a rock concert or a religious service; to Alan's mind, shared ecstasy was the ecstasy of sharing. It was a tribal drive that he understood to be a basic human need. On those occasions when he himself found a need to participate in a ceremony of life, the nearby Unitarian church satisfied this need without demanding he yield more than he comfortably felt he should. Alan reveled in the world, but enjoyed a sense of detachment in his enthusiasms. It was surrender that had always baffled him, even as it fascinated him to ponder it. Compared to the Lisa he'd married, he'd seemed a starry-eyed romanticist. Now she petted her neighbor's golden retriever and thought her fingers would dissolve in the living silk. There was color everywhere, and nearly every sound had its music. She slept and ate less, though both sleep and food tasted so much richer than they had before. Lisa had surrendered to a power greater than reason, and it had Alan baffled. Baffled could be fine. Men and women usually are baffled by one another. The problem was that Lisa was beginning to evangelize. She couldn't understand why Alan couldn't allow himself to embrace the wonder. It was tragic to think that they'd missed out on so much for all these years, and that so many other people had been missing out as well. Now that she knew the secret, she had an obligation to share it with the world. This national tour of Mam's was just the beginning, she vowed. She had promises to keep. Alan wouldn't stop her, in fact, he'd be there most of the way, but they wouldn't be rowing the same boat. That it was his own choice made Lisa no less sad when she allowed herself to think about poor Alan standing on the shore and waving his handkerchief. There always had to be a sacrifice, she supposed; it was actually fairly traditional.

It was that moment she'd unthinkingly compared Mam to Jesus that rocked Rosa to the core.

When Rosa Santiago had met Mam, one of the first people to do so, it had seemed to her to be a miracle of the kind she'd read about when she was at school with the nuns. The awe of that miracle had been pure and her heart certain. Even when Tara had called Mam a religion, she'd understood that to be something necessary for the government and nothing to do with Church at all. What Mam had to say was Good, and Rosa was proud to be with Her and spread the blessings of Her wisdom. Then those witches had come and Mam had gone to speak at their heathen ceremony, and Rosa began to be troubled. She knew what witches were. If Mam were as pure as Rosa had felt, the witches should not have been able to come near. Rosa had been taught she wasn't wise. She decided to wait and watch, to pray for reassurance and guidance.

In Lisa's media room, she was glued to the screen as those agents of Satan swayed in a kind of rapture before Mam, and Mam rejoiced in it. She'd tried to convince herself that Mam was saving their damned souls. If not, then she'd been deceived all these months into thinking she was the handmaiden of Christ when in truth she had been serving the black heart of the devil. Rosa could not believe that, and then she had to doubt her disbelief.

From a sociable, smiling person who'd always stopped to chatter with everyone, Rosa Santiago turned quiet and reserved. Even Carlito noticed, saying, "Mami's sad." Everything she did seemed to be weighed on some invisible scale. Was Mam a miracle of God or was serving Her a blasphemy? She had to make a private inventory. Rosa would pick up a T-shirt in the stock room and read its message. Was it as Good as first it seemed, or was there a subtlety she hadn't had the wit to smell before? On the mornings she worked, she came in after having gone to Mass, her delicate gold Confirmation cross shimmering in the hollow of her throat, and she would sometimes pop out to the nearby church on her lunch break. She prayed, and often fasted, seeking guidance. It was important, she decided, not to let her doubts become evident to the others. She needed to be inconsequential before Evil, if Evil there was, to make safe her escape. She hid in routine and cautiously pulled back her presence, and often during the day, she touched her throat, reaching for the consolation of the tiny gold cross.

It was watching the raw footage that made up Wendy's mind, but making the decision is only the first step. Sometimes it's even the easiest.

Wendy Smedstad was plotting out a chancy campaign. Wendy came in to the Mam Enterprises offices more often than before, darting her eyes enthusiastically around the space to seek out whatever might be new. She'd plop herself down in a chair in the Pool and help stuff envelopes, talking to whatever volunteers were around, asking all sorts of questions about their lives. At least once each visit, she'd duck into the conference room and stare up at the map, making notes in her laptop, which she now always carried with her. Material was rampant. Every instinct told her this tour would be that golden opportunity a documentarian often only dreams of, a fascinating subject with enough of a market draw to get financing.

There was no longer any "someday" to wait for; Wendy had decided to quit *Duh News* and follow Mam on the road now. That much was certain. It was the details she was mulling over. She didn't anticipate any problem with Mam, but she had to handle things carefully with Ziggy, to make sure she and the webcast team didn't step on each other's toes. She needed to analyze the itinerary and budget expenses for the road, as well as for little things like a crew and equipment rental. Most importantly, she couldn't afford to antagonize *Duh News*. She had a contract with a few months yet to run, and a freelance newbie documentary filmmaker could hardly afford to start out with a hefty legal bill. She also was a great believer in not burning bridges she might someday have to retreat over. She might believe in this moment with all her heart, but that didn't mean she wouldn't need a job at the other end of it. If the Mam tour turned out to be as hot as everyone involved seemed to sense it was going to be, it would be a major coup to be the official television outlet. Critical to Wendy's plan was finding a way to convince both Mam's team and the people at *Duh News* that it would be brilliant for everyone if she could fulfill her contract to the show by providing them with exclusive footage to use in a daily update segment on the tour— and to start by finding a cleverer name to pitch than "Mammogram."

It was the cool glow of silver bracelets in the moonlight that shook Raju back to a place so distant that he'd forgotten he'd ever inhabited its precincts.

For most of his adult life, Raju Nayar had cultivated the contradictory habit of privately honoring his heritage while outwardly presenting it, tongue-in-cheek, as an entertaining mark of distinction. He liked and admired his culture. He also liked blending in with the life he'd chosen, with his classmates at Yale, the lawyers and investment bankers with whom he did business, the people at the Racquet Club and at the chic bars and restaurants he enjoyed. Raju functioned as a typical high-achieving New Yorker of his generation, who just so happened to be Indian. Publicly, it only came up when it was interesting as a conversation starter or useful as a way of standing out from the crowd. How he felt, or what he did, privately was, well, private. Not that there was much difference between his private and public life. Raju had few hours of the day when he wasn't working. Even his tennis games and his periodic forays onto the dating scene were a form of work, because he took his leisure seriously. Girlfriends never stuck around for long, because he wasn't interested in making room for them in his closet or kitchen, or in spending hideaway weekends in romantic bed-and-breakfasts. He enjoyed a frictionless life of surface pleasure, finding serenity in a beautifully styled existence.

At an age when most people still cherish the illusion of being special, Raju had decided that what was special about him was the ability to be the same as everyone else but at a much higher level. He studied hard, because he knew a good education was the surest path to the type of money he wanted for the life he wanted to live. Intuiting early on that his own talents made him merely competent, he'd put aside his dream of writing in favor of a career in law, shrewdly turning even that into one of its more lucrative specialties. Once his comfort was assured, his condo paid, his closet filled with impeccable suits, his portfolio mounting satisfactorily, he could afford the indulgence of squandering time. Even so, he'd returned to writing with his customary practical approach, signing up for Harrison Levy's workshop and choosing to write what he knew would sell. Mysteries didn't interest him much personally, but thrillers by lawyers were known to sell like hotcakes. It was all running like clockwork, until he'd met Mam. From the evening of his first introduction, he'd found himself thinking more and more of those rare childhood visits to or from his grandparents in Bombay and of the aura of enchantment that always seemed to hover around them as much as the scents of sandalwood and spices. A craving to recapture this leads him to go occasionally to temple and to rent Bollywood movies. These were pleasant ways to pass the time, and his parents enjoyed the new frequency of his visits to Jackson Heights. He didn't see it as the beginning of a transformation, merely a brief touch of nostalgia.

When he'd stood at the edge of the woods to judge the effects of moonlight on his silver bracelets, he was unprepared to be swept away. Swept away wasn't in Raju's vocabulary. He'd felt something in his heart that he hadn't admitted was there, a connection to a world of colors and music that could lift him to a plane that made a summer weekend in East Hampton seem a paltry thing. There was magic in the world, and magic was as much his birthright as beauty and intellect. Why had he denied it for so long? Whatever Mam had done in that ring of trees had reminded Raju that he was more than he had chosen to become, and he was determined not to lose that self again. After the Beltane Confluence, Raju put aside *The Case of the Missing Brief*, never to finish it. Always methodical, he determined that the correct path to becoming accessible to the magic was to reclaim his inheritance in the most direct way—he became more aggressively Hindu than he'd ever been before. He gave up beef, and was seen wearing elegant silk kurtas with his jeans and Armani jacket. The bulletin board in his office was a collage of various avatars of Brahma, Vishnu and Siva, and the Vedic stories took their place alongside the *Financial Times* on his bedside table. In planning the tour, he envisioned opportunities to meet others who found his heritage as magical as he did, and to greet other cultures with an open heart beyond a studied tolerance. He didn't know what he would find or what might find him. It occurred to Raju that this might be the first time in his life that he could not guarantee the outcome of a project. He was opening himself up to disappointment, perhaps to embarrassment or hurt. Sometimes now he found himself alone at night, sitting on his Eames chair in the silence and nibbling from a bowl of bhakar wadi, filled with an exciting sense of trepidation as he contemplated the light of truth.

It was supposed to be the longest day of the year, and the shortest night, but Rosa felt the night had been going on forever. She never felt like she'd slept at all, but she must have because she found herself waking over and over again. Each time, she'd jolt awake, as if from a nightmare, except there was no dream that she could remember. She'd feel a pain across her chest, like an asthma attack almost. With her pulse racing wildly, she'd turn and see the blanket lump that was Ernie's back, snoring peacefully at her side. It was amazing he could sleep so soundly when her blood was pounding so loud. It made her crazy that he seemed so peaceful. The only way she could still her heart was to creep out to the living room, kneel in front of her real porcelain Madonna, and say a rosary. She must have done that maybe six times. It was a good thing Ernie could sleep through anything like an old dog. She couldn't imagine what she'd say if he was awake and asking questions.

She needed a sign; something to tell her what was okay to do. Guidance, that's what she needed. She'd been praying so much for guidance lately, but no word was coming down. She tried to purify herself, to be ready to hear, but it wasn't so easy to fast when you have a husband who likes curves on his woman and watches everything you don't eat. Tonight had been his night to go with his boys to the sports bar after work, and Carlito, who was getting big eyes and a big mouth to match, ate over at her cousin's. Rosa hadn't eaten since breakfast, and then only a piece of toast while the baby had his cereal. That one piece of bread was all that was between her and the chicken from dinner the night before. Maybe it was still too much. She kept imagining that piece of toast the size of a building, standing between her and the message she needed so much to hear. Maybe that was why she couldn't sleep. Her body kept waking her up in case the message was coming, but then that piece of toast would stop it like a shield.

Kneeling in front of the Blessed Mother, the carpet scraping against her knees through her thin nightgown, Rosa started to weep. She was so tired, not from the loss of one night's sleep but from a month of ceaseless anxiety burning away at her insides. Rosa loves God. She loves His Son and His ways. Always, since a little child, she knew in her heart that Jesus loves her, too. When other girls in school messed around with boys, when kids had beers or did pills or weed, Rosa had Jesus to keep her straight and away from all that. She'd been proud to be a virgin at twenty when she'd married Ernesto, not ashamed like some of the girls said she should be to be so old, and he respected her, too. He was a good man. He was her reward for keeping her faith. So was Carlito, all healthy and so smart. She had so much to lose.

"Sante Maria, Madre de Dios, ruega por nostrotos pecadores ahora y en la hora de nuestra muerte."

What had she done in return for all her blessings? Truly she'd thought Mam was a miracle of God's and so she'd believed in Mam's goodness. It was like listening to a priest almost, to hear what Mam had to say about honoring and respecting and all. Then things started to change. She was blind at first. She shouldn't have been, but she was. And then those witches came and she couldn't ignore it any more. God saved her. With one clear thought, He made the scales fall from her eyes. He wouldn't allow her to confuse His miracles, so if she was confused, then Mam couldn't be His miracle.

It wasn't like a priest, what Mam did. There was too much power. People who didn't honor Jesus and people who couldn't properly fear God were held by that power, and then good people, like herself or Tara, who honored Jesus as imperfectly as a Protestant could, they were being pulled in too. It was sounding a lot like worship, what was going on with Mam. But the commandment said "Thou shalt have no other God before Me." And if Mam was not His miracle, but a power separate from God, the only thing that could be that powerful was the Devil.

How could a voice that spoke of good things be the voice of the Devil? This was the kind of torture the martyrs used to feel, to wonder if something that seemed good might be concealing darkest evil. Rosa wasn't strong enough to bear it. She couldn't even bear the shame she felt whenever she imagined going to Father Martin and unburdening herself. If everything she had done for Mam had been a sin, it was surely of the blackest kind. How could Father Martin absolve her, if this were the sin she feared? So she prayed and fasted, and tonight she swayed sleeplessly on her knees and begged Jesus to send her a sign to tell her what to do.

She almost fell asleep at her prayers that last time. Just as her head became too heavy to hold up, she staggered to her bed and let herself fall into darkness. An hour later, Ernie heaved awake beside her and stomped into the bathroom. A few minutes later, over the sound of the shower, she heard Carlito call. It was morning.

Rosa rubbed the sand from her eyes and allowed herself to go through the morning routine. She put the TV on for the baby while she made Ernie's breakfast. After Ernie was gone, she gave Carlito his cereal. She skipped breakfast herself, telling the baby that she had a tummy ache. She smiled to reassure him, then got him dressed to take him to the Head Start.

When she got home, she still felt numb, as if her body wasn't hers. She called and left a message on the volunteer hotline that she wouldn't be coming in. She could have called Lisa directly, but then she would have had to talk to her.

"You better find someone else to cover for tomorrow, too," she said to the tape. "I got some kind of bug or something."

She tried to lie down for a while, but as tired as she was, she couldn't sleep. She pulled herself together and went over to Saint Agatha's to light some more candles. She knelt in her usual place, close to the statue of the Blessed Mother. It usually brought her such comfort to gaze upon that sweet, solemn face, the chubby hand of her Son reaching for her cheek.

Rose had been fasting for nearly two days, and hadn't slept in nearly as long. The air seemed to thicken with a veil of pearl that remained even when she blinked. As she watched, the slim hand of the Madonna glided down to open her robes. She offered up her breast, to nurse her Son. Seated on the palm of her other hand, the Baby leaned down and seemed to reach for His Mother's breast. Instead of bringing it near His mouth, His tiny hand pushed it roughly away, His face a pucker of infant anger.

Rosa blinked again. The veil lifted and it all went back to same chipped painted plaster as before. A cold sweat beaded her brow, like a fever breaking. She felt weak, drained. And she felt the first sense of peace she'd known in weeks. The message was clear. He had rejected the Breast.

There was no more doubt, no more pain, only a deep sorrow and repentance. She had been worthy of a sign. She prayed in her place for a while, allowing herself to be soothed by the certainty that she would be forgiven. Rosa rested a hand on the pew in front of her and pulled herself up. She smoothed her skirt and dabbed a tissue over her damp face. Slowly, with a growing calm, she walked towards the confessional.

It was the second day of summer and Susan was still wrestling with the angels or devils or whatever there might be out there tugging at her soul. IF there were a conscious Creator or whatever, it might be easier to imagine a day when she'd come face-to-face with "It" if she would only have to answer for her own actions. The problem with being a responsible person is that, when other people followed you, you felt responsible for their actions as well. Maybe this was how Helen of Troy had felt, watching soldiers die by the bushel. There'd been Gods in that disaster, too.

She took in the morning paper and poured herself a cup of coffee, wishing she could clear her head.

"You're awfully quiet," Mam observed, "but I know when you're awake."

"If I don't talk," Susan said, "I can almost be alone." She rustled the paper pointedly and started to read. The front page was hardly distracting. In the lead international story, a Kurdish group had claimed responsibility for the bombing of a hotel in Afghanistan "in retaliation for the slaughter of Kurds," while a group calling itself something that translated as "Sword of Islam" was taking responsibility for the same bombing as a warning "to those who loved the West."

In a sidebar, at the World Court, the former head of a nominally Christian state was being finally being prosecuted for ten-year-old war crimes that included the slaughter of vast numbers of the long-integrated Moslem population with the goal of "cleansing" the nation.

Nationally, the focus was once again on conception, this time specifically in regard to the so-called morning-after pill. "When does life begin? The debate continues over RU486." Susan paused over this one. It didn't affect her personally. She'd had such a pathetic sex life that the unwanted pregnancy issue hadn't troubled her much. The only time she'd thought she'd gotten caught, she'd actually been pretty happy about it. She'd already been old enough to think that if she wasn't going to have a husband, it didn't mean she had to forgo having a family. When it had turned out to be a false alarm, subsequent and less emotional consideration helped her decide that, while an accident would have been one thing, single parenthood was a luxury she couldn't afford to seek out. These days, of course, it was all pretty much moot. Even if she could find a man who didn't mind a breast that would kiss him back, she doubted she still carried many live grenades.

Nonetheless, Susan was enough of a feminist that the issues of birth control and abortion rights continued to wave like a red flag in her face. It was a political issue, after all. If RU486 were really about religion, then why didn't the Catholic French have a problem with it? Because, the less lovely aspects of their national character withal, the French, unlike her own compatriots, weren't committed bone deep to eternal adolescence. In America, it wasn't so much that sex and religion were in conflict as that they were two sides of the same coin: bad and good, cool and nerd; it was high school all over from sea to shining sea. Why was it so terrifying to acknowledge the world is made up of shades of grey? Susan didn't know why, but she knew that it was and that all American politics were predicated on this fear.

In the current climate, Susan could foresee only one logical conclusion to this endless tug-of-war between piety and prurience for the eternally teenaged American soul. The pious side would keep pushing the beginnings of human life further and further until they'd soon creep back to the point where thinking about sex and not having it would be considered abortion. Since it was usually the woman who was trying to prevent unwanted children, it would be the woman who, refusing sex, would face the brunt of the prosecution.

Maybe, Susan considered, this might actually make a good case for having a religion lead by a talking breast—a talking female breast. Probably not what Mam's power source had in mind, but when you give a gift, you give up the right to dictate how to use it. "Imagine beating them to the punch," she mused, "coming out with a statement that unless the man has sex with a fertile female woman for the purpose of propagation, taking Viagra is infanticide. And, wait," Susan's caffeinated brain was tripping merrily down the side roads, "if the argument against gay marriage is that marriage is a religious sacrament with the purpose of the procreation of children, then sterile people can't marry, or people who don't intend to bear children. And all couples whose children are past the age of 18 would have to divorce."

"Does this mean you're talking to me now?" Mam asked.

"I'm talking to myself," Susan said testily. She'd been enjoying herself there for a minute. "I'm thinking."

"Aloud?"

"People do that sometimes." In the old days of the roommates, she'd had more solitude than she had now. She'd lost her taste for the paper, but made a show of returning to her reading, which Mam seemed to accept as an unsociable occupation.

Locally, the MTA was in litigation with Sikh employees over their right to wear turbans at work. The reporter drew a parallel to the recent decision of the French government to ban female students from wearing headscarves in school. In both cases the ruling was described as a necessary attempt to protect the individuals from being viewed as targets for misplaced anger against terrorists.

In other stories, a member of Falun Gong had immolated himself in front of the UN, to protest imprisonment of others of his faith by the Chinese government. In Antwerp, to protest the slaughter of Tibetan monks, students had picketed the Chinese mission to a conference on trade. A reporter Susan remembered from a shared freshman English class had an article describing an upswing in travel to China thanks to perception of it as a country off the radar of religious extremists.

Susan flipped through in search of a story not connected to either terrorism or religion. She found coverage related to the First Lady's recent visit to Africa as part of a UN-lead international committee on children's rights and settled in. There was a lovely photo of Angelina Jolie smiling beatifically as Phyllis Hendron, in safari clothes, cuddled a starving baby in Niger. One of the related articles was about a panel discussion in Johannesburg on AIDS in Africa. Even there, Susan found politicized worship feeding the troubles. In speaking of the need for support—financial and otherwise—for AIDS education on her continent, a young South African activist told of the many tribal religious leaders who continued to believe and teach that AIDS was a curse and not a disease and that the only prevention was making offerings to the Gods. Without resources to spread medical information, this belief was the only information available to many people. More ghastly yet was that many who despite their devout offerings were astonished to catch the disease, were told that the way to lift the curse and be cured was to have sex with a virgin, which would purify their bodies. To insure virginity, the rape of children, even infants of little over a year of age, had become all too common.

Susan threw aside the paper in horrified disgust. The more she read, the worse mess she saw. How in good conscience could she contribute to it with yet another movement that people would follow like sheep? Crowds could not be controlled. People who wanted to be lead completely abdicated responsibility to anyone who would speak with conviction, but words corrupted so easily as they passed from mouth to mouth. Even those cults that began from the best of motives became mangled until they were unrecognizable. Whether or not he was a God, Jesus had always seemed to Susan to be a very good man, possessed of a benevolent wisdom. What would Jesus have done, she'd often wondered in reading of the Crusades, the Inquisition and the Ku Klux Klan, if he'd had an inkling of what would follow in his name? Maybe it wouldn't have mattered. Maybe she was the one thinking too much in blocks of black and white and paying too little regard to the drift of the larger shadowy mass.

What Susan really needed, what she craved, was the peace and quiet to think things through alone. As alone as she was able to be. She decided to call in sick, something she hadn't done since Mam Enterprises had begun operation. "Just a little under the weather," she told Lisa. She promised to show up in time for the Gathering and webcast, but she'd be out of the office all day.

"Seems like there's something going around," Lisa said. "Take care of yourself. If you need anything, just call."

"This is ridiculous," Mam said, when Susan had hung up, "you're absolutely fine."

"You have no idea how I feel," Susan said sharply. "I need a break."

The next logical step seemed to be to turn on the TV and surf the morning shows. That was what you did when you called in sick. Each station, big or small, provided a crew of carefully assorted smiling faces dealing a hand of stories from a similar deck. The deck had four suits, three of which were shuffled liberally. Lifestyle coverage, with its focus on home decorating hints, and auto shows and film reviews, provided the diamonds in the pack, allowing for judicious segues into advertising. Then there were the clubby local bits necessary to get viewers started on their day, the weather and traffic bulletins. The heartstrings plucked were those of the stay-at-home moms, with offerings related to weight loss, husband retention and child rearing. And, because the morning shows ran under the network news divisions, cutting the occasional grim furrow between the other segments were the bits of hard news.

Hard news was offered with the almost embarrassing politesse of a receiving line in the court of King George III. The presenters arranged themselves so as to imply respectful acknowledgement, while simultaneously moving as quickly as possible away from the eyesore and on to pleasanter orbits. As a result, the networks could point to having fulfilled their news quotas and yet the audience might come away from two hours viewing with nothing sticking that was any greater moment than how to choose a slimming pair of jeans.

The comfortable thing, particularly after reading the paper, would have been for Susan to zone out on the info-tainment, but she needed something to arrest her mind, not numb it. It was more like fishing than surfing, she thought, to flip through the channels with an eye peeled for the carefully sober mien that meant something real was about to be reported, then pause for the 30 to 50 seconds it took before once again having to flip through in search of a new feeding ground. It was the kind of fishing where you threw back most of what nibbled as being far too small. Still, she heard more than was comfortable to absorb, and everything she saw lead back to that same one place.

In Rome, the brand new Pope had come out vehemently against *Harry Potter* as an anti-Christian corrupter of young minds and souls, while in Boston, a pardon was being begged for the elderly priest convicted of abusing dozens of boys over the course of three decades. Apparently, teaching morality without sampling the Scriptures was much more dangerous than living immorally while preaching them.

A tearfully stoic couple in West Virginia assured a perky interviewer that they had no regrets for having refused to allow doctors to treat their little son's pneumonia with antibiotics. No artificial intercessions should be allowed to deflect God's will. That the state was charging them with criminal neglect in the child's death was a direct violation of their First Amendment rights. On another channel, President Hendron and Reverend Crockertt were shown at a prayer breakfast with the family of the woman who had died several months ago when her husband, after a lengthy lawsuit, had won the right to withdraw her feeding tubes. The woman's persistent and, according to the conclusive autopsy, irreversible, vegetative state had meant that only this artificial intercession had been keeping her alive. Her family and their chaplain were suing the widower for having authorized the withdrawal of the machinery, contrary to God's prohibition against the taking of life.

Susan nearly skipped past the interview with a perennially boyish actor, but paused because for once he wasn't grinning. He was haranguing—there was no other word for it—the interviewer with his religious views on psychotropic medication which were, ferociously, anti. He asserted that psychiatry itself, unlike religion, was ignoble and dangerous in the extreme. His religion in particular averred that there was no such thing as a chemical imbalance and then prescribed vitamins (implicitly, if impossibly, not chemical) to eliminate post-partum depression, bipolar disorder and any number of other conditions. It all might have been easier to at least partially credit if it hadn't been espoused with such wild-eyed frenzy.

A reporter in Gaza held a microphone to a burning-eyed woman in an orange cotton cap. She raised her voice to be heard above the background of shouting. "We will never withdraw!" she said, in an accent more Midwestern than Middle Eastern, fiercely shaking a fist at her own soldiers, who were holding a line between the angry mob and a row of houses marked for bulldozing. "God promised us this land!"

There was a jailhouse interview with the man who, the year before, had stolen a sleeping fourteen-year-old from her bedroom to make her his second wife, as God had instructed him to do. Another station had a follow-up story on the remarriage of a man whose ex-wife was in prison for life for having killed their children. An escalating chain of despondencies hadn't been offset by the treatment prescribed by their minister, a combination of serial pregnancies, home schooling the older children and pastoral counseling. Clearly they hadn't been taught about psychotropic drugs—or about vitamins.

Her final catch was a slice of a "goodbye" video made by a female suicide bomber who'd blown up a school bus in Rotterdam. She looked about 25, Susan thought, in her fatigues and headscarf, with a thin face and empty eyes. One arm cradled a rifle, while the other hand offered up a photograph of three beautiful, smiling children. As she spoke, Susan followed the subtitles that unrolled across the bottom of the screen. "I have always dreamed of being a martyr. I know that my children will be proud and that Allah will care for them." The newscaster's voiceover explained that the Saudi Arabian woman had been raped, convicted of adultery, and given the option of redeeming her family's honor by choosing to be a suicide bomber rather than suffering the traditional punishment of death by stoning.

Everywhere she looked, in print or on screen, Susan saw terrible things said and done in the name of God and holiness. It had been an exhausting two hours. She turned off the TV. "I could use some food," she said aloud. Mam made no comment.

She pulled on an old sweatshirt that completely covered Mam and walked to one of her favorite thinking places, a small, manicured park on a traffic island within view of the Hudson River. As usual, it was mostly empty and seemed, despite the urban bustle all around, still. Susan settled into one of the iron chairs, popped the top off her coffee, and took a deep inhale from the small white bakery bag before tearing off her first blissful bite of blueberry lemon angel food cake. Clapping on her headphones, in case Mam decided to grumble, she pulled out a nice cozy mystery novel where everything would have a purpose and things would come out tidy in the end.

It wasn't the penance she'd been expecting, if she'd had any inkling at all of what to expect.

That first horrible day, when Rosa had finally gotten up the courage to unburden herself in the confessional, the Father had thought she was mad. He didn't say so, not in so many words, but she'd known it by how careful his kindness was and by his leading questions. She'd told him to log onto the website that night. She'd even given him the price of a subscription as an offering.

The next morning, she came by appointment to meet him at the church. They sat side by side on a pew in the quiet shadows. She'd been ashamed to feel a slight smugness at the shock on his face. This time, he listened, and questioned, in earnest. He still didn't give her a penance, other than the rosaries she was already saying. He would be seeking guidance himself. He asked her to return the next day.

Despite her anxiety, that night was the most peaceful one Rosa had passed in nearly a month. The burden of decision had been taken from her shoulders. "Take responsibility for your actions, Rosa. There are always repercussions." For a second, Rosa though she heard Mam's voice in her ear. She waved it away like a buzzing fly. The responsibility for her Eternal Soul rested now in Father Martin's capable hands. Where it belonged.

The next morning, she prepared herself to accept whatever judgment the Father made. He had spoken, he told her in hushed tones, to those wiser than he, indeed as high the Bishop himself. They all agreed that Rosa was a gift and a blessing to the Church. She had sinned, yes. But the clouds had been lifted from her eyes. She had been pure enough to turn to God and His Son, and she would be redeemed by the service she was meant to perform on their behalf. The Church, he told her, was almost as confused as she as to the nature of Mam. She was unique in their experience. They needed to learn more, as much as possible. He didn't use the word spy, but Rosa understood that was what she was meant to do. She was instructed to return to work and to attempt to give no sign of her recent inner turmoil. She was to be an active and enthusiastic member of Mam's team, even as she had been before her doubts had begun. Each morning, she was to continue to attend services, after which she would meet with Father Martin to discuss the happenings, including the webcast, of the previous day. She was further advised to confess and take communion regularly, and to never be near Mam without wearing her gold cross.

Everyone was delighted to see her back at her desk, and so concerned about the flu they assumed had kept her home. There was something going around, Jonelle told her. It seemed Susan had stayed home much of the time for most of the same days. Rosa didn't know what that might mean, but she reported it to Father Martin the next morning. She was also able to give a full account of the tour itinerary. It wasn't like spying at all when Melissa flat out left a copy on her desk with "for Rosa" written on it in pink.

The first few days felt so peculiar, but once she'd settled into the routine, she didn't think about it anymore. Rosa began to enjoy her work again. Now that her spiritual safety was assured, she didn't have to fake her enthusiasm. It was almost like it had been in the beginning. She'd always believed in the goodness of what Mam seemed to be saying.

Thanks to Rosa's having been out sick, Susan's days of brooding made little impact on Mam Enterprises. It was simple. There was a bug. Lisa'd made sure to provide chicken soup for supper and a shrug to cover her shoulders in the overly-cooled Gathering room, but that was about it. Everyone was far too busy to notice anything unless their attention was forcibly drawn to it, and Susan wasn't much for drawing attention. She was just as glad to have it all slip by. All the reservations, all the fears, weren't going to stop things from moving forward. Susan knew that. Ironically, she thought, she'd only been trying to do what Mam advised: Whatever she was about to do, she needed to be able to look herself in the mirror and accept responsibility for having done it, even if she didn't think she had a choice. Now she was rolling along in the thick of things.

She and Mam spent most of a day trying to come up with a format for what she was learning to call (without breaking up into hysterical laughter) the "concerts." Susan had been to enough "An Evening With..." performances at the 92nd Street Y to know that bigger audiences wouldn't work the same as a Gathering. In a large crowd, you can't count on someone asking the provocative questions. They feel too exposed. Instead, you can pretty much bet money on people asking questions that are designed to prove how much they already know about the subject matter, hoping that the rest of the audience will be impressed. Ninety minutes of that would be torture.

"We need a ceremony," Mam said, unexpectedly.

It was the last thing Susan wanted. She was frankly scared of repeating the feelings that had overwhelmed her that night in the Berkshires. Mam might say she didn't preach, but Susan had begun to think that a little straightforward preaching might be preferable to crowd control via hypnotic trance. "I was thinking more along the lines that I introduce you, and then you speak for a while."

"Yes," Mam agreed. "But we also need a ceremony. That's something I've learned. People focus their energies when there's a ceremony. They listen to what they hear."

What are they listening with? Susan wondered. On the other hand, if they were calling them "concerts," she supposed the ticket holders might reasonably expect a little theatre. She sighed. "What kind of ceremony did you have in mind?"

"I have no idea," Mam said. "I thought we'd ask Alan. Isn't that his specialty?"

"Good idea." It made sense. And Alan would be over the moon. It must be an anthropologist's fantasy, creating his own ceremony. "Maybe we should ask Ziggy about that music he wanted to foist on us back when we started. Remember? The authentic third-world band from darkest Scotland?"

"Music would be good," Mam said, sounding pleased to have Susan working with her. "We had music at Beltane."

They agreed there'd have to be a little Q&A, of course. It was what they were known for. And there'd be a local audience of a few dozen people to be a Gathering at the webcasts each night. Lisa and Raju were already debating over whether to separate them from the concerts, or if attendance might be some kind of door prize for the first people to buy tickets, or who had the lucky seat numbers. This was the kind of decision Susan was glad not to be involved with. She didn't much think it mattered. The ceremony problem was passed to Alan, as Mam had suggested, and they turned their attention to other things.

People still didn't think she, or Mam, needed to be consulted every step of the way, but they liked to show what they'd accomplished and feel some pats of approval. Susan would sit in her office and people would pop in with proof sheets or color swatches for tote bags or whatever was on their front burner. Sometimes, she'd walk a half-mile to the home of the little old Romanian seamstress Jimmy had hired to work under Marta on her wardrobe for the tour. She'd also had a few outings with Raju to pick their space in New York. It had been Steffi, once again, who'd saved the day, reaching out from Arizona with information they should have known themselves—that

Broadway plays are "dark" on Mondays. If they could live with Monday nights, and deal with whatever was on the stage for whatever show was running, neither of which was a problem for them at all, they had a dozen theatres at their disposal. Susan discovered that it was thrilling to stand on the sweet spot of a Broadway theatre and imagine the velvet seats filled with upturned faces. It was as if all the thousands of performances had imbued the auditorium with a special energy that welcomed her and made her feel secure in a way conspicuously absent from an open moonlit field.

One Friday afternoon, Jack Rabb had been asked in for a meeting and Wendy brought him by to say hello before it began. He hadn't seen Susan or Mam since that fateful day in October. The dynamics were different. Then, they'd been a "thing." Now, they were a celebrity and apparently a respected one. Susan noticed the adjustment at once. Jack was almost shy as he shook her hand and he addressed Mam with a quiet gravity.

They gave Jack a tour of the offices, including the Gathering room and studio. He was clearly impressed. Better than most, Jack had a feel for how quickly it had all come together. They ended at the conference room, where the walls were thick with advertising tear sheets, program mockups and poster proofs, not to mention Raju's famous map. A rollaway bulletin board was pinned with copies of those of Jimmy's designs that Susan and Raju had approved for the various appearances, the gowns on which Ieva was sewing away, as well as a sample of the special edition Corpo Céleste bra that would soon be available. Overhead was the clothesline to which Lisa'd clipped sample merchandise; every time she walked into the room, Susan caught her hair on the tip of the official tour umbrella.

A smiling volunteer brought in a tray of beverages in official "Mamathon" mugs and sports cups, and a plate of home-baked cookies. Susan quickly picked one up and put it in her mouth. She needed comfort food. Looking around the table, she'd been struck by the understanding that, before making a single appearance, she was already at the center of a media circus. She whispered something to that effect to Wendy, who patted her hand gently and laughed. "These are your friends," she whispered back. "Wait 'til word gets out to the jackals and vultures."

Susan shuddered. She supposed she and Mam had been pretty sheltered up until now. Apart from a few smutty jokes on internet sites, there hadn't been much bad press. Wendy was right. That was going to change soon. She had to hope that the people in this room, who were there to support what Mam was doing, would be able to protect them. Wendy and Ziggy would of course, with their crews, actually be on tour every step of the way. Janet would be following from afar, as would the rep she brought from the publisher, who had a pre-sales campaign to execute. Jack, who Raju was introducing around, had been invited to join the meeting because Wendy had negotiated well, and *Duh News* would be doing a regular segment on the progress of the tour.

The arrangement was that Wendy would send them daily clips, which they would have a free hand to use—or not—as they saw fit. Jack was nervously determined to get things straight with the Mam team. The segment, which the writers had already decided to call "Mam-a-palooza," would be anchored by himself and Roger Haff. Anything would be fair game. Everyone understood the tour would become something of a running gag, but Raju felt, and Janet agreed, that it was better to be laughed at than to be ignored. What no one knew was that Jack had ambitions of his own. When Wendy'd approached with her idea, he'd seen it as the chance he'd been looking for, to upgrade the show from its frat-house humor to a sharper kind of satire that might make an impact beyond ridiculing its subjects. None of the news shows would be covering Mam's tour. She might be the story of their lifetime, but they'd be mocked for taking Her seriously. *Duh News* had nothing to lose. It was their job to not be taken seriously. How brilliant it would be if they could end up beating the news bureaus at their own game; how it would change the life of Jack Rabb.

"There'll be some rude laughs," he said earnestly, "I'm not going to pretend otherwise. But in the big picture, it'll all be good, I promise you." He radiated sincerity around the table. "I'm betting that by the end of the tour, Mam'll be the news story and the people who don't take her seriously will have become the joke."

It seemed like no time at all before they were in the studio for what would be the final webcast before hitting the road. After introducing the final caller, Melissa removed her headset and gave Susan a big thumbs up. Melissa seemed to be regarding the tour as a vacation and couldn't wait to get going. To Susan's certain knowledge, the girl had been packing and repacking for weeks. She seemed to be under the impression that there would be cowboys and movie stars along the way. It seemed improbable to Susan, but if there were any around, Melissa would surely be the one to find them.

"We're looking forward to sharing this experience with you," Mam said.

"We'll be streaming live every Monday through Thursday night from the road." That day alone, Ziggy had reminded Susan a dozen times to say this. "We're traveling across a few time zones, so be sure and check our home page for the times."

"If we're in your town," Mam added, "please come out to see us."

"And remember..." Susan said, as she always did on the air.

"Take responsibility!" Mam concluded.

The "On the Air" light went off and Ziggy started dancing in the booth, pointing elaborately downward, as if Susan needed reminding that there was a party starting downstairs.

There was no Mam-after-Cam that night. Instead, the Gathering room had been festooned with streamers and balloons, and Lisa had set out one of her famous Chinese buffets. All of Susan and Mam's friends had come. Even volunteers who didn't usually work on Thursdays made a point of being there to wish them good luck.

By the time Susan had removed her and Mam's makeup and thrown on a clean bra, the party was in full swing. She slipped through the back door and stood, half-hidden by the draperies, watching the fun. She hadn't had so much as a sip of wine yet, but her eyes misted with sentiment. The room was filled with the people who had supported her over the strangest year of her life, through situations too strange to even imagine. She swelled with love for all of them. Nearly everyone, she noticed, was wearing a new tour T-shirt. Some had already cut off the collars or sleeves. Melissa had done some particularly creative slashing and wrapping of hers. Susan could hear her asking Jimmy if she might have a career in fashion. Jack Rabb looked tempted to imply she might have other career options to explore, but the slightly uncomfortable woman he was with slipped in under his arm; Susan assumed this must be his wife.

"What are you doing in the corner, Sue?" Alan noticed her and pulled her out into the crowd.

"Being nervous," she said. "What do you think?"

"Me, too." Alan was taking vacation time to come with them as far as Telluride, to iron out any potential kinks in his ceremony. He passed her a plastic flute of some kind of wine and toasted. "Here's to it."

"I don't understand either one of you," Mam said.

"It's a human thing," Susan said.

"What is?" Lisa asked, coming up with a plateful of food.

"Nerves, babe." Alan opened his mouth, expecting Lisa to pop a dumpling between his lips. Instead, she offered the plate first to Susan who raised her eyebrows apologetically in his direction.

Lisa noticed the look. "Oh, please. Mam needs Susan to eat, don't you?"

"That's very thoughtful of you, Lisa," Mam said.

Lisa glowed as if she'd won a prize. "You're not nervous, are you Mam? You know there's nothing to be nervous about."

Raju came up behind Susan and started refilling glasses. "I think you and Mam should make a toast," he said. "Everyone's been waiting to see you."

Susan nodded. As usual, Raju was right. She took his arm and he walked her to the platform. He cleared his throat loudly until people turned and noticed them. When it was quiet enough for her to speak, he stepped aside.

"Thank you, everyone, for coming here tonight to wish us well. And for being here with us every day." Her voice started to quiver.

"Susan and I," Mam spoke up, "are very excited about the tour. Each time we start something new, something wonderful happens. We look forward to what we'll find this time, and to sharing it with all of you."

"And we know that none of this would have been possible without the love and faith and hard work of everyone in this room," Susan added quickly, raising her glass. "Here's to all of us!" Everyone cheered and hugged one another. Susan made her way down into the crowd. People milled around her, each taking their turn to come over and say a personal something to her and Mam.

"I wish I could come," Marta said when it was her turn.

It wasn't a unique comment, but she was the only person to whom Susan replied, "I wish you could, too." There was something so solid and comforting about Marta. It would have been wonderful to have her along.

"I tell you, if it wasn't for the union pension, I'd quit Corpo Céleste. But, you know how it is. A few more years, I can retire, right?" Marta gave Susan a big hug. "Now you don't worry. We went over everything, me and Jimmy, with Melissa. And Raju, he knows everything anyways. You're gonna be great, I know." She gave another big hug, then stepped back to look squarely at Mam. "And Mam, now you don't go starting something when it's time to get dressed, okay? You know that's when Susan she gets nervous and it's no time for messing with her head."

Mam laughed. "Marta, you're the only person who ever scolds me. Other than Susan, of course. We'll miss you."

"Speaking of missing," Susan said, "what happened to Rosa? She was in the office today." It seemed wrong somehow that Rosa was missing this.

Marta shrugged. "Sometimes she has to run home. I know she'd want to be here. I'll tell her you aksed for her, okay?"

160

9 – MYSTERY TOUR

Three weeks before Susan and the road crew boarded their plane for Arizona, a shockingly powerful hurricane hit the Gulf Coast, drowning swathes of Mississippi and Alabama and, by bursting the levees that held back the tides, turning New Orleans into the Lost City of Atlantis. In the aftermath of the storm, Mam's team held long and worried conferences. Should the show still go on?

As Raju explained, cancellation would not only mean immediate legal and financial ramifications, but the loss of goodwill at each cancelled venue, hurting them down the road when they'd try to reschedule. Of course, if they went through with it and people didn't show up, they might still lose their shirts (or, Lisa's point, fail to unload them).

Susan felt there was a moral issue involved. Unlike the rock and movie stars who were scheduling performances, they wouldn't be out there to raise funds for relief and repair. Would it therefore be insensitive—or worse, irresponsible—to draw the attention of caring people away from the plight of the hurricane victims?

Tara, who they'd all come to hear as the voice of the heartbeat of Values America, answered with an emphatic "No! In dark times, people seek guidance. They'll be looking everywhere. They may as well find Mam."

"We know we're better than the alternatives," was Alan's comment.

"And," Tara was always such a practical Christian, "we'll donate a percentage of the merchandising profits to a relief fund."

Not everyone was as comfortable, so they decided to put it to their audience. After all, these were the people who would—or would not—be turning out to see them.

"What happened in New Orleans was an act of God," the caller said, the one who settled it for them, his voice rich with the enthusiastic conviction of a young man who's picked out his next model car.

"I'm confused," Mam said, "by the term 'act of God.'"

"It was God's work. There was nothing we could do. We have to pray to understand and accept. And for His help in our hour of need."

"The same God you believe made a conscious decision to send the storm and wipe out those cities, that's who you turn to for rescue?" Mam seemed genuinely puzzled. "Why would you put yourselves in the power of your abuser? That makes no sense."

Whatever the young man may or may not have anticipated Mam saying, he was clearly discomfited by the image of the Deity in family court. "That's not what I meant," he mumbled. "I mean, there are reasons beyond our understanding."

"Yes, indeed," Mam agreed.

"We have to have faith and move on. It's not like the government could control a hurricane."

"True enough," Mam again concurred.

"But," Susan interrupted, "what about all those church-going men voting against the funding that would have shored up the levees a few years ago? They called it 'pork.'" By now she'd done enough broadcasts to know how to make her voice punctuate as richly as a keyboard. "And the same people said that tax cuts for the rich were 'budgetary necessities.' How come these so called 'religious conservatives' are so concerned about the spiritual health of the population that they want to dictate when and where to pray and where life begins and ends, but they considered measures that would save the lives of millions of people 'pork?'"

"They couldn't have known..." Tongue sucking against his teeth, he rummaged audibly for a reassuring sound bite. "We have to stop all this finger-pointing," he finally stammered. "We're wasting our energies trying to place blame..." Finding his confidence again, his voice rose triumphantly as he concluded, "We've had enough of the Blame Game!"

"If there is no blame," Mam considered, "then there are no mistakes. If you don't account for your actions, how do you weigh right and wrong?"

"I had a good Christian upbringing!" He sounded stunned by Mam's question. "I go to Church and bible study. I listen to wiser heads than mine."

"And they tell you to not to worry your own head about such matters, but to leave right and wrong in their hands?"

"You're confusing me." His voice quivered like an overwhelmed child's. "I only called to ask you to pray with us for the people down there."

It was Susan, to her own surprise, who replied rather sharply, "I suggest we all start praying, and pray hard. Pray that people stop pushing it all off on God and realize that God expects them to uphold their end of the deal by taking some responsible action."

The caller had been Jared Crockertt, a cellar level member of the White House staff and the nephew of the Reverend Dr. Hiram Crockertt. For the next two days and nights, Jared ran the conversation over and over in his head. He was troubled, and he didn't understand why. From the time he was a small boy, he'd been taught to meet crisis with prayer—crisis, sorrow and indecision (not to mention the pursuit of successful test results and good weather for a picnic). Jesus would provide aid, Jesus would provide solace and Jesus held all the answers. Your charge was to give yourself up to Jesus; the rest was in His hands. This was not mere theory to Jared. Even before his birth, Jesus had been there to direct the currents of his life.

Jonah Crockertt and his Cindy had been high school sweethearts, and determined to be chaste. Before shipping out to Vietnam, he'd been so very afraid. To make him forget his fears in those final hours on leave, she'd broken their vow. When she'd learned that she was pregnant, Jonah had written to his brother Hiram. On the floor beside his narrow white bed in the Seminary dorm, Hiram had prayed for guidance. The next day, at breakfast mail call, a fellow student received a package—a ring returned from a no longer fiancée who'd gone to the Devil by way of a summer internship at the New York City offices of *Mademoiselle* magazine. The distraught seminarian had hurled the ring out an open window, whence it landed in the vegetable garden. A few days later, picking beans as part of his scholarship job in the kitchens, Hiram had found it. It was a sign, he'd written to Jonah and Cindy, that God had seen their union was a true one. They were married in His sight, and so He had sent this ring in token of His blessing. Hiram sent the ring to Cindy, and made an impassioned testimony before the president of the Seminary. It was the first time that Hiram had brought himself forward; his belief in his Intercession had given him a fire that burned stronger than generations of sharecropper humility. The Reverend Doctor had been moved enough to send him to meet with a Congressman who was a member of the Board of Trustees and who, equally impressed by the impassioned young man, had pulled the necessary strings. The marriage had been performed by radio, helicopters thrumming in the distance on Jonah's end, while in back in Copper Bluff, the tearful gravid bride was supported by the aggressively beatific young man about to become her brother-in-law. Two months after that, Jared Jonah Crockertt was born. His uncle held him at the font, this time standing proxy for the infant's sponsor Congressman Jared Ludd. Not a week later, a sniper turned Jonah Crockertt into one of the final American casualties of the Vietnam conflict. He died never having even seen a picture of his son.

Uncle Hiram was the man of the family, and also the voice—and, when Jared transgressed as he often so innocently managed to do, the firm right strap-wielding hand—of God. To young Jared, his daddy was less real than Jesus (who had after all made him legitimate and the godson of a Congressman) and the uncle who commanded armies of souls in His name.

Cindy Crockertt raised her boy on an Army widow's pension which, as Hiram reminded her every Thanksgiving, was only hers to legally claim because he'd had the ear of Jesus. When Jared was six and desperately wanted a bicycle he'd seen in the Sears catalogue, she found a job as a receptionist for the dentist in town. The work was not taxing and the dentist, a funny little bald man with a foreign accent, was happy to have Jared play in the waiting room after school. Cindy enjoyed the feeling of getting a paycheck, and had begun to imagine a future in which she might train to be a hygienist and wear a white uniform. Then Hiram, who'd already started making a name for himself over in Little Rock, turned up on Memorial Day to preach at the cemetery. Picnics being nothing more than outdoor food and gossip, he'd soon found out about Cindy's job.

That night, tucked into his bed in the back room, Jared could hear the walls rumbling with his uncle's roar. Didn't Jesus provide for her in her time of need? Hadn't Hiram himself seen to it? Where was her humility? Who was she, who'd lain with a man outside of holy wedlock—even if it had been his own brother and even if Jesus in His terrible kindness had seen fit to afterwards bless that union—who was she to think she deserved more than Jesus had sent? Was she so puffed up as to think she knew better than Jesus? The boldness of her, a woman without a husband, to work alone with a man! And such a man for her to find! Didn't she know that man was a Jew? How could she risk her soul—and that of her only child—by working for a man who refused to accept Jesus as his Savior? If her son, her precious innocent son, needed a bicycle, then let him pray and if Jesus thought he deserved one, Jesus would provide it.

Cindy, who'd used up her lifetime stock of defiance in pulling Jonah down on the back seat of that borrowed Chevy, was thoroughly cowed by the Reverend Hiram. She sent Dr. Gruen a note; she couldn't bear to face him. For Jared's birthday, Jesus, through the earthly agency of the Reverend Hiram, had provided a rusted girl's Schwinn with a dented rear wheel. Cindy lived on the pension, and what hand-me-downs were sent from Little Rock, until the day she died from cancer and Jared went to dwell in the house of his uncle until college.

Lessons learned young are lessons learned well. Jared learned that when people don't wait for Jesus to provide, they make horrible mistakes that will damn them forever. He learned that the meek cannot be wise, and so must suffer in silent acceptance. He learned never to ask anyone for anything, lest it cause them to stray on his behalf, and to ask God for everything, even things that might seem to be within his own earthly powers to achieve. Because what he was or did or had was his to choose, but the Lord's to bestow. The Lord giveth, the Lord taketh away, and at times the Lord might partially giveth or withholdeth for no apparent reason. What, when and how was the Lord's prerogative, and woe betide the son of Adam who became puffed up and asked "why."

On his own, Jared would never have found Mam. He came to work one morning to find someone had left a voucher for a webcast on his desk. The giver was one of that jolly gang who'd never stopped laughing over Jared's reaction to the Janet Jackson Superbowl "wardrobe malfunction," when he'd jumped out of his seat, turned brick red, then started to hiccup violently at the three-second sight of an undraped breast. "Oh for fuck's sake, Crockertt," Chip had crowed, thumping him on the back, "it's just a tit. It's not like it's talking or something!" It had become a catchphrase around the office. "It's not like it's talking or something," the guys would laugh, when he'd hesitate to change the ink cartridges in the printer or pop the sushi in his mouth.

Sensing that the office was watching him and not wanting to be more of a joke than he already was, he'd held onto the voucher for a couple of months.

The night of his birthday, the one day of the year when he allowed himself to mourn for his Mamma, he felt especially alone and couldn't sleep. He thought perhaps the sound of a sweet woman's voice sharing the word of God might soothe his nerves, like a lullaby. He sat down at his computer and logged on. When he realized what he was watching, he was glad to be alone and unseen in the dark. It was unsettling and riveting. His stirrings were carnal and spiritual, both. He was awed and ashamed. He thought about it endlessly for weeks. He longed to log on again, but he recoiled from using his own credit card. There were files kept on such things, as well he knew. He wrestled with temptation, and ultimately, after the storm hit the Gulf, he yielded.

He never imagined calling. He'd logged on, his fingers trembling with the fear of discovery, to listen and be reassured by the miracle. It worked, better than the prayer service at the National Cathedral. It worked so well that he logged in again the following night. He began to yearn to share the calm and the hope. When Mam and Susan suggested they might be postponing their tour, he was too dismayed to wait and pray. People needed them. He was so sure of this that he acted. He called. He testified that the hurricane was an act of God, and that now was the time, more than ever, for prayer.

When they suggested that prayer might not suffice, it was a slap in the face of his bravery. His feelings were hurt. He felt like an idiot. He resented them for mocking him, and scorned their dismissal of what he held to be true. He tried to forget about Mam, but in quiet moments he would recall the miracle that She was, and needles of doubt began to prick holes in his world. His sleep and his waking hours were equally troubled. He felt too small for the burden. So he did what he'd been taught to do since childhood. He prayed. And he went to his Uncle Hiram for guidance.

On Sunday, after church, Jared went home with his aunt Sue Jean, to wait. He sat on the divan, nursing glasses of sweet tea so as not to nod off while she droned on about her bunion surgery and his cousin Isaiah's mission to Rapa Nui.

When his uncle finally arrived, he was accompanied by two senior cabinet officials, a Supreme Court Justice and a nubile blonde pop star who was in town on her way back from a USO visit to Iraq. Banished to the far end of the table, Jared had to wait through a long, overly heavy Sunday dinner until the interesting people had gone. Then, of course, it was time for the traditional Sabbath nap.

By the time they were finally tête-à-tête in Hiram's fusty study, Jared had had the conversation several times over in his mind, yet in the moment he didn't know how to begin. Compulsively humble, in his uncle's presence Jared tended towards servility. He would sit pitched forward, elbows on knees, his long body jackknifed so that his neck would bow back, ensuring that his look was ever upwards as Hiram would speak of this and that. This time, however, he folded himself slowly into the lumpy floral cushions and looked down at his hands. Hiram, blandly discoursing on the issues of the day as influenced by himself, noticed his nephew toying with his watchband and directed him to state what was on his mind.

Jared, though molded to presume his uncle's perspicacity, was caught off guard by being asked outright. "If everything is in God's hands," he blurted, "what are we responsible for?"

Hiram's eyes narrowed. "We are responsible, boy, for giving ourselves up to His plan, and praying for the grace to accept His trials as we accept His gifts."

"What if prayer isn't enough?" Jared covered his face with his hands, as if to hide from judgment. "It wasn't just that Jesus died for us on the cross," he mumbled. "He did things in life, as a man. He made things change."

Hiram stood, the lamp behind him casting a deep shadow. "Who have you been talking too?" It didn't sound like a question.

Mam sold out three nights at Mitra, and before the first in Santa Fe, they'd had to add a third Assemblage there as well. "Assemblage" is what Alan Stark had ultimately decided they ought to be called. Alan had also taken to emphasizing that they were a "discipline, not a religion". It was a bit of bolting the barn door after the horses had fled. Perhaps he was feeling the stares of those various official eyes, Roman eyes and eyes from Washington as well. Which, thanks to Wendy's deal with *Duh News*, were finding it easy to keep watch.

Coverage began the morning after the team arrived in Sedona. "Tonight," Jack said, after the last break of the night, "we launch a new segment we like to call "Mamapalooza."" An elaborate computer graphic was played in by a catchy theme, written and basement-recorded by one time New Wave icon, The Raisin d'Etre's lead singer Tash Loving, and found on YouTube by an eager *Duh News* staffer. "Over the next few weeks, *Duh News* will be airing exclusive footage of what might just be the climactic event of our times."

Roger smirked and wagged a finger. "That's right, Jack. And you know how much I love a climactic event."

"Let's just say that I don't." Jack swiveled to face camera three, over Roger's shoulder. "For anyone who's been living in a cave without Wi-Fi, the ovoid oracle, that divine diva, my own favorite American idol...Yes, Mam and her, um, associate, Susan Roth, are on the road and our own Wendy Smedstad has been embedded with her team."

Despite the tone of the introduction, there was little overtly jokey about the footage. The production team seemed to sense they were pushing the envelope enough by simply presenting this story as it unfolded.

That first night's clip showed the arrival at Mitra, looking like Homecoming Day. The big decorated tour bus followed Steffi's Land Rover with Susan, standing with one hand on the rail, waving as they rolled triumphantly under the archway. Banners (prayer flags mostly) and wind chimes stretched between the trees. People, smiling and cheering and wearing flowers, lined the road all the way to the main building where Bear, Patrick and John Robert stepped forward, beaming, resplendent and slightly self-conscious, their arms extended to bless and/or hug.

Delighted to see Mam and Susan, The Three were also aware of their new position in the world. Mam was affirming a special relationship by choosing to start her first tour here. Natural pilgrims, the Mitrans had been awed to realize that they were now slated to become a place of pilgrimage themselves.

Uri's camera ogled them with love: John Robert, bits of turquoise braided into his beard and Bear who, oiled like fine wood, had traded up to an especially white loincloth of extreme thread-count Egyptian cotton. Even Patrick, who'd always looked and smelled like he'd been washed in spring water and hung in the sunshine to dry, was wearing a caftan so crisp that it had to have been ironed. A new day was on the horizon, and they had been preparing to meet the dawn.

As Raju had decreed, thereby earning yet another nod of approbation from Marta, Susan was wearing robes of one sort or another throughout the tour. For travel and "off" days, Jimmy had provided some tunics that could be worn with jeans. Forewarned that Mam would always be in view, *Duh News* had whipped up a digitized version of the official Mam spiral logo (duly licensed), in lieu of the standard pixilated dot, to obscure what the censors wouldn't pass. To call attention to the fact that they were obliged to conceal what was effectively the face of the main character in the piece, the designers had created an entire galaxy of jarring color schemes to be used over the course of the coverage. In this first sequence, the dot was red with a lime green spiral.

"Looks like the lovely Susan had some of that famous Southwestern chil-lay for lunch," Roger remarked. "Tsk, tsk! That girl had better learn some table manners if she's going to be on national television."

"Whatever do you mean?" Jack broadly feigned surprise.

"Klocek!" Roger raised his chin to indicate he was talking to the control booth, "Can we get a close up of Messy Bessie here?" The footage froze and the shot zoomed obligingly in on Susan and The Three. The red dot screamed against Susan's pale yellow tunic. "Thank you."

"Oh, that."

"Mmmm. Shaming, isn't it?"

"Why no, Roge. Susan didn't spill anything. We did that."

"What?!" Roger blustered. "Are you telling me we deliberately smeared food products on a celebrity? Is this some new gag show we're spinning off? And if so, why wasn't I asked to host?"

"Calm down, Roge. That's not food. That's our special Mam pasty." Jack turned professorially into the camera. "Let me explain. As you know, we're not permitted to show Mam on camera—not on basic cable."

"We did once before," Roger furrowed his brow.

"Yes we did. With many disclaimers and some pretty nifty legal footwork. But we were warned afterward never *never* ever to do it again." Jack nodded gravely; so did Roger.

"Never. Ever."

"Exactly. So while we decided it was our responsibility to our viewers to provide coverage of these newsworthy proceedings, we are unable to show the main figure in the event."

"Well, she is a breast," Roger said righteously.

"Yes she is. But how can you report on a story without showing the key players? Imagine if the President were an ass." The screen showed a press conference shot of Roddo Hendron with a flower-garlanded donkey's head Photoshopped above his suit and tie. The studio audience screamed its appreciation. "Not that kind of ass," Jack said. The donkey head disappeared, to be replaced by a large pixilated blob of more or less fleshly tones. As the audience screamed louder, the press conference was succeeded by a rapid-fire montage of recent presidential newsbytes, each with fleshy pixels obscuring the head of the Leader of the Free World. "They get the point," Jack told Roger.

"The point that you're trashing our President," Roger bristled.

"The point that it's difficult to provide responsible news reportage without showing the subject you're covering. Now, as Mam herself is an image that falls under FCC regulations, our hands are tied. But we thought we owed her the respect of creating a suitable proxy to represent her throughout our coverage. We'll be seeing a lot of our Mam pasty in the days and weeks to come. And I hope that every time you see it, you'll remember that this is our only way to keep abreast of the news, and that you'll bear with us."

"Keep abreast? 'Bare' with us?" Roger rolled his eyes. "You couldn't resist, could you?"

"Roge, 'bear with us' is just an expression."

"Sure it is."

They were still bickering when the show cut to commercial. The point had been made.

Over subsequent nights, the Mam pasty became a phenomenon in its own right. Raju quickly licensed *Duh News* to use the strident patches of color on a series of white T-shirts, with "*Duh News* Presents Mamapalooza" on the back. The first run sold out before the tour made it to California, with savvy early adopters posting eBay re-sales as high as $100 a shirt.

Viewers who liked to make their own comments started posting variations on YouTube. Many of these featured the pasty superimposed over the heads of prominent politicians. The one that got the most attention began with a message on a black screen: "The following may contain images which, although disturbing to some viewers, your government thinks you have a need or right to know." The screen then dissolved into a brief montage of images pulled from network television, some real and some dramatized: bomb victims, political firing squads, a pile of severed limbs, a throat slashing, a morgue dissection and finally, some graphic close-ups of crucifixion from a notorious filming of the Christ story. From the nails being hammered into flesh and bone, the screen faded back to black and another simple white message appeared: "Your government thinks this is too much for you to handle." The silent footage must have come from a tourist walking along the Plaza in Santa Fe with his video camera. It was a cool day and Susan and Lisa were wrapped in shawls as they were noticed shopping for jewelry at the Indian Portal. Susan knelt to discuss a bracelet with the Navaho artist, who apparently recognized her and pointed to her chest. Susan nodded and opened her wrap. The camera caught Mam, gilded with sunbeams and the grave smiles of both Susan and the artist as they all spoke. The filmmaker froze that image and stamped a pasty over Mam, to the accompaniment of a well-known two-note coda from a long-running legal drama series. A final message displayed immediately over Susan's head: "What are they afraid of?"

Susan didn't know about YouTube. Nor did she know that Hazel wasn't the only one with a Mam-related blog. A dozen or so of the people who attended the Sedona Assemblages were featuring the experience on their MySpace or Facebook pages. She was a little old to think of looking at these sites, and those on her team who fell within the appropriate demographics were far too busy with the tour to do much online beyond checking their own e-mail. Apart from Wendy, they never even switched on *Dun News*.

In Santa Fe, they were, therefore, astonished to find the audience already familiar with the details of Alan's ceremony. When Mam began to speak of the need to not merely look but to see and acknowledge one another, there was a rustling in the audience of bodies and belongings shifting in preparation. Before she could ask them to stand, they were already mostly on their feet, and turning face to meet face. "You are not the only person on the planet," Mam began.

"I am as entitled to life as you are," they told each other, in unison with Susan rather than following her lead. "What you do affects me. Acknowledge my existence, as I acknowledge yours."

The whole city seemed to know Susan by sight. When she tried to explore the old town on their first "off" day, Susan was surrounded wherever she went. When one of the jewelers at the Portal invited her to visit his Pueblo the following day, she jumped at the chance for peace and quiet as much as the adventure. Even Uri wasn't permitted to film her on the Reservation, as her visit was considered a spiritual event. And for her private meeting with Elders of five of the Eight Northern Pueblos, only Alan accompanied her, and he only after relentless begging and a solemn vow never to write so much as a syllable about the experience.

Discretion was also necessary the next day, when they made their pilgrimage to El Santuario de Chimayo, a small adobe church also known as the Lourdes of America. Melissa, who'd been having her own adventures in town, showed up at breakfast, tousled and yawning, to propose it. "I promised Marta I'd get her some dirt," she said, "for her sister's niece who has lupus." Alan, who was having a glorious time in the Southwest, was quick to second the idea. Not everyone was so enthusiastic about driving 40 minutes into the mountains to see a hole in the ground with magic dirt, but Mam continued to be fascinated by certified miracles and some of the vortex sites she'd seen in Sedona had given Wendy an interest in researching faith healing in the US, so the four of them set off alone. Susan insisted that she could not walk into a church half exposed and borrowed one of Wendy's shirts to button over Mam before they left the car.

They walked from the parking lot to the church, past a series of shrines that seemed to have sprouted from faith and gratitude. Susan took a deep breath. There was a sense of calm and, yes, of healing in the air.

"There's something special in this place," Wendy said, surprised. "I can't put my finger on it but it's something."

"Maybe just the result of a couple of hundred years of intense prayer," Alan suggested. "You get that, you know. The energy builds up."

"Or maybe it was always here," Susan said quietly. "And that's why people came to pray."

"Good girl," Mam whispered into the pocket of Wendy's borrowed shirt.

As they reached the walls of the church, a loudspeaker broke the mountain calm, a carefully round baritone broadcasting from inside. They'd arrived mid-Mass.

After a slow circuit of the courtyard and its homely memorials, they took a respectful look through the door to the sanctuary. The benches were surprisingly full for a weekday morning. They watched the celebrants stand to face the carved painted altar with arms outstretched to mirror those of the red-faced white-haired priest. Feeling like intruders, they left the vestibule in silence.

Wendy noticed a few people coming out of a door in the side of the building. Two of them carried ziplock bags of what seemed to be dirt. "I believe you said you needed dirt," she said to Melissa.

The door pushed open into a cool, dim adobe room, crowed enough that people could only stand two abreast. A row of crutches hung by the door, some signed and dated, garnished with a cast or two and a single neck brace. There were numerous letters of thanks and a flurry of prayer cards. Glass shadowboxes held wax saints in silk robes, a crucifix blooming with a rose. Everywhere you looked there were pictures: photos of babies, often with their little worn shoes hanging by; photos of smiling children, of radiant brides; pictures of saints made with sequins or glitter, or embroidered with bright threads; the stations of the cross carved in wood. And clusters of milagros and rosaries hung from the beams and burst from every corner.

The alcove containing the miraculous dirt was reached through a door set into the rear wall of the room. Nearby, a low archway in the long wall looked onto the altar, where the priest was invoking the miracle of transubstantiation. He placed odd stresses on the syllables of the formula "this is MY body...this is MY blood." From what Susan had been told of Jesus, it sounded improbably egocentric.

Melissa cleared her throat nervously. "Would you go in with me?" she whispered. The room, or perhaps the proximity of the priest, was making her nervous. Susan smiled and squeezed her hand.

"Of course we will," Mam said, just as a young couple exited from the dirt room. The young man held a baby food jar full of reddish brown dirt. The young woman, clutching his arm, noticed Susan and stopped. She tugged her husband's sleeve and pointed.

Susan smiled and pushed Melissa past them through the door into a small cell, with a window looking out towards the mountains. On the thick adobe windowsill stood a few empty prayer candle glasses. Someone had tucked an index card between them: "use for dirt." In the center of the floor was the dirt itself, loose New Mexico soil filling a depression less than a foot across, stuck with a child's red beach shovel. One or two saints hung within, looking benevolently down, and an old wooden signboard, hand-lettered, with a prose poem tribute written by a blind man. Reading it, Susan felt her own eyes welling with tears. There was something so innocent about it all.

Melissa knelt to pick up the shovel and fill the small tin box Marta had given her. "Wow," she said when she stood back up.

"Wow," Susan agreed.

"There's something here," Mam murmured. "Yes."

The young couple was waiting outside the building. They stared as Susan walked by, then bent their heads together to whisper.

"What do you think that's about?" Melissa asked.

"They recognized me," Susan shrugged.

"Maybe they're wondering if the dirt 'cured' you of me," Mam suggested.

"Well, that would make my mother happy. She still thinks you're a tumor."

As they turned onto the path to the parking lot, the young woman broke away from her husband and ran up to them. Close up, her skin was like waxed paper and no hair escaped from her headscarf. She stared with pleading eyes.

"You're her," she breathed. She reached a hand towards the shirt pocket. "Please..." It was a statement, not a question.

Susan opened the shirt. "Bless you, my dear," said Mam. The young woman extended a tremulous finger and touched her gently. She began to cry. So did Susan, who hugged her before she ran away.

"I thought you don't do healings," Melissa sniffed.

"We don't," Mam said. "But something here might. And she needs to believe in miracles to make it happen. I'm the miracle she can believe."

"What did we miss," Wendy asked as she and Alan caught up with them.

"I am constantly awed by the power of human belief," Mam said.

"It's pretty amazing, isn't it?" Alan said happily.

"It's terrifying," Mam replied. "All that need. Button me up, Susan." She was silent for several hours after that.

As they rolled along, Uri captured general coverage of the scenic route—not just the red and ochre and cerulean and sage that were the painter's palette of the land and sky, but the stratified human history that was piled on top. He didn't know if Wendy would ever want to use any of this in the documentary, but he couldn't keep his eyes off the road. In Colorado, he became particularly fascinated by the ubiquity of gun shops in the tiny strip malls scattered along the highways. Most intriguing of all were the gas stations, liquor stores and pharmacies that advertised firearms for sale as an apparent sideline.

Somewhere outside Durango, Alan asked to make a pit stop for ibuprofen and the sign above the store read "Drugs/Guns." It was too good for Uri to miss. He jumped up to follow, his camera at the ready, chomping at the bit to finally get a lens on the other side of one of these doors. He fantasized a pharmacy counter with blister packs of bullets hanging on hooks right next to the diabetes strips and home pregnancy tests. The automatic doors parted. As he was about to walk through, he took a quick look back. The bus, with the big pink and black "Mamathon: Mam On Tour" banner, sat alone on the tarmac. Looming in the distance, the craggy mountains were already, in late September, dusted with snow. Susan and some of the others were taking advantage of the stop to stretch their legs. It was a good transition shot to have in the can for later; it would be foolish to miss it. He adjusted his focus. Out of the corner of his ear, he heard a motorcycle drawing close. He turned toward the sound, just as an enormous Hog pulled into the lot.

"Maybe we should just send our gals over there," Roger said a few nights later, following a *Duh News* piece on Sunni/Shi'ite clashes in Iraq. "Then we could say 'lo! The mountain comes to Mohammed.'"

"Painful segue, Roge," Jack shook his head sadly. "But since you brought it up, the ladies are indeed moving mountains."

An enormous black motorcycle was spotted, pulling into the parking lot. A dark burly figure jumped off and rushed, across Uri's frame, straight towards the Mam tour bus. While it looked hairy enough to be a small bear, it was a man in jeans and a leather vest. He stopped dead in front of Susan and fell to his knees. The camera zoomed in. Under his nail-head-studded vest was a baby blue Mam slogan T-shirt: "Evil Done in the Name of God is Still Evil." Under the sweaty tooled leather band that held back his hair, his eyes were streaming tears. Susan leaned down to hear as he whispered something. Uri was too far away and no one was miked, so only Susan ever knew what he'd said, but whatever it was made her sit down beside him and he leaned against her to talk to Mam. Shot from that distance, once the Mam-dot had been digitized where it had to go, the footage on *Duh News* seemed to show a biker nursing like a baby.

"And that," said Jack, "is our Mam-a-palooza byte of the night."

"And what a bite it was," said Roger. "Ouch!"

In the rectory in Brooklyn, Father Martin shook his head. His mouth set grim as he noted the episode in his diary: immodesty, mendacity, a flirtation with thaumaturgy and now the blatant blasphemy of this mocking Madonna and child. This false messiah and Her people were treading on some very dangerous ground indeed. Following protocol, he pasted the entry into an e-mail and ran it through an encryption program before sending off to a numbered box @vatican.org.

Father might have been more troubled still if he'd known of the footage that had never, and would never, make it onto comedy TV. If he'd stopped being affronted long enough to think, he'd realize that the images he was seeing, cut or twisted for an easy, possibly nasty, laugh, were merely insulting to him. There was nothing dangerous in them, nothing that the Church hadn't risen above time and time again over the course of two millennia. What might be truly insidious, were they to be shown, were the moments of genuine bliss and harmony that surrounded Mam in her progress through the American West.

Nobody knew what the biker had whispered, but after his conversation with Mam, he'd been thrilled to sit down with Wendy and the crew for a few minutes and talk openly about the change that come into his life since he'd first heard Mam online, and to detail why he'd driven 300 miles on his Harley for the chance to see her in person in Telluride. He was not the first whose experience of Mam made him eager to get something off his own chest, but he was one of a growing number who were doing it on camera.

Back in Sedona, Wendy thought it would be good to have some footage of people arriving for the first Assemblage. Not long after lunch, she and her team had wandered down the road to do some test shots by the entry to the Mitra Center. Crossing under the archway, Wendy was confounded by the sight of dozens of people sprawled on the grass, chatting or dozing. Judging by the food wrappers and occasional sleeping bag, some appeared to have been waiting there for hours.

"Who are all these people?" she wondered aloud.

A woman looked up from the blanket where she was cuddling with two gently grubby sleepy children. "Haven't you heard the good news about Mam?" she called to Wendy with a smile.

Wendy walked over to her, signaling for Uri and Baskar to follow. "Are all of you here for Mam?" she asked. "The Assemblage doesn't start 'til seven thirty."

"And it's all sold out," the woman nodded sadly. "We're hoping for some cancellations."

"All these people? That's what you're all doing?"

"So far's I know," the woman looked toward the man behind her, who gestured agreement from his folding bleacher seat.

"I waited 'til I had someone to cover my shift," he said. "By then everything was gone, even for that one extra one they added. But I figured, what the hell. I already had the shift covered, so I might as well give it a shot."

The elderly couple just ahead was listening from their lawn chairs. The husband nodded enthusiastically.

"Exactly," he said. "Nothing ventured, right? Usually we don't come down for another few weeks—we snowbird here from Michigan—but when we heard Mam was going to be here, Shirl said, 'Let's go early.' So we hopped on a plane."

"Just like that?" They weren't Uri's idea of spontaneous adventurers.

"Warren's a heart transplant survivor," Shirl explained. "We don't do a lot of planning in advance. Just live in the moment."

"The condo's ours so it doesn't matter," he added.

"But we never thought there'd be so many people," Shirl sighed.

"What about you?" Wendy sat down on the grass near the first woman's blanket. "Spur of the moment decision?"

"Kinda," she shrugged. "Oh, I found out about Mam way back, in the beginning. I listen to all the webcasts and everything. But when they announced the tour, the closest She was coming to where I live was LA. I'm in Chula Vista? So I never figured on seeing Her in person."

"What changed your mind?" Wendy smiled encouragingly.

"I can't say as it was my mind that really changed. Maybe more like my spirit. My husband...he's not the easiest man going, let's say." She gave a sidelong glance at her children, who seemed to be asleep. "He was always kind of a bad boy, but never mean. Not at first, not to me. I can't rightly remember when everything started being my fault, but it did. Did it ever." Once she'd started, it seemed she couldn't stop. Her burdens unrolled like a red carpet, laying down year after painful year of escalating anger and abuse. "Anyways," she ultimately said. "I never thought of myself as the kind that would take it," she was still surprised, "but it kept on happening and I kept thinking maybe it was something I did or shoulda done. Until this friend called me. 'Gail,' she said, 'this is something you just gotta see.' That first night, when I was listening to Mam online, She said something about how when they say 'save yourself' it doesn't mean by thinking that some other power's gonna save you. That really stuck in my head for like days after. We were always Christians and being saved was everything. I kept listening in and there was more about, well, responsibility, and dignity and things that just made good sense. I can't say why when Mam said things they hit me like they did, like something new. I've been going to Church my whole life..." Gail gave a sudden laugh. "Every one of them had some man telling me what do to," she continued. "And always his reason for being able to do that was some book that was written hundreds of years ago by some other man. Going back to like, no disrespect, Adam. Maybe it's gonna sound silly to you but I felt like, 'Alright! It's about time someone was in charge who looked like me!'" The woman had a great face, all bone and deep-set eyes that crinkled happily as she squinted up into the sun and Uri's lens. "I knew I wasn't gonna take it anymore. The next time Kev...my husband...started picking on me, like he would every time before, I just stood my ground. I even asked him to take a listen in to what Mam was saying. But a course he wouldn't. He said 'I don't see why I have to listen to some tit!' So I said, 'Why the heck not? I've been pushed around by a prick these last ten years!' Oh yeah, he went to beat the daylights out of me for that one," she said, grimly. "But not this time. I jammed my knee up into his business and while he was doubled over, I hit him over the head with the first thing I could reach, which happened to be the Yellow Pages. Didn't do any damage, but it shocked him so much that he just sat there on the floor staring up at me and crying like a baby. Then I told him I was leaving him, loaded the kids in the car and took off. That was two days ago. I'm heading for my cousin's, in Dallas; he doesn't mix with her. I was just outside Tucson when I saw a road sign for Sedona and thought well heck why not?! So I turned around."

Gail wouldn't sign a release. She was worried her husband might see something or someone might and tell him. But several of the others were happy to. Wendy got hold of Patrick, who let everyone move onto the lawns near where the stage had been set up, and arranged some speakers so they could at least hear the Assemblage. She also brought Susan over, so that Gail and the others got to meet Mam face to face.

After that, Wendy made sure to go out with her crew before every Assemblage and see if anyone wanted to talk. There weren't enough hours in the day for everyone to meet Mam, but she helped Melissa design a kind of lottery so that a dozen ticket holders at each performance would have a private fifteen minutes the next day. She sensed that it would literally be the heart and soul of the ultimate documentary, these testimonials being offered up by the seekers who crossed Mam's path.

What Mam said moved people to action, sometimes to making major changes in their lives. It wasn't that she was saying anything revolutionary. Over the months, Wendy had often found herself jawing with others who'd had upbringings equivalently traditional to her own. It was always with a sense of wonder that they'd reflected that nothing Mam said was any different than what they'd been raised to believe. It all boiled down to the Golden Rule and all that, the same old basic stuff they'd grown up hearing. Hearing but not heeding, since considering the repercussions of your actions could definitely get in the way of realizing your personal goals and visualizing your success. In a culture where loudly proclaiming your faith and parading your churchgoing habits was enough to excuse you from the rigors of actually practicing the tenants so inconvenient for success or comfort, the message dwindled to the point of irrelevancy. But when Mam said these things, they became important again. The message sounded fresh and inspiring, as though it maybe could change even today's world.

"It's because she's miraculous," said a young man on his way into one of the Telluride Assemblages. "She could tell you anything and you'd believe it. But she doesn't. She uses all that magic to tell you just this really simple stuff. So it must be super true and major important."

It was just as well that Alan and Lisa said goodbye in Colorado. Beyond her usual obsession with the merchandizing booths, Lisa had noticed several women walking around in T-shirts with holes hacked out of the breast area and started a blazing battle with Raju about how she'd been right all along to want to make a shirt with a sheer panel, a decision she immediately began to set right on a conference call with Jimmy and the factory in Puerto Rico. As if there weren't tension enough, she'd also become paranoid, swearing again and again that a blue SUV had been tailing them since somewhere just outside Abiquiú. It was a relief to kiss her goodbye before she got on Susan's absolutely last nerve.

Susan's nerves had become an endangered species. They'd been on tour for less than a month, and already she was tired of it all. She didn't know how they did it, those musicians who spent a year or more on the road like this. The sameness of the highways and pit stops, the unloading and setting up and knocking down, the packed assemblies of rapt strangers chanting the same words and clamoring to share the same unique insights, and the omnipresence of her own team 24/7, it all brought on a feeling of suspended animation. But as numbing as it was, the monotony of touring wasn't getting to her as much as the exposure.

At home, she'd managed to get used to celebrity at a remove. In the office, she and Mam were part of the family, even as they lead it. The people who came to the Gatherings there, well they came for a while and then they left, and while they were there they felt like part of the family too, because they'd come to the house. The webcast callers were voices, reassuringly distant voices. *Duh News* and the occasional other media coverage seemed to be about someone else; she could easily tune them out. At home, Susan didn't need to lock herself in the apartment to be offstage. When Susan wasn't in the office, she could throw something over Mam and get on a subway, or hike a few miles through the city and no one ever gave her a second glance. She could go shopping, duck into a movie, check out an exhibit at the Met, live the invisible life she'd always lived, except for Mam's running sotto-voce commentary and a disconcertingly robust bank balance. On tour, there was no "out of office." Wherever they went, whatever she did, she was on public view with a telephoto lens pointed down at her and a follow spot making sure no one could miss it, and all eyes turned to stare. To think that not so long ago she'd raged at being invisible. What was that old curse, "beware of what you wish for, for fear you might get it."

She could hardly wait for it to be over. Seattle, which she'd always looked forward to exploring, was a blur because she was too exhausted. The only time she ventured out was the night Janet arrived and arranged to meet at a restaurant of impeccable casual-elegance in a chic part of town.

Susan imagined Janet must have a whole address book of such places. She visualized them dotting a nighttime map of the world like stars, a network of culinary jewels. She looked around, admiring the warmth of the room and the chicté of the menu and couldn't help but reflect that it was not so long ago that she might have saved for a couple of months to eat in a such a restaurant and not have been able to get a reservation. Now she and her party were seated at what the hostess had assured them was the very best table and Raju was in discussion with a sommelier, approving the preordered champagne. It was lovely, and she felt a small pang that she was beginning to take it all for granted.

Janet reached for the uncharacteristic tote bag she'd been carrying and then refused to check. "Voila!" she trilled. "Your firstborn has been delivered!" She handed each of them a pristine copy of *Off My Chest*, hot off the presses.

In the two seconds it took for her to adjust her focus, Susan went from joy to dismay. "I don't believe it!"

"What is it?" Mam whispered discreetly. She, too, was needing a night off.

"They've covered you up," Susan whispered back.

The jacket photo on *Off My Chest* featured Susan in one of her most dignified robes, carefully selected for the purpose by the team. The legend "by Susan Roth, with Mam" had been strategically placed to obscure Mam.

"What chicken shits!" Wendy scoffed.

"I did my best," Janet shrugged philosophically. "Look at it this way. Now they can't stop us from selling it at Walmart."

"Ladies," Raju lifted his glass, "this deserves a toast!"

Janet agreed. "To Susan and Mam! Through the roof." They clinked and sipped. "Oregon," Janet noted Raju's choice of wine approvingly. "Not bad."

"One more," Raju stopped them from setting down their glasses. "To Susan Roth, published author. At last."

Without warning, Susan's eyes puddled over. His gleeful smile had flashed her back to Harrison Levy's workshop. So much had happened since that she'd almost missed the moment she'd been working towards all her life. Raju reached across and gave her hand a firm squeeze. "You did it, girl."

"Maybe if it does well, Janet'll publish one of my novels," she said. It was always good to try and put things in perspective.

"It's not just Walmart you know." Wendy, for whom Susan didn't exist prior to Mam, was looking at Janet with great respect. "With this cover, there'll be no problem holding it up on the talk shows."

"Oh yeah," Susan shook her head. "I can see it now. Me and Mam with Oprah."

"It depends if she can outbid Katie, Diane and Pearl," Janet said coolly.

"Barbara's dropped out of the bidding?" Wendy asked.

"Very funny," Susan said.

Raju nodded at Janet. "Tara's right. The woman really hasn't got a clue."

"People are following this tour in a big way, my dear," Janet wasn't very good at explaining without being patronizing. "Mainstream, not just your usual run of congregants. Wendy's little amuse bouches on *Duh News* are water cooler talk—Do they still say 'water cooler,' I wonder? They must."

"Does it matter?" Susan asked. "And don't call them 'congregants.'"

"You're the writer, find me a better word," Janet breezed along. "The other night, some socialite had a wardrobe malfunction at a hurricane relief fundraiser and *Woman's Wear* reported it as a 'Mam Moment.' And *Vanity Fair's* not only asking for an interview, but they're talking Annie Leibovitz, possibly a cover."

"The webcasts are through the roof. And we can hardly keep up with orders. Lisa's actually got a legitimate reason to be..." Raju thought for a moment, "well, Lisa. Oh, FYI, we've sewn up pay-per-view rights to the Assemblage at the Ahmanson."

"Melissa spotted a rumor that Madonna wants to meet you," Wendy added. "They say she's planning an 'Amazonia' tour, where all her costumes will bare one breast." There was a wicked laugh, which seemed to come from Mam.

"First, of course," Janet casually dipped her bread in the olive oil and sprinkled it with red Hawaiian sea salt, "there's one other tiny little matter we'll need to deal with before you leave San Francisco."

Raju took her hand again, this time with almost parental concern. "We've got a doctor's appointment," he said. Susan looked at him, confused. Was he not feeling well? Was something wrong?

"Stanford Medical Center," Janet explained. "With such widespread coverage, there was bound to be some allegation of fraud. We decided to take command of the situation, invite the experts in and get it on the record that we have nothing to hide. Best to nip things in the bud, don't you think? Only sensible. Plus," she grinned, "the publicity'll be a great kickoff for the book."

Susan felt as if someone had smacked her across the face. The excitement of finally seeing her name on the spine of a book completely disappeared. The food on her plate could have been poached egg whites on cardboard, for all she tasted it. The rest of the evening, which should have been an enjoyable break, went by like a slideshow of Purgatory.

"I don't know what you're worried about," Mam said, when Susan couldn't sleep that night. "There's no fraud for them to prove. And it's me they'll be examining, not you."

Yeah, Susan thought. Nothing to do with me at all. Look what happened the last time I went to a doctor.

It was unreasonable, but the very idea of an examination made her think of losing Mam and the possibility terrified her. Naturally, it had been difficult at first to accept the phenomenon of Mam. What never occurred to anyone else was that, after years of solitary life, it had been just as hard for Susan to adjust to the simple intrusiveness of a shared life. From the time the alarm went off until she slipped asleep at night, there was always another person—because she did always think of Mam as a person—with her. What she ate or drank, Mam ate or drank. If she whispered under her breath, Mam heard. Sometimes she thought Mam could even read her mind. She never knew whether Mam slept, but if so it was when she did, and she was certain that when she didn't feel well, Mam too was bothered. Gradually, however, this had become normal to Susan, and she'd even begun to enjoy having this "other" who shared everything. In more ways than the most obvious, Mam was a part of her now. Even if they never lead another Assemblage or hosted another Gathering, even if she buttoned Mam under a shirt and had to be an office temp to pay the rent, there was something in her life that was twice what it had been before. She wondered if this was how conjoined twins felt. Probably not. If something happened to make Mam go away, she'd still physically be fine, or at least she thought she would. But who would she be if her other half were to go away? What would she do without Mam?

The appointment at Stanford had been set for the day after the final San Francisco Assemblage and a dread hung over Susan throughout the week. After sharing Mam with strangers hundreds of times, she found herself the victim of a paralyzing stage fright. Raju and Melissa had to coax her into her robes, and Mam herself had to do considerable cajoling to get Susan to uncross her protecting arms when they walked out on the stage. Once an

Assemblage was underway, she'd detach herself and drift worlds away, only to snap back at some point in the proceedings and nearly lose her balance from the sudden disorientation. The webcasts that she'd come to enjoy so much over the year were occasions for alternating detachment and impatience as she longed to just get into bed, curve her body protectively around Mam and pull the blankets over her head. They tried to talk it over, with Mam saying all the logical things. The exam was an excellent idea, something that would only help the book and their work. They should have thought of it themselves and done it months ago. Being looked at by doctors wasn't going to make her disappear any more than being looked at by thousands of people. And what if she did go away as mysteriously as she'd arrived? Susan had managed to live a life before there was Mam and was bound to find herself able to do even better after (an argument Susan found the opposite of consoling). The warm, wise common sense that made open windows out of closed doors for all Mam's other adherents bounced off Susan like white noise, a classic case of the shoemaker's child going barefoot. With more reason than anyone else in the world to believe in the solid reality of Mam, Susan felt the last year was a fragile dream that could shatter in an instant. Now that she knew what it was like to share her life with Mam, how could she live without Her? Her stomach lurched at the thought. She was grieving for something she hadn't lost.

"Don't go borrowing trouble," was Tara's brisk response when she arrived from New York to accompany them to Stanford. "That's what my Gran always said. That and don't go crying over spilt milk."

"Don't worry, be happy," Susan said glumly. "Thanks for the platitudes. Makes all the difference."

"It makes sense." Tara was too cranky from the plane ride to play nursemaid. In any case, she was arguably the least imaginative member of the team and honestly couldn't empathize with Susan's fears. "You don't worry before something happens, because it might not. And there's no point in worrying about it after, because what's done is done. Period. Whatever will be will be, so just give yourself up to it."

That didn't quell Susan's fears, but it made her keep them to herself the next day. She sat silently and watched the highway roll by, only Mam aware of her heart as it hammered, over and over again, "Give it up, give it up, give it up." When they arrived at the hospital, Susan tried to shake the sense of déjà vu as she let Raju and Tara lead her through the maze of corridors.

It was a very bright white room in a part of the hospital that had eschewed clinically-tested reassuring colors. Few patients ever set foot in this part of the facility and those who did were not customarily conscious. The pack of doctors in lab coats carried tablet laptops in which they'd begun to make notes the moment they'd filed into the room.

The focus of everyone's attention, Susan sat on an examination table wearing jeans and a hospital gown they'd tied backwards. Dr. Snyder, who Susan had begged to fly in from New York, held her hand while the senior research physician, who hardly seemed forty, administered a local anesthetic. The medical center had balked at a film crew, but Raju and Janet had held firm: This day was for the public record or not at all. Wendy had Uri and Baskar recording every minute.

The senior physician placed a tongue depressor on Susan's tongue and shined a light down her throat. Her gag reflex, usually extreme, seemed to have been suppressed. He nodded his satisfaction to the room, then turned to her with a thin veneer of joviality.

"Ms. Roth? Have you anything to say?"

Susan opened her mouth to say something snarky and realized she couldn't make a sound. Her heart leaped out of her chest.

Dr. Snyder felt the pulse shoot up and shook her head. "It's alright, Susan," she said. "The paralysis will only last fifteen minutes."

"Excellent." The chief opened the hospital gown, and the rest of the doctors moved in closer to get a good look at Mam. Mam twitched. The chief did a double-take and most of the other doctors, gasping, took a step back.

"Well, I hope you're all satisfied," Mam said. "Let's get this over with before Susan has a heart attack. Questions, please?"

Being doctors of medicine rather than philosophy, they chose instead to lower an endoscope down Susan's throat to eliminate any possibility of a micro-speaker or mutated voice box. Susan was torn between the fascination of staring at her own larynx on the monitor and the horror of knowing that a cable she couldn't feel was snaking around her body. Mam kept up a steady stream of commentary, which seemed to annoy the doctors, as if she weren't the very phenomenon they were supposed to be exploring.

While Susan was still voiceless, a mammogram was performed, providing Mam with the opportunity to offer some constructive criticism as to technique, which caused an outbreak of snickering among the women in the room. This was followed by an MRI and a pair of cutting-edge scanning procedures that even some of the researchers had not yet experienced.

After several hours, they admitted that they could find no biological explanation for Mam (one doctor even hinted darkly that Susan should consider leaving her body to science), nor evidence of implanted technology. Raju had prepared a document that, while of dubious legal value, certified their findings and, by adductive reasoning and a slash of Occam's Razor, attested to Mam's unique, miraculous nature. This was duly signed by all present and witnessed by the cameras as well as by a research secretary who was a notary public, and within 24 hours it had appeared on no less than 30 websites, only one of which was authorized.

This seemed a trigger for the doctors to switch out of research mode and revert to the somewhat awkward men and women they were when they hung up their lab coats. They filed out embarrassedly past a hoarse and trembling Susan, who sat carefully sipping lukewarm chamomile tea. There was much handshaking, some headshaking and even one or two mumbled apologies, though it was never clear if they were apologizing to Susan or to Mam, and in either case, if the apology was for doubt or discomfort. The only elderly man lingered behind. He hadn't said a word during the proceedings, but had slipped in at the last minute and been given a respectful berth by the others. Now he sat beside Susan. "They don't know what to make of this," he said. "Their purpose in life is to find answers and you, you only make more questions." Unable to say anything, she pointed to her throat and shrugged and he patted her hand in what she felt was a rather comforting grandfatherly way. There was something about him that made her think of a sad old dog.

Mam spoke up. "Not every question has an answer."

He bent his head to speak directly to Mam. "This I know. A person wants to try, because for some questions to have no answer is not acceptable. But your question is part of the Great Answer. I stopped believing in that when I was young and angry to think I would soon die. I didn't die then. Now it gives me some hope, to know that the question, at least, is real." He stood up slowly. "Sehr gut! An old man thanks you." As he was about to leave, he paused to rest a hand gently on Susan's head. "And you, you should live a long and happy life," he said. She tried to thank him, but it came out in a croak and then he'd gone.

Dr. Snyder passed him at the door on her way back in and nodded to him shyly. "What did Zendtman have to say to you?" she was curious to know. Susan looked up questioningly and pointed to where the man had been. "Isaac Zendtman. Wrote the book on biochemistry. He really did; it has his picture on the back. That's how I knew his face the moment he walked in. I must have thrown it at the wall twice a day my junior year of college. We used to call it 'sandman' because it was so hard to stay awake. I didn't know he was still alive." Susan shrugged. "I know, obviously he is," Dr. Snyder continued, with that amazing facility that some doctors and dentists have for inferring what the patient was trying to say. "He must be emeritus here and have heard about this. Still, it's way out of his field. Not that you're really in anyone's field," she laughed. "But who knows what goes on in the mind of a genius."

Tara popped her head in the door. "Are you guys coming?" Dr. Snyder was taking the bus with them to Los Angeles so that she could go over the footage with Wendy on the way and answer any questions about procedures or equipment. "I'm starving. Are you going to be able to eat?"

Susan nodded firmly, Mam said, "She'd better" and Dr. Snyder said "As long as it's soft," all at the same time.

"Okay then," Tara said brightly. "Let's hit the road. Melissa packed us a picnic, so we won't have to eat hospital food. Oh, and she said I should give you this when it was all over." Tara pulled a folded note from her pocket and handed it to Susan.

Melissa wasn't taking the bus to LA but would be flying down to meet them after the weekend. Melissa'd been having her fun throughout the trip, but no one had expected her to find a straight man in San Francisco. "Trust me," she'd assured them. In the end, though, it was thanks to Mam that she'd been able to do the finding. Felicity Barnstock's brother, Will, had arranged to meet them before the first Bay Area Assemblage. After meeting Mam for himself, he'd offered to give them a tour of Skywalker Ranch and even set up a meeting with the prosthetics specialists there to certify that Mam wasn't a result of any of their technology. Will himself wasn't Melissa's idea of "boyfriend material," but there had been an abundance of men on site; none of the team was certain which one of these had been the lucky winner.

Thinking of Melissa enjoying her weekend made Susan think about Will. The makeup men and techno geeks, though no doubt as important a certifying force as the Stamford medicos, had taken most of the thrill out of touring Skywalker. Will, who'd several times taken her hand in his large, warm one, had redeemed the day. Tall, lean Will had grey eyes that seemed to be on a quest. He was affable, with a knack for making trenchant observations, and there was something oddly reassuring about him. There was no question that eighteen months ago, Will Barnstock would have been *Susan's* idea of "boyfriend material," but she didn't allow herself to have those kinds of thoughts any more. The complications were too great to even imagine. It was the trade-off; there always had to be one.

Susan unfolded Melissa's note. "Tell Tara she can say 'I told you so.' :D" She laughed painfully and passed the note to Tara.

Tara grinned. "Don't worry, be happy! That's all I want to say. Now let's go eat."

Los Angeles was good for everyone. They returned the bus and checked into a hotel in Santa Monica that was good enough (though Tara had drawn the line at the cost of "excellent") for Melissa to have happy fantasies. Susan was free of the dread she'd felt in San Francisco, which she now saw as "silly," and the first two Assemblages were rousing successes. On Wednesday, their off day, they were guests of honor at a pool party at the Malibu home of a power couple who were big Mam adherents but—no cameras please—not ready to make it public knowledge. Uri got to meet the cinematographer-turned-director who was his greatest hero, and Raju turned uncharacteristically giddy at the focus of attention from a desirable actress who'd just separated from her rock star husband.

At the end of a lazy Thursday morning, they were gathering for brunch on the patio of Susan's bungalow. It was time for the daily conference call with Janet and the New York office. Melissa came in, still dripping from the pool, with a message on her blackberry that Tara's limo to the airport had been confirmed for the next morning. After tonight's post-Assemblage webcast, Ziggy and his crew would follow. Then tomorrow's big finale at the Ahmanson Theatre and the rest of them could go home whenever they'd choose. The Mamathon was drawing to a close.

"So do I meet up with Pete, or do I hang out with Zach?" Melissa was taking a last long weekend on the West Coast before heading home but still hadn't decided whom to play with. Pete was the animation director she'd met at Skywalker. He was attractive and had a great job. But Zach, the actor she'd met at the Malibu party, was drop-dead gorgeous and just confirmed for a small but showy part in a film that, if it went as blockbuster as it was being designed to be, could be a major step on the road to the A list. It was a classic bird-in-the-hand dilemma.

"Who do you like better?" Mam asked. Mam seemed to get a kick out of Melissa and her road-test approach to finding The One.

"They both have their points," she was saying, as Tara ran up from the lobby newsstand, brandishing a copy of USA Today.

"Doesn't anyone here ever check the news?" Tara breathlessly threw down the newspaper and waved at Raju, who had a laptop open.

The headline screamed across the paper: "Pornography? Or Freedom of Religion?" Below came the tag: "Breast-Baring Schoolgirl Expelled." The accompanying photo showed a wholesome looking teenager wearing a baggie T-shirt. Though obscured by a printed "modesty patch," it could be inferred that a hole had been cut out above one breast.

"What is it?" Mam asked.

"It's that high school student, the one with the T-shirt," Melissa said. "She got expelled or suspended, I forget which."

Susan turned away from the paper to look at Melissa, shocked. "You knew about this?"

"It's been on TV all week."

"And you never mentioned it?" Wendy chimed in.

"You always say not to bother Susan with what the media says," Melissa reminded them. "And," she added in an injured tone, "you always make fun of me for watching tabloid TV."

"Well here it is in *The New York Times*," Raju grimaced. He spun the laptop around so that they could all get a look. "I'm going inside to turn on CNN."

Dakota Parker, a teenaged Mam acolyte, had been suspended from her Alabama high school for wearing one of the newer "peek-a-boo" Mam T-shirts to class. According to the story, the school dress code allowed for T-shirts with the sole restriction of prohibiting "inappropriate slogans." As the girl's lawyer pointed out, this did not apply to Dakota's shirt, which said simply "Take Responsibility," a sentiment clearly appropriate in every way to the education of our youth.

It took Raju some surfing to synch up with a news channel that was spooling this particular story at this moment. When he found it, they saw the girl, looking shyly down at her sneakers through a curtain of hair, surrounded by a crowd of reporters and bystanders in what seemed to be the school parking lot. To one side of her stood a lawyer, brandishing some papers in such a way that they obscured the breast area of the T-shirt. On the other side, a chubby woman in "mom" jeans and a "knitters leave you in stitches" sweatshirt had an arm wrapped tightly around the girl. Her mouth was wide open. Raju turned off the mute.

"I'm proud of my girl for taking a stand for what she believes in," the woman, identified in a caption as Bobette Parker, was shouting to the crowd. "And what she believes in is Values!" Some of the onlookers cheered, while others booed. "It's just plain common sense, what Mam says. It's how my mama brought me up and how I've tried to bring up my own kids, in spite of what they get from the media. Yes, the media! All those people who'll do anything on reality TV, and the booty girls on those videos. I'd rather have my girl wearing this shirt than being tarted up like all those hip-hop dancers and the like. Ain't nothing dirty about a woman's breast unless you have a dirty mind!

"I'll tell you what's dirty. Just look at the evening news. Those executives robbing people blind so as they can make millions of dollars they can't even figure out how to spend. That's dirty. The media keeps telling kids nothing matters but getting money, no matter what you gotta do to get it. It's a losing battle for decent hardworking people these days, or it was 'til Mam! God Bless You, Mam!!!"

Susan and her team stared at the screen, speechless.

"Who do I have to call to get hold of that footage?" Wendy murmured. The others shushed her as the network's own reporter segued to an "earlier that day" interview with the school principal.

The office décor featured an American flag, the state flag with its echo of the Confederacy and a stuffed, mounted fish. The principal, a red-faced man in a short-sleeved shirt and cheap tie, his hair carefully pomaded, sat behind an aluminum desk that, sleekly refurbished, would cost a fortune in New York or LA but here was chipping ill-chosen olive enamel and decorated with scout camp mosaic accessories and looked merely discouraged. Moving with exaggerated care, as if he'd been told that slow motion is better for the camera, the principal lifted up a T-shirt of the style under debate. He ran a hand inside the shirt and showed how clearly the articulation of his fingers showed through the sheer panel below the embroidered "Mam I Am."

"This has nothin' to do with religion!" he fumed, self-righteously. "The girl is flauntin' her body to get attention. And her parents, allowin' her to go out in public like that, baring her naked breast, well it's absolutely disgustin'!" He narrowed his eyes and hissed straight into the camera. "And it's child abuse, too, if you ask me! They may's well be pimpin' that child!"

The news cut back to the reporter, with a close-up. "The battle lines appear to have been drawn," she said. "What happens when freedom of religion seems to be at odds with other community values? Bill, I understand we've invited Professor E. Leslie Fennerman of the Cushing Institute to discuss this issue in our studios."

"That's right, Debra," the anchor took the cutaway. "Tonight, we'll be hosting a roundtable discussion featuring Dr. Fennerman, legal expert Star Jones and noted psychologist Dr. Phil McGraw. That's tonight at 10 Eastern, 9 Central. Check local listings in your area."

Raju flipped channels but it all seemed to be more of the same. Meanwhile, with Melissa's help, Wendy was checking out a week's worth of tabloid coverage online, and Tara checked the websites of the newspapers of record for several world cities.

The story was breaking everywhere. Mam was no longer the province of fake news or the slow but steady expansion of her own circle of adherents. It was irrelevant now whether it had begun as a typical teenaged head butt against authority or a true expression of religious fervor. Dakota Parker's challenge, her principal's response, and her family's legal reaction had politicized Mam.

When the conference call came through from Janet, Jack Rabb was also on the line, beside himself with joy. Mam was "real" news, and he was the first to have had the story. "I've got Dershowitz tonight!" he crowed. "He'll be here in an hour. We called him as soon as the story broke and he's dropping everything to be with us, because he says we're closest to the source. We told him we could get you on audio so he can ask a few questions."

"No problem," Raju said, excitedly. "We don't have to leave for the theatre until 5 our time."

Susan went back on the patio to tip room service and stayed out there. She poured herself some of the hotel's own energy water and began to nibble at a piece of pineapple, slowly breaking off little toothfuls of fiber.

"And you were worried about losing me," Mam said. "Is this more of that that 'beware of what you wish for...' you keep mentioning?"

"I don't know what this is," Susan said. She was as overwhelmed now as when Mam first began to talk or any of the other "firsts" that had punctuated the past year. It was hard not to accept you were leading a religion when someone was claiming First Amendment rights because of you. "Take responsibility," Mam and she were fond of saying. She was afraid to think what they might be taking responsibility for.

10 – THE BREAST OF EVERYTHING

ANEW suggested they come to Salem for Samhain and a Wiccan group in the Hamptons asked if they'd join them out East, but Susan had firmly declined both invitations. After weeks of touring, she refused to even consider spending Hallowe'en anywhere but home, and by home, she meant snuggly curled in her armchair with a cup of mulled cider, the West Village parade no closer than her television screen and the doors firmly locked against trick-or-treaters.

Home at last. It had been a long week back.

Wendy hugged them all goodbye at the taxi stand and said not to expect to hear a peep out of her. Until she met them in Chicago for the week-long Midwestern breeze-through, she'd be in the editing bay. The rest of them headed straight to Mam Enterprises where it was, in Melissa's words, "like coming back to work after vacation, except without the vacation." Even Raju, who'd been able to work remotely from the road, found himself facing a backlog of those face-to-face meetings so critical to the business of intangibles.

For Susan and Melissa, there was too much to do in not much time before Susan would be running out again. If the Dakota Parker story had hit the news sooner, it was unlikely Pearl Yuan would have won the bidding war for the first book interview, but the timing had been in her favor and contracts had been signed before the Mamathon had left San Francisco. Once Dakota's story broke, Pearl naturally pushed to have the interview sooner rather than later, so even before Chicago, there would be a critical day in Baltimore. Before that however, for the next week and a half, despite all the willing hands and good intentions of the staff during the tour, there were messages that needed a personal response, the extra Gatherings that had been scheduled to make up for the neglect of the loyal core constituency, and the basic but time-consuming effort of catching up on all the news at home.

Susan had scarcely returned Jonelle's welcoming smile when Lisa whisked her upstairs, where Diane was waiting for them.

"Rosa's gone," Lisa said, bluntly, shutting the door. "I came in early last Monday and she was packing up her desk."

Susan looked at her blankly "What happened?"

"I don't know," Lisa admitted. "All she would say was that she had to leave. I could see she'd been crying. Once she saw me, she just threw everything into a couple of bags and ran."

"When Lisa told me, I gave her a call," Diane took up the story. "I thought maybe it would be easier for her to talk to me." Lisa gave her a look and Diane shook her head. "Oh, get real. You know you can come on a little strong. Not that it matters. She wouldn't talk to me, either. Just mumbled something about 'a servant can't serve two masters,' said 'I'm sorry' and hung up the phone. And she was definitely crying."

"Julia thinks it has something to do with the news about that kid in Alabama."

"Dakota Parker," Susan supplied automatically.

"Right," Lisa said, rolling her eyes. "Dakota from Alabama. I guess the trailer must have moved around a lot."

Susan pressed her fingers to her eyelids and tried to think. In the weeks before the tour, Rosa had been more than usually quiet. One day, Mam had gently asked her what was wrong and Rosa had pulled back as if she were afraid of something. She'd made some excuse about being late to cover a relief shift at the day care center and disappeared. She'd kept a low profile after that. And she hadn't come to the bon voyage party, Susan recalled. At the time, Susan had been too busy to worry. Maybe she should have. She picked up the phone.

"She'll never talk to you," Lisa said.

"She's too polite not to," Susan replied.

"No, Sue," Diane said gently. "We've tried. She keeps her machine on. And she never returns our messages. Not even Marta's."

"Marta called her?" Diane nodded. "And she wouldn't talk to Marta?" Susan didn't know what to think.

"Maybe we should go and see her," Mam suggested. The others considered the idea. It had the virtue of being unexpected. It was worth a shot.

Diane drove them all to Brooklyn. She and Lisa waited in the car in the parking lot of the pizza place a few blocks away. Susan crossed the familiar red brick courtyard, trying to imagine what to say, or what Rosa might tell her. As she reached the door, an old woman with a walker was exiting the building. Susan held the door for her and slipped into the lobby without having to buzz upstairs on the intercom. One less opportunity for Rosa to refuse to see her, she thought. At the door to the apartment, Susan paused. She put her ear to the crack between the old door and the older warped doorframe. She could hear a vacuum cleaner; Rosa was definitely at home.

THE BREAST OF EVERYTHING

Susan rang the bell and stepped to one side of the range of the door's spy-hole.

"Who is it?" Rosa was forced to ask.

"It's me, Rosa," Susan said in as warm and casual a tone as she could muster. "I came to see if you were okay, if there was anything I could do to help."

There was silence from the other side of the door as Rosa frantically tried to decide how to handle the situation. "I'm okay," she finally said softly.

"Oh, I'm so glad!" Susan said. "Everyone's been worried about you."

"They shouldn't," Rosa said. Her small voice had a tremble in it. "I told them I was leaving."

"Lisa said you did," Susan agreed. "But we were still worried. It was so unexpected. And we miss you."

"You don't need me," Rosa choked. "You got lots of people now."

"I know we've got a lot of people helping us now, but you were the first..."

"And we love you so much" Mam added.

"Nooo!" Rosa wailed. "Keep Her away!" She began frantically to pray.

Susan tapped on the door with her finger then, as Rosa's praying grew louder and louder, knocked loudly with her knuckles. "Rosa, please. Won't you let me in so we can talk?"

"Sante Maria, Madre de Dios, ruega por nostrotos pecadores..."

"Please, Rosa..."

"Go away or I'll call the police!" She was clearly at the end of her rope.

There was nothing else Susan could think to do. "I'll go. Since you want me to. Goodbye, then." Rosa's sobs became less hysterical. "I guess you must have your reasons," she added gently. "And I'm sure, knowing you, that they're good ones. But it won't be the same without you. It just won't." It had gotten quiet on the other side. If there hadn't been a door between them, Susan would have reached out to give her a hug. Instead she had to do it with her voice. "Take good care of yourself, Rosita. We're always here if you need us."

It was so hard to walk away without knowing any more than she had before. It seemed to Susan that everything had begun with Rosa and that fateful meeting on the subway. At any time and under any circumstances, her quitting the team would have left a gaping hole that might get less noticeable with time but would never really close. This was more than that. It was the way she left, apparently out of nowhere, and that hysteria when Mam spoke to her. It was more than painful; it was frightening. What did it mean?

On the other side of the door, Rosa sank down on her heels and cried until it hurt too much to cry more. She'd hoped it was over when she cleared out her desk. Even though Lisa had shown up unexpectedly early that morning, she was sure that if she could only get out of the building, everything would be fine. It would all go away and her life could go back to what it had been before she ever heard of Mam.

For four months, she'd led a double life. Every day that she went to work at Mam's offices, she'd been spying for Father Martin. Spying was a nasty word, and she'd avoided it for as long as she could, but it was the right one. Once she knew that in her heart, it got harder and harder to go on doing it.

At first it had been a relief to give the burden up to Jesus. For weeks, Rosa'd felt lighter than air. Every day, she'd stop by the church and answer questions from Father Martin and then she'd go to work, with people she liked, and do what she always did anyways and what she was honestly pretty proud of. The questions were simple at first, things like who were going to be guests on the webcasts, or what kinds of questions people asked at Gatherings and what answers they got back. Sometimes, when Rosa was repeating things Mam had said, it would make her think them through again and she would feel more than ever how much good Mam was doing in the world. She tried to explain this to Father Martin, but his face would shut down and he would change the subject. She accepted there were things she didn't know or couldn't understand. And when she felt uncomfortable, she reminded herself that she had been chosen for this, it was her cross and her salvation. But the uncomfortable feeling started creeping in more and more.

Mam and Susan and Lisa and all of them, they trusted her and she was a spy. It didn't matter that she'd never snooped, that everything she passed along was something she'd heard or seen right out in the open. It was that everyone thought whatever they were saying and doing was in the family, when all the time she was telling it outside, to people who didn't know them and who were maybe even looking to find things.

The questions from the Church began to sound like what Rosa remembered from when she was on jury duty, what they called "leading the witness," and a lot of the time, they twisted her words when she answered. Like she was telling about this guy who stood up at a Gathering and asked if Mam thought the miracles in the bible was all real or like parables. What Mam said was, who was She to question miracles when, well, look at Her.

"And that was all she said," Father Martin had asked Rosa. "She didn't suggest that they were fabrications?"

"No." Rosa'd felt the priest looking at her real hard and thought some more. "Well, She did agree with him that sometimes stories are told a certain way that makes a point more than saying exactly what happened in history."

He'd nodded, like that was what he'd expected Rosa to say. "So she discounts the testimonies of the miracles of Our Lord as falsehoods."

"Nooo," Rosa had said, slowly, thinking she'd just said the opposite thing. "She just means there could be a lot of reasons for things."

"And did she give examples of this?"

"Well, the Marriage at Cana. Actually, this guy brought it up as something he didn't know if he believed. And Mam said that she wasn't going to say it didn't happen exactly like the Gospel tells it, but it was possible maybe the caterer was cheating them and Jesus caught him in the act and he had to hand over the wine. Or that maybe it was just that Jesus made the people so excited just being around Him that they felt like they'd had wine when all they had was water." Father Martin had kept silent, staring at her until she'd felt she had to fill the vacuum. "Um, She commented that people kind of get like that at the Gatherings, where there's no alcohol. Like Susan said, people call the switchboard all the time to aks the name of the 'delicious wine' they had the night before, when all they had was rosehip ice tea. They do, Father; I've had some of the phone calls. We laugh about it all the time."

"So she compares herself to Our Lord," Father Martin had said grimly, writing something in his notebook.

"No!" Rosa had said, frustrated, "That's not it!" But she'd been unable to explain why not and left the Church with a prickle that she'd been unable to shake for hours.

She'd thought that having Mam on the road would make things easier. She wouldn't have information any more special than what anyone could get by themselves, watching the webcasts or reading blogs. Instead, the Bishop's secretary called her in and asked a lot of questions about things that showed up in the blogs, like about the ceremony Alan had created, and what they meant by some of the things in it. Did Mam claim she could heal, the Bishop wanted to know. And what was her stand on homosexuality?

Father Martin said what she was doing was right, but it felt wrong, and she couldn't do it anymore. Not when some high school kid who didn't even look seventeen was standing up like a blessed martyr, getting thrown out of school and having them pushing her on all the news.

That girl could do it because she believed in Mam completely; she had no problem accepting Her goodness. Rosa didn't know what to believe anymore. She still thought she'd had a vision, that Baby Jesus had shown her He rejected the breast. But she didn't need to have a vision to see Mam. Mam was there, right in front of her. She could ask Mam a question and hear the answer with her own ears, out loud, and see the lips move to form the words. Mam knew her name, even the sound of her voice. And maybe it wasn't Baby Jesus who was rejecting Her. Maybe it was the Church. Mam said so much that was wise and good and true, but she didn't always match with the Church. And Mam was miraculous, no one could doubt that. Not even Father Martin, or he wouldn't be so afraid. Because he was afraid.

"He's afraid!" Rosa breathed the words out loud in wonder, breaking through her own tears and almost falling off her heels onto the floor because it was so much the truth. She'd felt this deep in her heart and but didn't really know it until she said it aloud. He was afraid, and the Bishop and the Bishop's secretary, and all of them. If they thought She was evil, then they shouldn't be afraid because with all their faith, their immortal souls should be safe and that was what was important. But it had to be that they didn't think their souls were so safe after all, or they wouldn't be so afraid. Were they afraid that it was Mam was who would be sitting in judgment on them? And if they were that afraid, what would they do about it? A frieze of terrible images rushed through her mind, things from history class and Sunday school and the movies. She squeezed her eyes tight and shook her head to dismiss them. She wasn't going to let herself get carried away by her imagination.

She didn't know yet what she wanted to do, but she knew what she didn't want to do. Whatever was happening with Father Martin and the Bishop, she couldn't keep being part of it. Mam was right, Rosa thought, you had to take responsibility. And that meant whatever you did, it had to be *you* doing it, not someone making you. And you had to know what you were doing, so that whatever came from what you did, it would belong to you.

Rosa got up and went to wash her face. She'd been hiding in the house long enough. It was time for her to get out and get on with her life. On her own terms. First thing she had to do was find a new job. There was a computer at the library she could use to make her resume. She'd never made a resume before. Until now, she'd only had the kind of jobs where you filled out an application. Working for Mam was the best job she'd ever had, and she could feel extra proud that she'd created it all herself. It might take a lot of trying, but she'd find something that was just as good or could someday turn into it. She could make that happen. It might not be so easy to find a Church where they'd leave her alone, but someday she'd find that, too.

It was cold in the studio. Susan hadn't expected that. The only other television she'd done had been *Duh News*, where it had been downright tropical from the lights. Pearl, for all that she was so famously "green," must burn a lot of ozone to keep it like this. If it didn't feel any warmer when she got on the set, Pearl's people were going to have as much trouble with the nipple that wasn't Mam as with the entity Herself.

Amazing as it was to Susan, Mam was in full view today. The message had been to wear "whatever Mam usually wears. Our people will worry about the rest." Raju had interpreted this as Pearl's plan to take on the networks and break away from the currently dense pack of alpha female interviewers.

Wendy completely disagreed. "It'll be another version of the digital pasty," she'd assured them. In most markets, *Pearl!* aired during school hours and her sponsors were mainly conservative food and drug concerns pitching to stay-at-home moms. "She wants to be able to say she had a face-to-face interview, but she'll never take a risk with the advertisers."

In any case, the team had taken Pearl at her word. Steffi, video-conferenced as the person most likely to pick something that could stand up against the sharply tailored pants suits and fragile stiletto pumps for which Pearl was known, had selected a white silk that draped and fastened with a clasp on one shoulder. "Pearl thinks she has classical taste," Steffi'd snorted, "well, this is the original classical style." Maybe so, but warm it wasn't.

Susan tried crossing her arms, but one of her silver bracelets grazed Mam, and Mam yelped. "What are you trying to do to me?!"

The assistant who'd been assigned to shepherd Susan from the green room dropped the digital clipboard that, together with a nearly decorative jawbone headset, apparently connected her to a Wi-Fi network. Pearl commanded a little army of these fresh-faced clones, provisioning them beyond their meager salaries with well-cut shiny hair, good black trousers and not-quite-white shirts in cotton so fine it might have been silk. Until this minute, this one had flaunted her self-possession while exhibiting how she carried the weight and sins of the world on her fragile shoulders. The sound of Mam's voice disturbed the mask with a ripple of wild panic that the poor girl couldn't suppress.

Susan wanted to laugh. The chronically smooth tended to be more than usually disturbed by Mam. It was small-minded of her, she knew, but she couldn't help feeling it was a bit of a karmic balance for a lifetime of being steamrollered by their tribe. She wondered meanly what Pearl herself would do when she finally met the subject of her interview, upfront and personal. There had been no preparation, no greenroom greeting. Pearl, who prided herself on a hard news background, liked to meet her guests for the first time on camera. She said it helped her keep her edge.

"Umm," the assistant's tremulous tap on Susan's forearm broke through her musings. "You're on," she gulped.

On the tasteful set, Pearl was completing her intro with "I am so very proud to bring them on now, Susan Roth and Mam!" She rose from what she always archly referred to as "Mama's chair" and gave her signature bow over clasped hands in the direction of the guest entrance.

Susan squared her shoulders so that Mam lead the way, and they entered to a storm of applause.

A number of Mam supporters lead the ovation. From his seat on the side, Raju noted a scattering of Mam T-shirts across the audience, though none of the newest bolder ones. He also noticed several versions of a symbol he'd never seen before. It was a line drawing of a vertical sign that began with a six-pointed star and unwound into a series of symbols, the bottom of which extended down to become the outline of a fish. From the fish's mouth depended what Raju thought at first was a hook but then realized, thanks to a close up on the monitor, was a spiral much like Mam's. He took a quick snapshot with his phone and forwarded it back to the office. Maybe someone, Alan most likely, would know what it was and what it might mean.

He was so absorbed in this train of thought that he missed the precise moment when Mam greeted Pearl. A silent hiccup in the audience's energy drew his attention back to center stage. Susan and Pearl were already sitting down. Pearl, who usually leaned forward as if to draw her guests out of themselves, sat as far back as "Mama's chair" would allow and as upright as if a brace were wired to her spine. With some amusement, he noted that she kept her eyes fixed firmly on Susan's while she recited, at length, the capsule history her researchers had prepared. Raju let his own eyes roam. As Pearl hit her points, Susan smiled attentively and occasionally nodded. Checking the monitor, he thought she looked lovely on camera. Steffi had chosen well. He also noted that there was no "pasty" in evidence. Whatever Pearl was planning for airtime, it was clear that during the taping, wherever they looked, everyone was to be allowed an unobstructed view of Mam, which was clearly what the audience wanted. As Pearl continued her monologue, there was some coughing and shuffling. These people either knew the background information or they didn't really care; they'd come here today to see Mam in action.

Raju tried to catch Susan's eye, but it wasn't necessary. By now she could sense an audience's pulse without anyone's help.

"Pearl, please!" Susan said with a bright laugh. "I'm flattered, but if you tell them much more, no one will have any reason to buy my book! And after all that hard work..."

"Yeah," Mam jumped in. "I didn't get a night's sleep for months!"

The audience roared with delight. Pearl, caught off guard, looked directly at Mam. "You sleep?!" she asked. The audience roared again, louder and with more applause.

"I'm not always alert or conscious," Mam replied. "If that qualifies."

The familiarity of an ovation had brought Pearl back to herself. She leaned forward and smiled. "Do you dream?"

"Sometimes Pearl," Mam said with all seriousness, "I think this is all a dream."

Once she got rolling, Pearl proved she'd pulled out all the stops in preparing for this interview. Even if there was nothing new to Mam watchers, it was a solid show. Dr. Snyder was brought in, remote from her office in New York, to discuss the findings of the Stanford Medical team. From the lobby at Mitra, seated on cushions beside the primordial goddess statue, Patrick went over some of the familiar philosophic paths with Mam and encouraged questions from the audience.

Finally, news clips were used to segue into the event that had brought Mam to the attention of the mainstream media. The audience watched carefully, then turned their attention back to Pearl who thanked the Alabama station and WNN for sharing their footage. Then she stood slowly and everyone held their breath. "Well," she said with a smile, "we don't have Dr. E. Leslie Fennerman here with us today, because we're not interested in *studies* and statistics, are we? We're interested in people." As often happened on *Pearl!*, the audience enhanced their applause with vocal sounds of approval. "So I've invited the young woman who's stirred up so much controversy to join us today. Won't you help me welcome her? Dakota Parker!"

Pearl pointed into the audience and all heads turned to follow. The audience encouragement only made Dakota, sitting in the front row with her mother, blush fiercely. Bobette Parker, beaming in her Sunday best, applauded while elbowing her child in the ribs. Dakota stood reluctantly and made her way to a third chair, which a stagehand had magically wedged between Susan and Pearl.

Pearl's people had asked her to wear "the" T-shirt, but this clearly warred with Bobette's idea of tel-appropriate wardrobe. The child did wear the shirt, but it was belted at the waist over a tiered lace-trimmed skirt, and a great many friendship bracelets jammed her arms. Makeup had scraped her hair back into a French braid so that she couldn't hide behind it, but she still managed to keep her eyes turned down toward her silver ballet flats as Pearl shook her hand and introduced her to Susan.

Susan smiled encouragingly, "I know. It's kind of scary to be on *Pearl!*"

Dakota nodded and gave a tentative smile as she raised her head halfway from the ground. She suddenly realized she was looking straight at Mam.

"But we know you're a young woman with a lot of courage," Mam said. "It's an honor to meet you."

Dakota's eyes filled with tears and she clapped her hand over her mouth, which had dropped open into a long O.

Susan touched her shoulder. "Don't be afraid," she said gently.

The girl let her hand fall to her lap. She blinked slowly and gave a wondering smile. "I'm not," she said. "I'm not afraid of anything at all. I'm just so happy to be here with Her."

"Dakota," Pearl inserted herself into the moment, "I see you're wearing the very same T-shirt that got you expelled from Scopus High School."

"Like y'all told me to," Dakota said with a nod.

"Yes of course," Pearl murmured. "Well, your principal and others claim that wearing this shirt constitutes indecent exposure."

"Her titties are that small you can't hardly see them 'less you're looking real hard," Bobette called out righteously from her front row seat. "Where's someone asking those men why they're staring at a young girl like that?"

"That's an interesting point you raise, Mrs. Parker," Pearl gave a tight smile and Raju imagined her being grateful that the woman hadn't mentioned any men by name. "But let's get back to the main issue. You and Dakota have both stated that the school decision, which I understand is supported by civil legislation on the books in your district prohibiting,.." she turned to her notes and read "ah, 'the immodest display of the bare female trunk or torso in any venue either public or supported financially by the public via tax dollars,' that this ruling is effectively unconstitutional, as it violates Dakota's right to freedom of religion."

"That's right," Bobette said. "Unconstitutional. And she wasn't bare or immodest. She was wearing a T-shirt. This T-shirt. Look at it! The hole is no more than the size of a biscuit, and it's got a bit of illusion sewn right in there, like a little veil."

"But you contend that if she did bare her bosom, it would be her constitutional right to do so."

"Exactly what I said."

"Her constitutional religious right." Pearl nodded thoughtfully, then turned, palm extended in a gesture of open communication, towards Susan. "And what do you and Mam have to say to this," she asked, baring her teeth in what a shark might be pleased to call a grin, "considering that, despite the registered tax status of your organization, you have gone on record as claiming you are not a religion but, in fact, consider yourselves to be heading up a *discipline*?"

Susan hardly had time to absorb this thrust. Raju was halfway out of his seat when Dakota took matters in hand.

"Pearl," she said with the calm of innocence and the intensity of faith, "when you're looking through your eyes, you have to let your soul do the seeing. Mam doesn't have to say who She is. She is here, is all. That's enough for me. Now if you can't see the hand of God in that miracle, or if you can't admit the truth, then I am truly sorry for you. And I promise I will pray that you will see the light and let it save you." Dakota shyly slipped one of the many friendship bracelets from her arm and proffered it to Susan who accepted it solemnly and gave her a hug. The audience went wild.

When the interview aired, Phyllis Hendron was in Qatar or Bahrain or on her way from one to the other. She always enjoyed spending time with the Arab emiresses, who universally reminded her of old fashioned movie stars and seemed gracious and well educated. She was also pleased when being seen at his side was somehow helpful to Roddo, like it had been back in the old campaigning days. On the other hand, she wasn't crazy about having to wear scarves over her head all the time, even if they were the luxurious tissues gifted by her elegant hostesses, trimmed with real gold and jewels. And no matter the why of it, she always felt just a bit put out when she had to miss *Pearl!*

During Rod Hendron's first term, the marquee "get" for the talk show and infotainment circuit had been an interview with the Vice President's wife, a former "first daughter," a special ambassador for UNICEF and the slim, blonde mother of adorable triplets. Pearl Yuan had been the one to instead invite the First Lady for an hour one-on-one to publicize her new "bikes for tykes" program and some heart-to-heart talk about her longstanding campaign to raise awareness on behalf of NASA (the North American Septoplasty Association).

Phyllis had never forgotten this. Loyalty was a major component of her personal integrity. From that day on, she'd never let an episode of *Pearl!* air without her watching. If she was traveling with Roddo, one of the girls in the East Wing made sure to TiVo it for her and she'd watch it on the plane heading home. Once Roddo and the Secretary of whatever-he-needed-to-talk-about were in the flying Oval office, Phyllis would tuck up her feet, have a nice cup of tea and reach for the remote. This time, her routine had apparently saved her from having to miss an especially interesting show. Pearl was interviewing this Susan Ross or Roth person and, if Phyllis understood correctly, impossible as it surely had to be, the woman claimed to have a bosom that could talk.

Not that it was easy to be sure. There was this kind of polka dot with the network logo that kept shimmying around in what, back in the day, Rod and his Greek brothers used to call "the chestal area." Phyllis assumed it was necessary. The Roth woman didn't seem to have much on her by way of a blouse and obviously they couldn't allow a display of nudity on the air, especially not a time of day when innocent children might see it, but it was frustrating to try and figure out exactly what was going on. Clearly a lot of the questions that were sent her way were answered without Susan Roth moving her lips. If it were on any other show, Phyllis would assume it was one of those ugly unfunny jokes that the Hollywood left wing like to use to try and undermine Faith. Phyllis was rock solid certain that Pearl Yuan would never do anything like that. If it was on *Pearl!*, it must be true. And yet, there couldn't really be a talking bosom. That would be miraculous. Not that Phyllis didn't believe in miracles. She did, but this wasn't the kind of thing that was meant.

It had to be a trick of some kind. Not a mean trick, though. Maybe she was big in Vegas. It had been years, Phyllis thought a little wistfully, since the last time Roddo was able to take her to Vegas. On the other hand, all the questions from Pearl and the audience were posed with great respect, not like how you'd talk to a ventriloquist or whatever, and they concerned the most unlikely things. It was all about morality and values, as if she was some kind of preacher, which was impossible, surely. Or maybe it wasn't. One of the women in the audience asked a question about a website, so maybe it was a computer ministry, in which case Phyllis could be excused for not knowing about it. Phyllis was an old-fashioned network television and newspaper kind of person. Unlike Mrs. VPOTUS, she didn't feel at ease with computers and the interweb and all that. She usually even bypassed cable TV—the violence and especially the language they got away with were just too much for her.

If it was a ministry, Phyllis wanted to know more about it. As a Christian, she had an obligation to do so. This Susan woman—and whoever else was talking behind that dot—was saying some interesting things. And she had quite a following. Phyllis had no idea what the numbers were, and she knew many people would say that it was only the numbers that mattered, but she could see how dedicated they were. That sweet little girl Pearl brought on, it sounded like she'd been thrown out of school for trying to pray according to Susan Roth's teachings. Shameful! This is why that school prayer amendment Reverend Crockertt was helping with was such an important part of their White House legacy. Phyllis was surprised she hadn't heard about this little Dakota girl from Roddo. Maybe it had all happened while they were in Bahrain. She'd talk with him tonight or whatever time of day it was when they'd be back home. She'd have to remember not to erase this episode, so she could show it to him herself and make sure he saw. She would learn some more, too, and really be a help to him. As soon as they landed, she'd set one of her girls to do some looking up for her. Maybe next time she had a Prayer Breakfast, this Susan Roth was someone who ought to be invited.

"Tonight's top story," Jack Rabb kicked off his show the next night, "Pearl You-know-who got the interview of the century. Right after us, but we're basic cable, so we don't count. This historic moment should have been your 'Mam-a-palooza Byte of the Night,' but the network in question—I won't mention their name but their middle initial is 'B'—wouldn't let us have a clip." The studio audience booed audibly. With a wry smile, Jack gestured for silence. "I'm sure anyone who actually caught the show would agree it was the last word in crusading journalism."

"Chicken!" Roger popped up from behind the desk with a cackle, goggling his eyes and wiggling his fingers wildly on either side of his face.

"Sorry, Roge?"

"The last word. It's chicken!" Roger repeated his antic grimace. "Pearl Yuan is chicken. Chicken, chicken, chicken!" He did it again. In contrast with his JFK haircut, chalk-striped suit and French cuffs, it was even more unnerving than if it had come from a real second-grader.

"She certainly wasn't very, um, bold," Jack agreed. "Pearl may claim to be 'the hard news journalist for the soft news audience,' but when it came down to challenging the network..."

"Chicken. Sweet-and-sour chicken. Lemon chicken. Chicken with cashew nuts..."

"Roge, please; the ethnic slurs are out of line."

"Southern-fried chicken, chicken cacciatore..."

"Enough, Roge. We get it. For those who may have missed the show, which I'm assuming is most of our viewing audience (somehow I'm sensing we don't do much crossover)...For those who don't yet know, Pearl pixilated Mam." Jack held up his hand to stave off more boos from the audience. "Now, now. After all, we here at *Duh News* use the Mam pasty in our regular coverage."

"You do know we're not really the news, Jack." Roger raised his eyebrows and shook his head pityingly. "Our so-called coverage? It's what we in the business call a 'bit.' A clever soufflé of satiric wit, pure entertainment. Wherein the pasty provides an ironic comment on the state of American media."

"Now that you make me think of it, Roge, when we had Mam here in person, we interviewed her face-to-face, as it were."

"And we took that FCC warning like men!" Roger said, pounding the news desk with his fist.

"Indeed we did. But Pearl and her people wouldn't take that chance. They went for one of those digital checkerboard things. Like an interview with someone in witness protection, except for the vocoder. Now can someone tell me what they were thinking? Mam's a talking breast! That's what makes it *news*. If you don't actually see Her talking, what's the point?"

"You know," Roger butted in, "if Pearl interviewed a talking dog, and I'm sure she would if she could find one, you can bet your bottom dollar they would have shown it talking it's little canine head off."

"It would have been reported with accuracy and integrity," Jack agreed.

"As would only be right. The public has a right to know." Roger addressed the audiences, studio and viewing, with his most pompous severity. "It's a violation of public trust to censor the news, whether it's digitizing Mam or maybe refusing to air the beheading of an American hostage or the dragging of American corpses by jubilant crowds through the streets of..."

"Um, Roge, they did air those last two." Now it was Jack's turn to address the viewers. He did it straight, with no twinkle in his eyes and nothing but conviction in his voice. "And regardless of who might be offended by that, and I have to say those other two offended me, the American people are mature enough to bear witness and make our own judgments. We don't need the networks or the FCC to be our babysitters. Their misguided attempts to 'protect' us are not good for us. On the contrary; as Mam is fond of reminding us, 'evil done in the name of God is still evil.'"

Roger looked at him with studied awe. "You used the G word, Jack," he rumbled, in his deepest register.

"I did," Jack smiled. "Mature of me, wasn't it?"

Jared Crockertt stared at his television set so hard that fragments of after-image floated in front of his retina. Jack Rabb had mentioned God, and he hadn't been joking. Maybe it wasn't bringing down the Walls of Jericho, but it sure was shaking the foundations. Jack Rabb and his team of so-called "reporters" were as perfect an example as you could imagine of that brand of godless liberal whose lack of values was ruining this great country. What they did and said ran counter to everything Jared held dear. Not only was he pretty sure they'd be burning in Hell someday, but he'd had serious concerns as to what watching their show might mean for his own salvation. He'd only started watching to catch the coverage of Mam's tour. Of course he'd prayed over it first. And it had seemed to him that, if they were the only heralds of Mam's progress, surely it must be permissible to heed them.

Because Mam was a child of light. Of this Jared was now certain, and he was bound to follow Her. He'd been deeply troubled at first, when She'd scoffed at his faith and challenged him to step away from the safety of his humility. He'd doubted Her goodness. He'd given his witnessing up to Uncle Hiram and had barricaded his heart with fear, but no matter how much he'd tried to hide from Her, he'd kept hearing Her call. Prayer just seemed to pull him more strongly towards Her. He couldn't keep himself from the website. He listened, and it was like a draught of cool, clean water refreshing his soul. For the first time since some long forgotten childhood moments, Jared had a sense that maybe he might matter and that in creating Man in his image, God intended Man to share responsibility for his own goodness. He felt a growing strength within himself, and an excitement in what this precious Good News might mean to the world.

202

And now, Jack Rabb had mentioned God on television. On *Duh News*, a place no one would ever think to turn to hear of God. Jared's heart brimmed full of joy. There was a movement in Heaven and his own soul was at peace with Mam and on the side of the angels. Like they said in Washington, it was good to be on the winning team.

Even if she hadn't been working this week, Rosa wouldn't have watched *Pearl!* It was nothing personal. She wanted to be seriously looking for a permanent job and not slipping into bad habits and turning into a daytime TV couch potato like when she was pregnant. She also didn't watch *Duh News* anymore. She was almost always asleep by the time it was on. She'd never been a night person, and she had to be up early, so unless there was something special like her and Ernesto having a date night, she hardly ever stayed up later than ten o'clock. She used to watch it for Mam on tape in the office, because she had to. Now it made her think of things she wanted to forget, and in any case, she'd never really enjoyed the humor. But Jimmy Touray had the podcast playing on his laptop and the speakers were up too high to ignore. She couldn't really walk away. For now, Jimmy was her boss. It was Market Week in New York for the Intimate Apparel Industry, and at Marta's urging, he'd hired her to help out at the booth.

Having divested itself of a Manhattan showroom during a mid-80s re-org, Corpo Céleste was renting space at the Javitz Center for the event. It had been a little eerie that first morning, when she'd tried to find her way through row after row of identical cubes. The hall was beige and cold and bigger than a football field, and even though her footsteps couldn't echo on the industrial carpet, she could hear her breath vibrating in the emptiness. Then the vendors draped their tables and hung their signs, and they blossomed into cozy open-fronted rooms of peach and pink and red and black. With music and scented candles and the rising buzz of conversation, the hall got friendlier. With all the bodies, it warmed up a little, too, which had to be a good thing for the models. That was the strangest part, the way there were girls walking up and down the aisles all day in nothing but underwear, high heels and a lot of makeup. A couple of years ago, Rosa would have been too uncomfortable to handle that. She wouldn't have known where to look. Now she was a little proud of how good she was getting at adapting to strange new worlds.

She was grateful to Jimmy for the work. It was only for a week, but it helped a lot to have a reason to have to get out of the house every day. She left home at 6:30 and went to morning mass at St. Michael's on 34th Street. Worship was much calmer when there was no possibility of seeing Father Martin or the Bishop. In just these few days she could feel it making an enormous difference in how she felt about herself. She could breathe again. Wherever her next real job turned out to be, she was going to whatever church was nearest the office. She'd keep to herself there as much as possible, though it might be kind of hard that way to have her Confession heard regularly. If she wanted to prevent the archdiocese from keeping track of her, she'd need to go to a few different churches then, rotate them. That was the only way to make sure it was nobody's business but hers and Jesus.

It hurt. She'd done probably the hardest things she ever had to do in her life, because she'd believed it was what God wanted her to do. The more she thought about it, the more it hurt because she was believing less and less that it was God who'd wanted it. Her Church had turned her into a spy, and now they were turning her into a sneak. People had done that. God couldn't have, wouldn't have. She kept remembering things Alan used to say about how religions were made by people, and how that was why religion was different from faith. Alan used to say a lot of smart things. And Tara. She'd envied Tara, who could follow Mam and give all her doubts and everything up to Jesus so easily and feel no conflict.

Rosa had put all that behind her now. She was making a whole fresh start. Here at the Lingerie Show she felt like a different person, and that felt good. Maybe she'd change her hair, too. Taking a sip of the fancy coffee they gave away in the lobby to exhibitors, she looked at the booth of the Israeli swimwear company across the aisle. One of the models had a very cute haircut and some interesting coppery streaks in front. Rosa was wondering if it would suit her, when Jimmy turned on his podcast of the previous night's *Duh News*. Usually he'd listened on his earphones, but Stan, the New York regional rep, was there today and also wanted to listen.

Since she had to hear it, she couldn't help finding it kind of funny that Pearl Yuan wouldn't show Mam. It was such a long time ago that Rosa had stopped thinking of Mam as a breast, as a woman's fleshy breast, that it seemed kind of immature to her that the networks were acting like junior high about it. She didn't need Jack Rabb and Roger Haff to tell her it was funny. Then she heard Jack say, "as Mam is fond of reminding us, 'evil done in the name of God is still evil.'"

Rosa put down her coffee. "Jimmy," she asked, "when it's done, could you play it again?" He did, pushing the laptop closer to her. She listened carefully this time. Watching her, Jimmy kept waiting for her laugh, which never came. Instead, the second time she heard Jack make the quote, she nodded gravely to herself and thanked Jimmy. Before he could say anything, the head buyer for an important Southern department store chain arrived with her entourage and he was fully occupied for the next half hour. Rosa returned to her coffee and her buttered roll, and to stuffing order forms and fabric sample cards into catalogues fast enough to satisfy Stan, who was expecting a flood of local buyers that day.

While she worked, she had plenty of time to think.

It used to be that she'd go to Father Martin when she had a spiritual crisis. Actually it wasn't until these last six months or so that she'd ever had a spiritual crisis in her life; moral issues and all the regular problems people have in everyday life, but not a spiritual crisis. For all her whole life, God the Father, Jesus the Son and the Holy Ghost, and blessed Virgin Mother had always had her complete and utter faith, the saints and blessed martyrs her belief and awe, and their shepherds on earth her trust. Whenever she'd needed guidance or comfort, they'd always seen her through. Now she needed help and Father Martin and the Monsignor and the Bishop and all them were the last people she could trust.

If she went to St. Michael's twice in one day, she'd be calling attention to herself, so at lunchtime she walked over to the river and looked out at the waters and the coast of New Jersey. It was windy and colder than her clothes were up to handling, but no one paid her any attention except a seagull who kept eying her sandwich. She threw the last bit in his direction and he grabbed it and swooped off. At least someone'd gotten what he needed, she thought, turning away from the piers. She wished she knew someone whose guidance she could trust. Then she realized that she did. Mam.

Mam had never asked her to lie or betray, Mam never asked people to do anything except accept responsibility for their actions, which was a way of saying they should think carefully about where those actions might lead. Why had she ever stopped believing in Mam's goodness? It was a vision that had started it. A middle of the night vision that had seemed so real but might have been, maybe, only in her head, while Mam was unquestionably real. Mam might be a hard miracle for people to accept, but you couldn't pretend She wasn't there. If you could, Father Martin would have done just that instead of asking her spy and trying to turn Her into something evil. "Evil done in the name of God," that's what Father Martin was doing. Even priests, even saints had their times of darkness. Maybe what God really wanted Rosa to do was lead Father Martin out of his. Instead of hiding like a coward, Rosa should be confronting him and making him see that his own fear was twisting his soul.

Rosa felt a click in her head; something had fallen into place. That's what she had to do, what she was meant to do.

The rest of the day passed without her noticing. After the last lookers had left the booth, she helped Jimmy tidy up and walked briskly to the train. Before the surge of adrenalin could ebb, before her nerve would fail her, she went straight to St. Agatha's. Father Martin wasn't in the sanctuary, only the new deacon she didn't like very much.

Determined to say her piece, Rosa walked around to the refectory. She put her hand on the knob and bumped her head on Mrs. Hogan, who was leaving for the day. "Oh!" Rosa said, trying to regain her balance. "I'm so sorry."

"Hello, Rosa." Mrs. Hogan nodded cheerily and patted the puffy coat she wore each year from Halloween until Easter, regardless of the weather. "No harm done. You'll be looking for Father," she stated.

"Yes," Rosa agreed.

"Did you have an appointment? He'll be sorry he missed you, I'm sure. It's just he would have forgot his own head today, he was in such a hurry."

"No. No appointment. I just wanted a few words." Rosa tried to act as if it weren't important. She wondered if she'd be able to keep herself fired up until tomorrow.

"It's the way they make them wait these days at the airport," Mrs. Hogan continued, taking Rosa's arm and leaning heavily on it as they made their way down the three steps to the pavement. "He was thinking he almost couldn't get there too early, don'tcha know."

"The airport?"

"You forgot it's today he's off to Chicago. Well, with all that's going on...and it's all thanks to you, dear." Mrs. Hogan patted Rosa's arm approvingly. "Not that I know anything official like, but I know what I know. We all have you in our prayers, you can be sure."

Rosa started thinking she needed as many prayers as she could get. She didn't know what Father Martin was doing on his way to Chicago, but the implication was that it had something to do with Mam. She smiled tremulously at Mrs. Hogan as they passed under the streetlight. "Thank you," she said.

11 – WEAPONS OF MASS DESTRUCTION

Susan didn't actually see the riot.

They flew in first thing in the morning, after a particularly long Mam-after-Cam the night before, and no one had gotten much sleep. Melissa and Raju, her entourage on these short hops, went to the hotel to get some rest, but Susan craved a few waking hours to herself. They'd been getting harder to come by of late, since *Pearl!* had put her on the tabloid radar. The hotel, which was known to be expecting her, was likely to be full of fans, rubberneckers and paparazzi. She took an anonymous cab from the ranks at O'Hare and went straight to the Art Institute.

Alan had suggested the Art Institute a few weeks back, but it wasn't until the morning plane that Susan had seen the hidden brilliance in the idea. Two-dimensional art not being something She could see, there was no guilt in keeping Mam buttoned away in the dark, presumably in the state that passed for sleep. No gawkers, if She couldn't be seen, and the only voice in Susan's ears her own. The hush of the museum wrapped around her like an afghan and fuzzy slippers. She knew it wasn't Alan's idea of how to "do" a museum, but it was pleasant to wander aimlessly from gallery to gallery. When something caught her eye, she'd stop or sometimes even linger on a bench for a while and stare with a little more attention. It was ironic, she realized, to be inches away from some of the most beautiful paintings in the world and feel the most gorgeous thing was the silence. It was so incredibly restful.

When she got hungry, she had a salad and coffee in the café, and read some of a story she'd picked up in the gift shop for Max Wilson. He'd been in a mystery phase last she knew, and his mom would be thrilled for him to learn something about Vermeer, so she expected the gift to be a big success. That was good. It was a long time since she'd spent any real time with Diane's kids. Another thing she missed.

She hated to leave the museum, but eventually she found herself constantly yawing in the climate controlled air and her feet getting too heavy to move. Still wanting to avoid the hotel, she self-consciously pulled out her expensive new smartphone. Raju had noticed her old dinosaur during the West Coast tour and had been, in his words, "disgusted and/or dismayed." As soon as they'd gotten home, he'd bought her one more like his new toy. She found it more intimidating than high school trigonometry. It did everything but make up her mind, though no doubt there was some kind of I Ching or Magic 8-ball application that could be added to do just that. For immediate purposes, it was enough to remember how to turn on the GPS, which Melissa had programmed with all the hotels and theatres on their itinerary. If she was reading it right—having a surfeit of disembodied voices in her life, she refused to let it talk to her—she was only a couple of blocks away from the theatre now. A little cold fresh air would do her good, and it was probably wise to check out the space before tonight and see what they'd gotten her into. The search for a Chicago venue had been a case of The Three Bears, except nothing had been "just right." The many small theatres available for hire couldn't seat enough to make the two-day trip worthwhile, so in the end, Raju and Tara had opted for a Broadway-sized house that was dark for the time in question.

The stage doorman had no problem letting Susan into the building, where Ziggy and his gang were hard at work with the local hired guns. She wandered onto the stage and looked out. It was enormous. To anyone in the balcony, she'd look like an ant and Mam like a breadcrumb. Not that there'd be anyone in the balcony. With all the tickets the same price, there was no expectation of releasing balcony seats unless there was a surprise overflow, "surprise" being the operative word. The theatre was larger than any they'd used, except for the Ahmanson, and that had been in LA, the land of crazy cults and celebrity worship, and for one night only. This would be two nights, in a far more pragmatic kind of town.

"Yodel-odle-lay-hee-hoo!" Susan called out.

"What in the world was that?" Mam asked. It was the first thing she'd said in hours.

"I'm doing my own sound check," Susan said. "This is some opera house we've got ourselves booked in. With all the empty seats, we'll be echoing off the walls tonight. Hey, Baskar!" she spotted Wendy's sound man in the auditorium, doing something to a mike from the top of a high ladder. He waved with his free hand. "I sure hope you know how to get rid of echoes!" He waved again, with an automatic smile that indicated he hadn't heard a word beyond his own name.

"I thought everyone was happy with ticket sales," Mam said.

"They sold well enough," Susan admitted. "It's just that when we said we wouldn't worry about filling the balcony, I never thought about what all that empty space up there would look like."

"There may not be as many empties as you think," Melissa declared a few hours later, waking her from her nap on the greenroom sofa. "It looks like we're still selling like crazy." She and Raju had arrived with the neatly steamed robes, Susan's makeup box and some dinner from the steakhouse across the way.

As would be expected on a Friday just around six, street traffic was heavy and a substantial of portion of it seemed to be lining up in front of the theatre. Melissa didn't understand why Raju wasn't more excited. These two days in Chicago could turn out to be their biggest box office coup yet.

Melissa's emotions tended to be as transparent as her enthusiasm, which was why Raju hadn't told her about the e-mail. When he'd turned on his phone after the flight, he'd found a message from Tara. Rosa, of all people, had called in tears with a story about some crazy priest from Brooklyn, who was apparently in Chicago, looking to stir up trouble. Tara had already alerted the Chicago Police Department, and had a contact name for Raju, as well as the identity of someone in the Mayor's office who had something to do with permits for protests. As soon as he'd gotten to the hotel, he'd made a few phone calls. No one seemed to take it seriously, but he'd made sure they'd taken his number. It did sound a bit far-fetched. Even after *Pearl!*, they were hardly in the mainstream of public consciousness. If some priest did have a problem with Mam, why would he come all the way to Chicago when Her offices were in New York? Poor Rosa had put herself through so much lately; it was probably some fantasy of hers. This made sense to Raju, and to Tara once he'd called to tell her how much was not happening in Chicago.

He'd so dismissed the idea, that he'd been taken aback to see the swell of bodies along West Monroe. Melissa was innocently delighted at what she assumed was a surge in ticket sales. To some extent, she might even have been right. A portion of the crowd did seem to be gravitating towards the box office. He could only hope they were fans or, at worst, curiosity seekers, and not a clique out to break up the Assemblage. What worried him more, were the people who were collecting in front of the office building down the street. He'd taken part in a few Human Rights marches near the UN and to his eyes, that group looked like it was being organized. He also wondered about the handful of men who'd been standing in front of the restaurant. There was a deep patch of sidewalk that, in the warmer months, was obviously used for outdoor seating. When he and Melissa had picked up dinner, these men had been arranging themselves as if to cordon off the area. When they'd noticed him watching, he'd gotten a stare back that drilled through his head. He thought, but he couldn't be sure, that he'd seen what might have been banners rolled around long poles.

It unsettled him. Maybe Rosa's panic had somehow translated to him secondhand and his imagination was making an associative leap, but something didn't feel right. He wished there was someone he could talk to, someone on the scene who knew more about Chicago. Alec Klocek, that's who he could call. The native Chicagoan had been determined to use this event to prove to his homies that his invisible Associate Producer job at *Duh News* really was as important as he'd said. They'd met only once or twice before, but now he'd flown out for the weekend, lined up a block of tickets and was hosting an after-show supper tonight, so Raju had his number.

Alec was gratifyingly receptive. Maybe it was his years working on a television show known for taking risks. Or maybe it was the memory of his former neighbor in Brooklyn, a member of the obscure Druze sect who'd worked on a Woman's Rights commission at the UN. Her gay roommate had come home one day to find her dead on the living room floor. Her throat had been slashed by an uncle who'd flown halfway across the world to do the "honor killing" after hearing she was living with a man. Not only was Alec willing to be mildly paranoid on Mam's behalf, but there was something he could do about it. Alec's cousin had married a cop, who promised to make a few calls and get Raju's earlier reports on the radar.

Feeling a little easier in his mind, Raju rang Wendy to give her a head's up. She'd be making her usual pre-show circuit soon and he didn't want her and her crew to stumble onto trouble unawares. Wendy sounded perversely thrilled that she might find herself in control of the only first-hand coverage of a hard news event. "Don't do anything stupid," he warned her.

"You mean like saying something like that?" she snapped and hung up.

Raju pocketed his phone. Before going down to the greenroom, he stopped by the box office. They'd sold the first few rows of the center balcony. That would be something he could actually talk about when he joined the others.

Wendy pulled Uri off the sofa and headed to meet Baskar at the rendezvous point. By the time they reached the intersection, things were starting to heat up. The first people Wendy spoke to were rubberneckers, drawn by the growing crowds. They didn't know what was going on at the theatre, but it sure seemed like something was. Maybe there'd be a celebrity, or a body. They were willing to hang around a while and see what they could see. It wasn't Mam-specific atmosphere, but Uri grabbed some quick footage as he always did—there was no telling what might be useful in a few months, when Wendy got down to editing the documentary.

The closer they got to the theatre, the more the sidewalk was crammed with people. If you could focus on the trees instead of the forest, Wendy found, the mass of bodies resolved itself into distinct groups. In front of the theatre itself, a modest trickle for the box office was separated from the street traffic by the traditional strap of tape. The platoon in front of the Grillroom had unfurled their banners and rallied behind their leader, a slight dark-haired man in priest's robes. "Blasphemy," one simply read. "Thou Shalt Not Worship False Gods," said another. Whether or not you knew what "Mark

13:22" meant, the ornate silver letters, painted on what looked like black satin, communicated the gravity of the message.

The group Raju had spotted in front of the office building identified themselves, with signs and buttons, as "M.A.MAM – Mothers Against Mam." Their slogans were shriller and less portentous that the priest's: "Stop Corrupting Our Children" and "Shame on You!"

Less organized, but greater in quantity, were the fans and supporters. This surprised Wendy. Unlike at other stops on the tour, where the theatres had been smaller, there were still tickets available and no apparent reason for anyone to wait outside in hopes of glimpsing Mam. Polling them, Wendy discovered they were a flash mob. Someone who'd come for a last minute ticket had registered the two protest groups and sent a fast blast to everyone on her call list, who had in turn repeated the call out.

Even Uri, a burly man with a camera like a missile launcher perched on his shoulder, found it harder and harder to shove a path through the crowds. Bodies pressed so close together that the wind didn't penetrate and the vapor cloud that followed every shout was the only sign of the first real cold snap. And shouting they were. Whether it was the appearance of a camera crew, or the early-arriving ticket holders milling outside the doors until they could get inside, something made the crowd switch from wait-and-see mode into action.

Between the street traffic and the muted rumble of the 'L,' people were raising their voices to do more than talk on their cell phones.

An amplifier screeched into life, piercing the swirl of urban clamor. "My children," came the blurred nasal baritone of the priest, his mouth pressed too close to the Mr. Microphone provided by the local parish house. "You provoke the Lord to a jealous rage. Is this ignorance? Or are you so puffed up, that you refuse to see the danger in this woman, this Susan Roth?"

The Mam supporters closest to the Grillroom started to boo, and pressed as close as they were able to come. The priest's supporters tightened their front line. His voice tightened with growing excitement. "I know some of you claim She works miracles. It is not your fault that you think this. Matthew warns us of false messiahs who will perform wonders so great, that even the elect are deceived by them. 'If anyone says to you "Look, here is the Messiah!" he warns, "do not believe it."' This woman is no prophet. This woman speaks with the tongue of Lucifer, not the tongue of angels."

"Damn Mam!" the M.A.MAM screamed. They turned it into a slow, rhythmic chant. "Damn Mam! Damn Mam!"

A cluster of Mam partisans overturned a litter basket and helped a large woman to climb on top. They steadied her so that she could raise her hands above her head without falling. "Mam doesn't work miracles, She IS a miracle!" Her voice carried surprisingly strongly over the din of the street, and even over the subsequent cheers from Mam's supporters. Later, someone said she was an opera singer, but that might have been a kneejerk assumption based on her size. "And She makes sense!"

The priest definitely heard her. He was ready for this and immediately cut her off. "Some of you will protest that what this so-called 'Mam' has to say is good," he said, pointing his free hand accusingly in the woman's direction. "I remind you of what Saint Paul told the Corinthians. 'You cannot drink the cup of the Lord and also the cup of demons,' he told them. 'You cannot be partakers of the table of the Lord's table, and of the table of demons.' Saint Paul gives a stern warning to those who think they can worship the Lord on one hand, and at the same time give credence to what the demons have to say."

The soi-disant opera singer took a deep breath and raised her hands to make a megaphone. "Saint Paul hated women!" she trumpeted. "Mam is your church's worst nightmare!!"

Meanwhile, the M.A.MAM group was still shouting. "Damn Mam! Damn Mam! Damn Mam!" One of them started beating out the rhythm on a mailbox. It's a federal offense to tamper with a mailbox and, unfortunately for the drummer, it was noticed by a patrol making a desultory sweep of the area as a favor to Alec Klocek's cousin-in-law. One policeman sprang into action and cuffed him (some of the M.A.MAM were apparently fathers), while his partner radioed in a report of a riot in progress.

Father Martin hadn't lost a beat. Eyes glittering, mouth pressed so close to the microphone that there was as much breath as sound, he continued his harangue. "It's not too late. If She has deceived you, let the veil be lifted from your eyes! A corrupt tree cannot bear good fruit! Turn away from this demon! Turn away, confess your weakness in being deceived and pray for absolution. God will forgive you!"

"Praise Jesus!" shrieked several of the M.A.MAM.

This was when the ululations began.

Like most post-911 Americans, Wendy froze at the sound. She grabbed Uri's arm. He smirked. "You wanted hard news?" he had to shout for her to hear. "Welcome to my world!" It was impossible to see where the sounds were coming from. She wasn't sure she was brave enough to look. Over the months she'd spent watching people of all backgrounds flocking to Mam, Wendy had become accustomed to focusing on the similarities that drew them together. Even today, she'd been invited to visit with a local group of Moslem women who met once a week to watch a Mam webcast. One woman had agreed to be taped, as long as her face remained off camera.

"They are truly the same ideals I've been taught all my life," the woman had said, leaning forward as if to convince the microphone, "excepting that Mam doesn't order obedience. She places no demands on the minute behaviors of life: what one ought to wear, or not; what one ought to eat, or not; what hours of the day one must pray. She enlightens and then allows one's own better self to receive and apply the knowledge. She is the teacher we have awaited." The other women had nodded firmly in agreement. Wendy had been incredibly moved by this sense of connection that could reach through the layers of differences humans had created for themselves.

Now Wendy felt like she was being woken from a particularly nice dream by a particularly nasty alarm clock. There were rabid Catholics on one side, militant Christians on another, and now Moslems of unknown stripe were somewhere she couldn't see. There was an ugly temperature rising on the street. She'd been so excited about Mam's challenge to an establishment that she'd long believed was failing the world, that she'd lost her grasp of the ferocity of religious differences. It was angry here and now on West Monroe, cacophonously, and possibly chaotically, angry. Wendy pressed closer to Uri. She could feel Baskar's itchy scarf in front of her nose. Somebody stomped on her foot and her scream was swallowed up in the greater roar. Stumbling along with her crew, she reminded herself that she'd be in sole control of footage that news outlets all over the country would be dying to get their hands on. That is, if she didn't get trampled on first.

Out of nowhere, some guy in a "What are the Repercussions?" T-shirt leaped over a hydrant and threw a firm uppercut to Father Martin's jaw.

After that, even in rewind it was hard to make out exactly what anyone was shouting. As people pushed and shoved and occasionally punched out, there were cries of "Pagan witch go home" and "Blasphemy!" as well as the deafening thud of "Damn Mam!" over and over. The other side had started to yell "Take Responsibility!" and "Mam is Love!" at the top of their lungs. Someone broke a car window. And the riot squad, Lexan shields and all, finally arrived to take control.

Neither Susan nor Melissa actually saw the riot, but Raju saw parts of it from behind the glass doors to the theatre.

He'd been on his way upstairs after dinner when he'd nearly collided with the house manager on his way down. Raju was glad he'd intercepted the man before he'd made it within earshot of Susan. He let Raju push him back up the stairs, burbling frantically about what was happening outside. Raju had to look for himself. He thought he'd go out on the street, but the tumult that met his eye stopped him in his tracks. Instinctively, he moved so that his body wouldn't be visible from the street, and he reached for his phone. He called the numbers Tara had given him and was told the police were already on their way. He tried Wendy and got her voicemail. Starting to feel sick, he called Alec to warn him.

"Have you spoken with Wendy?" Alec demanded.

"I got her voicemail," Raju told him.

"Do you think she's out there?"

"I warned her to be careful, that there might be some trouble. She didn't really appreciate it. We had no idea...I think she thought I was being patronizing."

"She's out there," Alec said with what sounded like satisfaction. "Look, I'll be there soon. I have to make a call." He sounded excited, not concerned.

His eyes never leaving the drama on the street, Raju automatically pocketed his phone. He hoped Alec was calling his police connections, but wouldn't have bet on it. The associate producer was probably calling the network.

Once the police did arrive and had created a cordon around the theatre, it was decided to open the house early so that audience members could get safely inside instead of lingering behind the vulnerable street-facing glass. People pushed their way into the theatre, bright-eyed and a little breathless.

Raju hadn't wanted to upset Susan and Mam, but this was obviously too big to ignore. Some kind of acknowledgement would have to be made. He slipped backstage, not a minute too soon. Melissa had already taken her customary pre-curtain peek into the audience and could feel the extra charge to the buzzing as people settled into their seats.

"What's going on out there?" she asked, her face alight with curiosity. "Is Oprah here or something?"

He took her by the hand and walked her over to Susan. Fortunately, they were so stunned by his news bulletin and had such a pressing need to focus on what to say, that no one thought to ask if Wendy was still outside. He left Susan and Mam hashing it over, with Melissa hovering nearby.

Standing at the back of the house, as he did for every Assemblage, Raju kept pulling out his phone and checking to see if he'd missed a call. Alec came looking for him, not with any reassurances but to tell him the results of his phone call with Jack. Arrangements had been made for her presumed footage. Whichever of them heard from Wendy first—and both of them were to keep their phones on vibrate throughout the Assemblage—should explain the arrangements to her. With a wink, Alec sauntered down to the prime block of seats he'd filled with his posse. As if he didn't have a care in the world, Raju thought. And people said *lawyers* were heartless. He had yet to hear a word from or about Wendy, when the houselights went down and the Assemblage began.

Susan and Mam made their entrance to more than the usual applause and some cheers. Susan held herself with particular dignity and raised her hands to quiet the room.

"Good evening," she said into the growing quiet.

"Greetings," said Mam, and the applause resumed.

"Please!" Susan said firmly. She gestured for quiet again. "We've only just learned about what's been happening out in the street tonight." The audience hushed uncomfortably, necks stretching back and forth between neighbors and the stage. Surely they weren't going to cancel the show? With the stage lights on, Susan couldn't see the audience, but she remembered what the theatre had looked like that afternoon and now she could feel a couple of thousand eyes filling those rows and rows of seats, all staring at her with apprehension. "Firstly, we'd like to thank you for coming. We're just glad that you're here and that no one got hurt." Someone started to clap. She silenced him with a shake of her head. "But we can't pretend that we're not disturbed by this occurrence. Before we begin the evening we'd planned for you, Mam would like to say a few words about what's just happened."

"Thank you, Susan," Mam said. "Since awakening among you, I've taken observation as my primary task, but in this situation I have no observation from which to speak. Unlike those of you sitting here in front of me, Susan and I didn't experience what's happened on the street. We've only been told about it. From what I've heard, I'm dismayed. Once again, I'm hearing about people closing their eyes and ears in the name of God, people closing their minds in the name of God, people willing to hurt one another in the name of God. Most of you here tonight probably have, yourselves, some image of God. Whatever it is, you probably use it to find guidance and comfort. That's a big difference between God and me. I am not comfortable and I don't come with a book of instructions."

Someone in the audience gave a "whoop" and Susan immediately raised her hand to signal a stop.

"I demand much of people," Mam continued, "and I offer little in return. I make you do the work yourself. Some of you belong to religions that use the word 'save' or 'redeem.' I say that if there is such a state of being, that you don't get it by asking some force to bestow it upon you, you have to make it happen. Don't ask God to save you, save yourself. You've got the tools. God, or who or whatever you believe did so, gave you three levels of consciousness: the consciousness of thought, the consciousness of emotion and that greater consciousness that you call Soul. Now me, I didn't give you these gifts but I expect you to use all three of them actively, every day."

Mam paused to let the audience consider this. "You're wondering what any of this has to do with the battle I'm told was taking place outside this theatre a little while ago. From what I hear, that battle was your world in a nutshell; people bullying people into agreeing with them, because of this odd human compulsion to believe that if I am right then you, by disagreeing with me, are wrong, and my righteousness gives me an obligation to convert you. I keep trying to understand this in you, but I can't. And so far, not a single person I've spoken with has been able to explain it to me. Why human beings, blessed with all those gifts of consciousness, will blindly battle, or even kill one another, in the name of forcing one another to be 'right?' How do any of you know for certain what is 'right?' Maybe there isn't only one right. Why is that so difficult for humans to believe? You don't think there's only one way to get from New York to Chicago, do you? And if there are multiple ways and they all do eventually get to Chicago, then how arrogant for anyone to think that the route he or she prefers is 'right' and the others are 'wrong!'

"I can't solve human behavior. I have no magic formula to give you, though apparently people outside were rather angrily protesting that I've said otherwise. It's your own human prophets who have told you, time after time, to treat others as you would wish to be treated yourself. That's as much of a magic formula as there's ever going to be. Stop nodding your heads and pretending to accept it. What's that word you're so fond of? Internalize? Internalize it. I've always said I am here to communicate, and as my time with you continues, I understand this more and more to be the essential truth. I've been talking with and listening to you. Maybe it's time for me to beg you to talk and listen to one another. Use those wonderful gifts of consciousness. Whether or not you do it with me is of no consequence. What matters is that every day there are more and more of you willing to do this and willing to let others find their own way. Let the bullying stop. Let the arrogance and the righteousness stop. Take responsibility for yourself and face the consequences of your own actions. Hasn't humankind had a long enough childhood? You could be such amazing creatures if only you would grow up."

You could have heard a pin drop but, like everyone else in the building, Raju was so focused on the stage that he hadn't even heard the door open. When Wendy touched his arm, he jumped and nearly hit his head on a fire extinguisher. He pulled her to where he could see her face in the amber glow of the emergency exit lights. She looked a bit haggard, but she was smiling. He smiled back with sheer relief, before surprising himself by grabbing her in an enormous embrace. They made their way down to the greenroom. Keeping the speaker on so that they could keep an ear on the Assemblage, they brought each other up to date.

Uri and Baskar were fine and at the police station. Wendy'd sent them on ahead in hopes they'd be able to shoot some people being brought in for processing, before anyone noticed and stopped them. Several dozen people had been arrested. A few with broken noses and severe lacerations had been taken to the closest ER. Property damage was not as bad as it might have been. Local news teams had arrived on the heels of the police, but only her team had full scale coverage of the riot in progress. She grinned widely as she handed Raju a stack of cards.

"We've got 'til 10:30! You negotiate, I meet my guys at the hotel and start cutting."

"You've got 'til 9:50," he corrected. "Whatever you cut by then, Jack's waiting to run it as a live feed."

"Then I'd better run." She kissed him on the cheek. "Good thing some friend of Alec's is waiting for me in a squad car outside."

Raju stared at the handful of business cards. Bloomberg, Fox, CNN, NBC, CBS, ABC. They were playing with the big boys now. With everyone he cared about safe and sound, he could afford to get excited. He reached for his phone. Better start by giving Tara a heads up, and then call Jack. He also should put Ziggy on alert, have him stream that welcome speech of Mam's to Wendy so that she could cut it in. He'd need some help to get it all done in time. He wasn't going to disturb Susan and Mam or the audience by making Klocek's pocket buzz; there'd been disturbance enough tonight. Melissa didn't need to wait in the wings throughout the Assemblage. If Susan needed a drink of water, one of those stagehands they'd had to pay to do nothing could help her.

By the time, Chicago time, that Alec had made it through the police cordon to the theatre, the live taping of that evening's *Duh News* in New York was already finished and in the can. His call had caught Jack in his dressing room. Jack had been quick to agree that they'd be idiots to drop the ball on this. They were *the* source for news on Mam. If Wendy showed up with some footage, it should be run tonight, not held for tomorrow when the other news outlets might get it. Jack had called back a skeleton crew and settled down to wait.

It was hard to wait. It was as hard as that time, before they were married, when Emily was "late" and had to pee on a stick. He'd thought nothing would ever feel longer than those five minutes. This was a lot longer and there was no telling how much longer it might be, or whether the results would be as happy. He tried to distract himself online, but he kept popping up and down, pacing back and forth. He was as jittery as if he'd had four double espressos despite his wife having taken him off caffeine a year ago.

If Wendy had something, an exclusive, it would be a major coup for the show and for him. It would be mainstream news and they would be the first to break it. No one would be able to ignore it. From day one, the whole

Mam story had been leading up to this. His bet would have paid off. Jack Rabb would be significant.

And Roger Haff would kill that he'd been left out of it. That made Jack smile enough to almost relax. He'd had it up to here with Roger's snarkiness and his bottomless sense of entitlement. He only put up with it because their on-camera chemistry worked for the show. It kept the pace fast and the tone light. Jack understood this. That's why he was a producer and Roge was just a hired hand. A hired hand with a chip on his shoulder. Roge had never gotten over being dropped from *Saturday Night Live* after only one season on the back bench. Now he acted like he'd single-handedly dragged *Duh News* out of the ratings basement instead of being one of a handful of new people who'd joined the show at the same time. Roge always thought he wasn't getting enough—enough credit, enough attention, enough money. He was always complaining, and he was always the first one out the door after each show. It wasn't Jack's fault that he was halfway to Connecticut before the call from Alec had come through, though he'd whine that he could have been called back. Oh, Jack could just imagine if he'd done that, and the tantrums if Alec's "possibly" came to nothing. It wouldn't come to nothing; he couldn't even think that. The phone was going to ring with the best news ever, and Roge would have to choke it down.

When the phone did ring, Jack picked it up as if it were an egg with his whole future held inside.

"It's a go," Raju told him. "Wendy's in the hotel cutting it now."

"Will I have time to see it?"

"No. She's going to call you when she's ready so you can work out what to do before show time. My hunch is that she'll be working up 'til the last minute, so she'll probably stream it to you live. Maybe you'll need her to do some narration. Alec's in the theatre, sixth row center, but if you think you need him..."

"I'll be fine with the crew here." Jack was loving the rush of adrenalin that came from rising to an occasion.

"Good, good." Raju sounded relieved. Jack loved that, too. It felt good for him to be the strong one with everything under control. "I can tell you that you're getting exclusive riot footage," Raju's voice brightened as he reached the comfort of legal turf. "At least part of it. I'm not letting any of the news outlets have more than five minutes worth for tonight, so you'll have plenty that they won't."

"Excellent!" Jack wondered if Raju could hear him smiling.

"Even better than you think." Now Jack was pretty sure he could hear Raju's smile. "You're also the only one tonight, the only one outside our own webcast, that is, who'll have the opening five minutes or so of tonight's Assemblage. Wait 'til you hear it, Jack! After your show tonight, there's not a network that will be able to deny that Mam is news. Breast or not, they'll have to put Her on the air!"

"And I'll be the first. I'll always have been the first."

It was difficult to say who was more triumphant.

Rosa'd had such a long day that by the time she got home she'd honestly forgotten all about it. After proudly complaining about how heavy Carlito was to carry home from Vanessa's, Ernesto dumped him in his new bed without taking off his things. Naturally the baby woke up while Rosa was easing him out of his puffy jacket and, in his not-really-awake confusion, he started kicking and his damp boots got all over the covers. Before she could settle him back down, Rosa had to change the new Thomas-the-Train duvet for the old baby blanket, which she'd pushed way in the back of the closet. She brought the laundry to the bathroom to do tomorrow, and got herself ready for bed. When she came out, after turning off the lights and keeping so very quiet, the last thing she expected was to find Ernesto sitting fully dressed in front of the TV.

"You had a message," he said, pointing a thumb over his shoulder at the phone. "That Tara from work. She said something about you being right, and thank you very much and all. And to watch what's coming on. She sounded pretty intense."

While he was talking, the screen split, with the credits for the show that preceded *Duh News* crunched into a box on the right-hand side. The larger panel filled with roaring flames.

"First it was Mrs. O'Leary's cow," came the sonorous voice of an off-screen announcer. The flames were overlaid with some 1968 newsreel footage of student protesters facing off with police in riot gear. "Then it was Eugene McCarthy. And tonight, Chicago's fired up all over again!" The vintage newsreel was replaced by a contemporary crowd, pushing and shoving. Rosa's startled eyes spotted Wendy Smedstad, narrowly missing being caught on the shoulder by someone wildly swinging a protest sign. "And *Duh News* is the only place to go for breaking news. Stay tuned for our Mam-a-palooza exclusive coverage of today's riot. You won't see it anywhere else but right here on *Duh News*."

Rosa ran for the phone and replayed Tara's message. It was what Ernesto had said, except he forgot to say how she ended: "Thank you for being there for the team." That felt good. Everyone was okay. Tara didn't say so exactly, but she sounded as excited as a booster at a home game, which she wouldn't unless everyone was okay.

Curious, but unworried, Rosa sat down beside Ernesto to watch, and also to watch Ernesto watching. She'd never said much about any of it to him. He wasn't all that interested in Church, only in his job, and the things he did with his boys. Even if she thought he'd be interested, she didn't know how to begin to explain Mam, so she'd said something vague about it being a woman's group that did community service, and that she worked in the office. It was enough for him that she was happy, had a good daycare for the baby, and was making a little money so they could start saving for a house.

Now Ernesto was glued to the set, with no idea of what he was about to see. Jack Rabb, sitting alone at the anchor desk, looked extra serious but with a kind of sparkle, like he was sharing Tara's excitement. In other words, he looked like a regular news guy with a big story. He even sounded like a regular news guy when he announced it without the slightest touch of a smile in his voice.

"Earlier today, as we do every weekday evening, we recorded *Duh News* in front of a live studio audience. However, while we were taping, events occurred that were both important enough, and of such personal significance to our show and our viewers, that we have decided to pre-empt the airing of that episode. Instead, tonight, *Duh News* will be presenting exclusive coverage of this evening's disturbances outside the LaSalle Bank Theatre in Chicago where Mam and Susan Roth are appearing," he appeared to check his watch, "even as we speak. Some of the footage we are about to show may be disturbing to some viewers. We also advise that as part of this news coverage, later in our broadcast, we will be airing unedited footage of Mam's response. This news footage," he elaborated with a touch of satisfaction, "will be shown exactly as it was recorded for Mam's own subscription webcasts, with Mam appearing in full, untouched by pixilation, digital overlays or any other obscuring device. Tonight's coverage will be presented by our own Wendy Smedstad, speaking to us live from Chicago. Wendy, over to you."

Wendy appeared, in coat and long striped scarf, standing in front of the theatre. To one side of her could be seen police barricades, behind which a steady stream of audience members was foaming out of the theatre. "Thank you, Jack. As you can see, it's calm here now outside the theatre, where Mam and Susan have just concluded tonight's Assemblage at 10 p.m. local time. My team and I happened to be on the scene a few hours ago, when things were very different, as you are about to see."

The screen changed, showing Wendy pushing her way through noisy, jostling crowds. A roughly cut six or so minutes of riot footage followed. Rosa and Ernesto were riveted to their seats as Wendy nearly got hit with the sign, as the M.A.MAM chanted angrily, as mailboxes were pounded and trash cans jumped on and as someone slugged the priest in the nose, precipitating an all-out brawl.

"That wasn't Father Martin?!" Ernesto rubbed his eyes in disbelief.

"Mmm-hmmm," Rosa said, "oh, yes it was." She knew it was uncharitable, but she was glad to see someone deck him. She would have liked to have done it herself, but she probably wouldn't have done it half as well. Even growing up with a brother on each side and a whole lot of cousins, she punched like a girl.

After the commercial break, Jack and Wendy spoke across time zones for a bit, and Wendy showed some more tape, including a shot of the bloody-nosed Father and his assailant both being ducked into a police car. There was an interview with a uniformed friend of Alec's Klocek's cousin-in-law, and one with a not-remotely-contrite member of M.A.MAM who barked full into the camera, "In the old days, they knew what to do with witches!" and spat on the sidewalk.

"What kinda place do you work?" Ernesto asked, awed. He didn't even seem to remember she'd mentioned quitting. Rosa was wondering if Tara was forgetting, too, or more if Tara was trying to act that way. Maybe they all were. Probably if she showed up at the office Monday morning, no one would say anything except "Good morning."

She was still pondering this when Jack set up the clip of Mam's opening comments at the Assemblage. She watched with admiration as Susan walked out like a queen. The only way anyone would know she was upset was if they knew her like Rosa did and could see the way her fingers were just a little clenched. Then Mam began to speak. Rosa listened hard to that clear, firm voice and experienced the same wonder she'd felt the first time Susan had sat on the dark red chair in her living room and addressed the bible study group. She made such good sense, Mam did. It all seemed simple and logical. Maybe that's why it had to be Mam that said it. To believe things so basic, you had to hear them from a miraculous source. For wild plans or unbelievable ideas to take hold, you needed to hear them from the most ordinary person around. Some of the stuff about this war they'd gotten into, maybe the country got roped in because President Hendron was such an average seeming guy.

She'd almost forgotten about Ernesto until she felt his eyes. With the show clearly over, he'd pried his attention away from the screen and was looking tentatively at her. "If I came to pick you up, you know, one night," he mumbled, "could I maybe meet Her...uh, them...whatever?"

"Sure," she said. "Whenever."

The *Pearl!* interview fascinated Phyllis Hendron. She'd made her girls do some research for her on the subject of Susan Roth. Earlier today, she'd watched the peculiar video they'd made for her of clips from *Duh News*, a rude show she'd never dreamed of watching. It was difficult to accept, surely it was impossible, but people did act as though the woman had a talking breast. "Mam," they called it. Phyllis wished that they didn't put those blurry dot things over the screen. It was quite frustrating. If she could only see it, with her own eyes, she'd know for certain. If it were only *Duh News*, she would have been positive it was a huge nasty joke, thumbing the nose at people of Faith. But, Pearl had implied the same thing and Pearl wouldn't make that type of joke. Still, it might be symbolic, a metaphor for something. Maybe about breast cancer, or was that in her head right now because of flipping by that article about self-examinations? Of course, if it were true, it would be a miracle, a miracle like never since the birth of Our Lord.

She took a deep breath and firmly admonished herself. It was too late to start thinking about such things now. If she did, she'd never get any sleep tonight. Tomorrow was another day, like Scarlett O'Hara said. She put a tissue in her magazine as a bookmark, took off her reading glasses and reached for the remote. As long as they weren't traveling, it was part of her bedtime routine to watch the monologue of her favorite late night comic. She always kept the volume down low so as not to disturb Roddo, who liked to go to sleep early, even on a Friday, "In case they have to wake me up in the middle of the night for a national emergency," and since she never laughed out loud anyway, that was fine. The last five minutes of the network news was still on. Even after so many years, Phyllis hadn't gotten used to that extra five minutes. When she was growing up and sneaking a peak while babysitting, *The Tonight Show* always came on at 11:30 sharp.

"And finally," said the anchor, "from our Chicago affiliate KNBC, here's Karen Williams with some unsettling footage of a disturbance outside a local theatre. Karen?"

"Thanks, Joe. I'm standing outside the LaSalle Bank Theatre on West Monroe where a performance has just let out. It's quiet here now but, earlier this evening, there was a clash between representatives of several religious groups and the followers of inspirational speaker Susan Roth."

Phyllis slapped on the infrared headphones the kids had bought her for Mother's Day and dialed up the sound. The video came from a tourist's camera and wasn't very good, but it was a shocking scene nonetheless. One thing was clear: There were many devout followers of Jesus who considered Susan Roth the enemy. Now wide awake, Phyllis clicked the remote feverishly, searching for more information. She didn't know what station *Duh News* was on, but she thought if she could find it, they might say something. She paused on one of those all-news channels that Roddo hated. They showed a different piece of amateur video, no better than the first one, and an interview with a man who'd been standing with the priest who may have started it all. It was a short exchange as the man was exiting from the police station and hurrying into a taxi to meet the priest at the hospital. The man was so angry that he didn't listen much to the reporter's questions but only said "Corinthians 10:20. They sacrifice to devils, and not to God and I would not want you to have fellowship with devils."

Phyllis kept clicking. When she found *Duh News*, it was only an advertisement. The show, it seemed, had already aired for the night. She'd missed it, and now she was too wound up to sleep. Slipping gently out of bed, she tiptoed out to the residence kitchen to make herself a cup of warm milk with honey. Maybe one of the girls had thought to tape it for her, that would be nice. Too bad she couldn't turn back time and watch it now. She put the milk in the little saucepan on the range. Heating it in the microwave missed the whole point, which was to get sleepy. Following the routine, taking the time to do it right, made all the difference. Maybe she'd call Sheila in Arizona, it was still early out there. Phyllis stopped with her hand on the plastic bear. It was two hours earlier there, and three in California. They hadn't seen *Duh News* out there yet; at least she didn't think they had. If she could watch television as if she were out West, she wouldn't have to wait for a tape. There was a way to do this; something in the back of her head told her that there was. When they first moved into the White House, before someone had programmed her remote, she'd asked why there were so many different CBSs, NBCs and ABCs and all on the TV, and one of the ushers had explained it had to do with the satellite picking up transmissions for all different time zones. She didn't need warm milk. What she needed was a young person.

Feeling adventurous, Phyllis wrapped her fleece robe tighter and went out into the hall. There was sure to be someone from the Secret Service or, barring that, a nice young Marine.

Jared Crockertt had been so tired all day. He thought he might be coming down with his annual November bug, and all he wanted to do was go to bed early and stay there for the weekend. After a slice from the place near the Metro and a couple of aspirin, he'd done exactly that. Then the television had come on and wakened him. He'd forgotten to turn off the timer he kept set for *Duh News*.

He was going to turn it right off, but what he saw caught him off guard and jolted him wide awake. It was like one of those soccer riots that always seemed to happen in Europe, except no one had their bodies painted in team colors. It was terrifying if you tried to imagine being in the middle of it but, if you were watching from the safety of your room, it was exhilarating.

He couldn't tear his eyes away from their faces. Everyone so focused and angry, and all of them so certain of being right. M.A.MAM sounded like people he grew up with. It occurred to him that, not so very long ago, he would have been one with them. Despite his distaste for the Church of Rome, he used to agree with the priest; now he rejoiced in watching someone give that man a bloody nose. Listening to Mam's speech, Jared felt himself getting all warm with pride at being one of Her flock and not any of theirs. He felt cloaked in Her wisdom and goodness. His heart was fully Hers.

As soon as *Duh News* ended, he logged onto the website to see what else Mam and Susan had to say. He zapped some water for tea. It was going to be a long night after all. At least he could sleep late tomorrow.

Having not seen *Duh News*, which wouldn't air on the Coast for a couple more hours, but alerted by the blast e-mail to subscribers from mamiam.com and by a phone call from his sister, Will Barnstock logged on to the webcast when it streamed live. It was a half hour after the Assemblage in Chicago, and began with a quick recap from Susan regarding the riot, followed by the tape of Mam's opening comments from that evening. Then Mam and Susan followed their standard format, talking first with one another before opening the floor to questions. Mam was in top form, he thought, pouring a glass of the good small batch bourbon and putting his feet up on Wilfred's back. The dog rolled an eye and blew a long, sleepy puff. Will sighed, too. Talk about an impossible situation. It would be easier if he didn't believe in what Mam was preaching. If he could discount Her, he could allow himself to be purely resentful with no mixed feelings. As it was, his head nodded along as She spoke, but his hand felt empty, wondering what it would feel like to caress Susan's other breast.

An hour later, a man calling himself Samael was watching television on satellite from his compound in Montana. His current favorite, a former child prostitute redeemed by his powers, had a fondness for a snarky adult cartoon that aired immediately before *Duh News*. As a treat for a particular display of obedience earlier than night, Samael had turned on the sole television, which was near his bed in the only room that had a door that closed. As the girl giggled at her show, he dozed, occasionally running his fingers through her curls, which had finally reached a satisfying length. He hoped it would not be too soon that he'd have to punish her by cropping them.

He drifted into that border state so conducive to visions and dreamed a dream of roiling crowds with arms upstretched and mouths gaping wide. The noise spewed forth at such a pitch, it was only his transcendent senses that enabled him to distinguish ignorant reviling from desperate pleas for his intercession. He felt a deep, stern pleasure as he anticipated the Judgment and his imminent rise, upward from this earth, a righteous flaming sword lifted in his hands. A low, rich, female voice emerged from the Babel, calling out "...people closing their eyes and ears in the name of God, people closing their minds in the name of God..."

When he grasped that the voice came from the television and not from a vision, Samael sat up and groggily tried to focus his eyes. There was a figure, wingless yet draped like Samothracean Victory (Samael had been doing a Junior Year Abroad at the Paris-Sorbonne when he'd first been called to his Mission). Had the Judgment begun? Why had he not been summoned to wherever this angel stood? He inched closer and closer to the screen, hands spread protectively across his face. Had he erred? Was there something he had overlooked? The picture changed to a close-up and he froze in terror. The voice, he saw, came not from the mouth of the brazenly undraped harlot on stage but from her breast. He held his breathe and watched the little crinkly lips move. That still, smooth voice poured on. "Don't ask God to save you, save yourself...Maybe there isn't only one 'right'...Merit is not entitlement...Just because you have questions doesn't mean there are answers...Prayers alone are only breath..."

None of this was true. Samael knew it; God had told him. He'd been told what was right, and had been assured that on The Day, the answers would come. He'd followed every instruction as God gave it to him, and in return, God had assured him he was Saved. This must be a hallucination, or maybe a devil. That mouth. He must have done something. He must have neglected to do something. He was being tested.

"I am being tested!" he roared.

Precious Blood untucked her head from the duvet and blinked. "Huh?" she yawned.

Samael grabbed her by her curls and twisted her to face the television screen. "What do you see?" he demanded.

The girl rubbed her eyes sleepily. "A woman dressed like in the Bible?"

"She's dressed like a blaspheming pagan! Look again!" he pushed her until her nose was almost touching the screen. "Now!"

Precious shook her head and her face crinkled up in a delighted smile. "Cool FX!" she giggled. "Wonder how they do that?"

"What do you see?!"

"It looks like it's talking. Her boob. Hey, is this *Duh News*?" She sat up and wrapped the duvet around her shoulders. "I used to watch this all the time. It's sooo random!"

"I'm not hallucinating," he mumbled. "Then it is a test."

"Jack is sooo funny! Roger, too, but he can be sooo annoying." The camera was back on Jack who was talking to Wendy. Precious cocked her head, as if it helped her concentrate. Her mouth slowly formed an "O." "Samael," she breathed, turning to face him, "I don't think it's FX after all. I think it's real!" She was so enthralled that she didn't notice his face turning red and his eyes bugging out. If she had, she might have been able to turn away again before the back of his hand smacked against her cheek.

"We are being tested!" he bellowed. "I need to address the family." Striding across the room, he flung open the door "Everyone, out of bed, now!"

After finally closing his eyes and getting maybe four hours of sleep, Jared Crockertt was hauled out of bed by a relentless buzzing at the door. His furry brain raced to remember where he'd stored his emergency suitcase, and whether he'd repacked it after gaining fifteen pounds and outgrowing all his trousers. He peered through the fisheye spy hole. Instead of the uniformed serviceman he expected, he was flummoxed to see Uncle Hiram tapping an aggressive foot on the stained grey-green carpet.

Uncle Hiram was not happy. Jared fumbled with the locks, trying to remember his latest transgression and drawing a blank.

"Get some clothes on," Uncle Hiram growled. "I'll explain in the car." Jared reached for the sweatpants he wore around the house but his uncle pointed to the kitchenette where his suit jacket was hanging over the chair. "Work clothes. And leather shoes. Bring a rag and you can buff them on the way."

Jared threw on the suit he'd taken off only a few hours ago and a clean enough shirt. He scooped the better part of a box of tissues into his backpack. Whatever bug he was fighting wasn't going to be helped by no night's sleep. On second thought, he threw in a couple of breakfast bars. Wherever they were going, he hoped he'd be able to get some juice or something.

Even before Uncle Hiram got around to saying it, Jared realized he was going back to the office right now, in the middle of the night and on his day off, too. Before he could imagine any end-of-civilization scenarios that might require the emergency intervention of someone with no unique skills, he learned the truth. It wasn't some mysterious rare blood type or an amazing resemblance to a foreign spy. His uncle needed him for his Mam subscription.

About an hour before picking him up in the government limo, Uncle Hiram had been awakened by a phone call from the White House. After seeing Mam with her own eyes, the First Lady had shaken the President awake and made him catch *Duh News* as it aired for the West Coast. Afterward, the President's reaction had naturally been to call his spiritual advisor.

Hiram Crockertt was one of those lucky people blessed with a brain that jumps from sound asleep to wide awake in the time it takes to pick up a receiver and mumble "Whoozit?" He wasn't angry at being woken in the middle of the night. He enjoyed this confirmation of his importance, that the leader of the free world valued his council so much. What riled him was the particular subject of this call. He knew little about this ridiculous blasphemy, and had no desire to pollute himself by learning more. When his nephew had first brought the subject to his notice, he'd shut the boy up and thought that would be the end of it. He hadn't thought to credit the story as anything other than a twisted fantasy. Since that time, he'd heard the occasional allusion, but never from any source that gave him concern. He had chosen not to dignify the story with inquiry. Now, he thought rapidly as the President droned on, it appeared he would be forced to take this seriously. He needed to give the President an impression of his mastery of the subject, while simultaneously making it seem inconsequential.

The President interrupted Hiram's bland dismissals without appearing to hear them. "I want to know more about this Mam woman," he said, with surprising energy considering both the hour and his usual lack of curiosity. "Phyllis says she's got one of those shows on the internets. I want to see it, Hiram. I want to see it now, and you're the only one I trust to get it done. I'm sorry about the hour, but this is big, you see? I'm sending a car right now."

Crockertt saw he had no choice but to do as the President wished. Thinking quickly as he dressed, he decided his task was to do damage control, and his first consideration in this would be to protect the President's reputation. Crockertt was deeply suspicious of technology and its ability to capture information. He didn't dare have the President of the United States log onto a dubious website on computer that might be traced to him. By the same token, he didn't want to risk a credit card charge showing up on any official account, including his own. Young Jared, he thought with some ironic relief, had already left his trace. His accessing this site wouldn't register as an anomaly. They could use his office computer. If anyone ever found out, it would look like one more case of a young idler wasting office resources. As he slid into the back of the long black car, Crockertt gave the driver instructions to swing by Jared's apartment.

Having worked in the White House for three years, Jared had of course seen the President many times, but he'd never actually met him. Now he found himself being ushered into the Residence before the sun was even up.

"Isn't this delightful!" the First Lady chirped, when Uncle Hiram introduced them, just like on TV, and the President gave his famous hearty slap on the back.

The First Lady even offered to make him a cup of tea, which was really nice of her and which was almost nearly ready by the time Uncle Hiram finished explaining his thinking to the President and pushed Jared to lead them all down stairs "Now, before any early birds start congregating on the telephone wire."

As much as he could have used the tea, and more especially, the honey and lemon, Jared could see his uncle's point. Even on the weekend, there were aides working through much of the night, and the Saturday shift would be coming in before eight. This was a private thing for the President. They didn't need the whole building hearing about it. Fortunately, the only person they passed was so engrossed in reading e-mail on his Blackberry that he never looked up, but just automatically flattened himself against a wall when he felt their shadow.

Mrs. Hendron seemed fascinated by the maze in the lower levels of the mansion in which she lived. She'd never had occasion to pass beyond the attractive offices used by senior staff, and even that had been rare as she wasn't one of the political First Ladies. She said "Oh, my!" every time they rounded a corner, and "Oh my goodness!" when they finally reached Jared's desk. The more they'd walked, the older the desks had become. Jared's seemed to be one of the oldest, and even when he switched on his aluminum goose-necked lamp, had less light than other parts of the room it shared with too many others.

Jared pulled out his once-beige chair to sit and, as always in the narrow space, it banged into the wall behind. Mrs. Hendron squeaked at the sound and he looked up. The three of the most important people he could imagine were looming over him. The lamp halo made them look like witches around a midnight cauldron, or would have if Mrs. H. hadn't looked too jittery. He jumped up to offer her his seat, but his uncle pointed sternly down at the computer.

"Get online," he ordered.

Jared obeyed, starting the protocol of unlocking the CPU, turning on the power and waiting for the tuning fork sound that meant he should present his biometric credentials. While waiting to be processed, he looked around the room, trying to think whose chairs would be the least unpleasant to offer his guests. It occurred to him that no matter which, it was impossible for more than two chairs to fit behind his desk and even that would make it too tight to shift your weight. He got up to rearrange everything so that he could swing his monitor around to face the other way. He had to move the lamp and the phone first, to make room for the keyboard on the other side. Nice Mrs. H. tried to help by grabbing up the chipped Georgetown mug he'd inherited with the desk and used as a pencil jar. Once they realized what he was doing, Uncle Hiram and the President dragged some chairs over themselves, absolving Jared of the need to choose.

His credentials verified, the White House logo wallpaper was enabled on his desktop. As Jared launched his browser and navigated to Mam's website, he felt the other three staring at him, as if he were doing something extraordinary instead of something he assumed everybody did every day. He keyed in his subscriber name and went to the program guide to select that night's webcast.

"This is it," he explained. "I'm putting it in full screen so you can see better. Let me know if you need the sound turned up." There wasn't really room for four chairs. He didn't need to see this webcast again so soon. Besides it felt strange to be watching Mam in the office. Instead, he stood behind the others, watching them watch. Mrs. H. seemed really excited. She leaned forward in her seat and often made little hums in the back of her throat. The President seemed confused. He was attentive, yes, never took his eyes off the screen, but he kept shaking his head from side to side like he was working out a crick in his neck. To someone who didn't know him forever, like Jared did, Uncle Hiram seemed to be focused calmly on what he was hearing, occasionally nodding as if in agreement. Jared, however, saw his right hand flexing and curling on his knee like a punch looking for an excuse to happen. There were too many times in his history that Jared had been the excuse. He vowed to himself that he'd move over to the other side of the desk real quick when the webcast was over.

He needn't have worried himself. When the video ended, the First Lady turned beseechingly and took Uncle Hiram's hand between her own two. "Please, Reverend Crockertt," she said fervently, "you must lead us in a prayer."

In an instant, they'd made a circle, linked hands and gravely bowed their heads. "I think what we need now is a moment of silent contemplation," Hiram began. "Dear Jesus, as we consider what we have seen, we humbly beseech you to grant us the understanding that we may act in your name." For almost five minutes, there wasn't a sound except for the couple of times when the President had to clear his postnasal drip. "Amen," Crockertt said firmly, with the exquisite timing of experience, exactly when the silence had gone on long enough.

"Amen," they all murmured. Jared hastily pushed the furniture back to where it belonged. Anyone working today would soon be shuffling in with their gym bags and insulated mugs of designer coffee. He didn't want them to find him here when he wasn't supposed to be. The President seemed to be thinking the same thing; he added some door-ward motion to his conversation with the Reverend.

Jared figured he'd check the vending machine in the lounge. If there wasn't any juice, he'd chomp down one of his breakfast bars with a co'cola before hitting the metro and going home. The First Lady, who'd helped him rearrange his desk, was still waiting by the door. "Thank you," she said, looking directly at him, like she would recognize him if she saw him again. "What a gift you've given me!" She leaned in for just a second and pecked him on the cheek.

He wished some of the guys had been there to see that, but then it was probably better they weren't there to see him blush. "I'm really glad I could be of service, ma'am," he said shyly. "Really."

"Why aren't you sweet!" She took his hand as if he were a little boy she was walking to school and led him out to the hall. "Let's go back upstairs

229

and have that cup of tea and get some breakfast in you, and then we'll have the driver bring you home." He tried to protest, but her maternal instincts combined with adrenaline were just too strong. "Anyone can see you're coming down with a cold, and I know you've had hardly any more sleep than I have." He couldn't really argue with her. He only hoped Uncle Hiram didn't notice.

Back up in the Residence, Uncle Hiram had more than enough else to occupy his attention. The President had been very impressed by what he'd seen of Mam, and the Reverend was having a hard time reining him in.

"Why haven't I heard about this before?" the President asked, pounding an enthusiastic fist on the arm of his chair. "It's a real miracle, isn't it?"

"We can't really know, sir," Hiram responded carefully, "can we? It might all be smoke and mirrors."

Hendron shook his head briskly. "What about all those people who come to her shows, wouldn't they notice that?"

"On *Pearl!* She was on *Pearl!* the other day," Phyllis explained to the men. "They talked about a medical exam. Isn't that right?" she turned to Jared as the resident Mam expert.

"Yes'm," he agreed, blowing on his tea. "One of the big medical centers in California. I can check on the website which one. They did a whole examination. No tricks, no makeup. She's all real, one hundred percent."

Hiram looked at his nephew through narrowed eyes. "That doesn't mean she's one of God's creatures," he said smoothly. "She might have been sent to tempt us."

The President cocked his finger and pointed emphatically. "You mean like that priest was saying."

"Oh, that poor man!" Phyllis tsked. "No matter what, it can't be right to hit a priest. Even a Catholic one."

"It won't be the first time that Lucifer has sent his demons to lure us from the righteous path."

Phyllis sat down across from Hiram and looked earnestly into his eyes. "How do you know she's a demon? What if maybe she's an angel?"

Hiram shook his head, pityingly. "Phyllis dear child, as a man of God, I would know. There would be signs."

Jared couldn't control himself. "But Mam is a sign!" he blurted. "Surely more than a ring falling into a bean patch!" The First Lady looked at him and blinked. She had no idea what he was talking about.

Hiram Crockertt pretended mightily not to be annoyed. "My boy," he said, his voice dripping patience, "I have dedicated my life to Jesus and finding his message, wherever He may choose to hide it. I have waited humbly, hoping only for the privilege of living to witness His return to the

Holy Land, and I pray daily that on the Day of Judgment I will be found worthy of being lifted up to bask in his Eternal Presence. His coming will not be heralded by a carnival act."

"She's not a carnival act!" Jared was so overtired that he didn't stop to wonder if he were pushing his luck. "She's a messenger!"

"Boy might have a point there, Reverend," the President said. "Something that hard to ignore, there's got to be a message in there somewhere. I'm thinking I might like to meet her and see for myself."

"Oh, Roddo, yes! Let's invite her here, please!" Jumping up to kiss her husband on the cheek, Phyllis nearly collided with Hiram, who'd risen majestically from his chair.

"No!" Hiram thundered.

"No?!" President Hendron wasn't used to being thundered at, not even by his pastor. He fixed the Reverend with an equally steely eye. Jared was amazed to his uncle shrink just a little bit.

"It's a risk we dare not take," the Reverend kept his voice strong, taking his seat so slowly that his retreat was all but imperceptible. "If you invite that...woman to the White House...if the President of these United States meets that woman on equal terms, the world will view that as giving support for whatever she represents. Until we know what that is," he whipped around to fix his nephew in silence, "and I mean what that really is, and not what she says in her pretty little crowd-pleasing speeches, until we can know that for certain, sir," he nodded at the President, "it would be far too dangerous for you to meet. My conscience won't allow me to let that happen."

"What then?" the President asked. Jared could see that he didn't look pleased, but he trusted Hiram Crockertt and would follow what he said. "This woman is going to be all across the news. We can't let that happen without offering some kind of response."

"Yes, sir," Crockertt smiled, sensing his hand on the wheel. "You are absolutely correct. It would be a mistake to ignore this." The Hendrons would never know how long Crockertt had done exactly that. "If she pretends to sanctity, I suggest we engage her in the same rigorous debate as we would any other religious pretender. And, for the sake of my country, sir, I am willing take that responsibility for my own."

"Reverend?" The President was puzzled.

"I'll invite her on my show," he explained with supreme satisfaction.

"On the radio?" Jared rubbed his eyes with the heels of his hands. "But that way no one'll see Mam. They'll just hear some woman debating scripture."

"Exactly," his uncle replied smugly. "No reason to confuse people by showing them something they won't understand. It's all sensationalism anyway. Without that, the fuss'll die down in no time. And no one can say we didn't give her a fair hearing."

The President nodded thoughtfully. He wasn't certain how this would work, but it had saved him from potential embarrassment. Phyllis didn't understand the Reverend's plan, but he was her spiritual advisor, and Roddo seemed satisfied. She patted her husband's hand and gave a tentative smile.

This wasn't the way it was supposed to be, Jared thought mournfully. There was supposed to be rejoicing. God had sent a messenger. Only it wasn't the messenger they wanted.

Reverend Crockertt's willful ignorance notwithstanding, the "fuss" was too far-gone to be tamped down. Following directly on the heels of the nudge from Pearl Yuan, the police action supplied the final momentum to push Mam from the margins of late night comedy and internet buzz and send her on a roll into the mainstream. By noon on Saturday, the fistful of business cards Wendy'd dumped on Raju had turned into a winning hand. Every major news outlet was begging for the right to air some of Wendy's footage, and nearly everyone agreed that it made no sense to show the riot without showing the source of contention. As one of the old school bureau chiefs said, it would be like making a movie about the Trojan War and never showing Helen. The phone lines at the FCC went into overload as division presidents, network censors and expensive attorneys battled it out over the right to air Mam's "face" on television news.

By five o'clock that evening, police cordons had been set up around the LaSalle, and a platoon of news vans were nuzzled up against them. Wendy swept up with her guys, causing a diversion that allowed Melissa and Susan to slip in, nearly unnoticed, through the fire exit. Several hundred gawkers duly assembled and craned their necks, but were disappointed to see nothing but the orderly stream of ticket holders arriving early and slowly filing into the theatre.

Most of the reporters philosophically had themselves shot standing so that the police lines were visible behind them, and said a few lines to the effect that "Everything was quiet today at the scene of last night's drama." Some chose to push the envelope a bit with provocative comments about the restrictions under which they were laboring.

"Many of you may be wondering what all the fuss is about," said the ambitious local reporter for a national news show. "Unfortunately, we can't show you. This is quite probably the biggest news story of modern times, and your only source for complete coverage is a fake news show on a cable comedy channel. Who's got the last laugh now?"

Sunday morning, while Susan caught up on some much needed sleep in a hotel in Detroit, the drama continued to unfold on American television.

A bemused Jack Rabb had taken the shuttle down to DC to appear on a venerable weekend interview forum. After submitting to the attentions of a green-smocked makeup artist with a shellacked bubble of beer-colored hair, he was escorted out to the studio. They seated him at one end of a lovely old piece of polished rosewood. His reflection looked up at him from the softly gleaming surface. It was difficult not to imagine the great men and women who must have been reflected there over the last forty years or so. He only hoped that he wouldn't embarrass himself. This was a long way from playing Francis Flute in Ontario. Taking a sip of water from the logo mug they'd placed on his right, he wondered if he could take it home. He'd surely never be doing this again; it would be nice to have a souvenir.

The host of the current generation, moonfaced and with a deceptively genial manner, arrived in a boxy pinstriped suit, a red tie, and a bustle of assistants. Before taking his seat across the table, he held out a large rosy hand to give Jack's a hearty shake. His porcine eyes made a quick assessment of Jack's sleek tailoring and product-enhanced coiffure. "So you're the comedian with the story of the century," he said, not entirely suppressing a note of disbelief.

Jack grinned weakly. "Yeah, I guess I am." That's right, he thought, I am. If I can keep remembering that, I'll be fine, even swimming in these waters.

"Amazing," the host said gruffly.

Jack could have chosen to interpret the tone as plain speaking rather than contempt, but he knew that feeling disparaged would give him stronger motivation. Anger always trumped insecurity. "Yes, it is amazing," he drawled. "Amazing that journalists have completely ignored a phenomenon like Mam for more than a year."

The host's eyes crinkled gleefully and he bounced like an oversized twelve-year-old who was winning at a video game. "Good answer! You don't mind if we repeat this bit on camera, do you? Get us off to a bang-up start!"

While Jack spoke earnestly about the obligation of journalists to air the news, and mainstream media's infantilizing of the American public, Father Martin was appearing on another channel and addressing a very different topic. He'd been invited to visit a contentiously conservative Sunday morning show on an unabashedly conservative news network. When the invitation had come the day before, the Bishop had questioned the wisdom of an appearance that he felt would only draw attention to their enemy. However, when the Father came to his office straight off the Chicago plane, stiff and purpled with his recent martyrdom, it was difficult to refuse his plea to trumpet a warning to the ignorant.

Supported on his left by the Church's New York press representative, Father Martin sat across the small Louis-something style desk from his host, rigidly splendid in a pristine cassock. His sunken black eyes glittered above the hillock of tape and packing that surrounded his nose. The rest of his face was swollen and mottled with bruises. The interviewer, his pasty face bulging smugly from his too-tight collar above his too-tight suit, introduced the priest with unctuous respect. He'd come on this show, Father Martin announced, because a great evil had appeared on the earth, and he had a duty to warn the righteous and the ignorant, both of whom might be vulnerable to the trap. He went on to pretty much repeat everything he'd said from his soapbox on Friday night, while the interviewer sat back with a smile and let him roll.

Fired up by Sunday morning channel flipping, Janet threw down her napkin to call one of her authors, the host of one of the major network morning shows, to line up an interview for herself. The following day, at an hour when she would customarily have preferred to be nibbling her morning croissant in bed, Janet instead perched elegantly on a bisque sofa, in full makeup, confiding her present chagrin. Her clients, Susan Roth and Mam, were having their names tarred by the conservative press without being given a fair, equal opportunity to rebut.

This went against the grain of the First Amendment in so many ways that it practically shredded it. Possibly the Sixth as well, as the stated right to confront one's accusers implied the extended right to publicly address accusations. How was it "righteous" (Janet didn't have to use air quotes to make her point) to permit Father Martin to go on a national news show and hurl accusations and yet prohibit equal face time for Mam, the accused? It was unconstitutional for the FCC to compel this restriction. More than that, it was immoral. By adhering to it, the journalistic profession was transgressing against its own proud tradition of telling the truth, and was breaking trust with the public they claimed to serve.

Not to mention that the bias was plainly ridiculous. Why she, Janet, couldn't even hold up a copy of Susan's book, *Off My Chest*, available in bookstores now, because the book's jacket cover was considered too suggestive for family fare. What could be more preposterous? Breasts were central to family. If they weren't, why would that wonderful old saying be "the bosom of the family?"

Before the week's end, nearly every news outlet in the country had jumped on the bandwagon. By doing so, they made Mam officially News, at last.

Once News, whatever else Mam might or might not be, the people had a right to know. And now that they wanted it, they wanted it now.

Janet and Raju decreed that, with the exception of *Duh News*, no one would be permitted access to Mam unless they could commit to showing Mam. They published a statement and distributed it in reply to every inquiry. No pasties, no pixilation, nothing cleverly interspersed between Mam and the lens.

The FCC held firm. So did Janet and Raju. Their client would be delighted, their client was eager, to share Her insights and experiences with the world, but only if She could do so face to face.

Off My Chest went into a second printing.

Deplaning in LaGuardia, following sold-out-to-standing-room Assemblages in Detroit and Minneapolis, Susan had to run a press gauntlet for the first time in her life. She wore a coat that zipped all the way up to her chin.

For successful professionals, this was a strange new form of frustration. The press was used to pushing the limits to get celebrity stories, but never limits that had been set from their own side of the fence. If only they could show the concert videos and webcast clips, they could get whatever their hearts desired. The subject was more than willing to do the interviews, with close-ups, as long as there were a guarantee they'd reach the audience.

Having a story that couldn't be told was untenable. If they couldn't cover the subject of Mam directly, they'd hit it obliquely and with a sledgehammer.

Tiger Beat interviewed Dakota Parker, and made sure she was invited to participate in a celebrity youth fundraiser for hurricane victims.

W Magazine, the fashion magazine well known for having artistic editorial photo spreads that never featured any garments, reached Mam's people and nailed down an exclusive cover story before Carter could get the *Vanity Fair* legal team out of the conference room.

A twenty-year-old PBS special on matriarchal religions was dusted off and frantically re-edited to include interviews with Stella Ravenswing and Alan Stark, and a shiny new electronic score.

The savvy technology reporter for a television news magazine tracked down the pseudonymous author of the YouTube "What are you afraid of?" video. It turned out to be a famous grizzled proto-boomer comedian and activist who was delighted to be interviewed at length about civil liberties. He showed up at the studio wearing a three-day growth of iron grey stubble and a black Mamapalooza T-shirt with a screaming watermelon logo. "I am as entitled to life as you are," he began the interview, with a solemn duck of his head. He thumped one fist, centurion-like, against the opposite shoulder, just missing the logo. "You affect me. Acknowledge my existence, as I acknowledge yours." Then he launched into what would be a nearly unbroken forty-minute concert-style rant that claimed the restrictions on mainstream media were compelled by "mankind's trivialization of religion."

"How small you make your Gods," he chortled, using his thumb and index finger aloft to illustrate the miniscule gap, "asking them for endless favors. Do they really care if your blemish clears up in time for the party? How petty is that? And how unloving to have to choose which one of you will win the ball game or the talent competition, or to give you a bigger condo while billions of people starve and the planet shrivels from global warning. That's not God, that's narcissism! We don't want to be made in the image of God; we want God to be made in our image. That's what's so scary about Mam. You can't imagine Her any way you want to, because She's already out there. And the FCC doesn't want you to see that. Why? Not because She's a breast. Oh, come on! They'd have her on every channel at prime time if She were advertising expensive cars. No, they don't want to give her airtime because what she has to say doesn't support commercial messages. She tells people to own up to personal responsibility, and that means thinking and going without, not buying a truckload of unnecessary things and throwing them on the junk heap a month later."

"So you're saying Mam is a socialist?" the reporter breathlessly interrupted.

"What, is McCarthy back? Are we having another witch hunt here?!" The famous humorist went ballistic. "How low will you people go?!" He ripped off his microphone, mumbling, "Just because you're paranoid doesn't mean someone isn't out to get you!" and stormed off. The reporter, who'd been born in 1982 and had no idea what he was talking about, could only stare.

The debate continued, kept alive by the media who'd wholeheartedly re-embraced the role of the nation's conscience. Europe, South America, India and Japan joined in the fun, their mainstream media taking liberal pokes at the always surprisingly and amusingly uptight United States. Overseas, Wendy's footage and Ziggy's webcast clips were aired unscathed, and Janet and Raju were in negotiation with French and Italian television for live interviews. The international coverage was spurring more serious interest in Mam as well. A Japanese edition of *Off My Chest* was already in the works, with several live appearances promised to coincide. Raju had also been approached by a go-getter with experience working the Eurovision Song Contest, offering his assistance in setting up a European tour.

Thanksgiving came and, seen or unseen, Mam was the topic of conversation at many a holiday table. At the White House dinner, President Hendron was seen to keep an unusual amount of distance between himself and his pastor. However, no official statement had been made.

At Mam Enterprises, they celebrated Thanksgiving with an enormous buffet. It was a family occasion. Ernesto Santiago wasn't the only spouse or partner to be introduced to Mam that day.

Rosa's return had passed without comment, as she'd sensed it would. That first Monday morning, Tara had tried to call her a hero for giving the warning about Chicago. It wasn't heroic, Rosa protested, but only a way to atone for her part in attracting Father Martin's interest in the first place. Over coffee later, just the two of them, Rosa unburdened herself completely, knowing that another person of faith would understand all that she was and wasn't saying. They prayed together, and then Tara gave her a hug and said to never think about it again. Amazingly, she hardly had, and when she did it was as the faintest most distant historic memory. Whether Tara had spoken with the others she didn't know, but it didn't seem to matter. She threw herself back into her work with a glad heart. As the media storm grew louder, she was proud to be on Mam's team and to be able to feel that she made a difference. She was happier than she'd been in months. Leading Ernesto up to Mam and seeing his face light up, she acknowledged that this year, even more than ever, she had a lot to be thankful for.

All at once, chimes and buzzers erupted across the floor. Tara, Raju and Lisa reached for their phones. Susan was closest to Raju. She saw him startle for the merest second before breathing his expression to a careful neutral. Turning, she caught Tara running out of the room, towards her office. Despite having had a couple of glasses of wine, she was suddenly vividly alert and began to wonder if she should be afraid.

Lisa had automatically picked up a serving spoon and tapped it against the rim of a Pyrex casserole where it rang out like a loud, flat bell. Everyone turned to face her. "I...uh, people..." Now that she had everyone's attention, she seemed uncharacteristically tongue-tied. Raju came to stand beside her and put a hand on her shoulder.

"Everyone, I need you all to stay calm," he said in the beautifully resonant voice he'd practiced when thinking he might like to litigate. "Please try not to panic. That was our local precinct calling. There's been an anonymous bomb threat and we need to evacuate the building."

Despite Raju's admonition, several shrieks were heard and a general buzzing rippled across the room. Those with children instinctively moved to gather them up, or at minimum to find them. Nearly everyone's head spun around, searching for Mam. "Please!" he said, several decibels louder. "We need to be calm and orderly. Chances are there's nothing to worry about."

"And we are all going to act as if that's an absolute fact," Susan said, loudly, rising to her feet so that everyone could find her. Her instinctive surge of adrenalin had been immediately suppressed by a distancing calm. There wasn't time for fear right now; this was the time for action. Fear would have to wait until later, if there was a later. "Right Mam?" The room quieted heavily.

"Exactly," Mam agreed firmly. "Now we all know I'm not very good at practical things, so I suggest you all stop looking at me and listen to what Raju and Lisa have to say." Some of the weight lifted in the room and there were even a few nervous laughs.

Raju nodded. "Thank you, Mam," he said coolly. "Now the police have asked us not to use the elevators. Instead, we're going to use the fire stairs."

With the prospect of constructive action, Lisa pulled herself together. "Are our fire marshals here?" A few hands shot up above the sea of faces. "Good, you know the drill. Check the restrooms and the offices. Everyone else, grab your bags and wallets and get ready to move towards the door. People with children go first."

Raju went to Susan and gave her a little prod in the right direction. "You're the leader," he said, "go lead. Tara and I will make sure everyone gets out." Before she could protest, he waved his handkerchief over his head and sang out at the top of his lungs, "Follow Susan and Mam!"

Rosa called out, "We're going to have to carry the younger children. If you have a child you can't carry, raise your hand now and we'll find someone who can help you." She was relieved to have Ernesto there and know that her own son would be taken care of. She pushed him towards the exit. "Don't worry," she whispered, "I'll be right behind you. Now go!"

They all went, in as orderly a fashion as ever a panic-stricken group executed a building evacuation. Nearly everyone stayed as close to the building as the bomb squad would allow. Those with small children took them down into the subway station to keep warm. No one wanted to go home.

Two hours later, the bomb squad gave the all clear. It had been a false alarm. Without discussing it, everyone filed back into the building to finish Thanksgiving. The squad captain caught Tara who, lugging the pair of laptops she'd run to grab, looked to be in charge.

"Were you people planning on opening tomorrow?" he asked. He didn't seem as happy as she might have expected him to, considering there was no bomb.

"No," she said. "We're officially closed 'til Monday. Of course, there's nearly always someone popping in to catch up on some work..."

"Not this weekend," he said brusquely, not allowing for negotiation. "Sorry, Miss. But there is someone who dislikes your group enough to want to give you a bad scare and risk jail time." Tara shrank in a bit and Michael put a protective arm around her. "Not a pleasant thought, is it?" He continued. "It may be nothing but a prank, but we don't want to be dealing with it on a holiday weekend if we can help it. First thing Monday morning we'll have a detective up at your place to go over some things." His headgear tucked under his arm, he waddled heroically towards his vehicle. He stopped suddenly and looked back at them with a sudden grin. "Happy Thanksgiving," he said.

It wasn't a detective who came by Monday, but an investigator from the FBI. Mam had long been on an FBI watch list. Not surprisingly, the Chicago riot had raised a red flag, and this bomb threat was, so to speak, the capper.

Agent MacAfee reported that the threatening call had been traced back to a disposable cell phone. He then asked if they'd been getting any hate mail. "I assume you have," he said frankly, "seeing who you are and all. Which I admit I didn't think was for real." He stared at Mam, who'd already been introduced, and coughed a nervous laugh. "Shows me. Anyway, you must have some, though I can't understand why you never reported it. So let's have a look."

"We don't," Susan said, puzzled. "Do we?"

"Well sometimes..." Lisa turned scarlet. "Oh it just seemed so ridiculous, I never thought...They weren't threats or I definitely would have said ...They were just so ugly!"

"Ugly how?" Agent MacAfee pressed her.

"Oh, you know, like 'burn in Hell, you witch' or 'God hates you,' that kind of thing." She wiped her eyes with the back of her hand and looked at Susan. "I don't want to bother you with such nasty crap," she sputtered defiantly. "I just throw it away!"

Melissa smiled wryly. "Come with me. I know you said throw them out," she said, starting back towards the reception desk, "but I don't know, it didn't feel right." Lisa, the agent and half the office followed. "I worked for a divorce lawyer once, did I ever mention? He always used to say, never throw anything out that looks like it might incriminate someone. You never knew when it might come in handy." She opened a supply cabinet that most everyone ignored when passing it each day. The bottom shelf had two large plastic mail bins, heaped with envelopes. "While I was out on tour, I asked Jonelle to keep it up."

Jonelle nodded apologetically at Lisa. "I know celebrities get hate mail," she said, "and that it's usually nothing. But I got my bachelors in criminal justice at John Jay. We studied some stalker cases. I thought Melissa was right."

"Oh my God!" Susan blurted. The agent looked at her strangely. "I had no idea! How could I have no idea?"

"For someone so cynical, you can be so innocent," Raju sighed.

"It's one of the things I love about her," Mam observed.

Agent MacAfee laughed uncomfortably and turned his attention to the mail. Crouching down by the shelf, he wriggled his fingers into latex gloves and fished out a handful of letters. He quickly flipped through the envelopes, eyeballing postmarks, method of address, whatever it was he was trained to notice in a single scan. "Good job, ladies," he said, lifting one eye in a kind of nod at Melissa and Jonelle, who were leaning closest to him of all the watchers. With the tips of two latexed fingers, he carefully extracted a sheet of paper from one of the envelopes. He glanced at it, then carefully folded it back with a sigh. "I'll have to take the lot," he said.

When he'd gone, a pall settled over the office. They felt a physical shock, as if they'd picked themselves up from a bad fall. People started to move because their bodies wanted to, or maybe they just couldn't help it. They paced restlessly, or sat on each other's desks talking about nothing. No one could settle down to work. They were all in a daze, and every cell in their bodies hurt.

It was a rude awakening. For most of them, the chaos in Chicago hadn't been real, but more like watching a movie that happened to be starring someone they knew. The bomb threat had been frightening at first, but once they'd known it was a false alarm it had been exciting too. It was another thing entirely to watching Agent MacAfee carry those two bins into the elevator. Even for those who had opened and read the occasional nasty letter or e-mail, it was different to see so many piled together in one place. That was a concrete accumulation of fear and loathing. That was real.

Someone, a lot of someones, hated what they stood for. And anyone who hated Mam, hated them. They looked around at each other and thought, how could someone hate our family? They thought back over their months together and everything that came to mind seemed so...nice. The success and acceptance, spreading wave after wave, had seemed so natural. They'd lost the imagination to view anyone who wasn't yet part of that family as anything other than unaware. Rosa, when struggling with her soul in all those dark hours, had considered only fear and rejection, but never hatred, neither on her own behalf or on a larger scale.

It was a hard, hollow feeling to know that they were hated.

And what were they to do about it now? Agent MacAfee had said he'd be coming back to go over some general security measures. Lisa, characteristically overreacting, was talking about signing up for armed guards and was ready to have the first security company in the phone book do an assessment at once.

Tara urged Susan and Mam to lie low for a while. "It's just as well," she said, in a rare show of "I told you so," "that you all listened when I said I didn't think it was a good idea to book live appearances during the Christmas season. If there's a crazy out there who hates Mam, that's all he'd need, to think we were laying down a challenge to Jesus. Thank goodness there's nothing until January."

"Except Miami," Melissa thought aloud. "But that's only one day, and anyway, who's going to make a fuss about another breast in South Beach? No offense, Mam."

"There's still the press," Raju reminded them. "There's no lying low if they're spread all over the media."

There wasn't going to be an easy answer.

"You didn't say much out there," Susan said to Mam later, when they were alone in their own office.

"Neither did you," Mam replied.

"I don't know what to say. Ever since you first showed up, every time I think I know what I'm doing and I start to feel comfortable, something happens to knock me sideways. Here we go again, something new that I have no idea how to wrap my head around."

"Did you really never think this would happen?" Mam sounded honestly curious. "Isn't this what always happens, when someone tries to change the way things are in this world?"

"Is that what we're doing? Trying to change the world? I've been so busy with the day-by-day, I don't know that I put a shape to any long-range plans. Especially since the few times I did ask, you weren't exactly forthcoming."

"It continues to fascinate me, fear and what's born from it."

Susan, more than a little fearful herself at the moment, didn't find it so fascinating. "You mean violence?"

"From the anger that comes from fear, yes. But also avoidance. Human beings play at being deaf and blind when they're don't want to learn something. I find that so fascinating."

"I've told you, people are afraid of the unknown, of change."

"But the lengths they will go to avoid it," Mam marveled. "If I disappeared, do they actually think all the things I've told them wouldn't matter?"

"What do you mean, if you disappeared?" For someone who often talked about repercussions, Susan found Mam to be fairly cavalier about how others might react to what she said.

"Susan," Mam sounded very dispassionate and wise, like a Reverend Mother in one of the nun movies that had been popular when Susan was a girl. "Isn't that what all this points to? What those people were saying outside the theatre in Chicago and in those letters? A bomb threat is hardly subtle. There are people in this world who want me to go away. And who are no doubt willing to go to some pains to try and make that happen. We have to consider this fact, and how we want to face it. After all, Susan, I'm a part of you. If someone is trying to eliminate me, it's unlikely they can do it without destroying you, too."

The words, once spoken, hung in the air. Susan circled them, trying to see them from all sides. They always said the same thing. Mam was right, as She always was. If Mam was a target, and it was possible that She was, then Susan was also a target.

What an odd thought to have to be thinking. How did she feel about dying for Mam? Susan had never thought of herself as being willing to die for anything. She'd never had that kind of passion. Ironically, before Mam, it might have been easier to think of dying for something in a general way. Before Mam, there had been little in Susan's life that she'd particularly valued. If something had come up where it might have made a difference, like pushing a toddler out of the way of a speeding car, Susan would probably have considered her life a fair trade. But since Mam, life had such richness and substance that now it would be hard to give it up. To give it up for Mam would either be the most ironic or the most appropriate sacrifice. Especially without being able to see if any good might come of it.

Then again, why should it matter if she ever knew? Even before Mam, Susan hadn't thought adult people should need rewards. In any case, she didn't believe people were guaranteed a reward because they were good, nor that they would necessarily be punished for being evil. A quick look at the news could tell you that, any day. Nor had she put much stock in an afterlife full of just desserts. That might be why she suited so well with Mam, who promised nothing.

Well before Mam and Her talk of repercussions and responsibility, Susan had developed a philosophy of personal responsibility. Without an equivalent religion, she'd always believed that the only dependable rewards could be knowing herself to have acted well, and peace in the knowledge she'd not deliberately done harm. She knew, about and personally, many good people whose lives had little ease or comfort. The good die as young and as horribly as the bad. Many vicious people enjoy every physical luxury. That was life; she acknowledged it, and it angered her to think about it.

Frustration and bitterness were familiar notes in her scale. Still, she considered them acceptable alternatives to the gnawing emptiness some people must constantly be feeling if they could bring themselves to do anything, regardless of how mean or even foul, just to get hold of something that in the end would never satisfy their bottomless hunger. She might resent their luxuries, but she would have never been able to live with the accompanying perpetual need to look over the shoulder, the persistent unacknowledged terror that, having gotten something through ill, it might similarly be easily stolen. If you don't love, there's no pain in not being loved, and no possibility of hurt from watching your loved ones suffer. In that way, the uncaring live pain free. Those with no honor must feel no shame. She thought that such people lead poor, empty lives. But she knew they wouldn't think so at all, and who's to say who's right?

Suddenly she felt very old, as ancient as she sometimes thought Mam might be. Not for the first time since Mam joined her, Susan wished she could find comfort in prayer. She picked up her mug and found herself staring at her own fingers. How amazing they were, her fingers. She was caught with a kind of nostalgia for them, as though she might soon be taking a long voyage and leaving them behind.

"This is ridiculous!" she said, firmly, aloud. "You're making me morbid. I'm not going to think about anything for now, not 'til I hear from Agent MacAfee. Anyway, it makes no difference. What'll be will be."

12 - A HERO GOING HOME

It had been especially hard on Jack not to be allowed to report the bomb threat. After acquitting himself so well with the Sunday morning pundits, he'd started taking himself seriously as a journalist. He'd known he couldn't do *Duh News* forever, but his career had never lent itself to a long-term plan. Now he was contemplating trying to land a spot on a weekly television news magazine or, even better, maybe he was so hot they'd let him host an edgy panel show on premium cable. Right now, it was critical that he do the best reporting job possible where he was, and prove he wasn't a one-trick pony. But the FBI had ordered him, ordered everyone, not to breathe a word about the bomb scare while they continued to investigate the hate mail.

Fortunately, the ripple effect around Mam was self-perpetuating. Even with Susan and Mam keeping out of the public eye, there was plenty else to report on in December.

Mam fever was burning hotter every day. People who'd seen Her or were otherwise willing to believe that She existed, were blooming in the light of public acceptance. Seekers who hadn't found Her on their own were joining the movement in droves. Atheists and paranormal skeptics of strong political bent were roused by the civil liberties issues.

"Hold onto your hats everyone." Two weeks after Thanksgiving, Jack grinned across more television screens than even Roger had ever imagined. "We've got a story so ridiculous, we'd never ask you to believe it if it weren't true. I mean even our crack writing staff can't make this stuff up. It's...wait for it, wait for it...it's the Million Mam March! One million women gathered in Washington today, each baring a single breast."

"Yes, Jack," Roger elbowed him as far to the side of the news desk as possible, frantic to grab his own moment in the sun. "One million magnificent naked bazoombas, in 42 degree weather. Now that's a march that makes me want to stand up and salute!" Roge threw a snappy salute and winked.

"According to organizers, who included Oregon Representative Martha Bishop, Michael Hoffman of the ACLU, and Mam chapter leaders Finity Barnstock and Hazel Marant, the women and the thousands of men who joined them marched 'in the name of personal responsibility and world cooperation.' And this," Jack added, "is how you saw it on the network news."

Whether the irony was inadvertent or not, the camera's perspective featured the Jefferson Memorial dome, from which an enormous crowd fanned out, possibly into infinity. A second, slightly closer angle, revealed the presence of banners and signs, but little else. The predominant colors in view appeared to be a rainbow of skin tones, but the shot was at such a distance that no details could be seen. For all the viewer could see, it might have been stock footage from any number of similar events since the advent of color film.

When Jack reappeared on screen, he was shaking his head sadly. "I'd be happy to show you more," he said, "but our lawyers are still up to their eyeballs in negotiating with the FCC about our Chicago coverage. However, as a service to our intelligent, and concerned viewers, our producers have negotiated with the BBC to make a link available to American audiences who want to see uncensored coverage of this important American news story. We're not permitted to post this link directly, but if you go to our website, you'll find instructions on how to go to bbc.co.uk and find the link."

Jared didn't need the link; he'd been down to the Mall in person. The organizers had said that Susan and Mam wouldn't be there, but that was okay with him. He'd splurged on a ticket to one of their Baltimore events, luckily before Chicago; everything had sold out so quickly after that. One of the White House interns who found out he had a ticket offered him $500 for it. When he turned her down, she was real nice about it. She said she understood; after all, he could get a lot more if he put it on eBay.

She came with him down to the Mall, Amy did. She was there to march. Jared hadn't known that until she whipped off her jacket and handed it to him to hold. Underneath, she had a scarf wrapped around her middle and tied at one shoulder. He felt himself go deep red and didn't know where to look. She just laughed and gave him a peck on the cheek "for being so sweet" before she skipped over towards the marchers.

Jared stood under the lamppost, holding tight to Amy's little fluffy jacket, his eyes following her as she joined a platoon and disappeared. He'd never seen anything so beautiful in his life. Way more than hundreds, at least thousands of women walking bared shoulder to shoulder. Many were using large brooches or belts to hold down their half-bodices. Every one wore a wide pink rubber bracelet on their "Mam" arm. All they were lacking were bows and arrows to be Amazons to the life. Jared's eyes filled with tears, and his face lit up with a smile.

"Move along there, sir!" A DC police officer looked sternly down on him from a Segue. He sounded strained, like someone primed to put down a brawl.

"But I want to be here," he said, "with them."

"Sure you do. Don't we all. No loitering here, sir. You're under the barricades." He jabbed a thumb over his shoulder. Jared stared, round-eyed. He was the most law-abiding person in the world. He'd never cross a police line. He'd just been so excited to be walking with Amy, that he hadn't noticed where she'd led him.

"But my friend," he protested feebly, holding up Amy's jacket. Even through dark glasses, he could feel the officer's glare. "I'm one of them," he stammered. "I mean, I'm with Mam!" He fumbled to pull his suit lapel past his duffel coat and pushed the little brass and pink enamel logo pin towards the officer.

"One of them," he grunted. "Then you should be over with those guys. Move fast or you'll get a citation." The officer rolled away. Jared looked over to where he'd pointed. There was a narrow band of men walking to either side of the women. A lot of them, like himself, were carrying coats or jackets. A few had signs of their own: "Mam's Men" and "Mam is for Everyone."

"Hey!" Jared ran to catch up. "Hey, how do I march?!"

The older man grinned. "Seems to me you are already," he said.

Samael did not attend the march. His radiance would have marked him and drawn the attention of all eyes, so he'd sent his chief lieutenant, Righteous Arm, to shepherd his three candidates. Righteous trudged doggedly in the men's column, keeping a watchful eye on his charges. Precious, as they might have expected, marched boldly, laughing and chatting excitedly with the women around her. Balm of Gilead seemed embarrassed. She kept her head down, her eyes fixed on her feet as they moved dutifully forward. But Rejoice in the Name, Righteous noted, marched like a soldier. Taller than most women, she held herself taller still, shoulders back, her pale eyes fixed straight ahead. And when Stella's speech floated out on the bullhorn, her cheeks glowed with anger. Back at the compound, Samael ended the call and allowed himself a brief prayer of thanksgiving. The die was cast.

It had been Finity's idea for Stella to speak. When the ACLU guy, Hoffman, had contacted them, she and Hazel had been gung ho to get the word out and make the event happen. They hadn't anticipated being asked to join him and the congresswoman on the platform. Neither of them was used to public speaking, and both found the possibility terrifying. Hazel had immediately suggested Patrick step in as an appropriate spokesman for her. Finity had no problem with Patrick, but she wanted to make sure there was another woman up there speaking for Mam and, after Mam Herself, Stella was the strongest speaker Finity knew.

Watching her on the platform now, Finity glowed with satisfaction at having made a good call. Stella, always majestic, looked amazing today.

She'd had a gown made up with an open front, similar to one of Susan's. Her sleeve rippled like a flag as she held the bullhorn to her mouth.

"Others today have spoken passionately about liberties and rights," Stella told the crowd, "and about a greater spirit of harmony and understanding that we all share. I agree that those are all very fine principles, and I applaud those speakers. But it takes more than ideals to bring one million of us together here on a December day. It took a miracle. The miraculous is by definition inexplicable. I don't seek to explain Mam today; that would be impossible. But I seek to explore the meaning of her sojourn among us. As women are half of the world's people, Mam also is half of a whole. Do you think it's an accident that She appears to us as one of a pair? Or that She appears to us in a form we identify as female? No! I say there are no accidents! For too long, we have listened only to the male voice of God the Father. Now Mam has come to restore to us the other voice, the missing half, our Mother. I say to you today, humanity is not a single parent family!" Her "Mam" arm, bare except for its pink cuff and her tattoo of the Pleiades, hammered the air to emphasize her words. Somewhere in the crowd, voices called out "Amen," "Right on!" and "Hallelujah!"

"Only if we listen to both parents, to both voices," Stella continued, "only with both halves in soul as in body, can we be whole. Consider the world that we have made, generation after generation, by following the dictates of those who believe God created them in His image alone. We have ignored the Mother long enough. It's time for a change!"

Pat and Vanessa had a lot to say about Stella's speech when Rosa met them for lunch at the hospital the next day. Rosa would have liked to have been at the Mall herself, except Raju, out of concern for potential liability, had asked that no one on the Mam Enterprises payroll attend. They'd all get to see Wendy's footage, of course, but it felt more firsthand to Rosa to be able to hear about it from her girls the next day.

"Some people cheered," Vanessa said, "but others, they yelled, like they were angry."

Pat nodded. "When she talked about body and soul, for example. I remember, because I always liked that song. My sister-in-law sang it at our wedding."

"Yeah, that was the first one" Vanessa thought back. "And a couple times after. I don't think some of them liked her talking so much about God, not by name."

"Not to criticize," Pat was apologetic. "Because, seriously, of all the speakers she was hands-down the best one. The political ones were boring and nothing they said was really about Mam. Patrick looks like a nice guy, and I'm sure he's smart, but it's hard to follow what he's thinking. But without Susan there, Stella was the only one saying anything that made sense about our side."

"She was representing," Vanessa agreed, "but it started to sound a lot like a sermon, you know? I thought Angela was maybe gonna bust something."

"Angela was there?" Rosa was more than surprised. Angela was one of Father Martin's stalwarts, as traditional as the Pope. She'd acted as though Mam were one of the Plagues, avoiding Her and advising everyone else to do likewise, and she'd never shown any concern about civil liberties in her life.

"Yeah, well she wasn't all that into it. I kept wondering why she came."

"I bet Father Martin made her go," Rosa said, knowing as soon as she'd said it that it must be true. "To spy." Then she had an unthinkable thought. Angela had nursed seven children and had a sagging pair of breasts that always brought to mind a net bag of grapefruits slung over her shoulders. "No! She didn't go taking off her top!"

"She had a T-shirt," Vanessa explained, "that kind of looked like it without having to do it. A lot of the older women had them. Kind of skin color, with a drawing of Mam that was like someone took a paintbrush and made a U," she took the pen from her smock and drew on a napkin, "and then, a dot," she punched it down in the lower third of cup shape, "right here."

"There was a group of Moslem women who were giving them out," Pat said. "A whole group, with scarves over their heads and everything. They had these T-shirts over their clothes so they could march in honor of Mam and still stick to their own rules. It was pretty clever, I thought. They got a lot of cheers." Pat's alarm beeped. She jumped up with a grin. "Gotta run. Later."

Vanessa held out her right hand, curved as if she were holding an imaginary cup. Pat made the same shape, but tilted her hand so that the two Us could brush against one another. She repeated the motion towards Rosa, who awkwardly mimicked her. Pat walked away with her tray, leaving Rosa perplexedly wiggling her curved hand.

"What's all this about?" she asked Vanessa.

"It's a new handshake. You know, like how the 'brothas' are always greeting each other by kissing fists? So we do this." Vanessa made the gesture again, slowly, "You see, it's the Mam shape." She emphasized her point by tracing the half-circle from thumb to forefinger with her opposite hand. "It shows we're with Mam. They were doing it at the march. Someone said they started it in Chicago, but now everyone's doing it. How cool is that?" Vanessa enthused.

"Pretty cool," Rosa agreed. It was news to her. She couldn't wait to share this back at the office.

"Shameful," Don Lee reported, taking his cup of tea from the tray and settling into the cushions, "that's what it was. All those bare naked hussies walking around with their signs and all, acting as if the Lord was some fairy story you could make up to your own taste. Oh, it was more than shameful, I tell you, it was entirely shocking. Plus," he added, raising a triumphant finger, "there was never a million of them."

Hiram pursed his lips and nodded at his deacon with grim satisfaction. "Lies and deceit. I expect nothing less from blasphemers."

"We can't go letting this pass, Reverend," Don Lee continued. "Like you said, this is Satan's work."

"As to that, Don, I've been struggling with it and praying for guidance. And just now," Hiram said portentously, "I'm counseling you to patience."

"Patience! Reverend, we have to stop this woman now!"

"Have Faith, Don. You know, when I first heard about all this, it was from my nephew, my late brother's boy. Well, he's just like his daddy. Not to speak ill of a dead hero—and he was a hero, my brother, and in Nam, when nobody gave you any parades for it—but he never had a lick of sense and nor does his boy. My nephew, out of nowhere—never had the gumption to swat a fly—he tells me about this..." it was difficult for him to spit out the word, "Mam creature. Oh, I saw red, you know I did. And I read him the riot act! When I found out he was keeping it up and was one of them, you know, Don, to me that was pretty close to a miracle all by itself. But I'm not pretending I was happy to see it. I didn't know what it all might mean. I was so angry and confused, I was frozen with it. It stopped me from acting, and that was God's plan. You see you wait, you pray."

"Yes, Reverend." Eyes blank, Don Lee nodded dutifully.

"I wrestled long and hard. And I resisted. Oh yes Don, I resisted! It's only a week since it finally happened, but it all came clear. I finally see the hand of the Lord and now, I'm content to sit back and watch it play out as He commands."

"Sit back?" Don sputtered, "We have to stop it is what I see!"

"No Don," Hiram leaned forward and Don Lee shifted uncomfortably under his most penetrating stare. "Let go of your fear and anger and think it through with me. Think hard. Here we are, Don, and the year of Our Lord 2000 has passed. And a b...yes, I have to say it, a Beast has arisen and commands thousands—if not truly a million—souls, leading them to certain perdition."

"End of Days?" Don's cup shivered against his saucer.

"Like yourself, Don, I was shocked when it came upon me. But what else could it mean, this Thing? It's real, Don; I believe those doctors. They're all damned atheists after all. And there's no magic on earth could make it happen."

"But the anti-Christ was supposed to be—"

"What could be more anti-Christ than this woman?!" Hiram brought his fist down so hard his ring jammed a bruise into his middle finger that nearly broke the skin, but he was too intent to notice. "The ways of the Lord are mysterious to behold Don, but when the veil lifts from your eyes, oh the beauty and magnificence! Think, Don, think! As Woman caused the Fall that forced us out of Paradise, what could be more fitting than for a woman to lead us, those of us who are worthy and have eyes to see it, back home!" Don watched, mesmerized, as Hiram creaked up out of his chair and stood in a slice of winter sun, smiling like a bloodhound-jowled Mona Lisa. His eyes fixed on a distant horizon. "We're entering the season of the birth of Our Lord," he intoned. "A time when our family, our people here and my radio congregation, all of them'll be thirsting for the Spirit. And I will stand before them and preach the Truth. The Truth, Don, is a flaming sword."

Raju took the call and burst into Susan's office with a radiant smile. "You'll never guess!" he said. She wouldn't, she'd stopped trying long ago. She nodded encouragingly. "*Time* magazine is naming Mam as this year's 'Being of the Year!'"

"Holy crap," she whispered, clapping her hand over her mouth.

"I know," he said happily. "It comes out next week. They just called to give us a heads up. I knew our profile was high, but this...wow!"

"Wow," she repeated. "More than wow. This is going to sound strange, Raj, but this may be the most unbelievable thing that's happened to me in the last year and a half."

He sat down on her desk and patted her hand. "I think I know what you mean. Everything else has a kind of dream quality to it. But *Time*..."

"Is this another of those cultural references?" Mam was curious.

"Yes," Susan agreed. "Another one of those."

Raju thought Mam deserved more of an answer. "It's one of the leading news magazines in the country," he explained. "Actually, in the world if you count the international editions. And it has been for, oh, I don't know...how many years? Since the Depression at least, I think. Let's say 70–80 years at a guess. And every year they wrap up the year's coverage by naming someone Person of the Year."

"It was Man of the Year when I was growing up," Susan observed. "Lately they've become more...eclectic. But I don't think there's ever been a 'Being' of the Year before. It's an interesting choice of word, don't you think?"

THE BREAST OF EVERYTHING

"It's a huge honor," Raju continued. "Whoever they pick is considered to have had the most significant impact on the year."

"Didn't they give it to Hitler once?" Susan asked.

Raju shrugged. "He did have a significant impact. It's a quantitative judgment, not qualitative. Being on any cover of *Time* is a big deal, Mam. Much bigger than any news coverage we've had before. And being on this cover, it's like winning the Nobel Prize."

"That's another cultural reference, Mam, but that one comes with cash."

Raju didn't notice. He had visions of Oslo dancing in his head.

When the magazine hit the stands, the cover featured a dramatic shot of Susan addressing an enormous, enthusiastic audience in Miami. From the angle of the photograph, her outstretched arms conveniently obscured Mam, eliminating the need for any uncomfortable editorial decision. Below the photo was the caption: "The Roth of God?"

The issue sold with the speed of a disaster commemoration. There were Mam International staffers who couldn't get hold of a copy until someone at Time Warner was kind enough to pull some back from a distributor in Idaho, where Mam buzz was less than a mosquito. After *Time*, as with the Washington March, came increased coverage by the mainstream news outlets.

The following weekend, on the Sunday before Christmas, the Reverend Hiram Crockertt switched into radio simulcast, hung onto his podium and roared out an electrifying sermon about the End of Days.

"So much for keeping a low profile," Susan said wryly during the regular weekly meeting. "Person of the Year..."

"Being of the Year," Melissa corrected her.

"Being of the Year and the anti-Christ. Imagine if we hadn't stayed home the last couple of weeks."

"If we could only get the venues, we could add another day to every one of the January cities and still sell out," Tara mused.

"I could kick myself that we ruled out a date in DC." Linda poked Raju emphatically. "And I bet Vegas would have sold out, too!"

"20-20 hindsight, babe," Alan shook his head.

"We'll just have to plan another tour for the spring," Raju said, rubbing his arm. "After Susan and Mam catch a breather. Maybe even take a vacation. Maybe we can all take a vacation. I know I could use one."

"We can easily add two or three more nights in New York," Tara ran right over him without hearing. She checked some notes on her laptop. "The Old Vic doesn't take the Belasco 'til February first. I bet anyone who was closed out on the Northeast Corridor would buy a ticket and hop a train. I bet people would come from all over, we're so hot right now."

"Hot is right. It's almost impossible for me to keeping anything on the shelves," Linda griped proudly. "And Rosa's having to train more new volunteers every day. Just to sort through the mail and e-mail."

"Do we know who these people are?" Raju asked.

"As much as possible. No strangers, that is," she explained. "They have to be recommended by someone we know, and we check to make sure they really know each other. Then Agent MacAfee takes the names and puts them through some kind of background check. It's not perfect, but it keeps out the criminals and the documented crazies."

"I've got a message from Janet," Melissa waved her Blackberry. "*Off My Chest* made two more best-of-the-year lists. That's nine I know of."

"Harrison Levy must be so proud," Raju said, with an evil grin.

Susan started to laugh, but it turned into a sigh. "You know, I haven't written anything in months. I hardly even have time to think about doing it. And I haven't the faintest idea what I have to say."

"Where's Wendy?" Mam asked. "She hasn't been with us once since Thanksgiving."

"Astoria," Melissa said. "At least that's the address Linda keeps giving to the takeout guys."

"She needs to eat!" Linda was defensive. "She's in a room with no windows. She probably loses all track of time."

"Nobody's arguing with you," Alan kissed her lightly on the forehead, "not even me. You think she'll have it ready in time?"

They all shifted in their seats and tried not to look at one another. When word of the march first broke, Wendy had been contacted by a distributor, who wanted to release her documentary the day before yesterday. Sight unseen, he promised that if she could commit to deliver in time, he'd manage the requisite "special engagement" at a downtown theatre to get it in for Academy Award consideration. "In time" meant before the end of the month. With equal parts of dismay and ambition, Wendy had taken a good hard look at the calendar. She'd planned to keep shooting through the New York dates, but this was far too tempting. Mam's momentum was racing now, who knew what it would be by spring? Luckily, Wendy's television habits and Jack's deadlines had kept her editing throughout the tour. The march would make as good an ending, maybe better. If she worked round the clock, she thought she might be able to pull it off. Maybe she'd send it off to the Berlin Film Festival as well. And, she rationalized, she could always turn New York into a short and make it an extra feature when the film went to video.

Privately everyone in the room thought Wendy had bit off more than she could chew, but they felt bad saying so.

"Well," Melissa said philosophically, "if she does we'll be able to show it at the New Year's Eve party."

To nearly everyone's astonishment, a proud and thoroughly exhausted Wendy did screen *Mam I Am* in the Gathering Room on New Year's Eve. It was rapturously received. No one could see any of the flaws Wendy insisted were there (while reiterating over and over that she'd really had no choice but to let it go out in this condition). They were far too enchanted to be critical. As Rosa put it, "I never saw a picture before where I knew almost everyone in it." Seeing it together, laughing and screaming as their faces appeared, was more fun than the opening weekend of a summer blockbuster. It was especially nice for Susan and Mam, since Agent MacAfee had categorically refused to let them attend any of the showings at the IFC Center.

"Why not just go paint a target around Mam!" he fumed when he'd heard they were planning to go to the opening. "Do you want to get yourself killed?"

The ugly letters and death threats had been mounting. The FBI thought much of this was due to the customary seasonal rise in religiosity. Regardless of when it was published, Mam's *Time* cover would have been controversial. At this time of year, it might seem like a challenge to all the Abrahamic religions and the most faithful might view it as a brazen taunt.

Some of Mam's people contended that tensions had been exacerbated by Reverend Crockertt's sermon, which spread through the media like brush fire. Tara, once she'd gotten over the shock of hearing the speech, had a different notion. "Crockertt's helping us. That speech neutralized a lot of extremists who might have been dangerous," she explained. "Anyone who wants this to be the End Time will leave us alone."

The profilers agreed with Tara, but continued to feel that the atmosphere was too emotionally charged for comfort. The FBI, and even some of her own team, urged Susan to cancel all the January dates, to take a few months off and wait for a quieter time.

"Like when?" Susan asked. "Easter?" There would always be danger. She understood that now and she thought she'd accepted it. Or, as Steffi had pointed out during a recent marathon phone conversation, perhaps she'd just gotten very, very good at denying it. She was certain of one thing: She wasn't going to let her actions be dictated by fear. Before Mam arrived, she'd had a long history of doing that. Now she knew what it was like to feel free and live life, and there was no going back. If she could let go of her own fears, the ones she'd nursed and crawled into since childhood, she damned well wasn't going to let some boogey man put her in a panic room. That was terrorism. Terrorism made her angry and anger made her stubborn. More than that, she and Mam had a responsibility to all their supporters. Thousands of people had bought tickets and not one of them was going to be disappointed on her account. And what about all the people who were finding something strong and admirable in Mam's words and her own conduct? Where's the moral ground if they walk away when things get rough? She had to have the courage of her convictions. This was her life and she was going to lead it on her own terms until the day she died. As to when that day would be, she'd decided to be fatalistic and leave it to the universe. She and Mam had made up their minds to continue with the tour as scheduled.

There was no breaking that decision, so everyone learned to swallow their objections and quietly go about the business of making Susan and Mam as secure as possible. The FBI provided a documented alias for booking Susan's hotels, and a discreetly armored SUV complete with drivers. Melissa, whose name and face were well known, was also provided with an alter-ego, including a wig, glasses and a very un-Melissa-like travel wardrobe of shapeless garments and clunky boots. Raju was advised to stay home. He was too much a known associate. They would be accompanied by family members who were entirely unknown outside the office, and by not so much as a point-and-shoot camera.

The last time Susan had been to Boston with Diane—well, Cambridge, really, that time—it had been Senior year and Diane's little brother was rowing for Harvard. It was a different kind of road trip this time. For one thing, unlike Diane's college rust bucket, the FBI vehicle had a floor. It also had a DVD player, seat warmers and a pair of stoic drivers who wore black coats and concealed weapons. For another, instead of bouncing riotously around town wherever and whenever the mood might take them, they were kept on a tight rein and, at least in Susan's case, to a narrow radius.

Thursday's drive took them straight from New York to the theatre. Melissa, in what she was mockingly calling her "dowdy drag," was there to greet them and share the dinner brought in by the local agents. Seven hours later, after the last person had filed regretfully out of the theatre, the women were hustled into the SUV and driven to the hotel's underground garage. The doors of their suite were under constant surveillance.

Friday presented as one of those rare diamond-like winter days, but Susan saw none of it. They worked from the suite all morning. After the room service lunch, she wanted to take a walk around town, but the agents forbade it.

"I walk around all the time at home," she insisted. "Even Agent MacAfee hasn't stopped me from doing that."

The Agency, however, felt the threat was greater around a concert-type appearance. Anyone who had it in for Mam would want as much publicity as possible. "They'll be clamping down on your movements before the New York engagements, too," one of the bookends assured her. Diane was sufficiently unknown to be allowed out to go to the Gardner Museum. That really chaffed at Susan, who had a particular fondness for the place and had planned on a visit. Instead, with Melissa's exquisitely patient assistance, she and Mam started work on the collection of annotated Gathering transcripts to which Janet had committed them. Diane came back just in time to share the room service dinner. After they ate, the SUV took them to the theatre, and from there back home at the end of the night.

Saturday would have been still more of the same, except that some of the Wiccans drove down to spend the afternoon in the suite before attending that night's Assemblage. Stella had been asked not to come to the theatre. Her increased visibility, following the Washington march, was considered to create additional risk. To prove otherwise, she showed up at the hotel in uncharacteristic jeans and a pea coat, and with her hair tucked under a Sox cap. Melissa, doing a double take ten minutes into the visit, finally appreciated the extent of the change uncharacteristic clothing could make to someone you only knew by sight.

Diane, who had a Parrish somewhere in her family tree and still felt awkward around Wiccans, slipped out to do some shopping. A few hours later, she burst into the suite, unable to contain her excitement. "I stopped for a cider in Faneuil Hall," she said, dropping a couple of pounds of Sweet Sloops and some souvenir T-shirts for the kids on the pseudo-18th century rosewood desk. "There were these women behind me. Someone stopped by their table to say hello, and I heard them—well I couldn't help it, they were practically screaming: 'Oh my God!,' 'You look so great!' That kind of thing. My back was to them, and it would have been rude to turn around and look, but I could tell that the woman who'd just come over, they hadn't seen her in a long time and she'd lost a tremendous amount of weight. It sounded like she'd always been heavy, tried everything for years, you know. Look, I wasn't eavesdropping, but sometimes you can't help but overhear. They kept asking her what diet she was on, and she kept saying none, but they didn't believe her. Finally..." Diane paused to swallow some water while the others waited tolerantly to see if there was going to be a point to this story. "Finally the woman said, 'I took responsibility. I was eating too much and exercising too little, and it was no one's doing but my own. So I did what Mam always said and I took responsibility.' Well, after that I wanted to go over and talk to them, but I was afraid I'd say something I shouldn't and blow our cover."

"Did you sneak a look," Melissa asked. "What did she look like?"

"Does it matter?" Susan wasn't sure how to react. Her first thought was simply that she didn't want Janet to get wind of it or they'd be churning out Mam's guide to weight-loss in time for Mother's Day.

There was no question as to what Stella thought. "They're using Mam as a diet! That's atrocious!"

"It makes sense if you think about it," Melissa said. "I think it's kind of creative."

"It's..." Finity was deeply perturbed. "Yeah, I'm going to say it; it's blasphemous!"

"Finity," Mam said sternly, "I've asked that no one use that word."

"Wait!" Diane said, finally unbuttoning her coat. "I wasn't finished. So then I left that building and was walking toward the other one, and I passed this man sitting at a folding table. With one of those huge water cooler bottles of loose change, you know? He was collecting for the hurricane victims."

"Sure he was," said one of the Wiccans, shaking her head and rolling her eyes.

"He was a well-groomed man in a Ralph Lauren parka," Diane snapped defensively. "I had change in my pocket from the cider, so I thought I'd drop it in. While I was standing there, I noticed he was wearing a kind of badge thing on his jacket that said 'Ask me how Mam changed my life.'"

"How did I?" Mam asked.

"I didn't ask him," Diane admitted. "I was too embarrassed. But the point," she raised her voice to be heard over everyone else's giggles, "the point is that he was wearing it. Regular ordinary people are paying attention to what Mam says."

"You mean we're not regular people?" Finity couldn't resist.

"Oh, you know what I mean!" Diane said crossly; she hated being teased when she had something serious on her mind. "People like these two, the man with the Republican hair and the fat woman...I mean the formerly-fat woman...I mean people who you wouldn't expect, they're genuinely changing their lives and saying that Mam is the reason. And then they're talking about it, sharing it openly." For some reason, this particularly mundane incident seemed to have knocked Diane for a loop.

"You don't get out much, do you?" Stella asked, kindly. "You should have been in Washington."

"This is Boston, for Pete's sake!"

The only thing that had made Susan sure she was even in Boston was that Finity and one of the agents made a run to Legal's for clam chowder for dinner. Otherwise, it was nothing but hotel to theatre and back again until it was time to be driven back home, only to move on to the next city.

Philadelphia, immediately after, was pretty much the same, except that it was cheesesteak sandwiches, and Rosa instead of Diane. And Baltimore was she-crab soup and Jonelle, who had a cousin in town who'd just had a baby. Three cities in ten days and only Susan's taste buds could tell the difference.

"Is this what it's like for you?" she asked Mam on the last or next-to-last morning. It had been a long time since she'd asked Her anything about Herself. There were never any answers, so she'd left of trying, but this thought had just hit her like a snapped elastic. "Is every place the same, like being packed in a box?"

"The world is just as big inside the box," Mam said.

"Do you really mean that, or are you just trying to make me feel small?"

"You know that's a foolish thing to say."

"Yeah, well, I'm human. We're foolish."

"Yes, you are," Mam agreed. "It makes me want to protect you, all of you." She seemed wistful.

"You sound so maternal. Was that what you expected, when you came here to us?"

"I've always said I had no agenda, and no expectations." It was a canned answer, closing the door to further discussion.

Susan mentally shrugged and moved on. A few minutes later, Melissa walked in and the workday began.

That evening, as they were walking from the dressing room to the stage, Mam spoke up unexpectedly. "What you asked me this morning," She said. Susan, having forgotten, remained quiet. Mam continued, deliberating over every word. "It's all so fascinating and exciting, you know. Human emotion is. Such a powerful thing. It awes me."

"It awes you?" Susan stopped in her tracks.

"If I understand 'awe' correctly, yes. It makes me feel small. But differently than what you implied when you used those words this morning." Her voice sounded like a smile. "Human emotion...so wonderfully complex...I'm glad I'm able to experience even a little for myself."

It pleased Susan to think that people had given something back to Mam; it made everything a little less one-sided. "Then let's go out there and get you some more of that." She walked out onto the stage and raised her arms in the light. The crowd went wild, and Susan smiled more broadly than was usual. "Mam," she whispered, "can you feel the love?"

Susan got back from Baltimore on Tuesday. Friday of the same week was the first of the New York events. There was hardly time to unpack and do laundry, but Susan didn't mind. She'd be sleeping in her own bed and living what she'd come to think of as "normal" life. It sounded downright restful.

For the rest of Mam Enterprises, New York was more special. When they'd first booked the theatre, they'd set aside a block of house seats for themselves. Everyone who worked in the office, Jimmy Touray's group at Corpo Céleste, Janet's assistant and other friends of Mam would finally be able to see what it was like to attend one of the big Assemblages. In addition, as in LA, it was anticipated that a number of celebrities would show. It was mostly guesswork, as few of the professionally fabulous could simply hand over a credit card and buy tickets for themselves. Looking at the seat-holders list, Janet had spotted the names of a couple of celebrity assistants she knew, and Melissa was certain that a name attached to four excellent orchestra seats was widely known to be an alias used by a former *People* magazine Sexiest Man on Earth.

Brokers and pseudonyms were not making it any easier for Agent MacAfee and company. Security for the New York engagement was a security nightmare. "It's like preparing for a State Visit," the NYPD liaison grumbled. Looking for red flags in the purchase lists was only the first stage. Each night that Mam was to appear, every foot of the theatre would be checked, and every entrance point locked down. The streets around the building needed to be blocked off with more police barricades than an A-list film opening. News trucks were to be kept as far back as possible. As they entered, attendees and theatre employees alike would pass through something akin to airport security, with x-ray scrutiny of every bag and backpack, and full body wanding.

And then there was the issue of getting Susan back and forth to the theatre. Not joking, Susan proposed taking the subway each way. "What could be more anonymous than that?" she averred, based on long experience. The security experts dismissed the idea of public transport as ridiculous and instead tossed around the various merits of bulletproof limos, police cruisers and decoy vehicles.

Jimmy, who had some ancient theatrical costuming experience on his resume, joked that they could cut that last headache by having Susan spend the three weeks camped out in the notorious Belasco apartment. "It's right in the building, you'd only have to walk down the stairs. It's haunted, of course," he added slyly, "but I'm sure Mam can hold her own." When MacAfee heard about David Belasco's legendary love nest, he saw red, but he learned that it had been locked and abandoned for years. Just to be sure, he sent a man to change the lock and bring back the only key.

Friday at Mam Enterprises felt like the last day of school. The air was too full of anticipation to get much done beyond the necessary. A dozen of them were going that night, with even more holding tickets for Saturday. People kept wandering over to one another to talk about what they were going to wear, or where it might be fun to meet up after the Assemblage. At three o'clock, they gave up pretending to work and officially called it a day, but no one wanted to leave; most people hung around until Susan and Mam left the building.

MacAfee had decided that routine would be a weakness on home turf, so there was a different plan for each night. For this first night, which was bound to get the most attention from the press, the schedule sounded like the plot of a caper movie. It would have been funny, if MacAfee hadn't been so fierce while he was explaining it.

Maneuvers began at four-thirty. Melissa, wearing her favorite black leather jacket and endless boots, strode out of the building, tossing her hair. A black limo pulled up. She peered in the window, nodded, and waved her hand. One of the volunteers, who was about the same size as Susan and wearing her coat and a scarf over her head, ran out of the building and ducked into the limo. Melissa got in beside her and closed the door. They pulled out, taking a convoluted route to the theatre that was guaranteed to make anyone who might be following them think that they were attempting to shake a tail.

Five minutes later, Linda walked to the corner and hailed a taxi, something unlikely in Queens unless the cab in question happened to belong to the NYPD. She said something into her phone and Raju hustled a blanket-draped figure into the back seat. The three of them drove off.

After that, Mam personnel left the building every minute or so, in gossipy groups of four or five or six. Some walked to the subway, others to the bus stop. Jonelle and another girl in a skirt and unseasonable high-heeled sandals were giggling so much that they didn't notice Jonelle's boyfriend pull up, even though the music was booming from his sound system. He had to honk his horn before they noticed and tottered, holding each other up. Still laughing, they fell into the back seat. Music blaring, they sped off on the most direct route to the theatre district.

"All clear," the undercover cop said to Susan and Jonelle. "None of the vehicles are being followed."

"Great," Susan said absently, rubbing her Achilles tendon.

Jonelle winked at her. "You sure were working that look!"

"Thanks. I don't know how the hell you wear shoes like this every day."

Jonelle shrugged. "It looks good."

The driver pulled up on the sidewalk and decanted Susan directly at the stage door. Another officer, and Marta, took her into their custody. Jonelle took a ride downtown to do some shopping before meeting her real boyfriend for a pre-concert dinner.

By five thirty, tonight's entourage had all made their way to the theatre, including Alan, who had been entrusted by his wife to pick up dinner. Wendy and her guys had also arrived, to capture the evening on camera while Ziggy's people ran a live feed of the Assemblage on the website.

Susan felt buoyant. "I don't think I've enjoyed an evening as much since the last night at Mitra!" she said, attacking her dumplings with unusual pre-show appetite.

"It's all family," Mam said quietly. "That's why."

At the traditional half hour before curtain, everyone who was going to be sitting out front kissed Susan and told Mam they'd see her later. Those who'd be watching from backstage trouped down to the greenroom, and Marta, delighted to be playing dresser again, took Susan to get ready.

Jimmy had insisted on making something new and special for the New York leg of the tour, so Marta had some final fussing and steaming to do while Susan did her makeup.

"Look at you!" Marta said fondly. "Remember how you used to get all nervous and everything? Now you're all calm and professional."

"I've had lots of practice."

"I still don't like the makeup," Mam said. "I don't think I ever will."

"Doesn't matter whether you like it," Susan had no sympathy. "It's like Jonelle says—it looks good." She was looking forward to looking especially good herself in New York. Hair was never going to be her thing. It was such a luxury to have Marta's help. If there was really going to be another tour, and Susan knew it was a when and not an if, she was thinking seriously of cutting it really short and asking Li Huan to teach her how he made his all spiky.

Five minutes before curtain, Wendy and Uri lead the way to the stage, Uri walking backwards to capture Susan's walk from the dressing room. Jimmy's new robes were white with crystals and the floor was none too clean, so Marta held the skirt up like a train. She didn't want it to get filthy before the night had really even begun. "I feel like a bride," Susan remarked. "Anyone have a bouquet?"

"Better not," Melissa joked, overhearing as they arrived in wings. "Mam might have hay fever." Lisa made a face at the image, then blew Susan a good luck kiss. Alan raised a thumbs up.

"If you can make it here..." Raju whispered, with a wink.

"Oh, yeah!" Susan whispered, excited. "Hey, Mam, we're on Broadway!" Waving to everyone, smiling so hard that it hurt, she strode out on stage and into the spotlight. The audience roared approval.

With the bright light in her eyes, she couldn't see a thing, but Susan knew the front row was filled with family: Tara, Michael, and Janet, Rosa and Ernesto, Diane and Bob, and Jimmy and his partner. A little further back, she could feel Jonelle, and Vanessa and some of the others. They were surrounded by love.

Susan raised her arms and the light splintered off her bracelets, making stars. The audience roared even louder.

"Hello New York!" Susan and Mam said together.

Something whistled past Susan's ear.

Rosa screamed and Susan looked down, moving her hand to shield her eyes. It was that motion that caused a second piece of stone to bounce off her bracelet instead of smashing into her temple. Even so, the impact made her fall to her knees.

An agent ran out from the wings to shield her with his body. Dr. Bob jumped up on the stage, yelling "I'm a doctor! I'm a doctor!" From backstage, Linda started screaming "Call 911!" even though she knew the theatre was full of police. The auditorium erupted.

Jimmy Touray stood up in the front row, called on theatrical voice control techniques he hadn't used in decades, and boomed "Turn up the house lights!" in a surprisingly resonant baritone. Either he was heard over the ruckus, or someone had already thought to do so.

The lights came on and everyone could all see her: an extremely tall woman with oddly cropped hair and pale, mad eyes, standing frozen in the fourth row. In her outstretched hands, she held, of all things, a slingshot. "Thou shalt not suffer a witch to live!" she was shrieking.

The police and FBI agents in the hall ran towards her, but not before two men in the row behind had grabbed her to hold her down. She kept screaming wildly, "For the wrath of God is revealed from Heaven against unholiness!" and, again, "Thou shalt not suffer a witch to live!" One of the men put his hand over her mouth and she bit him. With a roar of outrage, he smacked her hard across the face and she fell silent.

Insisting she was fine, Susan got to her feet. She pushed her protectors to either side and stood center stage. "Quiet, everyone! Mam and I are fine! Please, take your seats!" Her voice wasn't as steady as it needed to be.

"Listen to Susan!" Mam's voice cut through the auditorium. The theatre hushed and all eyes turned back to the stage. While attention was elsewhere, Rejoice in the Name was carted out of the building.

"We're fine," Susan repeated, sounding more confident. "Please," she said to the agent, "put your gun away. You're making people nervous." Having scanned the auditorium, he holstered the weapon and took a step back, but stayed ready. "Thank you. Now would everyone please take your seats? It's over. Everything is under control."

"Thank you, everyone," Mam said.

"Lights please," Susan called. She looked over her shoulder to where Dr. Bob remained standing, his lips pressed tightly together. "Thank you," she said, patting his hand. "It's okay, you can sit down." Not all that happily, he complied. As the houselights faded back down, Diane kissed him hard and snuggled up against him.

Susan stood in the spotlight. The audience, having settled down, watched expectantly. She wasn't sure what to do next. Her wrist, where the bangle had deflected the stone, started to throb. She rubbed it. "I feel like Wonder Woman," she observed. The audience laughed nervously. "What was that, anyway?"

Raju, who'd been on his hands and knees helping an undercover cop to find it, called out from the wings "Piece of rock!"

Susan felt the hairs on the back of her neck stand up. Someone had tried to stone her. It would have been easier to hear it was a bullet.

"You always said it would be exciting to be on Broadway," Mam observed, loudly. The audience laugh was stronger this time.

"Well, yes, Mam." Susan said, swallowing her panic, "but I never expected it would be this exciting. I sure hope the rest of the evening doesn't seem dull by comparison."

"No way!" someone called from the mezzanine. From somewhere in the orchestra, someone else called out "We love you!" The audience burst into applause.

Susan took a deep relaxing breath and smiled. "Well then, let's get on with it, shall we?"

Afterward, back in the dressing room, Susan was euphoric. Adrenaline washed through her veins like champagne. The audience had been so deeply invested that at times she'd thought she would levitate off their power. She felt as though she could conquer the world with one hand tied behind her back.

"You should be happy," she burbled giddily at Agent MacAfee. "It happened. Your worst nightmare. Now we don't have to worry."

He didn't look happy. "A slingshot!" he mumbled, rubbing the bridge of his nose until it ached. "Wood, like something out of Mark Twain. She had it stuck into a garter on her leg so it wouldn't show up in the bag check."

"Clever." Raju was impressed.

"Terrific," Diane said from Dr. Bob's knee. "She could have killed Sue and you're admiring her resourcefulness."

"Just don't tell me it was a bridal garter," Susan giggled.

"Bob, is there something you can give her to calm her down?" Mam asked. "Otherwise, it's going to be a long time 'til morning."

Whatever Bob gave her, it made Susan sleep late into Saturday morning. She slept, in fact, until Lisa called from down the street to say that brunch was on the way. Members of the family trouped in and out all day, whether to distract Susan or to stop their own imaginations from running wild, they didn't pause to consider. The memory of the previous night drifted off like a bad dream, surfacing only when it was time to leave for the theatre.

Saturday's transportation scheme had Susan sneaking out of her apartment building alone, disguised by a UPS delivery uniform, and being driven to the theatre by truck. The atmosphere in the theatre was very different from the previous night, edginess replacing excitement. The audience buzzed with a covert thrill, as if they half expected the person in the next seat to jump up brandishing a sword, and would be a little disappointed if it didn't happen.

Thinking ahead as always, Raju arrived early enough to give Susan one of his famous neck massages. Between that and Marta's indomitable calm, she was able to step out on the stage without panicking. She raised her arms in the spotlight, and nothing happened other than applause. The evening turned out to be an uneventful success.

Sunday, Reverend Hiram Crockertt followed his weekly radio broadcast sermon with a statement condemning the "misguided" actions of Rejoice in the Name and reminding his congregation that only the Lord had the right to take a life. Tara, the family's designated Crockertt-monitor, was astonished but delighted.

Naturally, Pearl Yuan quickly tied up an exclusive jailhouse interview with Rejoice in the Name and, just as naturally, she was already hammering Susan and Mam to comment. Janet was delighted to be able to say that the FBI would not permit it, and Pearl moved on to pin down a delighted Jack Rabb.

Monday, the entire office couldn't stop talking about "the slingshot nut." Those who'd been there were besieged by those who hadn't, and were pumped for every tiny detail. Agent MacAfee came by in the afternoon to bring them all up to date on the putative assassin and what had been learned about the religious community to which she belonged.

"Why not call a cult a cult?" Lisa asked.

"Then what would you call us?" Alan, the anthropologist, asked.

MacAfee wouldn't rise to the banter, but he seemed less tightly wound than before. Some of the letters that had concerned his analysts the most had been connected to the same cult, and measures were being taken. He'd be even happier on Sunday, when the New York engagement was over. His sixth sense, or whatever it was, told him that these big public appearances were the danger zone. Despite his urgings, he knew they were planning another tour. Since Friday's scare, he thought maybe they'd actually listen and wait a while. He certainly hoped so. He'd put off a vacation to handle this situation and he had every intention of rescheduling for March. Last time he'd looked he still had a marriage, but it was getting frayed. Fortunately there was no performance planned for Wednesday. He'd be taking his wife to a very nice restaurant.

By Wednesday, everyone was counting the days. The press was oppressive. They seemed to be lurking everywhere: around the offices, by the theatre, outside Susan's apartment building. At every corner, they vied with miscellaneous fans and, less obviously, undercover security. Some of it would end with the Assemblages, but a certain amount had become an unshakeable fact of life. Like MacAfee, Susan was thinking how nice a vacation would be. Maybe she'd fly to Arizona for a couple of weeks. Mitra was always full of people, but it was a comforting kind of crowded. No one took Mam for granted, no one ever could, but they were easy and accepting there, and they let her breathe.

With so many Assemblages, they weren't holding any Gatherings this week. Melissa arranged for the car service to come by early.

"I'm getting so spoiled," Susan said. "Look at me; it's January and I don't even need to wear a coat."

"You can imagine how I feel," Mam noted.

"And I order all your groceries online," Melissa grinned, opening the door. "You're a diva alright."

"Next time have them sent to the apartment," Raju grumbled good-naturedly, shouldering the carton.

It was really too cold to be out without a coat, even for the few yards to the curb. Susan broke into a run.

"Susan! Why haven't you called me?"

A woman's voice, somehow familiar. Someone she'd gone to school with, maybe? Instinctively, she stopped to turn toward the voice and wave.

"Susan, no!" Melissa called, just a second too late.

And a shot rang out.

Blood blossomed from Mam and Susan crumpled to the ground. Melissa screamed. Raju dropped the box, sending vegetables and canned soup rolling down the street. There were shouts and scuffles as people struggled to hold the shooter. Hannah didn't fight them, or the police who reached her seconds later. The limo driver called for an ambulance. People came running from the building.

Melissa knelt by Susan's side, pressing her scarf hard against the wound to staunch the bleeding. Raju, held her head in his lap, stroking her forehead. "Susan, stay with me."

She tried to focus on Raju. There were faces swimming overhead, some familiar, every one pale and concerned. "We're okay," she tried to reassure them, but the words stayed in her head and didn't come out.

"Mam?" Rosa's voice, breathless from running down the stairs, wobbled. "Mam, are you okay?"

"It is sufficient to say...," her voice trickled off, like rainwater, "to say that I...exist."

Susan blacked out, just as the ambulance arrived.

Raju and Rosa went with Susan in the ambulance. Melissa was about to get in the limo, to follow them, when she noticed the police car still standing at the curb. She walked over, pale and determined, and peered in the back seat window. An ordinary woman sat cuffed there. A woman so ordinary that, if the crowd hadn't grabbed her, she would have easily disappeared into the city leaving nothing but a cloud of witness descriptions too vague and confusing to ever track her down.

"You!" Melissa pounded on the window before the cop could stop her. Her voice rose to an anguished shout. "How could you do this?! How could you try to kill Susan?!!"

The woman turned. She blinked, as if astonished. "No!" she exclaimed, vehemently. "I would never kill another human being! Make sure my kids know that! Susan will be fine. It's only the abomination." With a grim smile of satisfaction, she turned from Melissa and closed her eyes. "Only Her."

Text messages and e-mails dispersed before the crowd did. Anyone with a device picked it up and started tapping.

From the back of the limo, Melissa sent the office broadcast e-mail she'd hoped to never send, so that everyone who hadn't been standing there would know. Most everyone who'd run downstairs returned to the office to wait, man the phones and monitor the website. Melissa also called Will Barnstock, who dropped everything and went straight to the airport, calling his sister while waiting for the next plane to New York. Lisa called Diane and

Steffi, and Steffi called Patrick. Everyone at Mitra stopped what they were doing to gather on the lawn and pray.

A flash crowd thronged to the hospital before local news got the word and sent trucks. By nightfall, someone had started a candlelight vigil in Union Square. Prayer circles, physical and virtual, linked hands and hearts all across the country and in every part of the world where Mam was known and loved.

In the hospital, Rosa knelt in the chapel and waited for an answer.

If she came to in the ambulance, Susan never remembered. There was nothing between the winter sky and the white ceiling tiles when they woke her in the recovery room.

"Do you know your name?" the recovery room nurse asked.

"Is she gone?" Susan croaked.

"Do you know your name?" she repeated.

"Does it matter?" she said, fretfully. "Susan, it's Susan. Mam, are you there?"

Behind her, she could feel someone else enter the room. "Let me," whispered a familiar voice.

"Dr. Snyder? Is that you? Is she gone?"

Dr. Snyder stood by the gurney and stroked her hand. "It's me," she said. "You're going to be fine."

They kept her a couple of days. Every time they changed the bandages and checked the drain, she closed her eyes tight and tried to hum so that the silence wouldn't hurt so much.

"You were lucky," Linda said stoutly, putting a full plate on her lap. "It was a lucky shot."

Susan shook her head. "No luck." She looked down at her favorite orange beef and wondered how to pretend to eat it.

"Sue," Alan squeezed her hand tight, "don't talk that way."

"I mean it wasn't lucky," Susan said dully. "It was deliberate. She told Melissa."

"She was building a defense." Raju sounded tough enough to pull the cork out with his teeth.

"I don't think so," Melissa said from her place on the rug. "She sounded like she really meant it."

"Oh it was lucky, alright," Diane brought in more napkins from the kitchen; there were never enough in the bag. "Bob says another inch and it would have been your heart. They'd be holding her for murder, not attempted murder."

"Agent McAffee says she was a sharpshooter in the army," Susan said, taking a deep gulp of wine and holding out her glass for more. "She trained others. She competed in the Olympics. She knew exactly was she was doing."

"She must be crazy" Melissa shook her head sadly. "Those poor kids of hers."

"Maybe they agree with her, that she should be applauded for taking out an enemy without collateral damage," Susan said. The others looked at her blankly. "Mam's dead, I'm alive." It was the first time she'd said it out loud: "Mam is dead."

Dr. Bob ambushed her with a psychiatrist who tried to put her on antidepressants. She didn't want their pills. "I'm not depressed because I have a chemical imbalance," she said testily. "I'm depressed because I've lost everything. I have a crappy life."

She was alive, but she didn't have a life. Not anymore. She'd been a vessel for Mam and now Mam was gone. Even her so-called writing career was entirely due to Mam. No one had ever wanted her for herself. She wasn't anything. She cut off all her hair with the only scissors she could find, then cried for an hour because she had cut if off in mourning, but there was no grave to throw it into. That was the only time she cried.

She couldn't imagine suicide because she already felt dead. She could disappear to Idaho under an assumed name and sell guns in a Walmart, for all anyone would know or care. What was the point of life, she wondered, and how much time would she have to mark, before it would all just come to an end?

All she wanted to do was hide in a corner until she would shrivel up and turn to dust. She wouldn't answer the phone. She couldn't stop people from coming to the house, because they all had her keys. She didn't want to speak with them but, hard though it was to admit, it helped to hear them talking all around her. When she was alone, the silence was deafening.

They kept trying to bring her back to the world. Wendy would talk about the buzz on the documentary, which was up for an Academy Award. She was told about the loads of baked goods and stuffed animals flooding into the office and asked Rosa to have them sent to soup kitchens and children's hospitals. Melissa was barely able to carry the large basket of roses that had come from the White House gardens with a letter from the First Lady. Will

Barnstock finally got tired of staring in silence and took himself home to San Francisco.

One afternoon, a few weeks after the shooting, Janet stopped by with a bottle of champagne to report that, with Alan's help, the book of transcripts was with the editors and advance orders were already huge. Tara was with her, bearing an invitation to give a lecture at the Harvard School of Divinity.

Susan exploded. "Don't you people get it," she shouted, ripping the letter in half, "It's over, it's all over! Time to close up shop and get back to real life!"

Tara gathered up the bits of paper and folded them into her laptop bag. "If that's how you feel," she said calmly, "then I suppose we should be closing the office."

Janet put a warning hand on her daughter-in-law's arm. "Tara, that's not what she means."

"Sure it is," Tara said, her voice staying soft and even. "How can there be a Mam Enterprises without Mam?"

"That's right," Susan was surprised, but relieved to be understood.

"It's not easy," Tara continued, almost hypnotically, "but Susan accepts that. It was nice while it lasted but now...It's like it was a dream. And now we're all waking up." Tara leaned in and kissed Susan on the cheek. "That's settled then. I'll see you in the office tomorrow morning." She stood and walked out, gesturing for Janet to follow. "Did you know, Janet, that this room was once my bedroom?"

Susan jumped up, nearly catching her foot on her wooly blanket, and stumbled after them. "Wait! What do you mean...? I thought you agreed..."

Tara turned and frowned, as if Susan were being deliberately thick. "If you're closing it down, then the only decent thing to do is come into the office and tell people to their faces."

The walk from the subway seemed to last for miles and yet took no time at all. The elevator, which took forever when you were in a rush, arrived instantly. Susan held herself tight inside the armor of her thickest turtleneck sweater and promised herself she wouldn't cry. It was the hardest thing she'd ever had to do, walk into this office. She'd been so happy here, she'd felt so alive and the world had held so much promise.

The door opened. Someone had hung some black bunting over the reception desk. Jonelle looked up with that automatic smile that somehow always seemed real. When she realized it was Susan, she jumped up with a wordless cry and hugged her tight. The phone rang and she turned, not certain what to do.

"Get the phone," Susan said, glad to have a reason to escape. "I'll be in our...my office."

She'd thought the place would be sad and quiet, but it was hopping. The Pool was as full as ever of volunteers, busily reading and answering mail. In the merchandise room, Lisa and her assistants were up to their hips, unpacking cartons, too busy to do more than wave as she passed. Tara didn't even wave when Susan passed her door; she was on the phone, checking something against the computer. Raju, also on the phone, seemed to be talking over a thick document. How was she going to tell them all that it was closing time? And why the hell did they need her to tell them? Why didn't they see it themselves?

She closed the door to her own office very quietly and sat down at her desk. There was her monitor and the station for her laptop, her phone, her inbox, her ceramic penholder that said "I lov U lov Sophie" in a pink heart. "It's like an ordinary day, Mam," Susan whispered. Except Mam wasn't there to ask why it shouldn't be. This not crying wasn't going to be so easy.

There was a knock at the door, and Rosa entered with Susan's coffee mug. "Jonelle said you were here. I figured you could use a cup. There's no cookies. Julia's on a diet so she bought these rice cakes and they're too nasty."

"Thanks," Susan mumbled. She didn't really want it, but drinking it was something to do.

"Did you see what the kids made?" Rosa asked, pointing to a large piece of poster board that had been propped up in the desk chair. Rosa lifted it carefully onto the desk so she could sit. She wasn't planning to leave anytime soon.

Susan looked at the poster. It was the kind of collage that young children made, with lots of stickers and pieces of foam and felt. It featured what seemed to be the floating figure of a woman—at least it had long hair and a triangle skirt—with black felt circles for eyes and a large gold tinsel pompom for a breast. When you looked with the eyes of a preschooler, you could tell she was surrounded, not by a cloud as it had first seemed to Susan, but by a "thought balloon," which connected, by many rows of puffy dots, to the heads of a circle of happy people standing below her, holding hands and smiling.

"It's supposed to be you...and Mam of course. They were feeling sad when we told them Mam had gone away. The grief counselor suggested they make a picture to say how they feel."

"Grief counselor?"

"Didn't Alan tell you? It was his idea. We had a grief counselor in the office, the week after. It helped a lot, for everybody. See how the kids, they're saying that they're happy because they remember her?"

"I didn't know about the grief counselor. I should have realized..."

"What, that you're not the only person on the planet?" Rosa gave a short, nervous laugh. "Yeah, well, you kinda had your own problems. We were worrying as much about losing you as Mam."

"But you knew right away that I was...you were at the hospital, Rosa. You knew and I'm sure you told everybody."

Rosa shook her head. "We knew you were going to live," she said carefully. "That didn't mean we weren't going to lose you." Her eyes were sad. "We still don't know," is what they were saying.

"I'm not worth very much here without Mam." Susan hadn't planned to say it that bluntly. It sounded self-pitying, and she'd wanted to be strong today.

"That's stupid," Rosa blurted. "I'm sorry, but it is. How can you say that when, without Her, we need you more than ever?"

"To do what? Just what am I supposed to do, Rosa? Me, Susan? Regular, plain...You know, before Mam nobody cared what I had to say. Janet, the first time I met her, she told me flat out that I wasn't interesting enough. And she was right. I was so ordinary, I was invisible. People would start to sit on my lap in the subway, thinking I was an empty seat."

Rosa reacted as if she'd said that green beans were orange. "But you're not ordinary. You never were or Mam wouldn't have come to you. You believe that, don't you?" She could see Susan didn't. "Okay," she regrouped, "but even if you was, you're not any more. Because of Mam. Because She was here, in you. Whatever you think you were before, you got to know what you are now. Okay, so now Mam is gone, you're thinking it's the end, but it's not, it's just beginning."

"Oh, Rosa, that's just ridiculous!"

Rosa pulled her chair closer, so that she could see the poster better. "That's nice, don't you think so?" she said, pointing at the pompom. "How they made Her all gold like that? It's because she was like magic, one of the babies said." Susan looked at the golden pompom and her eyes welled. "And that's so true," Rosa continued, relentless. "She was. She was truly a miracle. But you know, a miracle isn't supposed to be forever. It's to teach us something, to show us the way. And that's what Mam did. She showed us the way. We can never forget Her. And now we have to keep going. You have to keep going." Rosa took Susan's hand and stared directly into her eyes. "You started something with Mam. And like She always says, there are repercussions. You can't pretend it never happened. And you can't hide out. She wouldn't like that. She would be saying you have to take responsibility."

"Great! You're throwing my own...Her...okay, our words right back at me." It was a slightly hysterical laugh.

"And don't you believe them anymore? Just because now She's gone?" Rosa wasn't laughing, but she'd relaxed a little. She had a feeling she'd done something right, like when Carlito started saying "please" and "thank you" for things, without her having to tell him anymore.

"I do believe them," Susan said, because it was true. "I always did. But Rosa, what are we supposed to do, what can we accomplish, without Her?"

"The same as before," Rosa said stoutly. "You tell people what you learned from Her. It's just as real and important as it was last month or in the summer. People need to know. And they want to. So your job is to tell them, and the rest of us, we help you."

Suddenly, what Rosa was saying made all the sense in the world. Just because She's not here anymore, it's not as if She'd never been here. Susan had no idea what might happen next. Then again, she'd never had any idea where Mam might lead her.

"Rosa, I remember...you were there." It was one of the last things Susan could remember before the hospital, Rosa's face blurring above her against the grey sky. "She said something, before..." Her voice broke and she took a deep swallow. Rosa waited patiently for her to be able to continue. "What was it, the last thing She said?"

Rosa nodded. "It is sufficient to say that I exist." Her eyes were bright. "That's what She said. I promised myself I wouldn't forget, ever."

How like Mam. Sufficient to exist. From beginning to end, no answers, no promises. Susan felt a sigh ripple up from somewhere deep inside her. "We keep going?" she said, so quietly that it was little more than breath. Rosa squeezed her hand tightly and nodded. Tension, pain, everything tight and hurtful seemed to drain from Susan's body. Even if Mam were gone now, She'd been here. She'd existed. That was sufficient. Susan felt very light and very tired. She would go on. Maybe she needed to have some faith.

EPILOGUE

Jared grabbed his jacket. "See you tomorrow," he told the guys as he ran for the door.

Chip gave him a friendly wave. "Have a good service!"

"Come with me some time!" Jared called back, grinning, and sped off to meet Amy at the Metro station and get to Crystal City. Mondays being quiet for movies, they'd been able to negotiate a good price to use a theatre. They weren't late, but Jared still felt more comfortable having a while to prepare before speaking in public. Also, it was always good to check under the seats before the Gathering started, just in case.

They wouldn't need to make do with the multi-plex for much longer. Tonight, Jared was going to announce the great news. Not only had New York been delighted to grant them a charter—only the fifth in the nation, he thought proudly—but Ms. Santiago, the newly-appointed director of national assemblies, had informed him that the charter came with funding for a down payment on a permanent space and that they'd even fly in their own real estate consultant, Ms. Cicollilo, to help him find one. Mrs. Hendron would be especially excited. The Secret Service would only let her come to one Gathering a month in the multi-plex. Once they had a secure place of their own, she could come all the time.

There was going to be an official Vanishing ceremony, nationwide, on the first anniversary in January. It would be a tight deadline, but even if they had to rent folding chairs, how perfect would it be if the First Washington Assembly of Mam could open its own doors on that day?

ACKNOWLEDGMENTS

Writing is a solo act, but no writer is an island. My greatest gift in life is my circle of wonderful friends and family. I thank every one of you for your love and tolerance!

Special thanks always go to my Mom, Honey Seltzer, for unending encouragement and support over all the many many years that I've been writing, and to Thandi Brewer and Denis Hutchinson, my staunchest writing cheerleaders for over a quarter of a century. I may have given up regularly, but you never gave up believing in me.

For this particular project, I am grateful to those early readers whose interest and enthusiasm provided much-needed boosts at critical moments. Thanks to Robin Raines, who tried to get me a foot in the door, and Odella Schattin, who generously volunteered her copywriting skills (the oddities that remain are my own stubborn doing).

It would be remiss not to acknowledge Janet Jackson and Justin Timberlake for the infamous Superbowl "wardrobe malfunction," a few seconds in time that galvanized some observations and images that had been swimming randomly around in my brain for ages.

Most of all, Mam and Susan and I give thanks to three men who have stuck by us through thick and thin: Alan Salant, Michael McDonald and legal counsel extraordinaire Tom Wilinsky. You always believed this story could get to market and never allowed me to stop trying. It's a privilege to have you fighting in my corner.

Finally, A story isn't alive unless it has an audience. Thank *YOU*, Reader, for being part of mine

Lori Berhon, New York, March 2012

ABOUT THE AUTHOR

Novelist, playwright and sometime actor Lori Berhon lives in her home town of New York City where, technically, she makes her living writing. Over the years, she has had many interesting discussions with members of various major and not-as-major religions and did, at one point, work for a lingerie manufacturer. She is actually taller, slimmer and far more elegant than she appears to be.

www.ingramcontent.com/pod-product-compliance
Lightning Source LLC
Chambersburg PA
CBHW070856180626
46817CB00003B/795